EVERYONE
IS
WORRIED

A NOVEL

SANDRA J. PAUL

CASTLE BRIDGE MEDIA
DENVER, COLORADO, USA

CASTLE BRIDGE MEDIA
Denver, Colorado

Cover photo by Maria/Unsplash.
This photo has been modified.

This book is a work of fiction. Names, characters, business, events, and incidents are the products of the authors' imaginations. Any resemblance to actual persons, living or dead or actual events is purely coincidental.

EVERYONE IS WORRIED
© 2025 Sandra J. Paul
All rights reserved.

ISBN: 979-8-9917855-9-4

Before

Losing a child is probably the singular most horrible thing
—Laura Schlessinger

One

ON THE EVENING OF THE day my daughter would have been born, I woke up startled. It was the middle of October, and the city was bathing in autumn colors.

New York City streetlights illuminated the master bedroom of our two-bedroom downtown Manhattan apartment through the open drapes. I had left them open, before crawling into bed. At least this way, I didn't feel so damned alone. With the buzzing city below us, I could at least pretend that other people cared about me.

Philip wasn't in the room; his side of the bed felt cold. It took me a moment to remember that my husband hadn't slept by my side for a little over two months now. He would probably be fast asleep in the guest bedroom down the hall, snoring the way he usually did after taking a sleeping pill. I refused to take pills myself, even though they would guarantee a good night's sleep.

My heart pounded from anxiety. That damned recurring nightmare was killing me. I tried to compose myself but failed miserably. Crying out loud was not an option, so I bit my lip, fighting off the inevitable tears. Every single detail of the nightmare I was living in haunted me. Reality was as ugly as the dream.

In my recurrent nightmares, a dark-haired woman stood in front of me.

She held an infant, wrapped in baby blankets, with only a tiny flicker of soft baby red hair visible. The baby started wailing, but the woman did nothing to soothe her. The moment I reached out for the child, the stranger carrying her dropped her on the floor. The baby went still as soon as her frail skull hit the floorboard with a horrifying thud. The woman snarled audibly, laughing, and mocking me while the baby remained still. She just turned around and left. I caught a glimpse of her tattoo-covered arms before she pulled her coat tighter over her body.

The intruder hurried through the terrace doors, which she left wide open. She disappeared while I watched her, into the garden behind my house. My heart immediately went out to the baby. I cried while I knelt and held her gently against me. But I couldn't save her. She was eerily still in my arms. Her skull had cracked; blood seeped from her ears.

Over the past months, as the dream progressed and intensified, something shifted. In a matter of seconds, the still infant grew from a baby to a toddler and into a young child. Ultimately, I had to let go of her, because she became too tall and too heavy to carry. I placed her gently on the couch, where she lay perfectly still, eyes closed and limbs quiet. Blood still escaped her ears; her skull was still cracked.

The child stopped growing when she reached the age of approximately twelve. My daughter was a beautiful blonde girl, with green-blue eyes and a dash of freckles dotting her face. Her skin was fragile like china; she resembled a porcelain doll. I screamed at her to open her eyes, but she never did. I could never save her, no matter what I did.

Once awake, I realized once again that my hands were empty, and my womb gone. The all-too familiar ache that lived inside of me took over immediately. I was hurting physically and mentally. My daughter would never come to life; she would never truly exist. Those nightmares were all I had to remind me of her, even if they were ugly and nasty and choking. I started looking forward to going to bed at night, started considering the nightmares a blessing instead of a hellish experience. She was my daughter and sleep bound us together.

I knew I wouldn't be able to rest anymore tonight, when the dream had been particularly bad, so I slipped out of bed and walked over to the window.

Here, I could watch other people leading their normal lives. These days, that was the only thing that kept me going. The fact that I was surrounded by millions of people while feeling disconnected didn't matter to me.

People walked by the apartment building hand in hand, laughing, joking or arguing. The streetlights were bright, the bars in the invited guests in through open doors. I looked away and focused on the buildings across the street. The first person I noticed was our new neighbor. Her apartment was on the same floor as ours, which gave me some insights into her bare living space. I had watched the moving truck unload her things a few days before. The apartment must have been furnished, since they only brought in cardboard boxes. I had never seen the woman's face up close, since she was always busy doing stuff, moving around between her still-boxed-up possessions.

The woman stood quietly in front of the large bay window with her back turned towards me. Long black hair fell from her shoulders. When she turned slightly, I could see her profile for the first time. At the same time, I caught the tattoo-sleeves covering both arms. I nearly choked on air.

Oh god, no. For a scary moment, I thought it was her. That she had been released from jail, only to find me again and finish the job. When the woman turned and gazed outside, I quickly realized it wasn't. Her arms did have some tattoos, but they didn't cover her fully. My imagination got the better of me.

Our new neighbor lazily smoked a cigarette while leaning out the window, spotting me staring at her. When her eyes caught mine, she smiled broadly and waved with a friendly gesture. The colorful tattoos screamed at me. I shut my drapes, shutting her out deliberately. Her surprised look before I moved out of sight didn't go by unnoticed. The last thing I needed right now were new friends. They couldn't bring back my daughter either. Nobody could.

I was wrong about Philip sleeping soundly in the guest bedroom. He had come into the kitchen. He sat at the tiny table, with a cup of steaming coffee between his hands. He looked up, obviously surprised that I was awake.

"You couldn't sleep either, could you?" he spoke softly.

"Yeah."

"Sorry to hear that. Would you like some coffee, Zoey?"

Philip was polite. He would have asked a stranger the exact same question. Two strangers living together is what we had become. I had only myself to blame for that. We hadn't been on friendly terms for ages. I declined my husband's offer and sat down in front of him. It was hot in here; he hadn't switched the air-conditioning on. I was too tired to move and do it myself.

Philip returned to drinking his scalding-hot coffee and ignored me, obviously nervous now that I sat down with him. He was probably trying to come up with an excuse to go back to the spare room as quickly as possible without making an ass of himself. He winced when he drank his coffee too fast, burning his lower lip and tongue. I wanted to reach for my husband's hand in support. I ached to tell him that we could go back to living, now that the date had passed, and it was finally over. We could store away the memories and start all over again. We could finally start mending the broken pieces. Tomorrow could mean a new start for us both. If only we would allow it to.

I didn't move. Things would never go back to normal for us and we both knew it. Too much had happened for that to be possible. We had come to the point where we could barely speak to one another, let alone face each other properly. Philip looked at me with that eerily calm look in his eyes I had seen so many times now and hated from the bottom of my heart. For weeks, I had pleaded with him in silence to speak up and voice his sadness, but he never had. He never did. I hated his quiet, where I did nothing but scream. It felt better to lash out at people in anger, so why didn't he? Why couldn't he just voice what he was feeling?

My husband opened his mouth, as if he wanted to tell me something. He didn't. Never did, in fact. He closed his mouth again, focused on the rest of his coffee and continued to pretend that he lived in a world where things were not so bad. His expression was dark. He was in mourning, but he never showed that to anyone.

He would have been a good father. I would have been a good mother too.

I didn't believe in dreams-come-true fairy tales anymore. That used to be me, but not today. Philip would not come into my bedroom to comfort me any longer. We had lost that connection sixteen weeks ago, when he silently accused me of losing our child. I left my husband sitting at the kitchen table and moved back into our bedroom, slipping beneath the covers. I turned to the side and stared outside the window, looking at the skies above the other apartment building. For the rest of the night, I waited patiently for dawn to appear. Not that it would change much. Day or night never mattered anymore.

My hands instinctively protected my womb while I pretended that this was the night when I had just given birth to a beautiful red-haired child with green eyes. I even imagined the ache between my legs that would come with childbirth. I pretended that I was a normal mother, with a normal life, holding a perfect little child in my arms. Her name would have been Eve.

Two

I SPENT THE ENTIRE NEXT day in bed, listening to the drops of rain that tickled against the bedroom window. The unseasonable warmth had finally made way for typical autumn rain and wind. I was glad that the skies were weeping too. I didn't eat, sleep or even go to the restroom. I just stayed in bed feeling listless and useless.

Philip didn't leave for work, for once, but he didn't spend his day with me either. He shuffled around our living room, doing chores that had been lingering about for several weeks, even months. He was probably finally trying to make this place feel like a home, while I hated every inch of it. We had moved head over heels into this damned apartment, leaving the small town and the beautiful countryside house we had lived in before far behind.

The one thing my husband and I had in common was that we couldn't stand the sight of that town anymore. It was only two hours' drive away from the city, but it felt like another world to us, one we would never access again. Sometimes, it felt as if Philip had used the events as an excuse to move us Downtown Manhattan, as he always wanted from the moment we became an item. I used to be a New Yorker, but I had chosen the tranquility of a life beyond the Manhattan Skyline to raise a family. Now that we would never have one, there was no point in staying there.

After the incident, a medical emergency team flew me by helicopter from the ER of our small local hospital to a university hospital in New York, where I underwent several surgeries to save my life. The locals had quickly realized that I would not make it otherwise, and that decision most likely saved my life. While I lay in the ICU for days, first in a coma, then awake and in a gruesome amount of pain, Philip arranged the move from our house to this apartment without consulting me. It was his way of coping, to have something on his hands. He thought I wouldn't be able to stand going back there anyhow, and that he was doing me a favor by taking that decision away from me. Truth be told, it wasn't the last time he made decisions for me. He decided everything these days, from what I ate to what I saw on television, because I was too addled to do it myself.

My husband stored most of our personal belongings, including all the already purchased baby supplies, in a storage facility in our old town. We both knew we would never go back there. He only grabbed practical things like clothes, electronic devices and our laptops when he quickly arranged our housing in the apartment building where we now rented. He had wanted to give away everything we once had, but I insisted against it. Somehow, it felt comforting to have those baby things still around, even if we would probably never use them. The past sixteen weeks, I had never asked him what he was planning to do with it all, out of fear. In fact, I learned that he had already thrown everything out.

To me, it felt as if Philip had thrown away our old life, including our unborn child. To him, it felt as if he was protecting my sanity. Part of me understood that he simply needed this to ignore the all-consuming pain. He had to occupy his mind with what he felt were useful things. In a way, I admired him for that. I wish I could have been that strong. On the other hand: I wasn't as cold as him.

Late in the evening, I finally managed to get out of bed. I forced myself to do something. The back of my neck and skull ached from lying down all day. I needed to get some fresh air. My body felt numb and sore. Even after nearly four months, it still felt like a truck had hit me. I was suffering from unbearable pains, from my head to my abdomen and in between. At times the pain was so bad I would just crawl into myself and try to breathe the pain out, which hardly ever worked. I was often exhausted. I took too much pain medication. It was the only thing keeping me on my feet right now. Without my prescribed pills, I couldn't make it through the day.

I ignored the fact that I smelled and that my hair was greasy, changed into the first clothes I could find lying about in our tiny dressing room, still stacked with boxes, ignored the fact that I had worn this particular set of underwear for two days now, put on thick socks and shoes and headed for the front door without even looking at my husband, who sat on the couch watching some lame movie. I knew he wasn't really paying attention anyhow. A glass of wine stood before him; the bottle next to it was more than half empty.

"I'm going out for a while," I muttered.

Philip didn't offer to come with me; I didn't ask him to join me. We had grown apart in a way I thought would never happen to us. Nine months ago, we had been thrilled that we were going to be parents, or at least, I wanted to believe so. Philip had spent hours fixing up our house because I pushed him to do so. We had bought those supplies and baby clothes and had been discussing names. I never told him I had already settled on Eve. He only learned after I woke up from my coma and started asking about her.

Today, we were wrecked. Broken. Done. Over and out. We were a perfect couple once. Right now, we were the most imperfect pair I knew. My body, mind, soul, head and even skin felt raw, like I had clawed at it for days. My head pounded; my belly ached. The huge scars covering my abdomen and chest ached with every move I made. I felt sorry for myself. I felt sorry for him too. If misery could kill, we would be long dead by now.

It was raining heavily. My body, socks and shoes became soaking wet as I walked two blocks down, but I couldn't care less. I needed to feel the rain on me, to smell the acid covering my clothes. I wanted to be outside, where normal people lived and breathed and existed and were happy. Where nobody cared that it was wet and cold and autumn. Couples under umbrellas passed me by. Husbands protected their wives by shoving coats over their heads. Boyfriends held onto girlfriends, hugging them as if that would stop the rain with their caresses. A guy kissed his boyfriend gently. A woman held another woman's hand and pulled her laughingly beneath a silly, pink umbrella. Everyone seemed to have someone. It killed me not to be amongst them with my husband by my side. When had he ever stopped caring, anyhow?

I looked up to the skies and wondered why this was happening to us. What had we done wrong? Why hadn't Philip stayed by my side when I was going through hell? Why had he felt better leaving me alone for hours in that hospital room, while he occupied himself with useless things? Anything was obviously better for him than to stay with me. He didn't even attempt to help me get through this. Philip blamed me for being at the wrong place at the wrong time. He felt that I had killed his daughter. He was right. Who else could I blame, when I was the one carrying her in my womb when it happened? I hadn't protected her enough. Hot tears mingled with the acidic rain.

I was absorbed in my own misery when someone bumped into me. The pavement was wet and slippery. On instinct, I reached out with both hands so that the other person would not fall, grasping clothes and hands in the process. When she stood upright again, I noticed that the woman I was helping was balanced on uncomfortable, high-heeled shoes.

"Damnit," she muttered, grasping me tight.

I could feel her fingers claw into the skin of my hands and gasped lightly. The tinge of pain made me come alive. The woman before me wore an unbuttoned, bright yellow raincoat over otherwise black clothes. She stood out in the crowd. Her dark hair was covered, mostly by a huge cap that was connected to her coat. When she saw that I was soaking wet, she moved her umbrella over us both, holding back the rain. We stood underneath it, staring at each other for a moment. In a flash, I recognized our new neighbor from across the street, whose face I had seen for the first time yesterday. She didn't give a sign that she knew who I was. But I knew I wasn't mistaken when I saw the tattoos on her arms.

"Thanks," she grinned broadly, showing a set of perfect teeth. "I nearly fell on my ass there. Stupid heels. What was I thinking wearing those tonight? Who cares that it's date night anyhow, right? Where's your raincoat; don't you have an umbrella? Look at you, you're already soaking wet. Do you want to grab a cup of coffee and warm up a bit?"

Her rant stunned me into silence. Before I could form a reply, the fierce woman had already taken my arm and steered me into the first bar we passed, about five yards further down the road. Ten minutes later, I was warm again, on the inside and out. The woman's radiating smile broke through my cold shell. Her constant rambling about everything and nothing made me forget the dark thoughts inside my own head, if only for a short while. I paid for our drinks, while she removed her coat and shook her wet hair.

While living, breathing and existing in darkness, I had found an unexpected friend underneath a large umbrella. Her name was Vivian.

Three

MY DAD, ALWAYS THE AMBITIOUS one, told me once that life could be perfect for those who knew how to embrace it with the fullest of their abilities. That was why you had winners and losers. You just had to deal with whatever hand of cards you were given. When my parents moved away to South Africa and left me behind in the States, I took his remark seriously. Since their retirement, I saw them once in a blue moon; they might as well have been dead. I thought I had mastered my skills to embrace my almost perfect life. I had a wonderful husband who made a good living in the city, a more than decent marriage with only minor ups and downs, my own successful flower shop and a little girl growing inside of me, twenty-four weeks now. I couldn't have asked for anything more.

I was never an ambitious person. I could have started a business in Manhattan, something Philip had often suggested, but I was content with the little flower shop in our tiny town, just two hours away from the city. After finishing college with a language degree, I decided to follow several courses on flower decorations. Flowers always interested me and since I didn't know what to do in life, I decided to make a hobby out of them. While looking reluctantly for a job that matched my degree, I spent many hours at home improving my florist skills. Once I realized that this was what I wanted to do for a living, I gave up my boring daytime job at a small accountancy firm and applied for a job in a local flower shop. The owner was getting older and looking towards her retirement but had never found anyone who would want to take over her shop. I was eager, something she sensed.

I threw myself into the business. I made flower arrangements for weddings, funerals and everything in between, under the approving eye of my employer. Two months after my employer hired me, she offered to sell me the shop, and I seized the opportunity with both hands.

Rob, my former employer at the accountancy firm, became my financial consultant. He helped me to set up shop. I got a small loan, made some good investments and started off well. He's been advising me ever since. The clientele I inherited from my retired employer was vastly expanding. In the years that followed, the shop thrived, up until the point that I had to hire two staff members to keep up with the workload. We were called upon for store openings, for weddings, funerals and parties and had a steady audience that came for their weekly bouquets. We lived in a rich area, where the women still spent a lot of time decorating their houses.

Philip worked as a lawyer in Manhattan. He had a couple of large business clients in the city, so he commuted daily and often spent the night there. During the week, we didn't see each other all that much, but the weekends were always ours. Samantha, who quickly became a very good friend and trusted employee, preferred to work the weekends and have her downtime in the week, so we set up an arrangement where she took care of the shop when I was off. Simone, my other employee, helped from Thursday to Sunday. My employees were good women, both very eager to please our customers. I trusted them with the shop without hesitation.

In the beginning of July, Philip had booked an extended weekend at an exquisite hotel in Washington. He often told me that I should take it easier, now that I was twenty-four weeks pregnant. It was our anniversary weekend, and despite the busy time of year, I had reluctantly agreed to leave the shop in Samantha's hands for longer than a day. Unfortunately, we had some trouble with a late delivery for a wedding, meaning that I still had to make a couple of huge flower arrangements on Friday and couldn't leave earlier as I had planned. Philip had reluctantly agreed to rebook our hotel and flights for Saturday. The plan was to stay until Monday evening instead.

On Friday evening, right before closing time, I was finishing the last arrangement with Samantha's help, when someone walked into the shop. I looked surprised at the young, dark-haired woman that I had never seen before. I knew most of our regular customers, but we also had a lot of tourists who wandered from New York to the countryside and wound up in our gorgeous area of the country. Having a stranger in our shop wasn't that uncommon. There was something off about this woman though. She somehow seemed out of place, mostly because she didn't look like the average tourist that would end up in a quaint little town like this. She was dressed in a long, black skirt with a large gap on the hip, revealing her black boots and ripped stockings. The rip in her skirt was large enough to show the milky white skin of her tattoo-covered thigh. Her arms had tattoo-sleeves, not uncommon these days, but definitely noticeable in a small town like this.

What was off about the woman was that she was wearing a long white coat over her black clothes on one of the hottest days of the year. The air conditioning had been running at full force all day and even then, I still felt hot and sweaty, often stroking my bump instinctively. I longed for a long shower to cool off. Outdoors, the burning sun scorched people's skin, so most people stayed indoors. It had been a very quiet day at the shop, which I wasn't sad about, as we were busy preparing for the largest wedding of the year so far.

The woman seemed friendly enough. She smiled when she walked in. Her black hair danced over her shoulders. She wore discreet make-up, except for the dark purple gloss on her lips that made her look pale. She had a tattoo on her neck and a piercing through her nose and reminded me of a cousin who sported the same look. Her dark eyes scanned the inside of my shop. Samantha, who always stayed until the shop closed, moved towards our visitor and offered to help her pick out a flower bouquet, since she was obviously interested in the samples that stood by the window.

I watched while my employee showed our new potential customer around. At the same time, I finished the last flower arrangements for the exquisite wedding that would pay half of the salaries of my employees for next month and put them in the cooler. The wedding planner would pick up the large order in the morning, which meant that until then, we would have to keep the flowers as fresh as possible. Satisfied with our work, I closed the cooler.

When I came back out, something had shifted in the air, even though Samantha hadn't noticed this just yet. The woman looked around my shop agitated, while Samantha was performing her sales pitch like she always did. Her trusted soul didn't assume for one second that this woman was up to no good, but the woman's dark eyes betrayed her ruined common sense. My instincts screamed loudly to get rid of this woman straight away. There was something off about her, something intangible that had gone unnoticed earlier.

Samantha's back was turned towards the woman to reach for one of the most beautiful arrangements we had on display, when the stranger suddenly dug a small gun out of her purse. She aimed it at my employee's head and, in a high-pitched voice, demanded the contents of the till. Samantha and I were in the front of the shop, while Simone was in the back, cleaning up behind closed doors, something that went by unnoticed for now. I prayed she wouldn't suddenly pop up and set the woman off.

The intruder's voice spoke softly and gently, as if she was buying something instead of demanding it. She was in bad luck though: most of our customers paid with credit cards these days. She had picked the wrong shop to rob. Or maybe she was so desperate that she would go into the smallest shop in town to get what she wanted. Whatever the case, I would never find out the story behind her reasoning. Samantha turned towards me for help, pleading silently and obviously distressed. We had never been in this position before. This type of thing simply didn't happen in a town like this. I couldn't help but think that I should have been in Washington by now, instead of being threatened in my own shop. I moved forward, grabbed Samantha's arm and pulled her partially behind me, assuming that this woman would never shoot a pregnant woman.

At the same time, I fought the burning sense of dark foreboding building up, like a raging bout of nasty bile working its way up my throat. This would not turn out okay. The woman's unbalanced gaze was that of a drug addict. She came here to financially support her fix, and her hands were already shaking, telling us that she wouldn't leave without getting what she wanted.

"Stay calm," I pleaded. "I'll give you everything I have here, okay? I'll give you every last penny. Just leave Samantha alone. This is my shop; she just works here."

The intruder hesitated until she seemed satisfied that I was telling the truth. Then she nodded impatiently. With a wave of her hand, she ordered Samantha to sit down and stay out of the way. She barked at Samantha to keep her hands visibly in her lap. I prayed furiously that Simone wouldn't barge in unexpectedly after hearing the stranger's voice. It would set off this woman's drug-induced anxiety for sure, since she was shaking by now. I opened the till and showed her its contents, which was only about a hundred dollars in small bills and coins. The woman became visibly angry while she waved the gun under my nose. I knew she had expected a lot more than this. I didn't even have a penny in my pocket.

"Is this all you have?" she screamed, with the fury of an addict in need of an urgent fix.

Her eyes were dilated. There was no doubt that her tattooed arms would have plenty of needle marks on them. A hundred bucks would not get her far, perhaps enough to score a bit for tonight and tomorrow. She would be back robbing someone else on Sunday.

"I'm sorry," I spoke with soft voice, trying to soothe her by staying calm. "Most of our customers pay with credit card these days. I swear to God that this is all I have. Please be careful with that gun. As you can see, I'm pregnant."

My words seemed to shock her. Her eyes dwelled towards my belly. I was a skinny woman and the baby's form had filled me after nearly six months of pregnancy. Even through my wide clothes, my swollen abdomen was quite apparent, but she obviously hadn't noticed before now.

"I don't care," she snarled.

The woman reached for the till, grabbed the money and let every last dime slide into her jacket pocket. She turned and headed for the door, her gun still ready to use in her hand. That would have been the end of it, had it not been for Mrs. Peterson, who had the habit of showing up at the latest minute, two to three times per week. She was one of my best customers, but also the most annoying person in the world. She always took her time talking about flowers to me, because she only trusted mine and never Samantha's judgement. Nothing escaped Mrs. Peterson, which would ultimately cost her dearly.

The second she spotted the small, black weapon in the intruder's hand, she screamed so loudly I thought the glass would shatter. That cry for help would cost her that precious life of hers, where flowers were so important. The robber didn't even aim her gun properly at her. She just raised her hand and fired. The bullet hit Mrs. Peterson's throat, killing her instantly. She was dead before her body hit the tiled floor of my shop. Part of her body, anyway—the poor woman fell backwards, smashed her skull on the pavement and ended up lying half outside, half inside the shop. Her eyes were open. On the street, people screamed. I imagined sirens rushing towards us already, hoping and praying someone would get here on time to save us. I knew nobody could stop what came next though. Superman doesn't exist and all.

The girl turned and aimed the weapon. First at Samantha, then at me, then at Samantha again, who had stood up. She went back and forth like that, using that gun to stop us from reacting. The gaze in her eyes was icy cold. Her chest rose up and down underneath the black, slim fitting clothes she wore and that ridiculous long white coat that partially hid her armed tattoos. We heard noises outside, voices shouting and screaming. People came running towards us. Samantha and I knew they would come too late to save us both. My employee stared at me with tears in her eyes before the first bullet went straight through her forehead and out the back of her skull. She fell against the display of beautiful flowers, dead before her blood spattered on the bucket of white roses. I'll never forget that moment for as long as I live.

The baby inside of me moved faster than ever, probably sensing the adrenaline rush and fear that I felt. The intruder, now a murderer, aimed the gun at me and fired while I tried to get away from her, running towards the counter for a hiding place. She shot me in the back, but I didn't know that yet. I also didn't know that the bullet went through and through, because of the close proximity between us. The woman turned and ran outside my shop without looking back once. I fell forward shaking on the floor behind the counter, looked down and noticed blood on my clothes. I didn't understand where it came from. Somehow, my body wouldn't listen to my brain. I wanted to get up and run out of the shop too, but I couldn't move anymore. I lay on my side, paralyzed. Simone ran to me and screamed for help while she carefully turned me around so she could lift my head on her lap.

People ran into the shop. Samantha never got up. Mrs. Peterson still lay dead in the doorway. Phone calls were made, more people came in. Someone sat down next to Simone to help. It was our local doctor, who had been treating a patient two houses down. His fast reaction saved my life.

"It will be okay, Zoey," Simone whispered when she let go of me.

The doctor grabbed a towel from the counter and pushed it down hard on my abdomen to stop me from bleeding out. My hands were crossed around my belly, but the baby had already stopped moving. A cop appeared and muttered something encouragingly while he took over from the doctor and pressed more towels on the gunshot wound. With every drop of blood that left me, I knew that my baby and I were dying. They moved me to the front of the shop, so they had more space to work.

The last thing I remembered seeing and hearing, was the woman. She was lying outside, right in front of my flower shop, held to the ground by another cop. Her legs jerked while she protested. I heard her hard, cold voice screeching obscenities. She was dragged upwards and pushed roughly into a police vehicle.

The world just blurred into a strange whirlwind of sound darkness then. I was sucked into an abyss where I would stay for a long time. I don't remember how they flew me to New York by helicopter, where they performed three major surgeries on me to remove my womb and child and save my other organs after I suffered from sceptic shock caused by the bullet's passage through my body. I don't remember that they kept me sedated for days. I was in the Intensive Care-unit on a respirator for days, to allow my body to heal. All of that went by me unnoticed.

I didn't know that my baby had been immediately killed by the bullet that penetrated my uterus. The destruction had made it impossible for me to ever have children. I never remembered my parents-in-law sitting by my bed for days, or my friends coming back to see how I was doing. I do remember Philip not being there when I woke up. He would never be there again.

Four

STRANGELY ENOUGH, I REMEMBER EXACTLY what happened before and during the attack. I remember the clothes I was wearing and the perfume I had selected that morning. Something light, chosen by my increased sense of smell during my pregnancy. I still feel the necklace around my neck; chosen to match with the pregnancy dress I had picked out that morning. I still remember the very last time Eve moved inside of me in panic, as if she knew she was going to die. I remember that young, stoned woman kicking and screaming when she was stopped by that cop. I still scent Samantha's sweet-smelling perfume and the smell of blood that surrounded her after she was murdered. I know exactly how much money that woman stole. A hundred bucks was a bitter price to pay for three human lives.

I remember so much, but I don't recall the beginning of the subtle changes between my husband and myself. They were tiny until they grew out of proportion. Truth be told, I thought we were stronger than this. I thought that our loss and grief would bring us closer together, but they only made things worse. The resentment Philip showed towards me after I woke up, when he was forced by his parents to stick around, proved that he blamed me for our daughter's death. He never said the words out loud to me in person, but he did mutter them once to his parents, believing I didn't hear them since I was half-asleep.

"She was supposed to be in Washington with me," he had told them. "I had booked a nice hotel for us, but she chose to stay in that damned shop instead. Her customers always came first; I was always second. If only she had listened to me once."

There it was then: the ultimate truth. He was pissed off at me, blamed me for Eve's death. Had I not chosen the shop over him, our daughter would still be alive today. He was right of course, but I didn't need him to remind me of my faults. I blamed myself enough for everyone's death as it was. Had I closed the shop doors on time, then that drug addict would not have gotten in to score her final fix. Had I told Samantha that she could have gone home earlier, then she would not have been there. Had I told Mrs. Peterson off more clearly about showing up at the last minute in our shop so many times per week, she would not have been there. Had. Had. Had.

What ifs never did anyone any good. They shouldn't even matter, but they did. Looking back on it now, I wondered if Philip and I were as perfect as I always imagined. I had sunk further into the abyss, while he carried on with his life, his work and his friends. He saw his clients more than he saw me. I had lost a dear friend, my child and the prospect of ever becoming a mother. I had lost my husband too, even though I didn't want to admit that out loud just yet. When my head was finally clear, after being pumped full of enormous amounts of medication for weeks, I had too much time on my hands to think. The shooting repeated itself in my mind like a movie on repeat and I kept fretting about what I could have done to change its outcome. What ifs don't help fix things, but they are inevitable.

After three weeks in hospital, I was released, only to find that everything had changed. The home I so meticulously created in our town was gone forever. Philip had locked the doors to our house and moved us to New York while I lay in a coma. He said he did it so he could continue working while I was recovering, but that was just an excuse. Did he do it to punish me in his own way? He knew how much I loved our house; it would have helped me in my healing process. I would have found ways to avoid the shop, but at least I would have had the house. Instead, I was living in a strange Manhattan apartment, a prison of Philip's own making. It was obviously convenient for him, so he made the decision for me.

After the shooting, the few people in my life didn't know what to say or do. My in-laws couldn't stay long, since they had their own business to run, and they couldn't do much for me anyhow. We were never the greatest of talkers, and they obviously were too busy to stick around for much longer. I was also "just" their daughter-in-law, so why should they care, when my own parents didn't even bother to fly over? From them, all I got was a get-well card followed by a sorry-for-your-loss note. I threw them in the trash.

Simone came by a few times. She told me that the shop was closed and waiting for my return. She tried to do me right by avoiding too many details but seeing her only reminded me of that day, so I asked her to stay away. The few other friends I had came by and left quickly too. Nobody would be able to get through to me in the state I was in. I couldn't find it in my heart right now to ever go back to my shop, so I asked my in-laws before they left, to take care of things and to fire Simone with a more than decent bonus. I trusted my father-in-law a lot when it came to my finances. He was a good man, who did a lot of good things for me. I knew he would handle this whole process with Rob, so that I wouldn't have to face cold hard facts, something he was good at.

For months, I lived in shock, getting myself through every single agonizing day without giving a damn. I would stare for hours at the huge scars that mutilated my abdomen and chest. The surgeons had opened me up in three places to rinse my organs and remove the womb and Eve. Those horrible scars would forever remind me of lost happiness. Weeks later, they remained large and gritty, a reminder that when the surgeons were busy trying to save my life, they had no time to consider the esthetics of things. Even that didn't matter. I couldn't bear that my uterus was gone. I had dreamt of having children since the age of sixteen. My sole purpose in life had been to become a mom.

Philip had always been quite distant and superficial, something that I came to realize as soon as I started analyzing our relationship as it had been before all of this took place. Even when we were still a so-called happily married couple, we were not overtly happy. My husband often didn't get me. He had mentioned often that he didn't need to have children to be happy, that it wasn't because others had them, that we should feel obligated to raise a family. Before I became pregnant, my husband liked his carefree life and the freedom that we granted each other. We each had our own lives, and he liked that. I spent many nights alone at our house while he was away on business. It was one of the reasons why I worked so many hours too. No point in coming home to an empty house. I had asked him to change his ways as soon as the baby arrived. He never gave me a straight confirmation that he would adapt his lifestyle, apart from proposing to move to Manhattan. He asked me straightforward if I had forgotten to take my birth control pills. I hadn't, but I knew he wouldn't believe me. My pregnancy was an accident, but to me, it was a welcome one.

I know now that he was scared. Phillip was many things, but he never lied to me. Perhaps that trip to Washington was never meant to be. My husband and I never had that much to say to one another as it were. Taking me to some fancy hotel in a beautiful city meant we could spend the day wandering around instead of having a real conversation about our future. He could act all worried and caring, but he wouldn't have to talk about the time when we would have to take a stroller with us. I knew his dream was to live in Manhattan, something that people with kids don't often do. They stay out of the city, where subways are non-existent, and strollers can be shoved into family cars.

I know now that Eve wasn't convenient to him, yet he was pissed off at me for losing her. Looking back on it now, I realized that I was the only one preparing everything for the birth of our child. I had bought the furniture and picked out the clothes. I had done the practical things, while he continued with his life as usual. He had told me to hire a nanny, something I had blatantly refused. I had planned to take Eve with me to the shop instead. He didn't even know that Samantha and Simone had fought over who could take care of her the best, or that Simone had offered to work more hours to help me out.

Staring at my ruined abdomen, I knew why I so desperately wanted to have this child. She would have driven away that aching loneliness I had felt ever since I was a young girl. Eve meant life, after all. I had prayed that she would inject some love and affection into mine, something I had been missing for a long time, even with Philip as husband. When I was younger, I didn't have any friends. I had always been an introvert, especially as a young girl. I had difficulty making friends because I was so shy. I was a natural redhead, often bullied because of my amazing number of freckles, my startling hair, almost translucent skin and fierce green eyes. Boys loved to make fun of me, while girls openly discussed my looks and called me a walking stop sign. Even my dad called me Freckle-Face in front of his friends, who happened to be the parents of my classmates. Word got around fast.

My mom coolly told me not to care. She always claimed to love the color of my hair and the way that my skin stayed so pale, but I hated it. When push came to shove, she never went to school to talk to my teachers or principal. She always said it would pass. I was afraid of going to school and being bullied every single day. I preferred to stay home and create imaginary worlds, so I often used an excuse to stay at home sick. Since mom worked so many hours, she hardly cared. In my confinement of my bedroom, I felt safe. That was my haven.

I invented people to share my world with, mostly girlfriends that I could chat with freely, or watch old television shows with. I was crazy about an old eighties show called The Black Stallion, dreaming I was the one sitting on that horse. I wanted to learn horseback riding, but my parents never had the time to take me to riding lessons. Just like with many other hobbies, this one remained a dream. One of my imaginary friends was a good amazon, of course the best one in the world. She did whatever I couldn't, dared what I was too afraid of. I encouraged her in whatever she had to do to reach her goals.

My imagination frightened my parents, who even consulted a therapist. It was one of the few times they actually cared that something was off about me. The psychiatrist I spoke to a few times, told them that I would grow out of it, and I did. When I grew into my teenage years, my imaginary world slowly faded away. I still stayed lonely, still had no boyfriends and hardly any girlfriends. I would always remain the loner, but I got used to it. I found my way in school and no longer needed imaginary friends to protect me.

At the age of twenty, I was finally able to accept myself for who I was. I would always be a woman who stood out in the crowd and maybe that wasn't so bad as I used to believe. People started noticing me in a different way, even when my dad still called me Freckle-Face. During my college years, I had my fair share of boyfriends, thanks to the fact I got my huge amount of hair under control and found ways to cover up my freckles. Guys liked my looks and often called me a stunner. They showed me off to friends and family, which surprised me, because I never considered myself attractive. In my mind, I was still Freckle-Face.

When I met Philip, he was the first one who didn't brag about me to his friends, which was probably one of the major reasons why I trusted him immediately. He was a shy, quiet, polite man, who offered security. He was a calm personality, a man who let me grow into myself and accepted my quiet, introvert nature. He supported me financially when I refused to use my dad's money to buy the flower shop. Before moving to South Africa permanently, my dad set up a trust fund in my name that I refused to touch to this day. I was stubborn about it too. Everything came down to the fact that my parents didn't really like me enough to take me with them, so my dad paid me off, believing I could use his money more than him. My stinking rich father didn't get why I didn't touch it, so he had set up an arrangement that I would get it on my thirtieth birthday, which would be in a couple of months.

My decision had nothing to do with the money, but everything with their lack of interest in me. What kind of parents move to the other side of the world, without even asking their daughter if she wants to join them? They never did. They announced their retirement as if they were talking about the weather, after they had arranged it all. I was already dating Philip and had a job, so they figured I would be happier staying here. I was not welcome in their Cape Town villa. They never invited me to come over once. I was an unwanted child, an accident in their lives, which was made pretty clear over the years.

I didn't love Philip the way people do in movies. Philip was nice. Just nice. He wasn't sexy or overtly attractive and definitely not the type of man that I saw myself living together with for the rest of my life. He didn't crave sex all the time, nor did he demand my attention either. He kept on living his own life, while I did the same with mine. He was secure. The safe option. A friend. Easygoing. Not an asshole. He didn't like to talk about feelings and certainly never showed them to me. He offered to marry me before my parents left. We did. Not because I wanted to, but because it was the easiest solution.

Our marriage was a small, discrete affair, with only a couple of friends and our two sets of parents present, who hardly spoke to one another. My parents would be moving to South Africa one week later, so they left early with the excuse they still had some packing to do. I had yearned for the full-blown wedding thing since I was thirteen years old, but nobody bothered with it. There was no grand party in a fancy venue, no ten-thousand-dollar dress with matching shoes. I made my own flower arrangements, bought a dress with my own money. Philip didn't seem to care about the fanciness either. He didn't have that many friends and he disliked most of his co-workers. Inviting clients was out of the question. Our wedding was organized according to his low expectations, while I buried mine. What was the point in arguing with him about what I wanted, when he always assumed I thought the same about everything? I was so scared about losing him that I didn't dare to put my foot down. I just wanted someone to love me once.

Even the moment that I announced my pregnancy, bouncing up and down from sheer joy, my husband just quietly shrugged and told me he was happy for me. Not for himself. Never for himself. It all made sense now. Philip was cold of heart, and I had buried myself too deep into the life we had led together for years, sensing only now how damned lonely that was. It was fitting that I was now alone in my misery too. There wasn't even a grave to visit. According to the law, Eve wasn't even considered a baby yet, so she had no right to a funeral. Legally, I had given premature birth to a fetus that had not reached the full six months yet. I had been twenty-four weeks pregnant. Even if she had survived the shooting and they would have been able to bring her into this world alive, she wouldn't have stood a chance of survival.

To me, she existed. In my mind, she was an actual baby. Even though I never saw her or got to hold her, she was all I had after Philip, and I became estranged. She was all that I clung to. She kept me sane. To me she was a soul that had gone when her incomplete little body died inside of me. I imagined her talking to me, encouraging me to hold on, screaming at me to love life again.

I believe fiercely that somehow my daughter led me to Vivian when

I needed her the most. It wasn't a coincidence that I met her on the day Eve would have been born. Without Vivian, I would not have survived another day.

29

Thursday

Five

TWO MONTHS AFTER EVE'S SUPPOSED birthdate, I felt more miserable than I ever had before. It was mid-December, and the city felt extra-bright, lit with Christmas lights and decorated with too many colorful trees, as if people had nothing but good things to celebrate. It was still wet out instead of snowy, too warm for this time of year. A lot of people were hoping for a White Christmas, but I prayed the snow would stay away for once. I couldn't wait for the next four weeks to be over so that life could return to its dreary self. I was wallowing in misery, which radiated off me like an aura, something others around me noticed too. People automatically stayed out of my way. Having a stiff drink wouldn't help to lighten up my mood either, but I could at least try. Drinking myself senseless was one of the few things I hadn't attempted yet.

I envied people who could drink beer after beer and became light-headed and giggly as a result. I never did. Lately, my self-pity had become a source of negative energy that kept pushing me further into the abyss. I had driven everyone who meant something to me away. The very few friends that I had in the past never bothered to call me anymore. My parents and in-laws stayed away too. Everyone avoided my melancholy rather than trying to help me escape it. It was easier that way for them and I couldn't blame them. I chose to flee my problems, rather than to face discussions anyhow.

Yesterday evening, my dad called from South Africa to ask me bluntly about my future plans. After all, the day after Eve's birthdate, I had told him myself during one of our rare Skype calls, that I was going to bravely pick up the shattered remains of my life and move on. I was driven by the unexpected encounter with Vivian, who called me the day after our accidental meeting and told me she wanted us to stay friends. After the first high was gone, I never made a single attempt to live up to my vow to return to normality, which left my parents frustrated. Then again, they never bothered to come over from South Africa for a visit either, nor did they send me tickets to fly over to Cape Town, so why should I even care what they said about my life?

My dad started probing rather rudely. When was I going back to the shop? What was I doing with the rest of my life? Was I thinking of adopting children? How was Philip doing? Those were only a few of the questions that he fired at me. I knew mom was listening in, probably biting her fingernails. I knew that she had probably wanted to fly back after the shooting, but dad had refused since Philip was keeping them posted about my condition. He felt it was pointless, since I was in a coma and wouldn't even notice them around. After I woke up, I hadn't asked for their help, so Dad took that as a sign that I was doing just fine. He didn't even get I was so used to not having them around, that asking them for help didn't occur to me once.

Instead of going into a fierce argument with my parents about my non-existent future, I told my dad that I would call them back later. I didn't, like I never bothered. I had learned the trade of avoidance from the best and was getting pretty good at it too. Even my husband Philip stayed away rather than to face the mess we were in. He had made a habit of working late and hardly came home for dinner anymore. Then again, I never prepared any food for us, so why should he bother in the first place, when there were literally thousands of restaurants to choose from.

This evening was one of the first times I left our apartment for a dinner date. Before, Vivian and I always settled for a coffee bar or a small takeaway joint near the apartment, so that I wouldn't have to walk too far. Tonight, she had insisted on meeting me at Marcello's, only three blocks away. I had called the owner myself, since I knew him quite well. It wasn't easy getting a table there at such short notice, but I abused my dad's name for once. Even when Vivian was still living across the street, we never met up in her or my place. She hated that apartment, she told me once. It was cold, dreary and damp and she promised to find something else pretty soon, which she did. Only, she never told me where she moved to, nor did she give me a follow-up address. She kept to herself, which I respected. I had no choice in the matter anyway.

Vivian and I had grown close in a very short period of time. I had told her everything about me on that first evening, when we wound up sitting at a small table in a coffee bar. She just listened and then declared herself the person that would help me out of my depression. She'd been trying ever since. My current situation was unbearable; I don't think anyone would manage to free me from that. My husband and I lived apart together, with nothing in common but the furniture we shared. Part of me ached for the tension to end, to get things over with, but another part of my broken heart clung to the past and ignored the fact that that there was nothing left to hang onto. I read somewhere that a wife is always the last to find out about her husband's adultery, but I discovered the truth rather fast. I knew on instinct that there was someone else in Philip's life, even if I couldn't prove it yet. My husband had changed too much, too fast. His interest in me waned into a dull partnership that would result in lives of frustration should we maintain this status quo. My insides screamed loudly that he was still my husband, even if my body forgot what he felt like. We had devoted many years of our lives to making this relationship work. Any failure now would only result in a deeper form of depression I couldn't afford anymore.

Vivian was already at Marcello's when I arrived. When I walked in and shook off the raindrops clinging onto my clothes and hair, she turned in my direction, frowning. I knew she was not pleased that I again hadn't taken an umbrella with me. I attempted a smile and hugged her before she could comment on the negligence of my own health.

"What are you having?" she asked while I perched down on the barstool next to her.

"A Martini," I replied. "What do you want?"

"A cocktail."

The bartender ignored Vivian when I gave him our order. I felt his behavior was quite rude but didn't comment on it. The few times I had met Vivian for a coffee, she was often ignored by people serving us. It almost became a running joke that I would place our order. She usually just shrugged and told me she was the unnoticeable type that people walked by on the street without paying attention to. I didn't get that, since she was gorgeous, something she waved away when I commented on it.

The bartender came back with our drinks, placed them in front of me and told me that my table would be ready in a few minutes. Again, he never looked at her, which pissed me off. Vivian placed her hand on my wrist to stop me from speaking up. Lately, I had become more vocal in expressing my sentiments, which she didn't like. She told me to stay calm and ignore rude people, like she always did. Vivian had insisted on having this meal together, commenting that I was growing too skinny. Philip had told me this morning he would stay late at the office tonight. I couldn't care less. Days passed by unnoticed, and I still hadn't considered going back to work.

Vivian pointed a finger at my drink.

"A Martini. Are you sure that's wise?"

"Why shouldn't it be? I'm tired of drinking tasteless water," I snapped.

She shrugged and sipped her cocktail, pushing it aside before long. Her glass remained untouched on the bar. Even though we had only met by chance, Vivian knew me better than anyone ever did. I had come to realize that I was growing dependent on her advice. She was patient with me, more than I was with my own, rude behavior. I hated myself; she didn't. Somehow, she always figured out what I was thinking. I let her make decisions for me. To be honest, it felt good to have someone like her hovering over me. The manager, my father's old friend, walked over and smiled at me while Vivian checked her email on her phone. I prayed he wouldn't start in about the attack. Everyone seemed to know about it.

"Zoey, I'm so happy to see you here again," he smiled, giving me a brief hug. "It's been a while, hasn't it? How are you these days?"

He obviously didn't know, which made me relax a bit. I took deep breaths and put up my bravest face.

"I'm fine," I responded, a fake smile plastered around my lips. "How is your wife?"

"Perfect. And your husband?"

"He's fine too."

"I'm sorry to see he's not here with you tonight," the manager commented, looking around. "Is he still coming?"

"He had other things to do," I replied curtly.

"Your table will be ready shortly. If I can assist you in any way tonight, please let me know."

As a true gentleman would, the manager dismissed my husband's absence. Before my attack, Philip and I had been regulars at Marcello's. My father had earned that privilege for me, years ago. Philip was an excellent eater, someone who could really savor the taste of his food. He never left a plate half-stacked and often would clean up mine too, something a restaurant owner obviously likes. Tonight, I would leave half of my plate untouched, since appetite had escaped me for months. Even in this comfortable, beautifully decorated restaurant smelling like a home, I felt uncomfortable and eager to leave. For months, I had buried myself alive with my memories. When Vivian proposed this dinner, she told me bluntly that I was not the one who died, that I still had a life. I was too young to go through the motions like this. I owed it to Samantha and Eve to live my life properly.

"Stop feeling so sorry for yourself. It doesn't suit you."

I looked up when Vivian spoke to me. She knew me so well, my vivacious Vivian. Two months ago, I had sworn that I would move on with my life, but I had not been able to do so at all. Every time I tried to go outside, there was something holding me back. I lived with my ghosts and memories, waiting for something to end it all. I knew of course why Vivian never came to my house. She forced me to go to coffee places to meet with her, as her way of getting me outside, if only for ten minutes. The first time, I ran out before my coffee was even ready. She never commented on it.

"You're doing fine," she said. "Stop worrying."

Was I? My appearance had changed a lot, but underneath the pale skin and long, unkempt hair, I was still me. With a little help, Vivian told me constantly, I could sparkle again. She chose to ignore the fact that huge scars had ruined my abdomen. I had shown them to her in a toilet stable of our regular coffee place. She said they were reminders of my survival and that I should wear them with pride. Yesterday, she had given me a lecture on life and death over the phone. She told me bluntly she couldn't accept me going through the motions like that. I wasn't dying, nor was I sick. I just needed to dig out a decent outfit, walk outside and live again. I made the effort to select a dress but didn't put on any make-up. She still smiled.

The manager returned while Vivian complimented me on my outfit. The bartender looked at us while we talked with an eyebrow high in the sky, but he didn't mingle into the conversation. We were just making small talk after all. We were shown to a table by the window. It was crowded at the restaurant. There was a birthday party going on in the far corner, where a private table was set for about fifteen people. It caught my eye. A little girl blew out ten candles. She was beautiful, with golden hair that danced on her shoulders every time she moved and large blue eyes that betrayed her intelligence. You could already see the adult that she would one day become. She was perfect and when her mother hugged and kissed her, I couldn't help but wish that I were in that mother's shoes. I turned away when they sang for her.

The restaurant was as charming as I remembered. All tables were occupied already, except for the one we were headed for. I looked outside the window and observed people on the streets. The dreary rain had become a constant; most people kept dry under large umbrellas. It was comfortably warm inside. God, how I had missed this place. How I missed being amongst people. Some of the guests seemed to have come straight from the office, but there were also a few families with teenagers or younger kids. I looked briefly around discretely. Everyone seemed to be in control of their lives. I envied them. Suddenly I longed to go back to my shop. I had too much time on my hands and too little people to talk to. If I did something useful with my life, I might be able to deal with my constant sorrow as well. Vivian was right: I needed to move on and forget this had ever happened. Maybe one day, I might find happiness again, instead of this killer loneliness.

"Can I get you something to drink?" the waitress asked me friendly.

My martini still stood before me. I had hardly touched it, except to take a few sips. I looked up confused. I had no idea what I wanted to drink or eat.

My stomach felt like throwing up everything I put in it. Acid burned inside my throat and stomach, as if I had ulcers. Vivian looked at me and waited until I would order for the two of us, like I always did. My mouth opened and my unused voice croaked.

"White wine. Make it a bottle."

Vivian frowned when the waitress left to fetch my order. The menu lay closed before us on the table. I didn't feel like eating, even though I had to if we were going to stay here.

"You're drinking," my friend remarked. "First the Martini, now the wine. What's going on, Zoey?"

"Nothing. Why do you care?"

Vivian shrugged, only to continue in her familiar icy cold voice that she used when she didn't agree with me.

"You're right. Why should I care that you're ruining your life?"

We didn't talk again until the waitress returned with an expensive bottle of house wine. She put it on the table, poured some in my glass and let me taste it. When I nodded, she only poured my glass, rudely, and left hurriedly. I took the bottle and filled the second glass, which I placed before Vivian. What the hell was wrong with these people?

"Don't worry about it," Vivian said, smiling at me. "I'm used to this kind of treatment, you know that."

"That doesn't make it right," I snapped. "What's going on with the world these days anyhow? People are so rude and impolite. It pisses me off."

The waitress returned again, breaking through my rant with a nervous gaze in her eyes.

"Are you ready to order dinner?" she asked me.

"Not yet," I snapped.

The waitress stared past me at Marcello's manager, shrugged lightly and took off again. I couldn't even bear to open the menu, let alone decide on what food would make me want to throw up and which one would stay down. I stared at my glass for a long, long time. I was debating with myself about dinner, deciding not to order. Vivian didn't seem to be bothered either. She just sat there, watching me. I slugged down a first glass of wine. When I poured another one, she muttered quietly.

"Bottoms up, hon."

"Screw you," I whispered, knowing all too well that she still heard it.

God, my best friend was in a nasty mood today, as if she sensed how down I felt and was reflecting my anxiety through her actions. Vivian smiled lightly, leaned forward and pushed her chin on her folded hands. Her eyes narrowed while she examined the expression on my face. I knew I wouldn't have to count on much sympathy tonight.

"What's really going on, Zoey?" she asked.

I didn't feel like talking, realizing a little too late that this dinner was a bad idea. I should have been at home, fighting it out with my husband. I should be arguing with him, screaming at him for his sullen patience and complete disinterest in me. I should be battling to save my marriage, instead of sitting here in a restaurant complaining about it.

"Tell me, Zoey," she insisted.

"I'm in trouble," I blurted out.

My mouth felt dry. There was a sour taste capturing my tongue. Truthfully, I didn't like the taste of wine at all. God, why the hell was I even drinking in the first place? I felt sick to my stomach.

"Why?" Vivian prodded.

"I think Philip has finally had enough of me. He's going to kick me out."

My best friend looked at me with those startling eyes of hers that seemed to know everything.

"Good riddance," she reacted sharply. "He's been a pain in the ass for far too long."

"He's my husband, Vivian. I need him," I said weakly.

"You need comfort and attention, things that he is not giving you," she pointed out.

"He gives me that," I objected.

"When was the last time he was there for you, Zoey?" Vivian snarled. "How long has it been since you last slept together? By your own account, he hasn't touched you since you were released from hospital. He's busy, always too occupied with his work or anything else that keeps him away from you. He always has enough excuses not to pay any attention to your sadness. Don't you think that you have had enough of him?"

Her words were like a slap in the face. Most of the time, I accepted her snobbish remarks, but there were just as many times that I resented her for telling me the truth in such a harsh, cold manner. She was the person I turned to in times of need, but she could be tough as nails when it came to my estranged husband.

"He's suffering too," I spoke, lowering my eyes.

"Really? I hadn't noticed." She smirked.

"You've never even met him."

"Which says enough, doesn't it? I'm your best friend and speak to you more than your husband does, while you and I aren't even living together. Why hasn't he even shown interest in me, Zoey?"

"I don't know," I admitted. "Do you want to meet him?"

"No. I don't want to," Vivian said. "Your stories told me enough about his unbelievably selfish character. Where was he when you needed him, Zoey? When did he show you his sadness, his grief and his longing to set things right? Get rid of him. He's holding you back and he doesn't deserve you. He's one of the reasons why you're so down right now, do you even realize that?"

"So, what am I supposed to do?" I asked as hot tears flooded my face. "I can't move on without him either. He has lost his child too. If I let him go, I'll lose all that reminds me of Eve. She was meant to turn us into a family; don't you get that?"

"Oh really?" Vivian looked me in the eye. "Since when is putting kids in this world the perfect solution to fix what has already been broken?"

"Our marriage wasn't broken."

"Really?" she smiled. "Could have fooled me. Look at the kind of father he would have been for a child he didn't even want in the first place, by your own admittance, not mine. You said it yourself: you did everything, while he carried on with his life as if he was a bachelor."

Another slap in the face. I shoved my chair backwards roughly, causing everyone in the restaurant to look up and stare at our table. God, Vivian was in a nasty mood again today. Why did I let her into my life, when all she did was talk down on me? What made her better than my husband?

"Go to hell," I snapped.

"Sit down, Zoey," her strong voice ordered, while her hand rested on my wrist, holding me from leaving. Her fingers formed tiny circles on my skin. It calmed me down. "Please, take a seat," she repeated, calmer now.

I sank down again, still trembling. People returned to their dishes, ignoring us again. Vivian was right about every single word she ever uttered, which made her blunt words come across even harder. She was the strong one, like the person I had been after I discovered that I could overcome the bullying at school and move on from it all. It felt as if my former strength had been transferred into this woman's body. We could have been two parts of the same person: our own little Jekyll and Hyde.

"Don't ever speak to me like that again," I whispered hoarsely.

"I'm sorry, Zoey. I didn't mean it the way it sounded."

"I know."

I rubbed my temples. A pounding headache found its way through my skull. It felt as if my brain was going to explode. When I looked up, I saw Vivian in a haze. She got up and grabbed me by the elbow.

"You need some fresh air. Let's get out of here."

My head spun as I left the table, with the untouched menu and the bottle of wine as sad reminders of this evening. I threw some money on the table, told the waitress that I wasn't feeling well and left. The outside air sobered me up immediately. Vivian tucked her arm between mine and dragged me with her.

"Let's find a quiet place to talk."

Six

VIVIAN ENTERED MY LIFE OUT of the blue and I loved her for it. She was a god's gift; I had never met anyone like her. I could not have wished for a better friend. Truth be told, I wasn't sure if I would have been able to be so patient with her, had the roles been reversed. I envied her for her feistiness, because she represented what I had lost after the attack. She was a successful woman in every way, where I had become a neurotic little invalid. I often wondered if she saw me as a charity case, but you would have to have the patience of an angel to go to these lengths. My new friend's strength lifted me out of my stupor and kept me going. She didn't seem to care that I leaned on her in an almost suffocating way. When I was so down I couldn't trust myself anymore, we spoke over the phone for hours, even during office hours, where she laughingly told me she was hidden in a meeting room, just to talk to me. When she noticed I was so far gone I needed to see her in real life to keep my sanity intact, she dropped everything and told me where to meet. On the other hand, she would also disappear just as fast, sometimes even cutting off a conversation to go wherever she needed to go.

Perhaps one day, Vivian's lifeforce would give me enough support to move on and stop feeling sorry for myself. Perhaps then, I would accept I was no longer a successful woman running a flower shop in a quaint little town, but someone who had to start again from scratch. The smell of flowers made me sick to my stomach these days and the scars on my body still remained visible. I was far from doing okay.

We ended up at Jesse's Bar, a small place downtown, where five tables and a bar allowed no more than thirty people in. The place was filled, even when it was only Thursday evening. We got lucky and ended up at a small table near the toilets. The previous occupants had just left. Their seats were still warm. I ordered mineral water. Vivian smiled.

"That's a good girl."

I thought she was going to pat me on the back like she would do a dog. I was sobered up by now. The calm stroll through the streets of Manhattan had done me good. It had stopped raining, so we had decided not to take a cab, but to walk the five blocks to get here. Vivian said that I should look around and see what was out there. She was so convinced that I would love the city again one day, that her enthusiasm worked on me. I knew what she was trying to do of course. She wanted me to open my eyes to see the world for what it really was and realize there was so much more than sadness to full my days with. I glanced around and spotted hundreds of New Yorkers going about their business, enjoying their evening. I saw tourists taking pictures of the stupidest things.

"Close your eyes and focus on the smell," Vivian said.

I stopped walking, did as she said and focused on feeling something for real again. The scent of rain hung in the streets, combined with the typical New York smells. It was supposed to be snowing right now, but the rain felt so much better. I could even forget that it would be Christmas in two weeks' time.

"Life goes on," she whispered in my ear. "You just need to grasp it, reclaim it."

By the time we reached the bar, I did feel a bit better. The buzzing sound in my head had simmered to a low. I took off my Burberry and placed it on the empty chair next to me. We still hadn't eaten, but my stomach wasn't protesting painfully. I looked at my hands and noticed they were shivering. That old, familiar ache that hurt my abdomen, came back. Sitting down, hurt. Standing up hurt even more. Doing anything at all made me feel like I had been run over by a truck.

"What's wrong with you tonight?" Vivian asked casually.

"Nothing."

"Don't give me that crap, Zoey. You are not yourself."

"You've never seen me like myself," I pointed out.

"You're wallowing in self-pity again."

"Didn't I earn that right?"

Vivian leaned forward.

"There are thousands of people worse off than you are. People who lost absolutely everything and still managed to build a life for themselves. Why don't you get your head out of your ass and remember that you have plenty of good things to live for? Get rid of Philip and move on. That's what you need to do to feel better."

I winced in pain. Instinctively, my hands reached for my constantly aching lower body. Even after six months, I still couldn't survive without my pain medication. Last week I had another thorough check-up to find out what the underlying problem might be. My surgeon told me that my body was healing well and that I just needed to be patient. He couldn't say where the pain came from, nor why my head hurt where my chest and abdomen were the areas which had the surgery. He just said that the abdomen and head were linked and that they saw this phenomenon a lot with abdominal patients. He seemed to find it normal for me to suffer and frowned when I went into detail about my complaints. I'm sure he thought it was all in my head; he could be absolutely right too, but it didn't alter the fact that I needed pills to survive through the day. I took out the small bottle I always carried with me and dropped a tiny white pill on the palm of my hand. Vivian stopped me before I could swallow it.

"What are you doing?" she hissed.

"I'm taking this because I'm in pain."

"You are hooked on these pills, Zoey. You don't need them. How many did you already have today?"

I shook off her grip and swallowed the pill, downing a full glass of water straight after.

"Do you want my help or not?" Vivian asked coolly.

"I don't want you to do decide for me whether or not I'm in pain," I snapped. "Why don't we switch bodies, so you can feel what it's like to be shot in the gut?"

She winced and pulled back. Several people stared at us. I ignored them bluntly. I knew I was pissing Vivian off tonight, but I didn't care anymore. She was harsh to me tonight too. Payback's a bitch. Vivian sighed while she ran a hand through her long hair, rolling her eyes. She knew perfectly well I was in a nasty mood, challenging her to get rid of me too.

"I don't know why I even bother with you," she spoke. "You are not willing to listen to me or anyone else, and the only person to blame for that, is you. You need to start a war in order to win it, Zoey. That war isn't even with Philip, it's with yourself. Go home and talk to him. Get it over and done with. You are through with him. He's a waste. Move on."

"I can't," I muttered. "I don't want to go home."

"Why not?"

"I'm going nuts in that apartment. I feel suffocated, as if the world itself falls on top of me as soon as I set foot inside. All I have done for the past months is stare at empty, dreary walls. I get headaches all the time and these damned pills are not helping at all anymore. I feel worse every day, like something inside of me is still dying."

"Have you told your doctor that?"

"He doesn't believe me," I shrugged. "I just know something's still wrong with me, but nobody will listen to me."

"You're going to ask your doctor for heavier painkillers then? To get even more addicted?" Vivian asked matter-of-factly.

"I'm not an addict."

"You can't live without them. That makes you an addict."

"What do you know about it?" I snarled. "Do you really think I'm imagining my aches and pain? Do you believe, like they all do, that it's only in my head? I'm in pain, Vivian. I have to deal with this if I want to make something of my life again. Right now, I'm even too weak to confront my own husband because of this. I need to sort things out medically first, before I can even think about fixing the mess I'm in."

"So, you are planning on going back to work?"

"Yes."

I blurted the word out and immediately knew I meant it. I wanted to return to my flowers, but I was so afraid. I knew that from now on, I would stare at every customer as if he or she were the enemy. I would always look at the spot where Samantha had died and feel the overwhelming guilt. I would never be able to hear the bell charm, without seeing Mrs. Peterson's body lying there, blocking the doorway. No matter what any therapist would say or do to treat me, that feeling would never go away. I would never feel safe again.

"It's a start," Vivian said surprised. "You said 'yes'."

I blinked. Her voice was much calmer now.

"I'm proud of you," she continued. "And I'm sorry too. I don't mean to hurt you, but sometimes you need to be confronted with your own reality. You need to be through feeling sorry for yourself. It's over and done with. You need to restore your self-esteem and move on with your life. You're not even thirty years old, Zoey, do you even realize that? Don't let life hurt you like that anymore."

"You are hurting me," I commented softly.

"You come to me for advice, don't you?" she smirked. "You need me to act as your conscience. To force the decisions out of you that you won't take for yourself."

"Should I pay you for counselling me then?" I snapped. "You sure as hell act as if you are my therapist."

That smirk was back again, but it was a good one. God, she was acting like a shrink. The therapist I had seen at the hospital and with whom I was still meeting once a month, never even dared to address the actual issues of what I went through. The doctor who had performed those three surgeries on me only treated the physical aspects, but never the emotional ones. Because my scars had healed nicely and I no longer bled from the inside out, I was considered healed. The therapist focused only on my emotional state, but never on those killer pains. I had nobody linking the two together. Vivian was the only one that really noticed how badly I was still doing. Philip wasn't around enough to watch me spend seven to eight hours in bed per day, hurting, aching, begging for the nights to come earlier for once.

"What do you charge per hour?" I asked, suddenly laughing lightly.

My laughter shocked myself. God, I hadn't smiled for ages.

"That's what I like to see in you, Zoey," Vivian reacted, obviously relieved. "Anger instead of apathy. Fierceness instead of fear. You're stronger than you think. I really am so very proud of you."

I smiled nervously through my tears while I drank my glass of water. I even felt ridiculously happy for a few moments, savoring her compliments as if they were worth more than any gold in the world. She made me feel like I could face the world again. Why did I always lose that strength when she was out of sight again? Without her near me, I remained a wreck.

"It's time you get out of that prison that you're living in, Zoey," Vivian continued. "You should go out, have fun, laugh and enjoy life. You need companionship, someone who genuinely cares for and about you. Who listens to your fears and answers by taking them away. Someone who sees your needs and fulfills them. Someone who flirts with you and makes you feel as if you're the most important person in the world. Someone that connects with you on a whole new level."

"All of this at the same time?" I snorted.

Vivian threw her head back and laughed happily, making me smile again too. The tension between us broke. She patted my hand and leaned forward, whispering to me as if we were conspirators.

"I like you so much, Zoey. You're stubborn and hard-headed and oh so hurt, but you are, above all, strong and witty. I want nothing more than to discover the real you. You are still recovering from it all and you need time, but God, how I wish I could do more for you."

"You already are doing so much," I blurted out embarrassed, knowing all too well Vivian didn't do emotions. She usually shrugged my remarks away. "You bring me out of my shell, Vivian."

"I'm glad, but it should be your husband who is doing that for you, Zoey. Why did he ever stop caring? Or did he never care at all?"

"I don't know," I spoke truthfully. "I do know that I need go home and talk to him for real, for once. You're right about everything, Vivian. I can't go on like this. One way or the other, this has to end tonight."

"Good."

Vivian stood without even touching her drink once. She reached for her coat and placed it over her slim shoulders. I watched her pack her bag, totally surprised at her sudden move, not knowing she was going to drop a bomb on me next.

"I have to go," she spoke casually. "I'm leaving the country for a couple of days."

I slumped back and stared at her in despair. I had counted on her to be there for me after my confrontation with Philip. Why the hell didn't she tell me this earlier?

"Don't look at me like that, Zoey," she laughed. "I'm not going away forever, you know. I'm just catching a red eye to Paris tonight. I'll be back in a couple of days, I promise."

"Why?" I croaked.

"For work, darling, why else? There are no rich billionaires lying around, you know. That only happens in tacky movies. I told you before that I have a busy schedule for the remainder of the year, or did you forget? My flight leaves in three hours; my meeting with the client is tomorrow at two p.m. Paris time and will probably last until late in the evening. With a bit of luck, I'll be flying back on Saturday already. If I'm not that lucky, I might have to stay there for a few days."

"Can I reach you while you're abroad?" I asked in despair.

"Leave a message on my voicemail, you know what those time zones are like. That's the one thing I hate about them. Jetlag doesn't really bother me, but I always get lost in those hour differences. Look, I'll listen to my messages whenever I can and get in touch with you when it's urgent, alright?"

Noticing my disappointment, she pulled me up and gave me a warm hug.

"Come on, Zoey. Don't look so frightened. You'll be just fine, I promise. You've survived your whole life without me, and I promise you that you would continue to be fine when I'm gone again too, as a figure of speech."

Her words scared me. I was devastated Vivian hadn't told me this earlier. I couldn't for the life of me remember her saying she had to go to Paris. This was the first time since we met that she would be out of the country for a couple of days. Before, she was always in Manhattan, where I could get in touch with her whenever I felt the need to talk. The mobile phone number she gave me two months ago was all I had to get in touch with her. I didn't even have her email, and she had told me she abhorred social media. Plus, I didn't know where she lived. Hell, I didn't even know exactly what kind of work she did, just that it had something to do with financial software. She simply wasn't willing to share much information with me, claiming she was fond of her privacy. Since I had been in such a bad state, I had eagerly accepted her willingness to counsel me, no questions asked.

Vivian stroked the side of my face gently with the back of her hand once she released me from our hug. I wanted to hold on tight to feel human warmth. I wanted to tell her how important our friendship was to me, but I knew she would not have any of that expressed sentiment. We hardly ever hugged; this was one of those rare moments that we touched. I knew she hadn't told me about her trip earlier, to avoid any dramatic scenes in a crowded restaurant. Maybe she didn't even sense how devastated I was, or maybe she just didn't want to know. It felt like the lifeline she had thrown in my direction, was being pulled back without me hanging onto it. I screamed at her not to go, but my mouth didn't stop her from leaving either.

Vivian left me alone at the bar. I didn't make the effort to go after her. I watched her walk by the window without looking back once. She lit a cigarette while she stopped at a light. I grabbed my coat, pulled it over my frozen body and threw some money on the table, making my decision to go after her. I couldn't let her go like this, not when everything in me screamed to stop her, even if I had to sit on that plane with her. I rushed outside, only to find her gone already. She hadn't even waited for a proper goodbye, nor did I see in which direction she had gone. I wouldn't pull a "Ross going to the airport to stop his Rachel from getting on that plane." I wasn't in love with her, though I might as well have been. I felt abandoned and lonely like never before.

I knew this was the way Vivian had wanted our goodbye to happen. She told me some time ago that she didn't like building lifetime friendships. I was the exception because she felt how much I needed help. She spoke about nobody at all. She was blunt about her family, always brushed off any questions about them. She stated that she didn't care about anyone but herself, that friendship was an abstract something that she couldn't build her life upon. At this very moment, I doubted that she cared enough about me to stick around for much longer. She didn't want any strings attached to her, so that she could leave in the middle of the night, and no one would know the better. The constant moving around was a clear witness to that fact. She lived alone, made her way through life alone. No one would wait for Vivian's return back from Paris. She liked it that way. Sex without any strings attached, she said. Friendship built only on her conditions. Emotions never got in the way. Love wasn't something frail that could end at any minute. Maybe I should try out that way of living, too. It would sure as hell lessen the heartache I was experiencing right now.

Seven

EVER SINCE I WAS A little girl, I had one dream that I longed to live as an adult. It would have to make up for the bullying I endured in school, the one thing that kept me on my feet whenever the going got tough. One day, I would find a caring, attentive man. I would marry him, have his children and devote my life to my family. I grew up an only child and always envied the people who came from large families. I was convinced that with at least one sibling around, I might have been protected from the sharp words blurted out by the other kids at school. A big brother would have beaten up everyone who dared to talk to me like that, while a little sister would have stopped anyone from hurting me in front of her, asking them in her innocence why they were being so mean.

I swore that I would have several children, to make sure that they would not endure what I went through for years. I would have them love and protect one another and teach them that family always came first. My mom and dad used to workday and night, earning heaps of money that didn't mean a thing to me, which meant that they were hardly around when those kids hurt me. My dad brushed it off as insignificant and concentrated on his business instead; my mom noticed the pestering only when it was already too late and then bluntly told me that I had to sort things out myself. Already feeling out of place and unwanted by them, it didn't take me long to understand that they were too busy to care much.

To make up for the lack of love, I decided to create my own future. I wanted to have three children and often imagined what they would look like. They would resemble my imaginary friends: kids that had nothing in common with me at all. My kids, just like my friends, would have blond or dark brown hair, with hazel or blue eyes. I spared them my startling red hair color, freckled face and green eyes that made me look like a witch. I imagined them tanned from the sun, not pale as a sheet. More importantly, my children would be bright, intelligent and kind to others. They would cherish the values my husband and I taught them: respect for everyone, no matter the race, gender and sexual preference. Protect the bullied and never bully yourself. I dreamt of long strolls down Central Park on weekends, hand in hand with my husband while our kids ran in front of us, accompanied by our two dogs. I imagined love and care and a warm house.

My husband would of course be the kind of person I could talk to forever. He would respect me for who I was, love me for my freckles and kiss every single one of them on my body. Our lovemaking would be perfect: passionate, fierce, respectful and open-minded, with care for each other's wishes and enough excitement to make anyone jealous. We would work hard, party hard. We would share the most intimate moments at night, when the children were asleep, after spending beautiful summer nights with our many friends, talking about the joys of life. My husband would be someone that showed interest in me. He would respect what I liked, just as I would value his work and choices. We would be rushing home after work every night, eager to see each other, hungry enough to tear off each other's clothes. We would steal small moments when the kids were still at school to make love on our kitchen floor. We would live in a small town in upstate New York, where my husband and I would have our jobs, but we would vacation abroad. Financially, we would be able to afford the best of the best. Money would be no issue of course; we could do whatever we wanted. We would live in our dream house, a place with a huge living room and a fireplace.

Instead of all of this, I got Philip. A man who I thought was sensible, smart and caring, but who turned out mean nothing at all. He didn't share a single detail of my dream, and I still don't know why I picked him. Maybe it was because all those other men weren't interested in me. Maybe there was nobody in this world who would want to know me. Or just maybe, I thought that I had to be grateful that someone like him would like someone like me. After all, that bullied little girl still lived and breathed inside of me.

When it happened, at first, according to what I heard much later, Philip had reacted the way a grieving husband should. He rushed to the hospital, only to hear I was in surgery. Pacing the waiting room, he fiercely cursed the woman who had done this to me. He even called his best friend, a New York prosecutor that he often ran to in court cases, to make sure that she would not be released on bail. Since her actions were grave enough not to grant her temporary freedom, she stayed in prison where she belonged, until the day she would go to trial, which would happen sometime in the next year. Something happened during those hours and the days that followed. Things shifted to the point of no repair, but I still didn't know why.

Maybe it was the Intensive Care Unit where I was at first. Philip became upset when nurses came to bandage my injuries and asked him if he wanted to see them. He apparently couldn't bear to see the ugly scars, so he ran away whenever they came in. He was too much in shock to ask about Eve's little body, so he let his father handle that. She was cremated; her ashes were scattered in the local cemetery on a grassy knoll for unborn infants. He wasn't there. My husband fled into the practicalities of things, because that's what he did best. He even went back to work on the Monday after the attack, when they didn't even know if I was going to survive. His boss told him to take some time off; he refused. Work kept him busy, so he said. Besides, so he told my parents over the phone, there were plenty of people at the hospital to take care of me, so why should he stay, when he knew they were still keeping me in that coma?

When I woke up, he wasn't there. In fact, he was not at the hospital at all. I didn't blame him for that. It would have been unfair for me to expect him to put his life aside for me. He rushed in when the nurses called him to tell him I had opened my eyes, so the second time I came to my senses, he was there. The first impression I remember of him was a strange mixture of relief and pain in his eyes. He opened his mouth several times, as if he wanted to blurt out his feelings. He didn't. Instead, he cried silently and held my hand, before escaping the room again, long before I fell asleep once more.

He started coming in late at the hospital, so he would only have to stay for a couple of minutes. Most of the time, I was left alone in that room, with nothing else to do but sleep and eat. My father-in-law argued with him about it, stating that his place was at my side. At one point, they had a huge argument about it in the ICU-cubicle, where Philip shouted that I wouldn't make it anyhow. He believed that I would still die, even though my condition was stable at the time. He was angry at me for ending up in hospital. He was angry with me for losing our child.

I woke up dazed one evening, still lingering between sleep and reality without him noticing, when he told his dad it was my fault because I hadn't taken off to Washington with him that Friday. I never told him I overheard that conversation, but I think he knew. It took another three days before my husband and I could have a decent conversation. I was heavily sedated to give my body time to heal, so I spent my time dozing off, in between eating small bites of tasteless food and using the bathroom. After five days, I was brought to a private room to heal further.

I remember how he walked in with a huge bunch of flowers, a totally wrong arrangement without any care for the meaning of the flowers in it. The smell made me sick to my stomach. It brought me straight back into my shop, alongside two bodies and one dead baby. Philip spent minutes trying to fix the bouquet so that it would fit into the too-small vase. He refused to look at me, until he no longer had a choice but to sit down by my side and play pretend. He reached for my hand; his touch felt harsh and cold.

"I'm so happy you're okay," he started in that strangled, strange tone of voice he had donned after the shooting.

"What's wrong?" I croaked in return.

A tube had been down my throat for days and it still ached to speak up. My voice sounded raspy and different, just like his.

"Nothing."

"Are you sure?"

"Yeah."

I tried to kiss the knuckles of his hands. Strangely enough, my attention was fully focused on him at that moment, as if I already knew that I was about to lose my husband. He never spoke about the loss of our baby. He never called her Eve, despite the fact that I did that multiple times. He didn't ponder about her loss. He didn't propose to put up a gravestone for her somewhere. After all, the law said she didn't exist, so why should he? I could never forgive him for that, nor for the words he had uttered when he thought I was passed out. We never grieved together, because, I realize now, I never allowed him to. The downfall of our marriage continued in rapid steps after he took me to that damned apartment with the wrong colors on the walls and the couches that I didn't pick myself and the boxes we never unpacked. Until the climax of disaster arrived on the very night Vivian had to travel to Paris, when I discovered that my husband never was the man I took for granted.

Eight

WHEN I UNLOCKED THE DOOR to our apartment, I found Philip waiting for me in the living room. The television was turned off; the radio wasn't playing, nor had he put up some Spotify music. That's what told me he had deliberately shut off all sound, in order to focus on me. The street noise was audible through the closed windows. Christmas lights shone their brightness down in the streets, but I would never see them inside these walls, since none of us planned to put up a tree or make the least amount of effort. I resented every inch of this apartment. Coldness greeted me as soon as I opened the door. I hung up my coat in the tiny hallway, walked further into the living room and stared at my husband for a long time, wondering how to address him. He was tense and upset, barely even looking at me. He fiddled with his fingers.

I sat down on the other couch, facing him. I didn't attempt to kiss him, didn't try to touch him. The wine and Martini, combined with the painkiller I took earlier, played ball with my stomach. I felt unsteady on my feet. Even while I sat, it seemed there was a war raging inside of me. Philip noticed my instability. He didn't care enough to ask questions about it. My husband still looked amazing, all hipster, with his scruffy beard and trendy clothes. He was wearing a new suit I had never seen before.

One could never tell the man had suffered a great loss. At the age of thirty-one, he was extremely handsome, with a lean body he trained for, short-cut blonde hair that grazed his collar and stunning eyes under dark eyebrows. Usually, his facial expression was quite neutral, like Steve Rogers in those Marvel movies. Tonight, his face was dark and glum. His gaze spoke of the secrets he kept from me, hidden beneath those beautiful eyes that had always looked at me without lies in them, until recently.

I remembered when my parents split up years ago for a short period of time. It was the one time they actually seemed to care about me. They had waited for me to come home from school, to tell me honestly that they were going through a rough patch. Dad was moving out for a while, so they said, and I actually felt relief that he wouldn't be around for a while. Oh, I was so naïve back then. I thought my mom would spend more time with me, now that dad was gone, but that didn't happen. In fact, it got even worse. She spent her days at work and her nights pouring out her heartache to me. I was nine at the time. My parents lived apart for a month and then dad moved back in, as if nothing had ever happened. I knew he was having an affair with one of the women at the office. Guilt was written all over his face. In the end, my mom won. That's how she called it: a win.

It was my turn to face the same ordeal my mother went through at the time, but I knew that I could never win, since I had already lost. The headache that had started at the bar only worsened. I resisted the urge to reach for one of my pills to soothe the slumbering pain. It wouldn't help anyhow, so I did nothing. I sat there for over ten minutes, before he could bring up the courage to face me decently. I refused to start the fight myself. Let him fear me, I thought bitterly.

Philip looked at me numbly, swallowing the lump stuck in his throat. He did something I had never expected: he moved places, until he sat next to me. He reached for my hands and stared at the broken, bitten fingernails. I had picked up that habit during my long recovery. He moved my hands up and kissed my fingertips gently. His soft lips lingered on them for a long time. I swallowed away tears, remembering what it was like to make love to him. My husband's lips moved higher while he let go of my hands. His fingers touched my neck and throat and moved up even more, until his fingertips rested on my lips. His face came closer, and I knew he was going to kiss me.

I closed my eyes while tears escaped the corners of my eyes. They trickled down my cheekbones, to the corners of my mouth. He must have tasted them on his lips, but he never commented on it.

Philip's tongue opened my mouth and moved inside to explore me, tasting the mixture of wine and Martini, combined with the salt of my tears. His hands gripped my face; his thumbs stroked my ears. He kissed me like he hadn't done in months, maybe not even once during our marriage. He was hungry, eager and obviously turned on. I could feel his erection through his trousers. With a shock, I realized that this would be the last kiss we ever shared. I was not willing to have sex with him one last time as a goodbye present, so I pushed him away roughly when he crawled on top of me, trying to pin me down on the couch.

I tried to speak, but his mouth was still pushed on mine, his tongue still exploring my mouth. It hurt. I clawed at him, until I could shove him backwards. My husband's teeth grazed my lip just a brief moment, leaving them to sting painfully. He didn't care that I instinctively hissed in pain. He hid his face between his hands. To my astonishment, he started crying. I hadn't even seen him cry over the loss of Eve.

"What's wrong?" I croaked, moving my hand over my mouth.

"I don't know how to tell you this, Zoey," he began.

"Tell me what?" I blurted out.

Was he sick? Dying? In financial trouble? What the hell was going on in my husband's life that I had missed for so long? His voice sounded broken.

"I have rehearsed this so many times and every time it sounded so wrong, so I'll just have to say it as it is. God, believe me when I say that I wish this didn't happen, but it did, and I can't stop it anymore. You need to understand that, Zoey. I still love you so very much, even if you wouldn't believe me. On the other hand, I can't go on like this anymore and I can't watch you do it either. It's over."

My husband's mood changed from sadness to fury when I couldn't utter a single word. I just sat there in complete shock, numbed by his words.

"I've had it with you, Zoey," he snapped. "You've changed so much that I hardly recognize you these days. I know it has been hard, and I know that you've been suffering. You've been through hell, but so have I. I didn't marry the woman you are today; hell, I don't even know who you are anymore. I just can't live with someone who will never go back to the person she once was."

"You're leaving me then?" I asked stunned. "Just like that?"

"Yes, I am."

"Because of the loss of our baby?" I asked quietly. "Because I wasn't in DC with you that day?"

"Do you really think that low of me, Zoey?" my husband asked bitterly. "We could have made it through this, if you hadn't changed so much. You became weak, where I married a strong and independent woman. You wallow around in self-pity all day, while you constantly forget the tiny little fact that I needed help too. Everyone always talks about you and how you're doing, but what about me, Zoey? What about the fact that I have lost our daughter too?"

I was devastated, unable to remind him that he had plenty of opportunity to state his grief and never did. Not once have I heard him talk about her. I always assumed she was non-existent to him. Was I wrong all this time about his way of grieving?

"I don't have the time, courage or patience anymore to try and understand you," he continued bitterly. "I'm through listening to your moans and cries about what you've lost. You refuse to allow anyone near you. You ignore me; you don't see my pain. I don't even want to try anymore. I can't."

"You weren't there when I needed you the most," I whispered stunned. "Whatever happened to 'for better and for worse', Philip? Doesn't the worse count in your books? Where were you when I was suffering at the hospital?"

"I was suffering too!"

"No, you were blaming me for what happened. I heard you say it when you thought I was passed out," I pointed out.

"I was confused and in shock," Philip retorted immediately. "Nobody ever asked me how I was. They all only cared about you. Truth be told, yes, I did blame you for choosing your shop above me, but I never blamed you for getting shot and losing our child."

"That makes it better then?" I whispered, shocked. "What's the difference, really? I got shot because I was there, so how can you blame me for choosing my shop over you, but not for getting shot, when the two events are linked together? You're a selfish bastard, Philip. You're pathetic. Even now, you're afraid to face the whole truth."

"What is the truth, Zoey?" he asked me coldly.

"You weren't there for me when I woke up. You had already changed during those few days I was out, even then. You were hurting, I won't deny that at all, but there was something else going on. You stayed away from me on purpose - like you had someone else important in your life."

The moment I said it, I felt it was true. Something I hadn't dared to think about in these past months, popped its ugly little head and wouldn't let go anymore. My husband's features changed; he flushed scarlet red. How could I not have seen this earlier? It was too horrific to even contemplate right now, but still, here it was: the elephant in the room.

"Even then, you already had someone else, didn't you?" I blurted out. "You were seeing someone while I was fighting for my life."

Philip looked startled. He bit his lip like he used to do when something happened that he didn't like. He was ashamed. He got caught with his pants down, so to speak.

"You were seeing someone else. You had an affair while I was in the hospital."

"I am having an affair," he admitted suddenly.

My whole world collapsed. My husband was sleeping around. He had been for quite some time, while I was heading straight for the abyss. I wondered whether I should cry or simply scratch his eyeballs out. I knew I would never do the latter; I was not a violent person. I could have fought like a fury. Instead, I felt weak and powerless to stop these events from unfolding. I was losing it all. Everything that meant something in my life, was flushed down the drain.

"Who is she?" I asked, sounding like a cliché from a soap opera. "I have a right to know who you're fucking."

"No, you don't and please don't use such harsh words. It doesn't suit you," Philip muttered.

"Why not? Do you prefer banging, or screwing, or going down on her, or, having sex then, Philip? Does the work fucking scare you?" I hissed. "Tell me who she is. I want to know who you've been sharing your dick with."

He flinched for the second time, but I was on a roll, pouring out all the anger I had kept inside for months. The words just blurted out of me without filter. I had never used any cursing words or described sex graphically, considering it something sacred between one man and one woman. Right now, I felt like a whore, spilling out all the words her clients wanted to hear while they got off.

"Tell me who is sucking your dick," I screamed.

"Nobody!" he yelled.

"Oh, so you just have plain old sex then, without any foreplay?" I snapped. "You just shove your penis inside her vagina and be done with it?" I started shouting on the verge of hysterics. "When did you do it, Philip, while I was passed out? While I was recovering, or even at the moment that I got shot? When, Who, how? I'm going to find out anyhow, even if I have to hire a dozen Private Detectives to trace your every step."

"You don't know her," he spoke weakly.

"Does she work at your office?"

"No."

"Is she a friend of ours?"

"No."

"Liar."

"Like I said: you don't know her," Philip sighed. "Stop asking questions, Zoey. You won't find out, and I would like you to refrain from using those terms. It isn't like that. I'm not screwing around. I like her."

"If she's opening her legs for you, it sure as hell is like that," I replied sharply. "You're fucking her, like you used to fuck me. How's that?"

I wanted to shake Philip up and it worked. He hesitated. I read something on his face that was new. He had not seen this much fury in me since before the accident. Perhaps that was what he wanted in a woman: fury, anger, hatred and a bit of arrogance. He hated weakness after all. Maybe she was a feisty little thing that liked it rough, someone who could go on her hands and knees so he could do whatever he wanted with her. A woman without conscience or scruples, who had no remorse for her actions. After all, who would go after a man, whose wife had just been through hell? She must have known about me.

"Her name is Elisabeth," he finally admitted. "But like I said, you don't know her."

"Elisabeth?"

I let the name roll over my tongue, trying to recall if I knew anyone by that name. I had heard that name before, not even so long ago. It had a familiar ring to it, but my memory failed me.

"Elisabeth. Elisabeth."

I repeated her name twice, speaking it slowly the second time. What a difference in names we had. Elisabeth was such an eloquent, British name, like Queen Elisabeth, or Elisabeth Taylor. No wonder Philip preferred her; she even sounded stronger than I did. She sounded easier to live with too. She sounded … normal. Someone without any mental or physical issues. I couldn't help but wonder where he could have met her in the past few months, apart from the office. He said she wasn't a colleague, and I believed him. She wasn't a friend either. Then where did he meet her? At some bar perhaps, or at a party with colleagues?

A light bulb flashed on inside my head. Suddenly I remembered where I had heard that name before in the last six months or so. The knowledge hit me like a ton of bricks. My body functions failed on me; my knees trembled, and I would have slipped on the floor if I hadn't been able to grab the edge of our couch. My whole world fell apart. Philip tried to reach for me, but I shook him off roughly. He knew that I knew.

"She's a nurse," I blurted out. "She took care of me."

He paled, obviously shocked that I remembered her after all this time. How couldn't I, when I had literally spent days with her?

"Yeah," he confirmed with a weak voice, "She's a nurse."

"Bastard."

My mind dwelled off back in time. I tried to remember what she looked like, but Elisabeth blended in with a dozen or so images of that horrible phase of our lives. I couldn't distinguish her from all the other nurses who had taken care of me during those three weeks I was stuck in a bed, but I did remember that eloquent name and British accent of her. She was from the UK, and she wore her British roots with pride, even when she was wiping me off after using toilet.

"You met her at my hospital bed?" I asked. "When exactly, Philip? While I was in a coma, cut and sliced open? Or afterwards, when I was wide awake, and she had to take care of the scars on my body? When she had to help me pee because I couldn't even do that by myself? Did she offer you a shoulder to cry on, while your wife was fighting for her life? Did she hand you coffee and patted your hand, while I was crying for the loss of our child?"

His face flushed again. I felt sick to my stomach. Literally. I turned and rushed to the bathroom, where I threw up a strange combination of bile and other substances I didn't want to think about. I barely reached the toilet bowl. When the heaving was over, I flushed and leaned against the wall behind me, feeling sweaty, greasy and filthy. Sitting there on the cold floor, I realized how low I had fallen. Little did I know that my fall was far from over yet.

Nine

"ZOEY?" PHILIP KNOCKED ON THE door, but he didn't offer to come in. "Zoey, are you alright in there?"

It took me a while before I realized that I had no place to go. I needed to face my husband again, which would take me a lot of emotional effort. I rinsed my mouth, washed my face, brushed my teeth, pushed open the door, ignored my husband and practically crawled onto the couch that felt strange to me, even after all these months. He had picked out a furnished apartment, so he didn't have to move our old furniture.

Philip followed me into the living room and handed me something to stop my stomach from cramping up. A second pill was meant to soothe the pounding headache battling beneath my skull. I swallowed it dry, pondering for just one second if he was trying to poison me. It would be the easiest way out of this mess for him. Maybe he had subconsciously hoped that I would not survive the attack; that I would never wake up from my coma, or that I would be depressed enough to end my own life, so that he could go on screwing his little nurse and live happily ever after.

"Lie down," he insisted, as if nothing had happened.

He even dug up a blanket that he placed over me. I nearly blacked out as soon as my head hit the small pillow. I saw stars while I waited for the medication to work. By now, the headache was so bad, I thought I would die.

Migraine wasn't new to me. This feeling of losing it, was. Even the urge to shower Philip with nasty words evaded me.

Philip sat carefully on the edge of the coffee table, not attempting to touch me at all. My eyes were closed, but I knew he was watching me. What had I ever done wrong, that he would actually go and screw someone while I was in a coma? What kind of man did that? What kind of woman had I been before I lost Eve? Had our marriage been in such a bad place that he would do that to me? I was a living and breathing mess. A flurry of emotions, negative energy and a walking wreck. No wonder he hated my guts; I wouldn't want to live with myself either.

"Are you feeling any better?" he finally asked.

My husband was obviously relieved the truth was all out now. There he went, back to his polite tone of voice. I preferred the emotional version of him, where he at least would show some feelings. At least he replied honestly when he let go of his boundaries, showing that other side of him.

"Zoey, please talk to me," he sighed. "We need to get this sorted out once and for all."

I shook my head, closed my eyes and moved my arm over them, so that I didn't have to look at him. Every word I blurted out would spread the bitterness that built up at rapid speed. I wanted to relish my anger and lash out to get back at him. I felt humiliated. Lost. Betrayed. That woman had taken care of me. She bandaged me up and nurtured my wounds. She saw me naked, for god's sake, more than once. She had tried to cheer me up when I was down and told me there was plenty in life to go on for, like my loving husband. All this time, she was screwing around with him. She had handed me handkerchiefs and towels and wiped away the tears on my face when I couldn't make them stop.

My memories of her came back swiftly now. I recalled her vividly, since she was one of the first people I bonded with in the ICU. I had been forced to stay there for five more days after I woke up, so there was plenty of bonding to do. Elisabeth was small. She had a darker shade of blonde coming from a bottle. She wore glasses and slippers. She looked like a small, unimportant little mouse. Tiny, but strong. She spoke with a clipped voice. She had never once stood out to me. She was just someone in a white uniform, cleaning up my mess. She checked the IV-tubes pushing fluids into me. She noted down if I peed enough in a bag. She pushed new needles into me and monitored my heartrate and blood pressure. She fed me my medication. She held me when I wept.

"When did you screw her?" I whispered. "Before, during or after the hospital? Before, during or after my time in the ICU?"

"After."

"After what? The hospital or the ICU?"

"Both," he muttered. "It never happened while you were there, I swear. I would never do that to you."

"You're lying," I hissed. "You changed when I was there, fighting for my life. You fell for her even there, didn't you? Did she offer you a helping hand when you felt the urge to masturbate? Couldn't you even last a few days without me? Did you need someone to do the handywork for you? Were you too posh to fuck yourself?"

God, there I went again, shouting obscenities at him, as if I worked the streets. Philip blushed.

"Don't talk like that, Zoey. This isn't you. Please stop," he whispered.

"This is the new, improved me," I blurted out sarcastically.

"Look," he tried desperately, "I met her at your bedside, that's true, but it wasn't like that, not at first. She helped me through the worst in those first hours, when we all thought you were not going to make it. She was a friend when I needed one, someone I could talk to, an unexpected ally when I needed one. She understood my grief and helped me cope. Nobody cared about what I went through, but she did. There was something between us, that - God, I can't even explain it. Yes, I fled to her after you came home to escape the problems in our marriage. I had no choice; I was going crazy with what was going on here. She listened to me; she helped me to survive."

"And I didn't?"

"Frankly? No."

He did have a point there, but I wouldn't let him off the hook that easily.

"Let me get the timeline straight them. You started fucking her after I was released from the hospital?"

"It happened for the first time a few weeks after you came home and wouldn't leave our bedroom anymore. I sent her a text message on impulse, just to talk to her about all of this, and she called me. We spoke for a couple of hours. She called me again and we met for coffee. It felt so good to have someone to pour my heart out to. We became good friends. It was never my attention to sleep with her; I just needed someone to talk to."

"Someone else than me," I spoke bitterly.

"I couldn't communicate with you, Zoey," Philip spoke desperately. "Everyone, including me, was so worried about you. You were angry, in shock and too upset to discuss my state of mind. You were hurt and sick and I just shut down when it didn't get any better. I couldn't find a way to talk to you anymore. You ranted on and on about the baby and I didn't want to hear about her anymore. Eve became your focus, while I wanted to move on and explore other ways to have a family, but you shut me out every single time. This didn't feel like a marriage anymore. It just became a downward spiral into madness and grief. I realized I couldn't save us anymore, so I went to her."

"You didn't even try," I whispered. "Even now you're blaming me for this. You're kicking me when I'm already down. Our child died and you blamed me, so don't go and tell me now that you wanted another one. This is just your way of excusing your actions."

"I never blamed you," he interrupted me. "Not for the baby at least. I know what I said at the hospital and if I could, I would take my words back. You were not the one with the gun and you sure as hell didn't want any of this to happen. The truth is though that you are blaming you. Look at yourself, Zoey! You're a mess and you refuse help from everyone. How long will it last before you fall into the abyss, never to crawl out again? Are you planning to drag me with you? I wanted to move on, but what did you do? Nothing, but wallow in your grief."

"You never offered your help," I nearly screamed. "You backed out when it got rough. You never once talked about Eve with me. Hell, you even refuse to acknowledge her name!"

"Perhaps I did back out," he admitted. "And yes, I never called her by that name, because that was not the one I would have chosen for her. We hadn't even discussed proper names yet. Our marriage is over, Zoey, it has been for a long time. We already had some problems before the attack, but we were both too superficial to admit to that."

"I was pregnant with your child! How can you say we were in trouble?" I wept.

"You planned on that baby, not me, Zoey," Philip spoke quietly. "You stopped taking the pill without consulting with me first. Remember my shock when you told me? If you are honest with yourself, you would see that she was not my choice. I was looking forward to her once the shock died down, but I did not ask for her to exist in the first place."

He was right: I was the one who stopped taking precautions. I couldn't deny that, so I lashed out in rage and anger, trying to hurt him where I could.

"Didn't you trade me in for a woman less complicated?" I asked hoarsely.

"What else do you expect me to say, Zoey?" Philip spoke in desperation. "I tried to explain how I feel, but you simply will not listen. I wanted to make this easy on you but obviously, I'm failing. I am sorry about that. I'm sorry about all of this. I don't know what else to say. I've tried to reason with you, I've tried to talk to you about this calmly, but nothing feels right to you, so what's the point? As far as I am concerned, I've done what I needed to do. You know the truth now, which is all I can get from this conversation. We're through."

"Because you're screwing around," I spoke bitterly.

"Isn't that what you are doing as well?" came his retort.

A new shockwave of pain and anger rushed through me.

"Are you accusing me of fooling around too?" I stuttered.

"Yes, I am."

"I hope you're joking."

I bit my lip until it bled. He just shook his head.

"Am I, Zoey? You and Vivian, that's all I'm saying. That mysterious girlfriend of yours that I've never even seen, is driving me up the wall. You go to her all the time for advice and help. You're on the phone with her for hours. God, I can hear the conversations through the wall, Zoey, I can hear you rant on and on to her and you don't even realize I'm right here. Her words are sacred to you, but what about mine? I'm sure she has filled your head with filth about me, since you talk to her about things that only concern us. What did you expect? That I would not figure out how crazy you are about her? Why else won't you let me see her? You're having sex with her, aren't you?"

"You're insane," I spoke slowly, trying to force myself to stay calm. "Vivian's a friend, not a lover. I'm not even gay! She's just someone I can talk to whenever you're out 'working late'. Don't let me take the blame for something you have done. You're sick."

"Fine," Philip sighed. "Whatever. I just want to get this over with, Zoey. Enough with the pleasantries, okay? I've tried to reason with you. I've tried to stay calm, to give you the time to recuperate from this shock, because, believe me, I know that this is devastating to you. Maybe you needed this wake-up call. All you do right now, is dwell around in that little self-pitying world of yours, while I've been trying to act as normal as possible to avoid any panic attacks or screaming sessions from you. Whatever I do next, it will never be enough, and it will never be good. It's plain and simple, really: I want you out of my life tonight. There's no point discussing our failed marriage anymore, so let's just get it over and done with then."

"Fine," I replied, pointing at the door. "Then leave right now. If you hate me that much, just get the hell out."

"I don't think you understand," my cheating husband corrected me. "I'm not the one leaving. You are, tonight."

With those words, my whole world came crumbling down for the second time in an hour. Just like that, I was thrown away like garbage.

Ten

I STARED AT MY HUSBAND in shock, not believing what I had just heard. Did he seriously mean what he just said? Could he be that foul?

"Now why would I do that?" I croaked. "I'm not leaving my home willingly."

"But it isn't your home, is it? You never felt comfortable here," Philip pointed out, rightfully so. "You hate it, in fact. I bet you can't wait to escape this place."

"I don't feel at home, that's true," I admitted, "but it's still the only house I have right now. You can't just kick me out."

"This apartment and everything that comes with it, are mine," Philip said, tearing apart whatever was left of us. "I rented it on my name since you were incapacitated at the time and, unlike you, I actually like it. In fact, I've decided to stay here on a more permanent basis, so I've made the owners a generous offer, which they accepted. This apartment now belongs to me, and you are not entitled to it."

I was rough fully shaken out of my belief that my husband was a good man. My life just became a living nightmare.

"Fine. I'll go back to the house then," I responded, wounded. "I was planning to leave New York City anyhow and go back home. It's time to pick up my life again. You were right about that at least."

I turned around and headed for the door, as if I was planning to leave straightaway. My mind boggled; I couldn't think straight anymore. My legs trembled fiercely. I had to control myself not to scream out anymore unpleasantries.

"You can't go back to the house, Zoey," Philip spoke quietly, killing me slowly, but thoroughly. "Since you showed no intention of ever going back there after all that happened, I sold the place and used the money to put down the first payments for this place. How else did you think I could make the offer on the apartment? This is an upscale area and the profit from our old house made it affordable. I was planning on telling you in a gentler way in a later stage, but since you were in such a state of mind that made it hard to talk to you, I just went ahead and did it. I thought that we could still make it through the hard times, but it's obvious now that we never will."

"You … what?" I felt like I was choking.

"You heard me."

"You had no right!" I screamed, losing all self-respect. "We're still married, remember? What's mine is yours; the house was in my name too. You can't just kick me out and since I refuse to live with you ever again, you'll just have to go ahead and cancel your offer."

"Really, Zoey?" Philip snorted. "Remember how my dad put down the money to pay for the house, since you refused to use the trust fund your dad gave you when you moved in with me? You were adamant about it too, telling me over and over again that you didn't want his money since he never shared his heart either. Remember how you were planning on putting up your fair share the moment you earned enough money and how my name should be on the contract until then? You never paid for your share of the house, did you? We never set the records straight, so the house remained in my name, just like I was the one putting down the payments for it every single month. Not once have you paid your share, so I'm afraid your luck just ran out."

I opened and shut my mouth like a fish. He was right in every sense of the word. I had screwed things up myself.

"When I sold the house, I rightfully reclaimed what was mine to begin with, because of your stubbornness and determination to show your dad that you could do it all on your own. I supported you throughout our marriage,

Zoey, even when you started the flower shop, knowing it wouldn't do much more than pay for the bills. I endured everything, because I wanted to help you."

"The business was doing just fine," I said, defensive now. "You always told me to invest in the shop and even how to expand. How was I supposed to know that you still wanted my half of the payment for the house? You never asked for it."

"Was your business really doing so great, Zoey?" Philip asked. "Are you sure about that? Have you ever truly gone thoroughly through your numbers and figures? Because I sure as hell have. I know that you've barely earned a dime since you started the shop and whatever you received in profits, you invested in extra staff, even though I told you not to. Yes, I told you to expand and invest, but not to hire extra staff. I wanted you to thrive in a clean, easy way, to earn enough to support yourself and me. Instead, you hired people because you liked them so much. You simply never listened to me. You were so eager to make the world around you happy, that you forgot your common sense. The shop paid for their salaries and expenses, but you hardly kept anything for yourself. I'm sorry, Zoey, but you've survived on my financial security long enough."

"You abused my weak state," I whispered. "You arranged all of this behind my back and expect me to take it like a good, little girl? What kind of man are you?"

"I've been supportive and willing to listen to your sad self-pity for long enough," Philip sighed. "I've put up with your grievances and days, spent sleeping and mourning in bed, while I went back to work and made sure we had enough money to survive. I need to move on, before we start hating each other. Before this ends up messy for both of us. I just want to go on with my life."

"Go ahead," I whispered. "Go ahead then and kill me. You just did it mentally, so why not put a knife into me too? Get rid of the obsolete wife that means nothing to you anymore. It'll make things easier than a messy divorce anyhow."

"Zoey, please stop the dramatics," my husband sighed. "You know you don't need my money to cope, so it's not like I'm making a homeless woman of you. Use the trust fund your parents set up for you for once. You refused to use your father's gift out of blatant stubbornness when we got married, even though it would have been enough to help us through the hard times. Since you refused to spend your money on me, you can now start using it for yourself. You won't even have to work anymore if you don't want to. Let's face it: you can afford to lose this apartment. I can't. Divorcing you will cost me more than it will ever cost you. You should be happy that I'm the one requesting the divorce. All I want now – "

"I don't care what you want!" I screamed hysterically. "I don't care about your needs. It doesn't interest me if you can afford this place or not. You ruined our marriage, and you will pay the price."

"I knew you were going to say that," my husband answered quickly, of course predicting my anxiety. "I'm willing to grant you an easy divorce. I won't ask for a dime, but I will make your life a living hell if you start acting up now. I'm entitled to half of what is yours, since we married without contract. So, essentially, I could even demand half of your trust fund when you turn thirty in a few months. Don't think I won't do it, Zoey, because I will."

"What about her?" I asked, unable to use her name.

"She's moving in with me."

His words struck like sledgehammer blows to the chest. I felt like crawling into a corner and crying. What was Philip worth fighting for, when he had already made up his mind? I had to get away from here, but I wouldn't go without a fight.

"Okay," I spoke, forcing my voice to stay calm. "You can have the apartment for now, but I will fight you on this. No matter what you say or do, I am entitled to half of it, especially if we married without contract, as you put it so eloquently. This goes two ways, Philip, don't forget that. As a lawyer, you should know. I'm not stupid either and I frankly don't care if you have to sell this damned place or buy me out. I couldn't care less what happens to you next. You will pay me out and you won't see half of my trust fund. You may be a good lawyer, but there are plenty of those around that will support my case. I'll make sure you will not only lose this apartment, but you will also end up paying me an enormous amount of money for all the grief you've caused me. Don't think that a judge will make jokes about your sordid affair while I was in recovery. I'll put it all out in the open, I swear. Every single client of yours will know what you did."

"You wouldn't do that …," he started.

"I'm not finished," I interrupted him coolly. "You can have the car and whatever is in this apartment too, except for my personal belongings. There are a few items I want to keep. I'll pick them up when I have found a place to stay. In meantime, I don't want to come near you ever again and I certainly don't want to look at you ever again either. If I ever find you stalking me or even standing behind my back in a supermarket, I'll make sure you're sorry. Have you got that, Philip?"

He became so pale I thought he was going to have a heart attack. In all his bravery, he had forgotten that I was just as entitled to half of what he earned as he was to mine. Since I didn't have an income right now, he would fare a lot worse. The only difference was that I hadn't accepted or used my father's trust fund just yet and I wouldn't until the day that Philip and I were divorced. I turned thirty in three months, so with any luck, I could keep that out of the settlement. Whatever else, I would make sure that he couldn't touch a single cent of that money.

"I can't afford to lose this apartment," Philip spoke pathetically weak.

I knew I had won the first round, just listening to the tone of his voice. It gave me the strength to carry on.

"I know you can," I replied bitterly. "You can get a loan, like normal people do, or move into a smaller place that you can afford. Better that than to ruin your impeccable career."

Philip's shoulders slumped slightly, which made me smile, despite everything that was happening right now. I had a raging headache and aches in my abdomen that I would never forget, but right now, the adrenaline rush kept me on my feet.

"Why are you smiling?" he spoke bitterly.

"You wouldn't understand," I whispered hoarsely. "If I don't laugh, I'm going to cry and then I'll never be able to stop."

Philip seemed shocked by my admission. His attitude towards me changed slightly; I could feel it lingering in the air. My aggression was gone;

the room felt at peace again somehow. An opening was created for us to speak again like normal adults again, if we could only make ourselves mend the bits and pieces we just scattered around. My husband moved over closer to me in an attempt to hug me. I would never find out why he made that sudden, caring gesture. Maybe he was sorry for his harsh words, but it was too late now. All things said and done, there was nothing left for us, not even happy memories. There was only a rawness left that we would never be able to forget. I hated him right now, for ruining what was left of our marriage.

"Please Zoey," Philip whispered. "Please understand that I need to start over again. I'm thirty-one years old and feel like a guy going on sixty. I can't go on like this, don't you see? We both still have many years to go. Please don't take this away from us."

I wanted to kill Philip's damned innocence. I even envisioned myself murdering him, shoving a knife into his heart. Every fiber of my body wanted to make my husband suffer, to destroy him for what he had done, but I couldn't. I wasn't like that. Now I understood how love could change into anger so easily; how love became hatred, followed by complete destruction of fleeting happiness. I comprehended how former lovers slaughtered each other, leaving nothing in their trail of what they used to share. Sometimes complete annihilation felt better than survival.

I pushed my husband away and ran into the small hallway, reached for my warm and comfortable Burberry and shoved it over my freezing body. It felt warm and soothing, the only comfort that I had at this very moment. Not a single human being would be able to help me get warm again. I had nowhere to go, so I would have to spend the night at an impersonal hotel, wondering, waiting and questioning what my life was still worth right now, while Philip would be making love to that woman over in this apartment. He wouldn't even think of me again. It was an unbearable thought.

The only one I could turn to would be Vivian. I needed to contact her, but she would soon get on that damned plane to Paris. She might well have disappeared off the face of the earth. All I had was her voicemail. I was alone. I reached for my bag and tried to figure out what to do next. I had enough money and credit cards. I was a big girl. I could manage. I blinked against the onset tears, refusing to look Philip in the eyes. I wouldn't grant him the satisfaction of watching me fall apart.

"I'll be back tomorrow to get my things," I said.

"Will you be alright, Zoey?" he asked.

"Like you care," I whispered.

I walked out the door, with nothing but the clothes I had on me and my purse. This was all that I had left after my years with Philip. Our marriage was pathetic, a sham, a disaster. Would this have happened somewhere in the future if Eve had been alive today? Maybe, after a couple of years, Philip would have turned to someone else too, finding solace with another stranger. He never loved me enough; I knew that now. I wondered if he even loved her.

I closed the door behind me. A small thump followed, as if he threw himself against the other side of the wood. I had no idea what he was thinking, nor did I accept the possibility he might regret his decision. I closed my eyes and allowed my last tears to spill, before wiping my face and moving like a zombie towards the elevator.

Before I could push the button, the doors slid open. A woman stepped out, freezing immediately when she spotted me. She was small and slim, dressed in jeans and a black raincoat, with a cap covering her light brown hair. She looked away shyly, but I still recognized her immediately. Elisabeth tried to walk past me, keeping her face down, but not before I saw the guilt written all over her face. I blocked her way, forcing her to look at me. When she did, I saw regret and pity in her eyes. I recognized her from all those days at the hospital, which still felt like yesterday. The memories flooded back into my mind. If I hated anyone more than Philip right now, it was her. And she knew. I imagined her taking care of my bruised and battered body during the day, while sleeping in Philip's arms at night. I imagined her hands washing my body. The same hands that stroked my husband's erection. I felt sick to the bone.

I forced myself to stand straight up and returned her apologetic stare with a haughtiness I had never felt before in my life. I despised her so much. I felt violated. Raped. She had seen every inch of me, while I had never known better. She obviously came by too soon, not expecting me to still be here, judging by her awkward behavior.

"I'm sorry," Elisabeth felt compelled to say. "It just happened; we fell in love. It's not because of you, Zoey, I promise, and it has nothing to do with what happened to you either. Believe me, if I could, I would take away all your pain."

"Go to hell," I snapped. "I hope he does to you one day what he just did to me."

Before Elisabeth could even gasp, I stepped inside the elevator, with my back turned towards her. As soon as the doors closed behind me, I leaned against the wall and stared at myself in the mirror. Who was that stranger staring back at me? Who was that cold-eyed woman, that felt nothing but hatred and pain coming from the deepest betrayal possible? I closed my eyes. I didn't want to look at myself anymore. Philip had resented me so much that he screwed around while I was hurting. Was I really someone that deserved this type of betrayal? Was I such a foul creature that he would throw me out like this? I guess I was.

Fury bottled up inside of me. I wanted to kick something or someone. My entire body seemed to burn with the urge to destroy whatever I could get my hands on. I couldn't allow this to happen to me. I just couldn't! Something happened to me while the elevator went down. I was riddled with anger, furious, upset, dazed, depressed. And I felt very much alive. Somehow, despite the mess I was in, that felt damned good.

Eleven

WHEN I WAS A CHILD, I found a bird in my grandmother's backyard. The poor thing had fallen off a branch of the oak tree that stood in the far corner of her small garden. The poor bird had broken its wing, and it was too young to survive on its own just yet. It had just learned how to fly. I rushed to my grandmother's kitchen with the bird in my hands, willing it to stay alive. I was young, but even then, I knew it wasn't going to make it. My grandmother came towards me, took the bird from my hands and said it was going to die. She told me he couldn't let it suffer for too long, that she wanted to shorten its misery. I ran into the living room and begged my mother to stop him, but she didn't feel like stepping in, until I kept on screaming that she should save the animal. When she finally walked into the kitchen, my grandmother had already killed it by snapping its neck.

I was angry at the two of them for days, while I refused to listen to their logical reasoning. My grandmother had killed an animal, and I hated her for being as coldhearted as my mother. The woman who put me into this world didn't bother comforting me, while my grandmother just sat there and listened to my ranting. Until she suddenly paled and looked away from me with distressed face and scared eyes, muttering that she was having a stroke. The pain passed quickly, and she acted as if nothing had happened to her, while my mother hardly looked up, used to my grandmother's often dramatic antics. Nevertheless, I apologized for my rant. That evening, before we went home, my grandmother told my mother that she was going to die, that the death of that bird was a premonition and that her end came near. That I was right to be upset with her. My mother mocked her, like she always did.

That night, my grandmother suffered a major stroke. She was hooked onto machines that kept her alive, but her brain was dead. The only reason her body still breathed were those dreaded machines. When they removed her life support unit, I knew that she had been punished for killing that bird. My mother signed the papers and arranged the funeral, and we never spoke about that day again. I spent the evening surrounded by my imaginary friends, who told me that it would all be okay in the end.

I walked through Manhattan without anywhere to go, until I noticed a small bird lying on the sidewalk. It was still alive, but barely so. A car had most likely hit it. I knelt and took the frail body in my hands. The bird felt cold already, as if it was struggling to survive, but never stood a chance. It took its last breath in my hands. I placed its little body in the park nearby, beneath a tree. I couldn't bring myself to throw it into a dumpster. Someone was going to die; I hoped it was me.

Rain poured down in buckets. The Christmas lights hanging soullessly in the streets looked ruined. People ran through the streets, without even gazing up at the splendor that should be part of this city right now. They had predicted snow in a couple of days, but right now, the world felt too wet and cold. I had to find shelter for the night. I had already tried to call Vivian several times, each time reaching her voicemail, as expected. I wondered if I should try to contact a relative to track her down, but that would be fairly impossible. A high school friend that wasn't that nasty to me, was also named Trent, but there were probably hundreds living in Manhattan alone. Vivian's name was too common to start a search in a city like this. All I could do was hope that she would call me back soon.

I stopped at an expensive looking hotel, smiling suddenly when I remembered that Philip and I had credit cards linked to a mutual account. Since he had been the sole provider for months, that basically meant he would be paying the bill. I was soaking wet and chilled to the bone; my hair stuck to the back of my head and was plastered against my face. Despite all of that, I just walked in and pretended I belonged here.

The night doorman nodded politely and asked if I had any luggage. I shook my head, before walking through the glass turnabout doors, heading straight for the reception area. There was one receptionist, a young woman with a Russian accent, who looked at me just as politely as the doorman had done. I knew I must have looked strange, like a stray cat looking for a place to sleep, but he hardly seemed to care. Credit cards worked wonders, and I couldn't give a damn about appearances. Once the card was approved, neither did she. In fact, she seemed quite concerned about my well-being.

"We have a laundry service that works 24/7," she offered, nodding at my wet clothes. "If you want, I can arrange something for you?"

"That would be great," I smiled. "Thanks so much."

"Are you okay?" she asked hesitantly.

"Well, my husband screwed around while I was in the hospital recovering from the loss of our child, so I'm guessing I'm not doing so well right now," I said, giving her my brightest fake smile.

"Oh."

"Don't worry about it. I'll be paying him back in full. Credit cards and all."

A slight smile showed that she knew exactly what I was referring to. She gave me a small nod and pointed me towards the elevators while arranging the dry-cleaning service.

"There's a nice little shop on the ground floor that opens at eight," she said, holding the phone in her hand. "They have beautiful things and they're expensive. Maybe your husband's credit card could help a hand there too?"

"Sounds like a plan," I smiled. "Thank you."

"Oh, and there's a cash machine over there. Maybe you should withdraw some money for the next few days," she winked.

"That sounds like a perfect plan," I grimaced. "Thank you so much for your tips."

"You're more than welcome. Just holler if you need anything else. I'm at your service all night."

I felt faint by the time I walked into my huge hotel room on the eleventh floor, clutching my back against me, now with six hundred dollars in cash in my wallet. The bathroom was almost as large, with a hot tub that felt very inviting, but I couldn't care less right now. I closed the door, threw my Burberry on the floor and dropped on the bed, feeling very much alone and upset. The New York City lights weren't that friendly tonight. They mocked me for being alone. The small Christmas tree in the corner of the room made it even worse.

I needed to call my parents at some point, and tell them what had happened, but I didn't want to just yet. I couldn't listen to their 'I told you so's'. Then they would tell me to swallow the humiliation and to give Philip another chance, because divorce is something that happened only to failures. After all, my dad had screwed around too and he had come back, hadn't he? Hell, my parents even lived in South Africa together now, as if nothing ever happened between them. Well, I wasn't like them and I sure as hell wouldn't forgive Philip.

This night would be the first one of many lonely ones to come. The isolation frightened me. What if I didn't make it out there, in this huge city where people got lost all the time? What if I couldn't survive on my own out there? I had never been without someone else in my life. I had gone from my parent's home to the home I shared with Philip. Yes, I'd had many nights alone at the house, but always with the knowledge that my husband was still out there. I had nothing now. God, I was weak. Pathetic. An ignorant idiot.

"I can't handle this," I heard someone mutter, only to realize it was me talking.

To add to the insult, I was talking to myself. Another sign that I was totally losing it. A glimpse in the mirror told me I was a total mess. My hair stood in every direction; it felt damp and fell in lumps down my shoulders. The bit of make-up I wore had smudged all over my face. I looked like a ghost, a shadow of my old self. I missed that person, whoever she had been. I stared at my ruined clothes. I had dressed up a bit to meet Vivian, the perfect occasion to pay some attention to my appearance again. Look at me now.

I threw away my bag furiously. The contents scattered on the floor. A small plastic bottle fell out and rolled under the bed. I dropped on my knees to retrieve my painkillers and remembered how numbing they worked if I took more than two per day. I opened the bottle and emptied the contents on the palm of my hand. There were over a dozen left. If I took them all at once, my pain would be over forever. I would fall asleep and be rid of this dreadful life. It could be so easy to just let go now and get it over with.

No. No! I wouldn't quit now. If I did, Philip and that bitch of his, Elisabeth, would win. Nobody would know about our problems, and he would play the grieving husband, who had lost his wife after a tragedy. No, he was not going to push me in this direction. I wouldn't allow him to. I threw the bottle back into the bag and shivered when I realized what I had considered. I wouldn't do right by Eve's memories if I would let go now. Without me, nobody would remember her. After all, Philip had already buried her.

A knock on the door startled me. It was after two in the morning, and I was so tired. So terribly tired.

"Who is it?" I asked cautiously.

"Laundry Service," a soft male voice spoke.

"Just a minute," I yelled, realizing I was still wearing my wet clothes and shoes.

I walked into the bathroom, found a towel that I could wrap around my hair, and a bathrobe that felt as soft as anything I had ever felt beneath my fingertips. I removed my shoes, pantyhose and clothes, kept my underwear on and tied the robe around me. It was too large, as were most of the things I wore these days. My make-up was still running and my hair stuck everywhere, but I didn't care.

I opened the door for a young, attractive man, who entered the room with a basket to put my wet clothes in. Our eyes met briefly. His smile betrayed a set of perfectly white teeth. Small wrinkles around his eyes made him even more attractive. I knew he probably smiled like that at every guest at the hotel, but it still got to me. I hadn't seen friendly faces for quite some time; I felt touched by this one. After the receptionist and the doorman, who had both treated me like a human being, he was the third one to act normal around me.

"Can I have your clothes, Miss?" he asked, pointing at the bathroom.

The door stood open, showing my things. Before I could move, he walked over and took them all: my coat, my trousers, shirt and coat. He even took the scarf and my shoes and lastly picked up the Burberry from the bedroom floor.

"That's okay," I said, pointing at my shoes. "They'll dry by themselves."

"We've got a machine in the basement for that," he said. "With the weather we've been having lately, it has already paid back its investment, trust me."

I felt embarrassed watching my clothes treated like they were worth millions, when in fact, they were old and rubbish. He folded them carefully and placed a white towel over them. He put my shoes on top of that towel, wrapped inside a plastic bag that he brought with him.

"We'll have your things ready for you by morning," he said. "When can I return your clothes? Do you need to be somewhere early in the morning?"

"No," I said. "I've got time. I'll probably be staying here for a few days and I'm feeling a bit drained, so no early appointments for me."

"Alright," he smiled. "My colleague will bring them back around ten a.m.; is that alright?"

"That's perfect, thank you."

I stood still in the middle of the room while I watched the hotel employee deal with my clothes. I almost wished for him to stay longer and have a chat with me. He was going to leave me soon, to wallow in my sorrow once more. I wouldn't sleep a wink tonight anyhow, stuck here in this too large hotel room. I was so lonely. Despite its splendor, it still remained a hotel, and I was just a guest. Nobody gave a damn about me.

I gave him a twenty-dollar tip, which he accepted graciously. His eyes caught mine again; his hand hovered mid-air, with the twenty dollars crisped between his fingertips. For a brief moment, he didn't look like someone who worked here. There was a flicker of interest in his eyes. He broadened his smile, but there was also concern in it.

"I hope you don't find me impolite," he started, "but you look awfully sad. Is everything alright?"

"Yes."

"Then why are you crying?"

"Am I?" I asked surprised.

He moved his hand towards my face and folded his thumb, as if he was going to wipe those tears off my cheeks. I backed away, before he could touch me.

"Sorry," he said. "It's just that - you're not okay, are you? Can I help?"

"No. Just leave me alone," I said.

"Are you sure you want me to?"

"I don't know what I want," I admitted.

"I could keep you company, if you like. My shift is ending in fifteen minutes. I just need to get your clothes to Laundry Service and then I'm off duty. Do you want me to come back?"

"Why would you do that?" I asked surprised.

"I could offer you a helping hand, or simply a shoulder to cry on. It's so sad to see a beautiful woman like, you cry like that."

I smiled cynically.

"Let me guess: and you are going to offer me help with my loneliness, is that it?"

"Why not?" he shrugged.

"You're a hired hand working in this hotel. I'm a guest."

"So? As soon as I'm off, I can do whatever I want," he smiled. "I could help you take a shower or wash your hair for you. I can do whatever you would like me to do."

I laughed bitterly, realizing what he meant. Did he really think I was the type of person that had casual sex? The look in his eyes told me exactly what he wanted. He didn't lick his lips, but he came damned close.

"You are actually offering to come back here after your shift is over and have sex with me?" I snapped. "What the hell is wrong with you? You're all the same, aren't you?"

He smiled without losing his composure. "Do you really want to put it this bluntly?" he spoke quietly.

"It is the truth, isn't it? Why not put the words to it then? You want to fuck me, and you expect me to pay you for that," I remarked coolly.

The man reached inside his pocket to fetch a business card. I stared at him in shock. God, so that's what his kindness was about: he was an escort, finding his rich customers in this hotel. He didn't look away once, while I couldn't help but stare at his beautiful hands with their slender fingers. Philip had stumps for hands that hated massaging me. This man, God, I could just feel the way he would knead the knots from my shoulders, how he would let his fingers walk to my lower back, towards -

I shuddered. What was I thinking? A stranger came into this room, offered me sex and I got turned on by the prospect of it? I wasn't a slut. I didn't have meaningless sex with anyone. I never had anyone but Philip. How could I even consider this? Then again, why wouldn't I treat myself? After all, Philip was doing it too. He may not pay his charming little nurse in cash, but he was certainly buying her presents and offering her a place to live. In fact, he had already paid her far more than I would ever put on the table for this man's services. If Philip could sell his body to the devil, then so could I.

I shivered, when I suddenly remembered I was standing in a hotel room in front of a total stranger, contemplating paying him for sex. He noticed of course that I was considering his offer.

"Look," he said, soft and gently, "I'll be at the hotel for another thirty minutes and I promise you that I don't have any other plans tonight. If you are still feeling lonely before I head home, just give me a call. My mobile number is on that card. I promise you that I'm discreet and professional. Nobody will ever need to know."

I accepted the fancy card, staring down at his name in embossed golden letters, Matthew, and his phone number on it.

"I assure you that my name really is Matthew," he smiled, tapping his hotel nametag. "I don't lie to my clients, I promise. I want to keep things strictly business, with a personal touch. I'm doing this for me too. I like what I do, and I promise you that I will make it worth your while."

"Do you even work in this hotel?" I asked. "Or do you use Laundry Services as a ruse to attract your clients?"

He smiled.

"My work at the hotel helps to pay the rent. As an escort, I have good days and bad ones, since I'm quite picky about who I choose. You need to survive in this city, you know, so why not do it in the nicest way possible? I also promise you that I'm clean since I always use precaution and I don't just have sex with anyone. You are a beautiful woman, even if your make-up ran out and you are kind of looking like The Joker right now."

"I'll think about it," I blurted out, before opening the door. He picked up the bag with my clothes, coat and shoes and walked over casually.

"Why don't you take a hot bath? You'll feel all better," he said. "Relaxation makes you look at things in a different perspective. The offer stands: you know where to find me."

Like an old-fashioned gentleman, Matthew tapped his forehead and left me. I stared at the card in my hand. I walked into the bathroom and let the hot water run in the tub. While soaking between bubbles, Matthew was on my mind every second of the way. Could I do this? Could I really, really sell my soul like this? I knew it already. I had made my decision the second Matthew left the room. I was going to call him and tell him to come over, as a way to punish Philip.

This had been the strangest day of my life so far and I knew there were plenty of rough times to come. I needed someone with me right now, someone who could understand what I was going through. I knew Matthew would not be that person, but at least he could hold me and give me warmth while we pretended we were in a relationship together. I would ask him to stay for the night and hold me, even if I had to pay him to do so.

I reached for my phone and called him.

Twelve

I NEEDED WARMTH AND AFFECTION. I craved it, longed for it. That's what I told myself when I waited for Matthew to answer my call. He answered immediately.

"Matthew." Curt and polite, which I liked.

"I want you to come over," I blurted out.

"Room 902?"

"Yes."

"I will be there in half an hour."

"Perfect."

He hung up. We were closing a business agreement, I told myself. I placed my phone back on the chair next to the tub and pondered about myself and the heat between my legs. I hadn't felt like this for a very long time. Was all that Philip and I had to do to fix our relationship, was have sex? Was that really what life was about? I wondered about that once I stepped out of the tub, feeling better.

He arrived right on the dot. I had washed my hair and ignored that I was warm and tingly all over. Two hours ago, my life had been shattered and here I was, contemplating having sex with a total stranger. I wanted to run away from it, but I didn't. That same soft knock on the door, told me he was here. I opened the door, dressed in the same bathrobe, this time with my long hair down and my face bare of make-up. I ignored that nagging little voice inside my head, telling me that this was one big mistake, and I should just kick him out. Matthew closed the door behind him.

"My fee is a hundred and fifty dollars per hour," he said. "I brought my own precaution. Anything goes really, but I don't do kinky stuff. No S&M, no bondage, just straightforward, in different positions, oral included. I accept cash only. Payment upfront. If you didn't come, I'll pay you back."

"You're expensive," I said, knowing I would have paid triple that amount.

"I'm worth it."

"I'm sure you are. Can you stay the night after we –?"

He raised an eyebrow.

"Do you want me to stay until dawn?"

"Yes, but only to sleep together on the bed. I could use some company tonight. Just name me your price, like that hooker in Pretty Woman."

Matthew gazed at his watch, uncaring about the fact I had compared him to a street whore. It was after two a.m. by now, but I was alive and kicking.

"How about five hundred?"

I gave him the full six hundred I took from the ATM, using the same credit card that Philip would end up paying for.

"That's too much," Matthew replied, handing me back a hundred, which I refused to accept.

"I'm sure you'll be worth the extra tip," I smiled.

The man shoved the money carelessly in his jacket pocket and removed it. I didn't know what to do next, since I had never done this before. I had only seen stuff like this happen in movies, where it was usually the woman who got paid instead of the man. I would be on the receiving end. Whatever I wanted would be done. I would be the focal point of his full attention, and I had no clue what to do next.

After removing his jack, Matthew stood in front of me in a plain black T-shirt and black skinny jeans. He was lean and in good shape, without being too bulky in the arms or legs. I was sure he would have a happy trail and some chest hair, but not too much. In other circumstances, he would have been my type. My paid escort asked me to stand up and face the window. I looked outside, ignoring the city and Christmas lights as I closed my eyes.

He started kissing me on the back of my neck and throat, while his hands worked their way softly towards my strained shoulders. His fingers hooked into the rope that kept my bathrobe tied over my body. I wasn't wearing any underwear this time. I shivered, while I pretended that Matthew was Philip, the only man I had ever had sex with. When he kneaded my shoulders, I realized startled that he was not my husband. It felt wrong, all of this. I opened my eyes in shock and shook Matthew off me. His hands let go immediately. He backed away as I turned around.

"No," I whispered hoarsely, "I can't do this; it's not right."

His beautiful eyes stared blankly at me.

"Why not?"

"I'm not that type of person. I can't sleep with you pretending that you're someone else."

"Everyone else does," Matthew remarked.

"I'm not everyone else."

I moved away from the escort. His hands lowered, resting unmoving next to his body. He stood in the middle of the room like a statue, waiting for my next move. I hid my face between my hands. What had I nearly done? What was I doing, for god's sake? This wasn't me. Vivian might be able to sleep with men she didn't know, but I couldn't.

"I want you to leave," I spoke softly. "I'm sorry, but it is not going to happen. I'm really sorry about your trouble. Please, just go."

He looked at me inquisitively, without asking too many questions about my dilemma. I wasn't the first one who obviously changed her mind at the last minute.

"You said earlier that you were lonely," he said. "I can stay. We can just watch television or something, until you fall asleep. It doesn't have to be sex if you don't want it to be. I promise you that I won't force this. You're the one who decides what you want."

I looked at him, surprised by his kindness.

"You're serious?"

"I am."

To my surprise, Matthew reached for his jacket and retrieved the cash that I had given him. He placed the bills on the table.

"I don't need it," he said, "and I have no place to go tonight. I'll keep you company, free of charge. You do look like you could use some company."

I stared at him in shock.

"You would do that for me?"

"Yeah."

"You don't even know my name."

"You can tell me, if you want to," he smiled. "Your choice."

"It's Vivian," I lied.

He smiled again.

"What a beautiful name, Vivian. I should look up the meaning of that someday." He offered me his hand. "I'm Matthew, but if you read my card, you already knew that."

I laughed, shaking it.

"Pleased to meet you, Matthew. What do you want to watch on television tonight?"

"Apparently, there are reruns of Dr. Phil on at night. I'm pretty sure his guests are all messed up even worse than you are. That will definitely brighten your mood. What do you think?"

"Sounds like a plan," I laughed, for the first time in days feeling lifted. His sense of humor appealed to me.

We sat down on the couch together, while Matthew reached for the remote control and searched for Dr. Phil. Once he found it, I leaned against him with his arm around my shoulders and just stared at the screen. We ended up laughing and joking about the psychiatrist's guests, wondering who would ever go and tell a national audience about their deepest fears. After a while, I fell asleep.

When I woke up, I was in bed, beneath the covers, still in my robe, without my underwear. Untouched. Matthew was lying next to me on top of the covers, snoring gently. He was still wearing his jeans and T-shirt. It was eight a.m.; I had actually managed to get some sleep. I slipped out of bed and ordered breakfast, making sure that the man who brought it in, didn't see Matthew, by accepting the tray at the door. The escort woke up from the smell of coffee and looked surprised at the huge amount of food on the tray that I ordered for him.

We ate together in silence. He devoured most of the meal, while I picked on a slice of toast. We never spoke a word. After breakfast, Matthew put on his jacket. I gave him back the money, folding my hand over his when he refused at first.

"Why are you giving this to me?" he asked.

"To thank you," I said.

"What for? I didn't do anything."

"Yes, you did. You restored some of my self-esteem."

Matthew left me before one of his colleagues brought back my clothes. I knew I would never see him again. Later, I would remember this night as something that happens only on a blue Monday. This past night wasn't real; it couldn't have been. I must have dreamt it all. I laid down on the bed again, while I ignored my cleaned clothes hanging in the closet. I pulled the blankets over my shivering body and closed my eyes as I remembered Matthew's tender touch on my shoulders. He had also restored a big part of my soul.

Friday

Thirteen

I WOKE UP FOR THE second time around noon, my thoughts filled with newfound courage and promises. This Friday morning would be the first one of my new life. At least, that was what I promised myself after I brushed my teeth with a brush and toothpaste provided by the hotel. I hated putting the same clothes back on, but I had no choice. The first thing I would do was get some of my own things from the apartment, even if it meant facing Philip. I needed my clothes, if only to feel like myself again. For a moment, I contemplated taking that receptionist's advice and going shopping downstairs in the boutique she recommended, but I decided against it. I would punish Philip in a different way.

In order to so, I needed to go to the bank to get my finances sorted out. Truth be told, I had no idea what my financial status was right now. I still had debit and credit cards linked to our mutual bank account, but for how long? Philip would undoubtedly make sure I would be cut off soon enough. Then there was also the issue of finding a place to stay I could afford. Rental sounded like the best option, but this would be costly. I wouldn't contact my father or touch his trust fund for as long as I could avoid it.

Busy afternoon traffic was catching up. It had finally stopped raining altogether; the clouds were grey and showed the first signs of snow. It was extremely busy outside and I felt even more isolated, sitting alone in this room. I wondered how Philip felt right now. Was he sorry he had kicked me out, or relieved that he could be with Elisabeth without having to hide? Whichever way, I had to make plans to move my life forward.

I searched for apartment rentals on my phone. There were plenty of furnished rooms and apartments around Manhattan, some more affordable than others and in better areas than others. I would have to look for something temporary while I considered my future options. I wasn't sure yet if I wanted to stay in New York or head back home and try to reopen the flower shop. Part of me wanted to, but I was too scared right now. The memories would be too suffocating, and Simone probably hated me for firing her. Besides, I had no idea what had happened to the shop, apart from the fact that my father-in-law had taken care of it. Besides, walking into the shop would be a killer in my state of mind. I would see Samantha everywhere and still feel the baby kick inside my womb.

I checked my bag. I could get more cash from the ATM, which I definitely needed to do first. My phone was low on battery, but I could manage for at least a few more hours before I would need to recharge. I would buy one or get an extra battery for my device. I tried Vivian again. I called three numbers that I found online, offering apartments. The first one went straight to voicemail; the other two picked up immediately. I made appointments for this afternoon and thanked them for being so flexible. Life in this city wasn't cheap, so I needed to find a job fast.

I checked my business bank account on my phone. Despite Philip's comments that I hardly earned any money from the flower shop, I actually did save up quite a bit, which had been sitting on that account for months now. Philip had no access to it, on the recommendation of Rob, my accountant, who had always told me not to mix business with personal life. He must have been psychic. I was grateful for that decision now. There was a substantial amount of money on our mutual bank account, coming from Philip's job and there were two savings accounts that knocked the wind right out of me. The first one was almost empty, but the second one held a huge amount of money, which I didn't understand, until I realized that it must have come from the sales of the house. I grabbed my things together and left the hotel, to never come back here again, with Matthew on my mind.

Around three p.m., I walked into the bank where Philip and I had our joined accounts. One of the three clerks welcomed me and asked me to wait when I requested to speak with the manager, Mr. Jones, who happened to be my father's old bank manager. I gave the clerk my name, which opened doors. I knew they would indulge my unexpected visit. Two minutes later, I sat in the manager's office. Mr. Jones, a sturdy fifty-five-year-old man, greeted me courteously, asking me politely how my father was doing. The trust fund that was waiting for me, also laid with this bank, ready to be used. In meantime it was building up high-rate interests, which of course pleased Mr. Jones.

The bank manager listened sympathetically while I explained my current situation. I told him how my husband had decided to end our marriage and that I was here to divide our mutual assets, since I was legally entitled to half of them. I needed the bank's permission to do so since we were talking about a large amount of money. Little did Mr. Jones know that my husband wasn't even aware I was here, probably too naïve to assume I would do such a thing.

"I assume your husband knows about your visit?" he asked.

"Of course," I spoke haughtily, like I often saw my father do. "The problem is that my husband left me no other option than to arrange this quickly, since he threw me out and I have no home at this moment. If I don't get the money, I will be forced to move out of the country and therefore close all my accounts. You do understand, I hope?"

My words made impact on Mr. Jones, who obviously wasn't stupid. He knew all too well I was playing emotional blackmail on him, but he didn't care, since I promised to open two new accounts with his bank. Two could play these games and Philip was losing big time.

"Well then, let me just verify how we can arrange the transfer of funds the easiest way, Mrs. Walters," he spoke.

"Miss Mitchell. Please call me Zoey."

"Of course," he smiled broadly. "Who else gets access to your new accounts?"

"No one but me," I said.

"Of course. Let me see what we're talking about here."

The man went over the bank accounts into the last details, summoning up the profit from our house and savings. He shoved a note towards me with half of the outcome scribbled on it.

"Actually, I would like to have sixty percent of these amounts," I smiled broadly but sadly, putting up the best act of my life.

"I see." Mr. Jones hesitated. "Well, that's quite unorthodox. Can I confirm this with him?"

"There's really no need," I interrupted him. "I wouldn't want to bother him anymore with these trivialities. Besides, as I said, I am planning on keeping the money and my business accounts with your bank. I'm sure that you appreciate this gesture? After all, my father was one of your biggest clients too."

"Of course, Miss Mitchell," the man smiled nervously.

Mr. Jones did everything I wanted, because of my father's name and working on his mood. After setting up a debit and savings account on my own name, I had my name removed from Philips, destroyed my old cards and received two new cards. I shook the bank manager's hand, thanked him for his help and left. I felt like a bitch, but a happy one. Philip wouldn't know what hit him.

Outside, I took a deep breath, feeling better than I had done all morning. Little revenges were sweet, and I had come to realize that I wouldn't be short of money anytime soon, which gave me some time to recover from all of this. For once, I was actually not sad that Christmas was approaching rapidly. Maybe I could find a nice furnished place and put a tree up. It might brighten my spirits.

Snow had not started falling yet, but it wouldn't be too long now. I had another couple of hours before my appointment with the first real estate agent and I wanted to make use of them. I debated whether to go to Philip's first to get my things but realized soon enough that I would have nowhere to bring them to. The only thing I really needed was a fresh set of clothes. All the rest could wait.

I suddenly felt a painful sting in the back of my head, reminding me I had overdone myself. A killer headache was on its way to taunt me for the rest of the day. No wonder. I hadn't swallowed a single pill since last night. With a sigh, I took two, without water. I needed to learn how to survive without these damned pills, even if it meant dealing with these headaches for the rest of my life, but that would have to wait for now. I sat down on a bench in Bryant Park and waited for the pain to subside, before focusing on my tasks at hand.

People were everywhere, walking by me without paying much attention. I wasn't alone, which did me good. I felt alive again, despite the headache what my husband had done to me. He had dumped me like second-hand clothing, but I felt vivid and ready to face my new life. It was the strangest feeling I had ever experienced in my life. For the very first time ever, I had no idea what was going to happen tomorrow. I didn't even know where I would be tonight. I felt excited in a way I had never been.

I should probably thank my husband for his betrayal, I thought ironically, as I stood up and left the park. Philip had forced me to come back to life. Maybe he had even done me a favor.

Fourteen

MY SMARTPHONE NEARLY RAN OUT of battery, and I couldn't be reached at all, which felt strangely exhilarating in a time where people were expected to be online at all times. Selfies, Instagram and the likes had never been my cup of tea, so I didn't care that I was offline. I still needed to make some calls, so I walked into the first shop I passed and bought a Power bank and cable. My phone charged quickly. I needed my phone to make sure Vivian could get in touch with me. It wasn't a good idea to vanish off the grid completely right now.

I walked into a quieter street and lingered near a shop, where I called Rob. He was surprised to hear from me. I told him briefly what was going on, which shocked him. I left nothing out about Philip's betrayal, knowing he would find out soon enough what was going on. I asked him if he could investigate the option of moving my business to New York, so I could start up again somewhere in Manhattan. Flowers had always given me peace of mind, and I needed to regain that feeling. I still had the skills and the talent to do some magic with them, so why throw that away?

Rob promised to dig deeper into my finances, but he also reassured me that my father-in-law, a trusted man, had done right by selling the shop for me at a good price. I was financially set for the time being, so I had time to find a decent location to start all over again. The money was apparently put aside for me on a separate account that I didn't even know about. Philip hadn't spoken about it either, but he must have known.

"You need to talk to your dad, Zoey," Rob said. "You should tell him everything and allow your parents to help you out for once."

"You know what my dad is like, Rob. He'll freak out first because of his ruined good name. Then he won't bother flying back and he'll tell me off over the phone about everything I did wrong in these past months. I don't want that. They never cared about me when I was a kid or when I lost Eve, so why would they now? No, I want to stay here and start all over again. I don't need him."

"I get that," he said, "but that doesn't mean I'm not going to worry about you. Do you have a place to stay? There's plenty of room at my house, you know that. I can help you out for the time being."

I thought about Rob's two small children and knew that I couldn't go there. Being confronted with kids was still too early for me. Besides that, I would only get in the way and feel awkward as an unwilling, temporary member of his family.

"I'm covered," I said.

"Are you sure?" he asked concerned. "You can have one of the guest bedrooms. You would have all the space that you need. We can keep the kids away from you."

I smiled, sensing that Rob knew exactly what my motives for declining were. I loved him dearly; he had always been a good friend, even if I had refused to see him while I was recovering.

"I'm sure," I said. "I'm currently looking for a temporary apartment for a couple of weeks or so, until I find something appropriate. Thanks, I really appreciate it."

"Zoey," he hesitated, "I have to tell you something about Philip."

"You knew," I said matter-of-fact.

"I guessed."

"Did everyone else know too?"

"There was a lot of gossip going around about him in town. He was spotted with her a few times. I'm sorry, I didn't feel it appropriate to tell you, since it was just gossip and you were in such a bad state of mind. I'm sorry,

I feel like I've betrayed you now by not telling you."

"Did his parents know?" I asked.

"I have no clue."

"It doesn't matter anymore," I said. "I'm not angry at anyone, Rob."

"Despite it all, you do sound better, Zoey. The last time I saw you, you were in very dark place."

"I know. I'm sorry I refused to see you."

"Which is totally understandable," he waved away my apology. "Just find your feet again, Zoey. Opening a flower shop in the city might be a good place to start. I'll look around for areas where you could consider starting up your business again. How's that?"

"Sounds like a plan," I said.

"I'm happy to hear that," Rob smiled, satisfied that I sounded so self-assured and confident in my future. "If there's anything I can do, give me a call. Just give me a shout beforehand if you want to meet."

"Will do."

I hung up feeling a lot better. How stupid was I not to believe I still had friends left in this world? How silly indeed.

Fifteen

A WOMAN BY THE NAME of Anne Carlisle opened the office door to a small, independent business downtown Manhattan. She ran a business that rented affordable apartments all over Manhattan. The woman was friendly enough. Motherly, without being too smothering and quite businesslike. She asked me politely if I smoked or had any pets or children. I said no to all three with a lump in my throat. She offered me a cup of coffee and a slice of home baked cake, before getting down to business.

It seems that I was running on a lucky streak. Not only did her agency have rental apartments on offer. When she inquired about a budget, I gave her a number I could afford to spend for now. When she asked me about a preferred area, I had no answer. There were so many beautiful corners in this city that I hadn't even considered, simply because I didn't know them. All I knew was that I couldn't leave in a ten-block radius of Philip. That was my only demand.

"Can I make a suggestion?" Anne asked.

She showed me some exterior photos of a recently restored Brown Stone in the Meat Packaging District, only three floors high. It immediately called out to me.

"I can assure you that the neighborhood has shaped up quite a bit, with a lot of renovations and new apartment buildings being constructed as we speak. This whole area became quite popular over the years, thanks to The High Line, which is very popular with the tourists, so there is always some activity there. This apartment is fabulous. It has two bedrooms, a large open kitchen, an L-shaped living area, with a large bathroom, separate toilet, a small hallway and a small terrace. It is quiet and, as a bonus, located on the top floor. I only signed the contract to rent it two days ago exclusively, so not many people know about it yet. I want the right person to get this one. Hell, I even considered moving in myself for a while because it's so beautiful. All the furniture is new and barely used; the building itself has been restored three years ago."

I studied the interior photos. The apartment was indeed gorgeous, hardly needed any changing and the furniture appealed to me at once, could I afford it? It looked way out of my league. I was scared to hear the price, knowing I would have to tread carefully with what I would spend for the next few months.

"Now I should be honest with you," Anne continued, sensing my cautiousness. "I have shown this apartment to three other couples in the past two days, but none of them appealed to the owner, who is very picky in his choice. To be honest, they didn't really connect with the place, so I recommended against signing the contract with any of them. There are two more couples booked for a viewing tomorrow, so if you want to look at it, I'd advise that you do so today and make your decision quickly. I promise you that this one will be gone in a week."

"How much is the rent?" I asked.

"I suggest that we discuss this after you have seen it. You gave me a budget, and I can guarantee you this apartment stays far within that price range. In fact, you will find it very suitable to your needs, both location-wise and apartment-wise. I promise you that I won't show you anything you can't afford; that would be a waste of time for the both of us. I'm here to help you, not to make you feel bad."

"Really?" I asked surprised. "I would assume an apartment like this would go for quite a bit of money."

"Not necessarily," Anne said. "The owners are an elderly couple that just want to find a good tenant for it, which is why they chose me to do the work for them. Look, I'll be candid with you in order to save time," Anne smiled, while showing me a figure on paper. "This is the rent they expect. If you decide to pay this amount after seeing it, it could be yours to move into today."

"My luck," I smiled. "Can I see it right now? Do you have time to show me around this afternoon?"

"Of course. There are a few other places you might want to look at too, but I have this feeling this apartment has your name written all over it. It suits your personality." Anne smiled. "It was the first thing that popped to mind when you walked in, and I promise you that my instincts never fail me."

I looked at her surprised. The woman smiled mysteriously. "You seem curious to know why I said that."

"I am, since you don't know me."

"In this business, Mrs. Walters, you need to be a good saleswoman, but above all, a good psychologist. I believe that every house or apartment has a personality, as we all do. You are someone who walked in with the saddest look I have seen in someone's eyes for a long time, but you also came in searching for new beginnings. The moment I showed you the first photo, you smiled, as if you hadn't done that in quite some time. That's what I need to see when my clients walk in. If it clicks with this apartment and the area that it's located at, you will live happily ever after. If it doesn't, you will never feel at ease, even if it is the apartment of your dreams. Perhaps the house you used to live in wasn't the happy home you always thought it was. If it had been, you would have fought to your dying breath to get it back."

"That is an interesting thought, Mrs. Carlisle," I said, knowing she was right. About my previous home and my husband. I didn't want either back.

Before I knew it, Anne Carlisle and I were in a cab, heading towards the apartment she had in mind for me. She insisted on showing me three apartments as well, but I declined, convinced that I needed to see this place first, before she would take me to the rest of them. The moment I walked into the apartment, located on the third floor and reachable by elevator and staircase, I realized this was the one I could see myself living in. It had my name written all over it. A small step divided the kitchen and living room area, which was quite spacious. Even the kitchen was big according to New York standards, even though I would probably barely do any cooking.

The windows were large and overlooked a small part The High Line, which I loved immediately. I saw people passing by and felt like I was part of them, even though they couldn't see me. Large curtains prevented that. I could picture my flower shop in one of the streets nearby. This was an up-and-coming area that was expanding rapidly, still away from the crowds that usually hung around Times Square and Fifth. The garden terrace was large enough to hold a table and two chairs and overlooked a park. The bathroom was brand-new; the second bedroom was almost as large as the master bedroom. There was enough space to put a small desk in the living room, but the second bedroom could also function as office space. The furniture was perfectly chosen: two grey couches, three small tables, and a small dining table and four chairs.

I knew I would never find an apartment like this again. Just like Mrs. Carlisle had stated before, it fitted my personality to the core. Most importantly, it also fitted my budget and the fact that I could start all over without having to bump into Philip all the time, who would be living on the other side of the city. The apartment was high, with enormous, restored ceilings.

"The building dates from the early 1900's and had been bought by an architect and restyled, according to the area it was located in," Anne explained. "He has combined a more traditional style with some modern details. It's one of the smallest buildings in the area, situated between larger ones, but with the privacy every New York citizen craves. You see why I contemplated taking it myself?"

This being the top floor, was the quietest one. It also had the most windows and an air-conditioning unit. It was perfect. Just perfect.

"The owners lived here themselves, before moving to another area," Anne explained, "which is why it's so well-maintained. The other neighbors won't bother you, so you'll be leading a quiet life here. Like I said: you'll have to decide quickly to get it, Zoey. I see you living here, so if you want it, it's yours."

Anne used my first name, as if I was her best friend. I loved her for that. A spell of dizziness overwhelmed me in my enthusiasm. Carlisle grabbed me before I could fall over. For a moment there, I nearly passed out.

"Are you all right?" she asked worried.

"Yes, I am," I muttered, rubbing my hand over my eyes in embarrassment. "I'm so sorry about that."

"That's all right. Do you want to sit down?"

She practically forced me to take a seat on one of the two couches. I closed my eyes for a moment until the dizziness passed, while she went to get a glass of water.

"I'm really all right," I smiled after a short while. "It's just the excitement I suppose. I'm still recovering from surgery, probably overdid myself a bit."

"I understand," she smiled, obviously genuinely concerned.

She sat down beside me and waited until I felt better, which fortunately happened quite quickly. As soon as the dizzy spell was over, I stood and looked around, knowing that this had to be mine, no matter the cost.

"I'll take it."

Anne seemed taken aback that I had made such a quick decision, despite the fact she had encouraged me to do so.

"Are you sure you don't want to think this over, Zoey?"

"No. I'll take it. Like you said: it has my name on it and the rent is right. I want it."

"Perfect. I will make up the contract and I also three months in advance from you as standard policy, as you already know. I promise that we Skype with the owner, who will want to talk to you briefly and when he gives his agreement, we can have this over and done with by Monday evening. I need the weekend to get the apartment prepped for your arrival, just to make sure that everything's fine and then we're settled. We can do all of that back at the office, if you feel like going back with me right now, or we can do it on Monday, if you prefer that."

"Perfect." I smiled, almost eager to hug this woman. "You are heaven-sent, Mrs. Carlisle."

We shook hands on it. I knew that fairy tales sometimes really did happen. I had gained this woman's trust, and she had mine. She then surprised me by telling me that she might have a good location for a new flower shop in the Meat Packing District.

"A friend of a friend of a friend is retiring, and I happen to know that he's planning on selling the property, which is very conveniently located by the way, near your apartment and within the heart of this district. I can set something up if you like?"

"That would be great," I said, "but let's wait with that for a few weeks. I need to get used to my new life as a single woman first."

"Got it," she smiled.

I asked Anne to be left alone in the apartment for a few minutes, to get a feel of the place. She smiled in understanding, handed me the key and told me that she would wait outside. She walked out with her phone in her hand, always the businesswoman. I took the opportunity of going through the apartment quietly, taking in the rooms, the views and the atmosphere. I tried out the furniture and checked the kitchen cupboards. If I could have chosen something from scratch, it wouldn't be so different from what I was offered here. She was right about everything, to the very last detail: it already felt like a home to me, a place to feel happy again. It seemed that my lucky streak was not coming to an end soon, even though I didn't know what was happening to me. I was living in a dream state of mind, but I wasn't about to complain about it. I needed this, after all that had happened over the past few months. I needed this to be right.

I took the stairs instead of the elevator and was deep in thought, when I walked to the front door. A man entered the building, just as I was making my way out. He was cute, but not my type. He was quite tall and lean, had dark brown hair and intense hazel-colored eyes. I guessed his age to be around forty. He was dressed in jeans and a black turtleneck sweater and wore a navy-blue jacket. His hands were large, his fingers slim. Grease was all over those hands, as if he had been working on a bike or an old car.

"Hey," he said, "did you come to see the upstairs apartment?"

"I did," I smiled. "Zoey Mitchell. If all goes well, I'll be moving in pretty soon."

"Wow, congratulations. I'm Mac Ramsey, your downstairs neighbor and occasionally the janitor of this building."

I offered the man my hand and he grinned, flashing his perfect teeth, while showing me his greasy hands apologetically. He grinned boyishly, which made me like him immediately. He seemed like the type of man that wouldn't be phased by anything. The type that became good friends in a short period of time.

"Just fixing some pipes," he said. "I'm afraid a handshake will have to wait until later. Do you need some help moving in?"

"I'm fine for now," I said. "The apartment is furnished, so all I need to move, are some personal things. Thanks for the offer though."

"If you need anything fixed in the apartment, just let me know, okay? I'm happy to help. The owners are friendly folks and I'm happy to help out."

"Thanks. I'll be sure to contact you when I need you then," I replied.

I watched my neighbor dig a set of keys out of his jeans pocket, without getting too much grease on them. He pushed his front door open with his elbow, sliding into his apartment quietly. The door slipped shut after him.

On the way back to Anne's place, I sent Rob a text message about the apartment. He replied saying he was happy I had that sorted out so fast. I called Mr. Jones too and asked him to transfer the advance rent for the apartment, which he did over the phone. Earlier today, during my call with Rob, I had told him truthfully about what I had done with our mutual bank accounts and how I had lied to the bank manager. Rob didn't comment, but I knew he disapproved of everything I was doing, even though he would never say so. I reassured him that I wouldn't touch Philip's money and that I only wanted to teach him a lesson. I wondered in silence if my husband had already discovered by now what I had done to him. It wouldn't be long anyhow.

Anne set up a Skype call with the owners of the apartment building, who turned out be a very nice elderly couple. We connected immediately and they approved me while on the call, even though I didn't have a job right now. I had the money to pay the rent upfront for a whole year, so they didn't seem too bothered by that. Anne had the documents ready in no time. After I signed a one-year lease, she offered me a glass of champagne. When I signed my name, I realized I was signing off on my marriage too. There was no turning back now; Philip and I would never get back together. I could feel it.

Something tugged at my insides, telling me that everything was happening too fast, but I still signed the lease. I needed to put my life back on the rails and rise from the ashes my husband had created. If I stopped, or held back now, or if I even contemplated a reunion between us, I would face the same ordeal again. It would be just a matter of time before he screwed me over again.

"May this be the very first step towards a new life," Anne smiled.

You could still make things better again between my husband and I, something screamed at me. You've been too fast, too quick, too hasty in decisions. I refused to listen.

I was a free woman now; nobody would ever hurt me again. For once, I was happy. Of course, that couldn't last. It never did.

Sixteen

AFTER ANNE AND I SAID goodbye, I wound up alone again. Anne still had some work to do and promised to contact me soon to officially hand me the keys to my new apartment. It was getting late, so I had a club sandwich in a small diner near Central Park. It was cold outside and even though the air was dark grey by now, there was no show predicted for tonight. While eating, I made an inventory of my current state of affairs.

All I had with me were the same clothes I was still wearing from last night's dinner date with Vivian, a phone, power bank and cable, and some money and bank cards in my bag. I didn't feel like going back to the same hotel, but I hadn't decided on where I would want to stay tonight, so I left that out in the open for now. I watched the tourists in the park, who had come over for the weekend to watch the city bathing in light. I used to do the same in a previous life: just hop on a train to come here for a few days, in the company of my husband. It didn't affect me as much as I thought it would to see these couples stroll around the park, with or without children and dogs. Anne gave me a call about an hour later, to set up a new appointment. Since I had told her I was staying in a hotel for now, she had promised to rush things for me.

"We're all good to go," she said. "Let's meet on Sunday morning at the apartment, so you can help arrange the furniture just the way you want it. How's that? In meantime, you can drop off anything you already want to leave at the apartment building. You can use the storage room in the back, like I showed you. The key I gave you allows you entrance through the front door for now. I'll give you the final keys on Sunday then."

"Like I said: you're a dream, Anne," I enthused. "Thank you so much."

"You're welcome. Let's have drinks next week or so. Talk to you soon. Congratulations again, Zoey."

After she hung up, I realized I had no more excuses left not to go to my old apartment. I had avoided the confrontation for as long as I could, but I needed my clothes and personal things. Philip would be there, watching me pack up. I was exhausted and knew I should get some rest, but I didn't listen to the signals my body gave me. First, everything had to be settled with Philip.

I threw away the garbage and hailed a cab. I settled in the back and closed my eyes briefly while the cab driver took me to my old address. I fell asleep for a while, allowing my body and mind to rest. He woke me up a few minutes before we got there, looking at me inquisitively after he parked his cab. I pulled my hair backwards and tied it in a knot.

"Are you okay back there?" he asked.

"Perfect," I smiled. "Would you mind waiting? You can keep the meter running of course."

"Sure."

The driver pulled up in front of the building I had spent the past months grieving. I gave him a big tip already, so he would surely wait. He smiled broadly, revealing his crooked teeth. I felt his curious eyes pierce my back after I closed the car door and walked up the steps leading to the building. Using my key, I gained access to the hallway and took the elevator up to the sixth floor. Nerves acted up.

"Don't be home," I whispered. "Please be gone."

I opened the apartment door, only to find Philip standing in the middle of the living room. He had a glass of wine in his hand; the fireplace was lit. Elisabeth, the one he was with now, sat in front of it, reading a book. He had never lit the fire once when I was still living here, I thought stunned. They looked like a classic English couple. Elisabeth seemed quite comfortable, with her legs folded up on the couch and a glass of wine by her side. Her shiny hair lay in perfect curls on her shoulders; her glasses were gone. She was hardly recognizable.

Maybe she wore contacts, or maybe those glasses she had on her face at the hospital were just for show. This woman hardly looked like the little mouse I had seen last night, and at the hospital. In fact, with the right light and in this seated position, she looked stunning. She looked up at me with beautiful blue eyes, looking all innocent and happy, while Philip moved closer to stand by her side, as if he was afraid I would attack her. No wonder he fell for her. She was exactly his type, the kind of woman he turned around for on the streets.

If there ever had been a chance of making things right, it was blown away within a millisecond. A few simple gestures, a few moves and actions from their side, destroyed the hope that might still have lingered in the back of my mind, even when I had rented my own place and vowed never to return to him within a day of our split. Despite my purchase and my persistence in building a new life that didn't revolve around Philip, I had probably still cherished vague hopes that all of this had been part of some eerie nightmare.

For the first time since last night, I felt bitter tears streaming down my face. They were unstoppable, despite my determination that I would get through this. In this split second, I recognized the fact that this woman had taken my rightful place, without even blinking an eyelash. My self-confidence was destroyed. This was the family I should have had; the relationship I should have been in. She could still have children; I was broken forever. Philip never looked at me the way he gazed at her right now, like a lion protecting his lioness. He was afraid that I was going to harm her, pull her out of that chair and scratch my nails over her face.

I couldn't do it. I couldn't get past them, so I turned and slammed the door behind me. I practically ran to the elevator and pushed the button furiously, but the damned thing was on the ground floor and still needed to come up. I ran down the stairs, going so fast that my feet could barely follow. I ran and ran, until suddenly I missed the second bottom step and tripped forward. I went down hard and cried in pain, when my wrist hit the cold marble tiles. I stayed on the floor, crying so hard that I didn't hear a door open and close above me and footsteps running down.

Someone helped me up. I thought it was Philip and clung onto him. Only when my head rested against the man's shoulder did I realize that this was not my husband. It was a total stranger who lifted me off the ground and asked me if I was okay. My own husband wouldn't even come to check on me, but a guy I had never met, did. I growled at him in anger. He backed away and muttered I was a crazy bitch.

I was.

Seventeen

I SAT OUTSIDE IN THE cold for at least ten minutes, trying to catch my breath, before I felt able enough to head back inside and get what was mine. I needed to get this over with, so backing out was not an option. Before I could take the elevator back up, I bumped into Philip, who stood in the hallway, looking at me. I quickly shoved my sleeve over my wrist, refusing to let him see I was hurt. I didn't look in his eyes.

"Can you please come back upstairs with me?" he asked. "You didn't have to run like that."

"Is she still there?" I asked coolly.

"Yes."

"Then tell her to leave now. I won't set foot in there with her in it."

"Okay," he sighed. Give me ten minutes."

He left me alone in the corridor while he took the elevator back upstairs. I knew he was going to do as I asked, because he owed it to me. The nerve, I thought, of having her live here already. How could he do that to me? Anger was building up again. Anger was good, I told myself, much better than fear and anxiety.

The elevator doors slid open again after ten minutes or so. Elisabeth walked out with Philip. She glanced angrily at me before leaving, dressed in a warm coat, with fur on the sleeves and collar. Her footsteps were barely audible, which bothered me somehow. She was the type to sneak around. I followed Philip inside the elevator. Once the doors slid shut, he looked at my wrist. It looked black and blue; I had forgotten to keep the sleeve down.

"My god, what happened? Did you hurt yourself?"

"It's nothing."

I felt so tired I just wanted to drop on a couch and sleep, but I needed to get this over with before things got ugly again. His casual attitude betrayed the fact that he hadn't realized yet that I had taken half of his money. I hoped to avoid a confrontation about that until next week, once I was settled down enough in my new apartment. Philip ignored me once we entered the apartment. He walked into the kitchen to get a cup of coffee. He didn't offer me anything. I had to strain to hear what he was saying.

"Have you got somewhere to stay?" he asked.

"A hotel."

"Where?"

"Don't know yet."

"What about Vivian? Can't you stay with her?" he asked tense.

"She's out of the country; I couldn't reach her. She doesn't know yet what's going on."

"I see."

Philip looked at me briefly. I could tell he was shaken up by the fact that I had to spend the night in a hotel. My god, I thought, he had expected me to have a place to go to. He didn't think he was shipping me off to nowhere, probably assuming that Vivian would have opened her doors for me and let me in. After all, he had practically accused us of having an affair. His voice broke.

"I'm so sorry, Zoey. I had no idea you had to go to a hotel."

"Would it have made a difference?" I asked bitterly.

"Yes, of course. I wouldn't have handled things like this. I would have waited, so you had somewhere to go."

"You're a bastard, Philip," I snarled. "A coward, a liar and a bastard. Just for the record: I told you that before. Nothing's changed since yesterday."

"Don't start this again, Zoey," he sighed. "You knew our marriage was over. We have both changed too much."

"You have changed. You went and screwed that woman. Don't put this on me! I didn't choose for any of this to happen."

"Let's not go back there, Zoey. It's too late to make things right now. We can't undo this, even if I wanted to."

"Would you want things to be right again then?" I asked shocked, hearing doubt in his voice.

For one moment, I thought my husband was going to wrap his arms around me and hold me tight, so I backed away. He took a deep breath, straightened his shoulders and looked just as cold again as he had done the night before. The power he had felt when he threw me out, took over again. The man I had once married and loved was gone.

"It's over," he said out loud.

"I'll be getting my things then," I reacted coolly.

I turned away from him to prove my point. Philip followed me into the bedroom, where I went to work. There were three suitcases in the walk-in closet that we hadn't even used since we moved in here. I picked out the largest one, removed my clothes from the dressing room and started folding up every single piece, to get as much as possible in the case. I had lost much weight after losing Eve. Most sweaters and slacks were baggy around my skinny bones. I would have to get new things soon, but that would have to wait. Even so, I vowed not to leave any piece of clothing here for her to take. She had no right to touch my personal belongings. She wouldn't get a single thing.

I started selecting my shoes and put them in a large duffel bag, while Philip folded his arms over each other and leaned nonchalant against the door. I couldn't take them all, so I stashed some pairs in a pile in the back. Philip watched me intently while I worked, leaning casually against the door.

"It didn't take you long to plunder our bank account, did it?" he said. "Are you satisfied with what you got?"

I raised an eyebrow, refused to pay notice to his accusing tone of voice. He wouldn't rattle me, no matter what.

"It was good for starters," I said. "You know I earned my fair share."

"You got more than I did, and you put me in a bad position. You do realize that, right?"

"I want what I'm entitled to."

"Are you saying you deserved more than I did?"

"That's not the point, Philip," I snapped. "You still don't get it, do you? You threw me out, remember? You sold our house behind my back, bought this apartment, kept the car and got yourself a lover. Despite what you said earlier and your claims that my shop didn't do well, I have paid my share for years. I've earned a good income that you profited from too, or did you forget how you used my VAT number to buy stuff? Yes, I didn't pay for half the house, but you never asked me to after we moved in, so don't use that as an excuse. So yes, considering what you've done, I will fight you for every penny that you have. I'll drag your ass into court if I have to, in front of the judges and lawyers you work with."

"Is that what you want then, Zoey?" he asked quietly. "To sue me, so you can pay me back in full? I thought we were going to do this the easy way."

"We are doing it the easy way," I replied sharply.

He laughed bitterly. "Could have fooled me."

"I haven't told anyone that you're a lying bastard who had an affair with his wife's nurse. How do you think your clients will react?"

"How do you think everyone will react when they find out you're a messed up, psychological case, Zoey? A drug addict, living on pills to make it through the day, that's all you are these days," he lashed out.

"I'm not on drugs."

"What do you think that medication does to you? You've been popping pills for months now. Don't you think I haven't noticed how you numb yourself every single day, up to a point you can't even remember your own name? You're hooked."

"Really?" I raised an eyebrow. "Then how come I haven't taken a single pill today?"

"You're lying."

"I'm not."

"You took one. I can see it in your behavior."

"I didn't," I muttered, until I realized he was right.

I did take something at the park. I remembered having a headache. But I didn't take any pills, ... or did I? God, I couldn't recall if I took one or not.

"I rest my case," Philip smirked.

I wasn't the type of person to use foul language, but Philip had forced me to, both yesterday and today. Something inside of me snapped. I let go of the duffel bag, turned to him so that we were only inches away from each other and breathed out in the hardest tone of voice I could produce the words that I had wanted to say for ages.

"Fuck off, Philip. Fuck you. I wish it were you who died that day, not Samantha and not Eve."

My husband turned and left the room. I swayed and nearly fell on the bed. Sharp pains stung my temple. I reached for my head with both hands and tried to stop it from hurting. The only thing that could help me were my pills. I reached for my bag. After all, if I was already an addict, why shouldn't I just take them?

After a few minutes, I had filled up two suitcases with clothes and threw everything else in the duffel bag. I headed for the bathroom, where I threw all my former make-up in the bin. I kept only one hairbrush and threw away most of the rest. My toothbrush and paste were also thrown in the duffel bag. My wrist hurt like hell. Philip came in when I was nearly finished, barely looking at me. He removed all my bottles of pills from the medicine cabinet. There were more left than I thought, and I knew I needed them all. The largest bottle with small white pills, called out to me. I wanted to leave them here, but I knew I couldn't. I needed that medication to survive the day. My hands shook, even now.

"Don't," Philip spoke gently. "You need them, and I get that, Zoey. I get you, more than you think."

I allowed him to shove the bottles in my bag while I gathered my shampoo and soap, but dropped my old perfume in the bin. Philip watched me when I spotted a bottle of perfume that wasn't mine. I picked it up and smelled it. It had her name written all over it. It was a modest perfume, barely noticeable. I let out a bitter cry and threw it in the garbage can, on top of mine. Both bottles broke. The scent permeated the bathroom.

I left my books and some vinyl records but removed my personal documents from the small room we used as an office. I needed the paperwork to restart my business. I also remembered to take the phone charger. I decided not to take anything from the living room either. Many were mementos from our travels: crystal from Prague, glass from Venice, some exclusive items given to us by my parents and decoration pieces I had carefully chosen for our house. They all seemed misplaced in this much smaller apartment, but I didn't want them in my new place either. I wanted nothing from our past.

I lingered by the piano and touched the keys briefly. To my big surprise, Philip had moved the instrument from the house to the apartment, even though that must have cost him an arm and a leg. He could have easily gotten another one, but he didn't. We both used to play on it, but Philip had stopped when he began to work for bigger clients. It was one of the few hobbies that I really cherished, so I debated how to get it moved to the apartment, until Philip stepped forward and touched the wood with his hand, blocking the way.

"That is staying here. Besides, where would you bring it?"

"I found a place in the Meat Packing District," I whispered. "I'll be moving there soon."

"Why there?" he asked surprised.

"Why not? It's a nice area, with nice people."

"That seems pretty fast, doesn't it? Shouldn't you move in with someone else first? You said you were looking for a hotel tonight, so – "

"I rented it and I'm moving in on Sunday," I interrupted him. "That's all you need to know right now. The rest is none of your business. Why not give me the piano? You don't play on it anymore."

I looked at him with tears in my eyes, and he softened.

"I'm sorry," he spoke gentler, "but you know that was a gift from my father. I can't give it to you."

Just like you couldn't give me your love anymore, I thought in silence. We returned to the living room, where Philip helped me move my things to the door. Here we were: two people standing in between what was left of their life together. A marriage, buried in a few suitcases and one duffel bag. It was pathetic really. The old Philip appeared again for a moment, trying to find the right words to apologize for his own actions.

"I wish -"

"Don't."

I stopped him by placing my fingers on his lips. The moment my fingertips touched that softness of his mouth, I shook uncontrollably. Furious with my own weakness, I picked up my things and headed to the elevator, placing my stuff inside the small box on my own. I refused his help. The cab driver put everything in the trunk, while Philip stood there, watching us.

"I hope you are going to be okay Zoey," he spoke friendly, touching my face for the last time. "I didn't mean for any of this to happen. It just did."

"Goodbye Philip," I replied, too tired to argue anymore.

I shed my last tears over my husband in the cab. My new life waited for me, and I would never look back.

Eighteen

THE CAB DRIVER STOPPED AT my new apartment building so I could leave my things there in the storage room, like Anne had suggested. He helped me graciously move my things inside the hallway, where I gave him a large tip and watched him take off. I had spotted a small hotel nearby and decided to head there to book a room for two nights. The door of the apartment on the ground floor opened before I could even pick up my first suitcase. My new neighbor, doctor/janitor Alex Ramsey popped out.

"Hey," he said, scratching his hair. "I saw you struggle with those suitcases. Need a hand?"

I wanted to say no, but his help would be welcome since I barely managed to keep myself standing on my feet.

"Sure," I said.

"What's that?" he asked, pointing at my hand.

"What's what?"

"Your wrist."

Before I could protest, his slender hands took my painful wrist in his to explore the damage.

"That looks sprained or even broken. What happened?"

"I fell."

"Must have been quite a fall. I think you might be lucky, it's definitely a sprain, but it doesn't feel like you've broken a bone. I'd suggest we get you to the hospital for an X-Ray and go from there. It definitely needs treatment though."

"An X-Ray?" I asked dumbfounded.

"Yeah, you know? That thing that they do to find out how badly you hurt yourself. Don't worry, they're painless and it won't take too long to get you to the ER and back here."

"Are you a doctor?" I asked. "I thought you were a janitor."

"Only in my spare time. I'm actually an abdominal surgeon, but I did an Orthopedics internship before I realized that I preferred to operate on stomachs instead of fixating broken bones."

The man let go of my wrist and looked at the suitcases, probably trying to calculate in his mind how heavy they were.

"Where do these need to go? Upstairs? Are you moving in already?"

"No, they need to go to the storage for now. I won't have a key until Sunday. You're a surgeon who loves to work on pipes too?" I asked surprised.

"Walter, our landlord, is getting too old to fix everything by himself and I love to work with my hands, so I help him out now and then. They live across the city, so when there's an emergency, I do my thing. If you want, I can keep your stuff with me until Sunday. I have a spare room, so it's no hassle."

"Thanks, but I'll manage," I said, debating his offer.

He sounded like a really nice guy, and I felt I could learn to trust him, but it was too soon to start relying on others again.

"Look," he said, stopping my thoughts. "I can tell you've been hurt by someone, so I won't pry and interfere with whatever you decide, but it's okay to leave your things with me. Like I said, I have a spare room that's gathering dust anyhow. You could even stay with me until you get your key. I take it that you are homeless right now, so I'm just offering some help."

"How do you know I don't have a home?" I asked, pushing back tears.

When he stated it so bluntly, I sounded like one of those people on the streets, begging for some change and a place to stay.

"Well, it's a bit strange that you would be moving suitcases here, putting them in a storage room when you have another place to go to. My guess is that you took off from wherever it was that you lived, right?"

I nodded before I could stop myself. It would feel so good to have a place that felt more like home for a couple of nights.

"Okay, so that's settled then. Come on, let's get these things moved inside, o I can take you to the hospital next."

"What hospital are we going?" I asked, suddenly horrified he would take me to that place that had nothing but bad memories for me.

"St. Mary's, where I work," he said. "Why?"

"You're not working with Elisabeth, are you?" I blurted out. "If you are friends with her, I don't want you touching me. I swear she won't ever lay a finger on me again." My words shocked him.

"Who in the world is Elisabeth? Zoey, are you alright?"

I didn't even notice that I was crying for real now. Mac moved forward, but he didn't touch me. Somehow, he sensed I couldn't handle that right now.

"Who is Elisabeth?" he repeated. "God, you're shaken all over. Come on, I'll make you some tea. I can take care of your wrist here, if you trust my judgement that it's probably a sprain and not a break. I've got a medical bag with me at all times. If hospitals scare you that much, you don't have to go. I don't want you as a steady patient though, not when we're obviously becoming close friends. A doctor should never befriend his patients, don't you agree?"

I couldn't help but smile at his words, knowing that he felt the same about me. We could be friends. Maybe we already were.

"You don't believe in doctor-patient personal relationships then?" I asked.

"Not if I want some psycho patient chasing me with a knife after we broke it off," he laughed. "They always know where you work, so stalking sounds like a pretty realistic option to me."

I studied Mac for the first time, taking in his features. He was the genuine kind type, the one that didn't want anything in return, but a good chat, shared over a nice cup of coffee. Did men like that even exist anymore these days?

"Okay," I finally gave in. "I suppose you can make me a cup of coffee. And I would love to sleep in your spare bedroom tonight."

"Great," he smiled. "Are you sure you're okay?"

"I'm fine."

Mac showed me around me inside his ground floor apartment, which turned out to be quite nice, with dark furniture and lots of colorful tones brightening up the room. He had a small, neat back yard and a kitchen stacked with modern appliances. He obviously cooked too; the smell of fresh soup sparkled through the room. God, it smelled so nice. As if he could read my mind, he started talking again.

"Why don't I get you a cup of soup instead of tea? Homemade, my mom's recipe."

"Sounds wonderful," I whispered.

Mac settled me down on the couch to get his medical bag. His skilled hands were soft while they worked on my wrist. He used a salve that soothed the ache and wrapped a tight bandage around my wrist and hand, to stop the injury from throbbing. He offered me a painkiller, but I told him I had taken one earlier. I didn't want him to know I was hooked on these damned things.

He settled me down at the kitchen table next, heated some soup and offered me a spoon. While eating slowly, I blurted out what had happened to me, not leaving anything out. If we were going to become good friends, I wanted him to know the whole story, even if it meant already losing him before it even started. Mac listened intently while he folded his hands underneath his chin, a habit he often practiced, so I would find out later. He never smiled when I made ironic remarks about my husband and his mistress. He didn't show whether he genuinely cared or was simply listening to my story from a professional point of view. Right now, he might as well have been my psychiatrist. It felt so good to say it all. Not even Rob knew as much as Mac did now.

"You still love him," Mac finally remarked. "Which is not so odd, of course, considering the circumstances. You still haven't dealt with the fact that he threw you out. Even while you rented this new apartment, albeit very fast, you still had hopes that he would come back to you. At the same time, your mind screamed for you to move on. You're torn between what you feel is right and what you really want to happen, which is, that Philip will come to his senses. You may say you don't want him back, but you haven't truly said goodbye to him either."

I looked up in wonder and laughed.

"Am I that obvious?"

He smiled and shook his head.

"No, you're not. I've been there, Zoey. I'm a surgeon and have been for years, but I was different when I first started out. I used to work long hours and save many lives. To be honest, I thought I was God. I was good at what I did. Some people even called me brilliant. I had everything going for me: a career, a good future and prosperity. I was on my way to becoming wealthy and respected. I thought those were the most important things in life. During that time, I hadn't even noticed that my wife and I had become strangers. I didn't notice when she started an affair because she was lonely. One day I came home, and she practically threw me out. I didn't need to bother trying to fix things, so she stated bluntly, since I was married to my job, not to her. She was right."

"What happened then?"

"That first night alone, was hell. I had never spent a single night away from her, even if those nights were often quite short. After emergency surgery, or after I was on call, I always went home to sleep by her side, despite the fact I often had to go back in a few hours. She didn't see that as a token of love. I had neglected her too much, so she left me for someone who was willing to spend enough time with her. She needed to be treated like a queen, with the necessary attention, even if it meant being with someone she didn't love as much as she loved me. Her words, not mine."

I felt Mac's pain when he discussed the failure of his marriage, feeling what he went through, realizing why he had offered me a place to stay for the night.

"I spent that first night in a hotel, believing my dreams had been crushed. What was life worth, when I didn't have her? It took me that devastating news to learn that she was worth more to me than any job. I had never had another girlfriend in my life. She was my high school sweetheart. I walked around with suicidal thoughts. I wanted to throw myself out of a window and get it over with. I called her and begged her for forgiveness, but that man's voice could be heard in the back, and I knew she had already let him move in with her, because she couldn't stand to be alone. He had taken my place. I was angry and upset and started working like crazy. I did even more shifts and didn't bother finding a new place to stay. I practically lived at the hospital. Until one day, everything went to hell."

I was afraid of what he was going to tell me next. I reached forward to touch his hand on impulse, wanting him to know I was listening. He didn't even notice, sunken deep into his own thoughts.

"A mother and daughter were brought in after a serious accident. The girl's life was on the line. It was after midnight and I had been on call for the past twenty-four hours, deliberately pushing myself to the farthest edge of the world. It was the summer season, and I was the only doctor there who could perform the operation. I opened up that girl, knowing I couldn't handle it, but I was too stubborn to ask someone else. She died on the table."

Mac had tears in his eyes. He looked away from me, guilt radiating from him.

"No one blamed me of course. How could they? The girl didn't stand a chance as it was, the medical examiner's report said, but I knew that I could have saved her, had I been clear minded enough. She wasn't the worst case I had ever done; she still stood a chance. The truth is that I lied about my hours in the report. I had taken on the daytime shift too, showing up unexpectedly, not even signing in. I had been on call at the ER, and my supervisor didn't know because I didn't tell him. I told him later of course and he protected me, as did the rest of the staff at the hospital. I worked many hours because I didn't want time to think, since my soon-to-be ex-wife was in Italy, enjoying the holiday I had booked for us three months earlier. She had gone anyway, with her lover instead of me. If I had not taken that daytime shift, I would have been clear-headed, and that girl would have lived."

"But she was critically hurt," I stated. "How can you blame yourself, when you tried to save her? You don't know if you would have been able to save her life."

"That's the whole point, isn't it? I'll never know," Mac spoke bitterly. He shook his head ruefully. "I hated what had become of me. When I spoke to her mother afterwards, the woman thanked me for at least trying. I started to cry, collapsed and broke down in front of my colleagues, peers and patients. My superior said I needed to rest urgently, so he put me on an obligated leave of absence so I could deal with my personal things. I was suffering from a burn-out, Zoey. That girl's death took me over the edge."

"What did you do?" I asked quietly.

"I just took off. I drove the car up north, ended up somewhere in Canada and picked out a small hotel room. I didn't leave the room for three days. I couldn't even remember how I got there. Those were the darkest days of my life, Zoey, just contemplating what to do next. And then one morning I woke up and realized I had to decide right there and then what I wanted to do next. Which was, either to live, or to end up dead, there and then. If I moved on, at least I would know by the pain that I was alive and breathing. I could spend the rest of my life making up for that girl's death, instead of moaning about my own grief and sorrow. That's what I settled for. I returned to New York, spoke for hours with my supervisor and told him things had to change drastically. I wouldn't just help people anymore and move on, so I chose to take on lesser patients and spend more time with them, post-surgery. I even set up a small clinic where I could see my patients and help them cope with post-surgery trauma, along with some of my colleagues."

"I remember something about that," I murmured. "After I woke up in St. Mary's, someone gave me a flyer of this service and said I should try it, but I never did."

"That's us," Mac smiled. "Why didn't you make use of it, Zoey? You never ask anyone for help, do you?"

"I am not the kind of person you would want for a patient, Mac," I whispered. "I'm too complicated, too messed up."

"Aren't we all? That doesn't mean you're not entitled to talk about your problems with someone. If you want, I can set you up with one of my trauma specialists to have a chat. Even so, I will never take you on as a patient, so you don't feel like you have to share your life with me. Let's start by being good neighbors and friends, how does that sound?"

"So, you're not only a replacement janitor and surgeon, you're also a psychiatrist," I smiled quietly. "You're an interesting man, Doctor Ramsey."

He smiled and touched my hand lightly.

"You are going to be a good friend, Miss Mitchell."

I blushed.

Saturday

Nineteen

AROUND SEVEN A.M., I WOKE up startled in the confinement of the small spare bedroom Mac had offered me. He also told me that he had to go to work real early, so I knew I would wake up in an empty apartment. I was shocked he had trusted me enough to leave me alone in his home, but he never seemed to question my motives, not once wondering if I was some crazy homeless person.

Sleep didn't come back. I felt dizzy and out of sorts, but that improved slowly once I took a shower, used one of Mac's towels to dry me off and drank some water while downing two pills. Not an intelligent thing to do on an empty stomach, but I hoped that they would ease the pain I felt all over. My body felt stiff and sore. My wrist hurt like hell. It felt swollen and sensitive to the touch. I had to put up a brave face for Mac, since I didn't want him to feel obligated to take care of me. I skipped breakfast altogether, feeling too queasy to bother.

New York was waking up; people were already outdoors, going about their business. It was cold outside, but I liked that. I decided to take a long stroll in the area to get to know it. Perhaps then the pain in my stomach would improve and I might even be able to eat something. With Mac's spare key in my pocket, I walked outside in my Burberry. The beautiful morning improved my mood considerably. I wandered around and got familiar with the area, loving it immediately. Three blocks down, there was a market. I heard people selling goods on the market speak loudly; their voices blurred together, until they were a flurry of sounds. I tried to make out what they were saying but couldn't follow most of the conversations. My head felt like it was stuck in another universe. I felt sick to the bone.

I ended up buying a croissant and an apple at a food stall and ignored the small second-hand book stands and typical vintage goods. I ate the croissant while pushing myself through the crowd. The apple stayed in my pocket for now. There were a lot of people around, but one stood out. I froze when I spotted the back of a man standing in front of me, gazing at one of the food stalls. It was Philip, or someone who looked very much like him. I stopped and waited until the man turned slightly so I could see his profile, gasping when I recognized him beyond a doubt.

How the hell did he even get here? He never came to the Meat Packaging District and yet, he was here, when I happened to have moved here. God, that meant that she must be here too somewhere, but I couldn't see her. I became frantic while my confused brain tried to figure out what was going on. Did he find out somehow where I was staying? Did he come here to track me down?

I turned around quickly to get away, but it was already too late. He made his way through the crowd towards me. I walked away fast, not caring if he was following me or not. I ignored him calling out for me. I felt dizzy just smelling other people near me. My feet carried me away, without my brain catching up on the situation. When someone accidentally touched me, I backed away; I couldn't stand anyone bumping into me. My skin crawled every time someone came too near. I shook my head while the world became cacophonous. She was here too, dressed in black, tattoos over her arms, holding a gun. I could just see her, could see her piercings blink in the winter sun. I gasped for air for the second time, pushed someone away and started running. Someone bumped into me; I dropped the duffel bag I had with me.

I walked into the first small street I passed to avoid the crowd, where I bumped into the only woman I never wanted to see again: Elisabeth. We both stood still in shock. I could see devastation wash over her face. She was thinking the exact same as I was. Why, in a metropolis like New York, could we not avoid each other? What was she even doing here, and why was I? I wanted to move past her, but she grabbed me by my sore wrist to stop me. I hissed in pain. God, I was so afraid of her as I battled to free myself.

"Leave us alone," she murmured in a strange tone of voice. "Stop following us and get the hell out of our lives."

"I'm not following you," I replied weakly. "You came to my new area. Don't tell me it's a coincidence that you would wind up here, when I told Philip last night I was moving here. Let go of my arm right now."

She wouldn't, nor did she give answers to my questions. She was completely out of control, acting exactly like the bitch I thought she was.

"You have no idea how much I suffered these past weeks," she hissed. "You're only out to make our lives miserable from now on, aren't you? All I wanted was to have a good life with Philip, but you destroyed everything. Don't you understand what I went through?"

I laughed out loud and then snapped, losing control again. This time though, I wouldn't show my tears. Not anymore.

"I lost everything, and you are miserable?" I spat. "What's the matter, honey? Didn't I leave enough money behind for you to spend? If you thought Philip earned enough to support you for the rest of your life, you were wrong. He's not a rich man. He has barely enough to pay for the apartment. You'll have to keep on working. Tough luck."

"It's not about the money," she spoke passionately, "It's about the man I love. It's about supporting my sister and me. You're punishing Philip for the choices that he made out of love, but you ruined everything by screwing him over financially. You're pathetic."

I didn't know what Elisabeth's sister had to do with this, nor did I care. As far as I was concerned, she could move in her entire family. She showed me who she truly was: a money seeker, someone who used others to get what she wanted. This was a woman with a quest, and she had played it perfectly. If she could, she would probably erase the memory of me from Philip's mind forever. She wanted it all and she would get it, no matter what.

"Let go of me," I repeated.

Her fingers dug deep into my bandaged wrist. It hurt like hell; her grip was extremely strong.

"You like playing the martyr, don't you?" she whispered angrily. "You blame Philip for everything, while you were the one who messed things up in the first place. You shouldn't have been in the shop that day. You brought this onto yourself."

She might as well have kicked me in the face. He had told her every single detail? How could he do that to me? Her eyes were so close now that I could see tiny sparkles in her pupils, and even her contact lenses. Her black eyebrows accentuated those strange eyes of hers. She was beautiful in a strange, striking way. I felt awkward, small and insignificant. Why hadn't I seen this earlier? I thought she was a mouse, but in truth, she was a tigress. Elisabeth could easily knock my head against the wall and call it an accident, none the wiser. I shivered; I stood unprotected and within her reach and I was damned scared.

All of a sudden, we weren't alone anymore. Philip stood behind her, moving his hand on her shoulder to pull her back. I realized only now that she had practically forced me up against the wall. Her hands were still around my wrist, until he forced her to let go.

"What's going on?" my husband asked. "Lisa, what the hell are you doing?"

He called her Lisa, not Elisabeth. He had a pet name for her. He never had one for me. Bitter jealousy struck my heart, while horrible dizziness returned in full. I leaned against the wall and closed my eyes as I tried to get a grip on myself. If I didn't stay alert right now, I didn't know where I would end up.

"Tell her to back off," I muttered dazed.

I clutched the side of my head in pain. I was suffering when sharp pain rushed through my temples. I couldn't help the moan escaping my mouth.

"Zoey?" I heard Philip say.

There was a shuffle and then Elisabeth was out of sight and Philip's hands were touching me. I opened my eyes and stared at him, discovering that I had buckled through my knees and was practically lying on the concrete, in his arms. His hand supported my neck, while the other one rested on my arm. It felt as if someone had pulled the strings holding up my legs.

"Zoey," my husband urged me. "Zoey, talk to me. What's wrong?"

Elisabeth didn't move an inch, even though she was a nurse. He turned and shouted impatiently at her to do something. Someone else called an ambulance; I could hear the words. When others came closer, Elisabeth knelt by my side and tried to touch me. I shoved her away. I didn't want her by my side; I didn't want her hands on me, ever again; I didn't want her to take care of me.

I had no choice in the matter. The world turned black before my very eyes and there was nothing I could do to stop that from happening. The last thing I heard was the constant wailing of my mobile phone.

Twenty

A MIXTURE OF BLURRED IMAGES, the sound of screeching sirens and panic followed. I came to several times. I remember my husband telling the paramedics that I passed out without any forewarning. He explained my medical history to them in a rapid and speedy choice of words. He also told them truthfully that we were separated and that he had no idea of where I was staying right now. He didn't go into further details.

The paramedics spoke to me in an attempt to get an idea of what happened. I remembered answering questions but had no idea afterwards what I had said. I just let myself slide into darkness for a second time, only to wake up in a small room in a hospital. I recognized the color of these walls immediately. God, I was back at St. Mary's, the same hospital I had been in months before. The hospital I had vowed to avoid for the rest of my life. Philip had probably told them that I was treated here before. It seemed like a logical thing to have me admitted here.

Someone was in the room. Even with closed eyes, I could hear a soft scuffling of feet. I turned my head slightly and saw Vivian sitting by the window, scanning her phone. Next to her on the table, lay my duffel bag. When I stirred, she looked up.

"Vivian?" I asked stunned.

My friend moved away from the window and came closer, so that I could see her better.

"It's me," she smiled. "How do you feel?"

"Like crap. How did you get here? What's happened? I thought you were in Paris. How in the world did you get back so fast?"

She smiled while she sat down on the side of the bed. Despite her concern for me, her everlasting self-confidence was still there. Whatever movement she made, it was always gracious. I was so jealous of the easy way she held herself up in this harsh world.

"I came back on the first flight out after my meetings ended," she said. "I got your voicemails pretty soon, but our flight got delayed and I arrived just in time to the client's office to manage the planned sessions. Honestly, I was so angry when they were unprepared; I might as well have saved me the trouble of flying over. Truth be told, I spent more time at the airport and on planes than in actual meetings. I swear to God these people have never heard of Skype calls. Anyhow, once I heard your frantic voicemails, I decided to fly right back instead of staying until Tuesday as originally planned, so I had my flight rebooked. As soon as I arrived at the airport, I tried to call you a few times, but you never answered. I finally got through to a nurse who picked up your phone and told me you were here, so here I am."

Even though I was glad she was here, I also felt disappointed that Philip wasn't by my side. Then again, he had no reason to be. Why would he stay when he had Elisabeth to tend to now? It's not because I became sick that he should feel obligated to stick with me. He had done his duty.

My body felt sore and painful. I shifted in bed and tried to lean back better against the pillows. Why was I in a private room and not in the ER? It's not like I was seriously ill; I just passed out. Or was there something else going on that I didn't know about yet? Vivian helped me to lean better against the pillows and gave me a glass of water.

"What happened to me anyhow?" I asked.

"I don't know, Zoey. I came straight to your room. No one's been in here yet, but I'm sure a doctor will come and see you in a few moments. I'm afraid I can't stay long though. I just got off my flight two hours ago and my boss wants to have a word about the way I left Paris in such a hurry."

"It's still Saturday, right?" I asked, figuring from her explanation that

I hadn't lost a day.

"Tell that to him," she sighed.

Again, disappointment took over when I realized I would be alone again. Vivian's fingers stroked my face, stroking my right cheekbone.

"Hey, I'll be back to keep you company tonight, I promise. Just don't scare me like that anymore. I'll give you a call and we'll find out where and how to meet, okay? If things go well, I'm sure you'll be released pretty soon. If this was just a fainting spell, you'll be out of here in no time. Just don't do stuff like this anymore, okay?"

"I won't," I promised.

I hesitated, debating whether to tell her about the last few days, or to keep that for later. Had it only been two days since we had last seen each other? So much has happened since, a lifetime ago.

"By the way, shouldn't that lousy husband of yours be here to take care of you?" she asked, "or is he too busy working again, also on a Saturday?"

"We're separated." I whispered.

"You mean he threw you out?"

"How did you know?" I asked in shock.

"It doesn't take a genius to figure out that much, seeing the look on your face. You didn't choose this separation, that's for sure. I remember you telling me he wanted to talk to you. Is there another woman in his life?"

"Yes."

"What's she like?"

"Possessive. Cold. Scary. One of the reasons why I ended up here. We bumped into each other, and she threatened me. I guess I kind of passed out because of that."

"So, he finally found someone giving him the attention that he wants," Vivian remarked coolly. "Where are you staying?"

"With a new friend," I muttered, trying to avoid bringing the subject to Mac. "I did something radical though: I rented a furnished apartment in the Meat Packaging District, near The High Line. Can you believe it, Vivian? I saw the place and just needed to have it. It's all been sorted out; I'm moving in tomorrow, once I get the keys."

She seemed pleased by that and fortunately didn't ask any tricky questions about Mac.

"That's fantastic, Zoey," she enthused. "You're starting all over again; I'm so proud of you."

"Thanks, Vivian, that means a lot."

She frowned suddenly, fiddling with her fingers.

"I wasn't there for you," she murmured. "Had I known, I would not have left for Paris, but I didn't think it would be that serious. I never thought he would do that to you."

"Don't blame yourself, okay," I stopped her. "I managed and I'm doing great. I just want to get out of here now and move on. I'm really feeling okay."

"You're staying put," she ordered, when I tried to slide out of bed, IV be damned. She pushed me back down.

"Don't be so worried, Vivian," I protested. "I'm fine, honestly. I just fainted like some damsel in distress."

"Are you trying to convince yourself, Zoey?" she asked. "You're not okay at all. Look at you: you're all skin and bones. You need rest, right now. No excuses, no getting out of here. You're not taking care of yourself at all."

"I'm fine," I repeated stubbornly. "I need to go home."

"If you're fine, you wouldn't be here in the first place. Find out why you passed out, Zoey. For some reason, it feels too important to just let it slide," Vivian ordered me. "Please, do that for me?"

"I will," I said, disturbed by her concern.

Vivian leaned over and kissed me softly on the cheek. Her eyes were so close to mine that I had to look away. There was worry in them, but also something that I couldn't really describe, like a sense of worry about things I didn't want to face just yet. I didn't want to accept that something more might be going on with me than just some fatigue and those damned headaches. I was on the verge of a total breakdown, which she knew all too well.

"I have to go." Vivian picked up her coat from a chair near the window. "Face my demons, so to speak. Listen, call me if you need to talk, okay? I'll get in touch tonight to find out where you are."

"I will," I promised. "Thank you so much for being here, Vivian."

"Don't mention it."

She was gone. Two seconds later, Mac Ramsey walked in.

Twenty-One

ALL THE PLAYERS IN MY life seemed to come together continuously in a strange vicious circle that had started on Thursday evening. My third encounter with Mac Ramsey was obviously a lot more serious one than the previous two. I knew he felt the same way. He was dressed in casual clothes, which made me believe he came here as a friend again, not in the call of duty.

"Zoey," he spoke worried, "I honestly didn't think I would find you here. I came as soon as I found out you were admitted. What happened?"

"I passed out. Stupid, I know," I sighed. "I'm so sorry, Mac, I didn't mean to scare you."

"That's okay. I'm not here as your doctor, but I can tell you a bit about what happened, if you want?"

"Yes, please."

"You gave your husband quite a scare, it seems," he continued. "My colleague was on call and first looked after you when you were brought into the ER. You were passed out and unresponsive. He was worried for a while that your fainting spell had something to do with the emergency surgery you underwent months ago. Fortunately, it had no relation whatsoever. Your surgical wound is nicely healed, and they did a CT-scan to make sure that there were no leftover infections, which your bloodwork confirmed. He moved you here after they checked you over at the ER, so you could get some rest. You woke up a couple of times, but you probably don't remember. Your speech was incoherent, and you were confused."

"How did you find out then?"

"One of the ER-nurses told me someone was brought in from the Meat Packaging District with a labeled key in her pocket with my name on it, so they figured out that we knew each other and notified me. I was in surgery all day, which is why I only found out now."

"What time is it anyhow?" I asked.

"Around four p.m. You've been out for a couple of hours."

"What about my doctor? When is he coming in to see me?" I asked. "I'd like to get out of here."

"He'll be in later, but I wouldn't be a good friend if I didn't come in to see you too, right?" Mac smiled. "Truth be told, I think you'll be stuck here for a while though. Do you remember what happened?"

"I don't know exactly," I frowned. "One minute I was in an argument, the next I was on the ground. It's all quite blurry."

"They ran a blood test, like I said earlier. Apparently, you have an abnormally high amount of medication in your system. What have you been taking?"

"The pills are in my bag," I said. "I'm taking a daily dosage of Meperidine."

"Why?" Mac asked surprised.

"My body still hasn't recovered completely from surgery," I explained. "I suffer on a constant basis from abdominal pain and heavy headaches. The doctor who last treated me explained that the pain will slowly subside, but he prescribed Meperidine to help me get through the worst. It should be in my medical file."

"How many pills do you take daily?"

"Two per day," I lied. "To be honest, I already took two this morning. I had a horrible night, couldn't sleep and started feeling pain before I went to the market."

He knew I was lying of course, especially since they could trace the amounts in my bloodwork.

"So, you're suffering from chronic pains? You didn't tell me that yesterday."

"Yes, I am, and I didn't tell you because we decided last night that you were my friend, not my doctor," I remarked.

"True. Did your doctor never give you a concrete diagnosis?"

"Not really. During my last check-up, three weeks ago, he prescribed the same drug again and told me that it seemed to be the only thing that worked. Since I was responding well to the medication, he said to stick with that for now."

I didn't tell him about the diagnosis of the other doctor, claiming that it was all in my head. I'm pretty sure that was in my medical file as well.

"I see." Mac frowned as he glanced at the label on the bottle. "Meperidine shouldn't harm you, even though I find it curious that you are still taking them after all these months, when they are only meant to be used post-surgery. Have you tried alternative ways to work around the pain? There are alternative ways, like acupuncture or working with a physiotherapist."

"Dr. Peterson didn't give me any alternatives."

Mac jotted down the name of the doctor I had been seeing outside of this hospital in his private practice. He obviously knew him, looking by the frown between his brows. Something told me he didn't agree at all with the man's vision on things.

"Why don't I discuss this with him and get back to you on this?" Mac said. "For now, I will blame this collapse of yours on your low blood pressure, bad sleeping habits and physical exhaustion. I remember you telling me that you haven't been eating properly for a while, which is, considering the circumstances, not abnormal. You have to take it easier, Zoey. You're not giving your body the rest that it needs. Don't forget that you're still in recovery. You've had major surgery, not once, but three times. Some people take over a year to recover from a trauma like that."

"Can you blame me? You know what situation I am in," I whispered.

"I know, but I have to urgently advise you to rest for the next few days. You have been through a terrible ordeal, Zoey. You need to start building up strength again. You're severely underweight and have clearly been neglecting your health."

"I thought I was doing okay," I muttered.

"Well, you're not."

Mac's professional appearance changed into a more personal one. I read something in his eyes I had seen in Philip's too once, albeit in a diminished manner. God, it would be so easy to throw myself in Mac's arms and let him comfort me, but I couldn't. I wasn't ready for another relationship, nor was he even my type. He was a friend, not a lover. I couldn't contemplate this. He was not a paid escort whom I could use for a one-night stand. This was a man I could genuinely care. He had already proven his friendship and loyalty to me.

"This is serious, Zoey," Mac reprimanded me gently. "I don't know if you are aware of how seriously close you are to an emotional and physical breakdown. I saw the signs in you yesterday. Do you remember what I told you then? You have to realize that you are in a fragile state of mind. You've just been through a rough break-up. Your life has changed for good. You need to learn how to cope with that and you still need to deal with the loss of your baby. You haven't done that yet; I can read the pain in your eyes. You need help, Zoey."

"Are you being a shrink or a doctor right now?" I asked.

"I'm being a friend."

"As a friend, you should know I'm doing perfectly fine."

"You will manage one day," he agreed, "but not right now. I don't want you in here again, Zoey. I don't want to find you on the streets one day, unconscious or worse. This is the harsh reality you are in. If you tell me that you're going to leave this hospital today, only to neglect these problems again, I will keep you here for a while to recover. You need to be taken care of for once."

"You can't do that," I protested.

"As your medical doctor, I can."

"Look," I spoke calmly, "I'm not going to argue with you about this, okay? I'm fine, Mac and I need to move on, to deal with the rest of my life, which I can't do here. My new life starts tomorrow, when I get the key to my own place. I'll be fine, I swear. I'm dealing with things my way."

"That apartment can wait a few days, can't it?" Mac spoke gently. "You can stay with me for as long as you like. The spare bedroom is yours."

"I don't want to be a burden. I'll check into a hotel," I said.

"Don't." Mac raised his hand. "I would love to have you around longer, Zoey. You're a good listener and I could use some company. Besides, we're friends, right?"

We both understood the underlying meaning of his last remark. We were both so very lonely, so eager to have someone to talk to.

"Listen, why don't you rest for a bit now? I'll be off in less than two hours. If you feel okay enough then, I'll get you out of here under my supervision. How's that?"

"Thank you, Mac."

"Don't mention it."

He tucked me in, gave me a small pat on the hair and left the room. Before I fell asleep, I wondered why I trusted this man so much. My husband had become a stranger to me, while this interesting stranger had come into my life and turned it completely upside down. My vow that I would never love another man again, was pushed into the back of my mind.

I believe that every move we make in life is premeditated. For every bad thing, a good thing happens in return. This man was heaven-sent, just like Anne had been. I could only be grateful for that.

Twenty-Two

I MUST HAVE DRIFTED OFF, because the following moment, Philip was standing near the bed. The blinds were lowered, and it was darker in the room than it had been earlier, which made it all the more surprising he was standing there.

I never thought my husband would come in to see me. My surprise was even bigger when I realized that he stood close enough to stroke the side of my face with the back of his right index finger, like Vivian had done. He thought I was asleep when he touched me. It was a small gesture he had often made after we had sex. He hadn't done this when I woke up after losing Eve. He didn't even notice I was awake. When I stirred, he pulled back his finger and smiled faintly, as if it was perfectly normal to touch me so intimately.

"Hey there, how are you doing?" he asked, friendlier than I had heard him speak in a long time.

"I'm fine."

My throat was dry, and I was dead tired. I noticed that the IV-pole was gone, which made me happy. It was a sign they would probably let me go.

"I'm parched. Could you hand me that glass of water?" I asked.

"Here, let me help you sit up first," he offered.

Philip lifted the head of the bed a bit, fluffed the pillows and supported my neck while he helped me drink from a straw. I coughed when the water tickled the back of my throat.

"Thanks," I croaked.

"You gave me quite a scare, Zoey."

"Did I?"

"For a moment there I thought -" he stopped and shook his head. "Thank God you aren't seriously ill."

"I'm sorry about the scare. Thank you for coming by."

"I never left."

"Oh?"

"I had a late lunch at the cafeteria and then your doctor came over to tell me that you were fine and asleep. I was in the ambulance and at the ER with you, until they moved you here and said I should leave you alone for a while to recuperate a bit."

"You were here all the time?" I asked surprised. "Why?"

"Why wouldn't I be? You're still my wife."

"The one you dumped."

He frowned, sinking down on the side of my bed.

"I wish I could change our past, Zoey," he confessed. "I wish I could go back in time, to a point where we could still change our future, but I can't. I know I made some big mistakes. I wasn't there for you when you needed me the most and I sure as hell didn't help you cope with the loss of our daughter. Instead, I destroyed our marriage singlehandedly."

"Philip -"

"No, let me finish, please. I've been thinking about it all for two days now, about all the stuff that I did to you. I thought it would be so easy to hate you for what had become of us, for what I believed you had done to ruin us, but I can't find any fault in what you did, and I can't blame you for anything. You were the victim here, but I was too blind to see that. I can't forget you, Zoey. How can I, when everything in my life reminds me of you? When I wind up in the Meat Packing District without even realizing I was out there, searching for you? How can I let you go, when my heart broke the moment I thought you were going to die?"

"What are you saying?" I asked troubled.

Philip looked at me awkwardly and then back at his hands, his voice emotional as he continued.

"I know that we can never be together again after what I did to you, but I want us to stay friends. I want things to change; I want to change myself. I want to become a better person. I can't go on without you in my life. You're a big part of who I am. You made me into who I've become, and I realized over the past two days that I have thrown away the best thing that ever happened to me. You were right when you said I blamed you for losing our daughter, while in truth, you were the one that fought for her life. I cannot believe you came out so strong. I thought you were weak and pathetic, but you were the strongest of us all. I'm not so sure if I would have survived such an ordeal. I want us to be friends."

"It doesn't work that way, Philip," I stopped him. "You can't just switch emotions on and off like that. Besides, Elisabeth will never want me in your life, even if I were to contemplate the possibility of a friendship between us. I can't even think about that right now. It's all too much, too fast. I can't switch off my feelings either, simply because you apologize for what you did to me."

"Elisabeth doesn't hate you, Zoey."

"You didn't see her in that alley."

"She is afraid that I will go back to you."

"Will you?" I asked him. "If I told you now that I still loved you, would you come back?"

"No, I love her, Zoey, but I still love you too. It's so difficult. Why does life have to be so hard?" he sighed.

I smiled, while a sense of bitterness boiled up inside of me. He found his life stressful? Philip had changed everything we worked for in a heartbeat. Two days ago, I was still living in his apartment. I still believed that we had a marriage, no matter how bad it was. It gave at least the option of improvement sooner or later.

"What do you want me to say, Philip?" I said. "I can't just forget everything that's happened to us. What you did was unforgivable and I frankly don't know if we can ever be friends. It's way too soon to even consider that, since I'm not even sure if I can deal with you in the same room as I am. You broke my heart. Do you even realize that?"

"I know," he admitted.

"God knows I've screwed up big time," I continued hoarsely, "I know I'm an emotional, sad mess, ready for the loony bin, too self-absorbed in her grief, but I still didn't deserve what you did to me."

"I know," he said in shame.

"I have to think about this. I can't give you an answer right now on where we stand," I sighed.

"I get that and besides, I have to go anyhow. It's getting late. Are they going to let you go home? Do you want me to stay with you?"

"They said they would. What time is it anyhow?"

"Little after six."

I wondered if Mac had finished his shift yet and if he hadn't changed his mind about taking me home with him again. I contemplated sending him a message, when Philip leaned over and kissed me. His lips touched the corner of my mouth, and I didn't back away. He turned, put on his coat and left, just like that, as if nothing had happened between us.

There I was, stuck in a hospital bed, with millions of thoughts rushing through my mind. What had happened to Philip that he was singing another tune all of a sudden? Only two days ago, we had been enemies. Yesterday, he had watched me pack up and leave, without making a single attempt to stop me. Now he seemed to want to step back on that decision and gain a place in my life again. Was there something wrong in his relationship with Elisabeth? Something that made him regret throwing me out? Or did he use this tactic to get me to calm down, so I would stay meek and quiet for the rest of my life, after returning back his money?

I felt powerless. Powerless about this whole situation that I didn't choose. Frustrated because there were things happening in my life that I couldn't control. I swore to myself I would never go back to that dark place I had been stuck in for so long after Eve died. From now on, I would be in full control over what was happening to me. I needed to regain some of that power.

A doctor came in a few minutes later and signed me off. I was ready to go home, but he warned me I should not go home alone. I smiled and told him a good friend was going to pick me up and stay with me tonight. I didn't want him to know it was Mac, hoping to avoid hospital gossip that way.

The man smiled, shook my hand and wished me all the best. I got dressed, gathered my things, sent a text message to Mac and sat on the side of the bed while I waited for him. He showed up a few minutes later, smiling happily because I was ready to go. I had truly found a good friend in Mac, who seemed to genuinely care about me. And I knew that maybe I would not have to be lonely for much longer.

Sunday

Twenty-Three

I WOKE UP FEELING OKAY. Today would really be the first day of my new life, that was a promise I made to myself. The morning sun broke through the large windows in Mac's spacious spare bedroom. I stretched out underneath the warm blankets, felt the crisp white sheets against my skin. My feet could touch the wooden edge of the bed. It felt comfortable lying in this large bed, until I heard sounds coming from the living room. I wanted to thank Mac by making him breakfast, which meant that I needed to get out of bed. My bare feet touched the warm carpet; my toes curled. I felt warm, happy and pleased.

Last night was something of a blur to me. Mac and I took a cab back to the apartment building. I was still feeling extremely tired and no matter how much I wanted to have a chat with my new friend, I found I couldn't keep myself awake. I fell asleep in the cab, just listening to the humming of the engine and the soft music playing on the radio. The ride didn't even take that long, but I was out like a light.

I woke up when Mac tapped my shoulder. I felt like an old woman, barely able to walk as we made our way in. He carried my bag and supported me. Mac insisted that I should sit on the couch, while he went into the kitchen to prepare dinner. He changed his mind before he even got started on the food, muttering something about an empty fridge and too little ingredients in the house. Typical bachelor, I thought. I was barely listening to him, practically falling asleep on the couch.

"I know this great Chinese restaurant," he said. "It's right around the corner. I'll order some takeaway. It will be your first taste of our beautiful area."

I watched him order won ton soup and chicken noodles online, not asking me about my choice of food, as if he could read my mind. Nothing too heavy on the stomach, but still hearty enough to make me feel better. Mac left to get the food, which gave me some time to really look around his living room, which was identical to mine. I could hear his upstairs neighbors walking on their parquet floor: a woman's heels clicked at a soothing rhythm. I didn't get the chance to fall asleep again, since Mac was back in less than ten minutes with the most delicious Chinese food I had ever eaten.

We ate together in silence. He ordered me to eat slowly, so that my stomach could digest the food properly. I had nibbled on a toast at the hospital, which was, apart from the croissant I had at the market this morning, the only thing I had eaten all day. With every bite I took, I felt my spirits lift, but the tiredness stayed. Around nine, I excused myself and went to bed. I hugged and thanked him. He didn't know how to react to that.

Inside the spare bedroom, I fell asleep almost instantly. The moment my head hit the soft pillow, I dozed off. Mac had turned the television on. The soft murmur of voices in the background made me feel comfortable. I had a strange feeling of happiness and safety, even though I spent the night in the apartment of a man I barely knew. It was my second night here, and I had yet to discover who Mac really was. He might be a rapist or a murderer, for all that I knew, but I felt in my heart that he was one of the good guys. Every single moment I spent by his side, I felt he was genuinely kind. He was a better man than I deserved in my life.

I left the haven of Mac's bedroom, dressed in slacks and a T-shirt that he left for me on a chair. They weren't mine, but his. He had probably felt too awkward rummaging through my personal things, so he gave me some of his that were way too big on my small frame. I found him in the kitchen, making breakfast. I was too late to surprise him, so I sunk down on a chair at the kitchen table. The smell of bacon and egg welcomed me. I couldn't remember having a decent breakfast for a long time. He must have gone out to get the ingredients while I was still out.

"Good morning," he greeted me.

That soft, soothing voice was there again. It gave me the impression that he was content with everything life had to provide. He wasn't lying when he said he had considered death at one point, but the moment that he decided to live, his way of thinking had changed completely. Mac Ramsey was a happy man, an example to how I should perceive life from now on. One day, I might be able to look back on all of this and know that it had been for the best. Philip was happy now with his lover and I would become happy again too, without him and without Eve, but with people like Mac, Vivian and Rob in my life. My daughter would not have wanted for me to grief for her forever. I knew that now.

"Good morning," I smiled back. "These smells are fantastic."

My hair was a mess, and I knew I looked like hell, but he didn't seem to care. He put two plates on the table and handed me a fork and knife.

"I made you some toast and jam for starters. If you can digest those, I might even allow you some bacon and eggs," he challenged me. "First you have to prove your worth though."

"Yummy," I grinned.

Mac smiled back, but I could tell how he was exploring my face to make sure I was doing okay. This whole situation was strange for him too. I wasn't even sure if he felt the way that I did, as if we had been living together for ages. We were friends, even if we barely knew each other. It felt nice, comfortable, good and easy.

"How are you feeling?" he asked casually.

"I'm okay. I'm feeling quite a bit better," I said.

"Did you take another pill last night?"

"No, I fell asleep almost instantly."

"And you don't feel any pain right now?"

"No. I feel good, Doctor Ramsey."

He laughed.

"I'm sorry, but you know I had to ask. You are under my care right now, remember? I can't afford to have you pass out on me again. My colleague only let you go under the condition that you would come with me and listen to what I say. I'm not sure if you're capable of doing so, but we can at least pretend to try."

"I thought I was only in your care until this morning?" I asked with raised eyebrow. "I'm moving upstairs, remember?"

"Nope, I'll be watching you until I say you're good to go. I did tell you I'm a very strict doctor, right? Only when I say you're okay to sleep in your own apartment without supervision, I'll let you walk out of here."

"No, you neglected to mention that," I snorted, nibbling on a piece of toast. "I'm not going to take advantage of your hospitality for too long though; I am serious about that. If all goes well, I should be able to move into my apartment this afternoon, once Anne hands me the keys. You can come and pay a visit there if you insist. At least then I can treat you with dinner."

"I saw some cleaning crew pass down the hall this morning," Mac said. "They should be finished soon, so you can go up whenever you want to. I think your electricity and water supplies should be settled too, since we're all on the same lines and tubes anyhow. You just need to sort your internet access and get some devices in, like a television and radio. That wasn't foreseen, was it?"

"Actually, it was. The owners left some devices behind for use, since they didn't feel like moving them," I said. "Cable and internet are about all I need to arrange. Anne was going to give me a call to meet somewhere today. She doesn't know I'm here of course. Once I'm settled in, I can take things easy in the first few days, before I start thinking about finding a good shop location."

"Sounds like a plan."

Mac seemed almost disappointed that I was not staying at his place for another few days. It radiated from his face, which I really appreciated, but I didn't want to be a burden to him either. He had his job at the hospital. He shouldn't be looking out for me all the time.

"You're so sweet, Mac," I said. "I really appreciate everything you have done for me, but I need to take charge of my own life now. If I don't leave now, I might never leave again."

He laughed. "My door will always be open for you, Zoey. For your information, I don't mean that in a romantic way, but you know that, right? There's this woman that lives down the road that I really like and … God, you didn't think that you and I -"

"Hang on," I stopped him. "No, I didn't, Mac, so don't worry about that. I'm totally not ready for a new relationship, so rest assured that friendship is what I need right now, like Joey and Rachel have."

"Joey and Rachel?" he asked, dumbfounded.

"Yeah, in Friends. They like each other and … oh my god, you've never seen Friends?"

He looked serious and then he burst into laughter.

"Nope."

"You're not kidding," I remarked. "Okay, so that's something I'll arrange for you: television nights to binge-watch Friends. On what planet were you living, Mr. Ramsey?"

"The planet that's called hospitals and overtime," he snored. "This is so weird, Zoey. You entered my life two days ago and it almost feels as if I've known you my entire life. You feel like an old friend that I bumped into again after years of absence. I like being with you."

"I like being with you too," I whispered. "Maybe I'm already counting too much on you as it is, which is hard for me."

"Are you really though?" Mac asked, turned serious. "You're the most independent woman I've ever met and you're stubborn as a mule too. There are things from your past that you need to deal with soon, or you'll be heading for a fall. There's something going on with you and you don't even know it yet. I've seen the way you act and the radical, impulsive decisions that you make. On the outside you appear to know what you're doing, but on the inside, you're all over the place. You rented the first apartment that you came across. You give your trust to me, while I could be a wanted felon. You are all over the place, Zoey. You hate your husband, but you still love him too. You fall apart at the seams when he sees you and you definitely are not okay with the fact that he was screwing your nurse while you were recovering. You're so locked up inside that protective shell of yours, that no one can come in to talk to you about all these things. Do you get that, Zoey?"

"You came in," I replied dazed. "You gave me back my confidence."

"Is that true, Zoey? Or are you pretending to be in control, because that's what you need me to see?" he asked quietly.

"What do you want me to say then?" I asked dumbfounded. "You seem to have made up your mind about the irrationality of things. What else can I say to defend myself? I thought we were friends."

"True friends don't have to defend themselves."

"Then what do you expect from me?" I asked. "I don't get what you want me to do, Mac."

"I want you to show more emotion than you are doing right now, Zoey. The way you act right now isn't normal behavior. It's almost as if you're constantly high on medication, even though you haven't taken anything. You're walking around like a ghost, and you don't even see it. You just let everything happen to you; you let others take advantage of the numbness that breathes and lives inside of you. I want you to scream when you feel like screaming; to cry if you want to cry. I want you to show emotions that are related to what you are experiencing right now. This bravado of yours will only get you so far. Truth be told? I'm scared that something is very wrong with you, and we haven't figured out what that is just yet."

No matter how much I tried to deny it, his words did make sense to me. My skin did feel a hard, unbreakable shell, yes. After Eve, I was damaged goods. Not just from the single bullet that destroyed my baby and ability to have children, but also by the man that was supposed to help me. Philip had bounced back on the wall he had helped to build in the first place. Instead of support, I received hostility, probably subconsciously caused by Elisabeth, even then.

Thanks to that silent aggression, my husband and I had become strangers to one another. He had unwittingly kept me cooped up in the house, perfect for him. As long as I was at home, I would not be in the way of his relationship with Elisabeth. I wasn't even aware something was wrong. Mac, the doctor who only knew me for little over a day, saw that truth in the blink of an eye. He saw what Philip had been ignoring.

"That shell is my protection," I tried to explain. "It helped me not to break down for months, and it has helped me to put my fate in my own two hands. Without that shell, I would probably be dead right now."

"You are nearly thirty years old, Zoey," Mac remarked. "Your life has just begun despite everything you went through. You can live on without your husband, and you can finally put Eve to rest. Don't believe you will spend the rest of your life feeling like this. You need to let people in."

"I don't want to feel this way anymore," I admitted. "Like I was drowning, with nobody offering me a lifeline."

"Then think about how you can shake your shell off. It will be worth it, Zoey. Take it from someone who has been there. I know what it's to like to stand on the ledge and consider jumping off. Trust me, once you take that step back, you will have taken the greatest leap you'll ever have to take."

"There are already people in my life who broke through that shell," I whispered. "There's you and Vivian."

"Vivian?"

I realized he had never heard of her before and told him in a few words who she was. I could tell he was surprised that I hadn't called her to help me out, but how could I explain to him that my best friend loved her freedom more than anything else in the world? That she would never offer me to stay, not even when my life depended on it? She simply wasn't like that, which was perfectly fine by me. I had grown used to her independence.

I opened my mouth to explain and then stopped. I had never discussed Vivian's character with anyone. Philip had known very little about her. She was part of my life, but she belonged to something that no one else had access to. She was mine alone. I have never shared her with anyone.

Mac frowned, but he didn't ask anything further. Instead, he filled up the dishwasher and started the machine, before settling down next to me again at the kitchen table.

"I want to help you, Zoey," he said. "I won't counsel you myself, nor will I offer you professional advice. I would be mixing my personal feelings with my professional ones. I can refer you to someone who might be able to unravel that complicated life of yours. Trust me when I say that this isn't about you going crazy, because you aren't crazy at all. You are someone who needs to sort some things out and it's okay to ask help to do so."

"I'll have to think about it. I have never seen a counsellor before," I admitted.

"Why are you so afraid of them?"

"I don't like having people exploring my mind."

"Not even when they help you to see things clearer?"

"I'm an introvert, remember?"

"You can still be. No one is going to take that away from you. You talk about the things that you want to talk about. It can be that simple."

"Just let me consider it and I'll let you know," I said. "It's just not that simple as you make it sound, Mac."

I moved forward and pecked him on the cheek. He smiled and touched the skin where I had kissed him.

"What was that for?"

"For being who you are."

Twenty-Four

THE MORNING PASSED BY QUICKLY. Anne sent me a text message to let me know that she would come by around two, which gave me plenty of time to relax. I took a refreshing shower, washed and dried my hair and changed into another set of slacks and a sweater I had bought about a year ago, when my pregnancy became clearer. My clothes were much too large, like Mac's had been, but I felt comfortable in these clothes. I returned to the living room, where Mac was on the phone with the hospital. My fear that he would have to go to work became reality when he hung up with an apologetic look on his face.

"I'm so sorry," he started, "there is an emergency, and they need all available doctors. I'm on surgical call today. It's serious."

"Of course."

I waved away his excuses, convincing him that I really didn't mind, even though he probably wouldn't be able to help me get settled.

"Why don't you stay here and rest a bit until Anne comes? You can prepare a light lunch; there's plenty of food in the fridge. In fact, you can stay here for as long as you like, you know that. I'll be back in the afternoon to help you get settled in."

"Don't worry about it," I replied, "Honestly. I'll be fine."

"Are you sure?"

"I'm very sure. Go. You're needed at the hospital."

Mac grabbed his coat and left, dressed in blue jeans and dark turtleneck sweater. The jacket he chose was dark too. Mac left me alone in an apartment that wasn't mine but had his stamp all over it, again without even giving it a second thought, as if I was his roommate. I sat down on the couch, looked around and wondered what it was like to come home to an empty apartment every single day. Mac did that and he didn't seem to care, but I did.

I didn't want to live alone. No matter how much effort I would make into decorating my apartment to make it my own, I knew that I wasn't the type of person to spend the rest of my life as a single person. I needed someone to come home to, someone that would make me feel special. Someone who didn't mind that I would never be able to have children. Someone who could do better with anyone else but me. Who would ever want me, this broken and mentally bruised?

I spent the rest of that lazy morning reading one of Mac's books. Christine, one of Stephen King's classics. It was the tenth time that I read that book, but I never grew tired of it. Engrossed in the story, I almost forgot that it was lunchtime until my stomach started to growl. Rob called me before I could start on lunch and asked me how I was doing. I didn't tell him I had spent my second night at a stranger's house and had ended up in hospital yesterday. Thirty minutes later, I was picking food from a plate filled with vegetables, chicken and pasta, losing my appetite after even one bite.

Mac sent me a text message, saying he would be stuck for another hour. Tired of hanging around, I changed into warm clothes, took out the same duffel bag I had been carrying across town for a couple of days now and left the building, with Mac's spare key in my pocket again. My mobile phone rang as soon as I started my walk around the block. It was Vivian, sounding quite worried.

"Where are you?" she demanded to know, "I've tried to call you all night."

"I'm so sorry," I said, hitting myself over the head for not sending her a message to let her know I was doing fine. "I turned off my phone to get a good night's sleep."

"You aren't at the hospital anymore, I gather? I didn't have time to come by anymore last night."

"No. I hitched a ride."

"From whom?"

I hesitated, not wanting to tell her about Mac just yet. I would do that when she came to see me face to face.

"Why don't you come over?" I proposed. "I'm moving into my new apartment this afternoon, but I'm already staying in the same building right now."

"Are you alone?"

"Right now? Yes, I am."

"I'll be right over then. I'm in the neighborhood; give me the address."

I gave her the details and walked back to the apartment building, where, to my big surprise, Vivian was already waiting. She leaned against the wall, casually checking her phone.

"You really were in the area," I smiled.

"Yes, I was." She gave me a quick hug. Surprising, seeing she didn't like physical touch all that much. "You're looking well. Well, at least better than you did lately."

I was surprised by her actions. During all the time we had known each other, she had basically never shown any emotion. I had always considered her to be quite cold.

"Come in," I invited her, showing her the key to Mac's apartment. "I'm staying downstairs, with Mac Ramsey, a new friend of mine. My real estate agent will come by with the key in an hour or so."

She looked at me oddly but didn't react any further. Instead, she walked through Mac's apartment and whistled while she touched the furniture and checked out his kitchen. I felt embarrassed that I had let her in, praying silently that he wouldn't show up yet. He might not be so happy with the additional company.

"The guy who lives here, earns decent money," she said. "Sounds like a good catch. Which floor is yours?"

"The third, and it's not like that. He's just a nice friend that I met only the other day. I'm into someone new, Vivian. I can't just shut off my feelings like that."

"It's a good building for you," Vivian said. "I like this apartment, so I'm guessing yours will be identical to it. You'll fit in just fine. By the way, shouldn't you be resting? Why were you outside anyhow?"

"To catch some fresh air," I muttered.

"Well, you shouldn't be alone out there; you still look white as a sheet. What did the doctor say?"

"That I should take better care of myself. I'm trying," I smiled.

"Good for you."

We drank coffee together in Mac's kitchen, while I tried to get the attention off me and onto Vivian, but my best friend wasn't in a talkative mood. I asked her for more details about Paris, which she brushed off immediately, as if it wasn't important that she flew eight hours there and then back for some meetings. She also didn't mention the fact she had to see her boss and explain why she had come back so suddenly.

"So, you've left Philip for good then?" she asked me suddenly, staring into her cup.

"Yes, I did."

"No chance of reconciliation?"

"No."

"But he was at the hospital, wasn't he?"

"How do you know?"

"I heard someone mention it. A doctor said your husband was waiting to see you, so I gathered he was there with you all the time."

"Why didn't you go over and speak with him?" I asked. "You could have introduced yourself."

"Why would I? We've got nothing to say to each other. We don't even know one another, you know that. Stop trying to get me to meet the man, Zoey. I don't care about him; I only care about you."

That's right, I remembered again now. Vivian and Philip had never met once. Their resentment towards each other always seemed to keep them on opposite sides of me. The moment I told my husband I had met someone really nice and supportive, he closed up. He wasn't so happy that I had a new person in my life I could talk to and often asked me how I could even trust a complete stranger. He also resented the fact I went out for coffee with her, while I refused to go out to dinner with him. I wondered why I had never brought Vivian home to meet Philip. Did I subconsciously want to keep her to myself? She was, after all, the only true friend I had, someone who never judged me, but took me the way I am. I had Mac now too, so I hoped that they at least would try to meet. Something told me they would get along quite well. Mac was different than Philip in every way possible.

"Where did you spend the night?" she asked bluntly. "You obviously didn't sleep in a hotel, and you seem quite at home here. Did you sleep in this apartment?"

"I did," I said. "Two nights even."

I told her about Mac, up to the final details, including the fact that he wasn't looking for a new relationship. Her reaction, as always, surprised me. I thought she would be happy for me to have made a new friend. Instead, she frowned and asked me if this was such a good idea. A hint of jealousy shone through her voice.

"You just got out of a bad relationship," she said. "Don't do something you'll regret later."

I was shocked at her suggestion that I was after Mac. As if would do that. I opened my mouth to object and then realized she was right to assume. I had nearly slept with Matthew, so why not sleep with Mac? She had every right to believe I could have sex with a stranger. She must have seen the danger in my eyes. I had a darker side to me that I came across more often these days.

I saw sudden jealousy in Vivian's eyes. Oh god, what if she did love me, like Philip insinuated? Did she believe somewhere in the back of her mind, that we might get together once? I wasn't gay; I had no feelings for her. If she were a lesbian, she should sense that I had nothing but respect for her. I looked at her with pity in my eyes, betraying my thoughts.

"No, Zoey," she smiled, softer now. "Believe me, I don't want anything more from you than I'm already getting. All I want for you is to be happy. Women aren't my interest at all; I prefer men, trust me."

"Are you sure? They say that many women like to experiment once and – "

"Definitely. Unless you want to experiment yourself?"

I relaxed and placed the empty cup on the table.

"No," I laughed. "I'm sorry. I just thought -"

"Let me guess," she interrupted me, turning harder again. "Your darling husband put this thought inside your head, didn't he? Did he imply that I have a crush on you, that I might want to end up in your bed?"

I blushed, remembering Philip's accusation during that horrible argument we had last Thursday. The stony expression on her face proved that she knew exactly what had happened between us. I couldn't help but wonder if she went through these accusations before, if someone else had accused her of breaking up a relationship. I knew so little about her and I had no idea what kind of people she befriended, or if she ever had any serious relationships. How could I get a clear picture about her, when I didn't even know where she lived? No, I couldn't think that. She was good to me. Mac might be helping me now too, but without Vivian, I would have been far worse off. I wouldn't be here today.

"I'm sorry," I repeated.

"You'd better be," she smiled, before she stood up, grabbed her coat and glanced at her watch.

"I have to go. I'll call you later."

"Hang on," I said. "Mac will be here any time now. Don't you want to stay and meet him?"

"No time now," she said. "I've got a few appointments this afternoon I can't skip. See you later."

"Thanks for your visit," I said, even though I was disappointed she wouldn't stick around to meet the man I was staying with.

"Any time."

Ten minutes later, Anne showed up with the keys and some additional information about the apartment. She left me alone in a hurry, wished me all the best and took off again.

Twenty-Five

MY NOW SECOND-BEST FRIEND watched me stand in the middle of my new living room, surrounded by furniture I hadn't picked out myself, but was perfect. I couldn't have wanted it any other way. I still remembered every single detail of this apartment, and it was even better now than it had been the first time. Again, it felt as if someone had drilled a hole in my head to dig up the details on what would be my own dream apartment.

"It's official now," I declared dramatically. "I'm single."

"Welcome to the club," he laughed, patting me on the back.

Mac closed the door while he silently approved of my new furniture, touching fabric and wood along the way. He whistled through his teeth when he saw the kitchen appliances the owners had left for me to use.

"It looks fabulous. Walter really does have great taste, like I always suspected."

"Thanks," I smiled, looking happily around my furnished apartment, before turning to him. "How about dinner tonight? I'll cook."

He laughed because my request was blurted out after all the rest. He bowed graciously.

"I accept."

"There is one condition though," I said, raising a finger.

"Oh?"

"Dinner should be at your place since I have any supplies yet. I need to go shopping urgently. We could go right now, if you have time?"

"That can wait until tomorrow," he said. "But I don't want you slaving away in my kitchen while I'm doing nothing, so how about dinner someplace in the area? Or we could do takeaway again."

"No takeaway," I said, "we need to celebrate. Let's have dinner someplace close, but I'm paying for it, and I don't want you to object, okay? We're not going Dutch and you're not going to be old-fashioned about this. It's my apartment, so my celebration and my treat."

"I wouldn't dare to suggest otherwise," he smiled. "Now, why don't you unpack your bags while I go take a shower?"

We promised to meet again at the front door in half an hour. I looked around my new home with sadness and joy at the same time, wondering how Philip would have felt if he were to move in here. The apartment was furnished as if I had been the decorator. Everything felt right. This was meant to be, and I had Anne to thank for that. I stepped inside my bedroom and pondered my new life. I would sleep here tonight, in my own bed, all by myself. God, it was amazing. Thrilling. Crazy. I hadn't felt this excited about anything in years and at the same time, I had never felt so depressed. I sunk down to the floor and burst into tears.

We chose a small restaurant nearby that neither of us knew. Mac let me do the picking and I went inside on a whim. The place only held ten tables and was quite dark, giving its guests enough privacy. The decor was old-fashioned and quaint, but we both liked it immediately. I spoke to our host, who told me it was a quiet evening, and she had a table in the back, where she pointed me to. Mac stayed at the bar while I arranged for our seats and looked around, not talking to anyone. I had noticed he was a rather introvert person, who preferred to keep to himself.

For the first time in months, I minded what I was going to wear for dinner. I wore a dress that I hadn't touched for months. It was a white dress that wasn't really suitable for this time of year, but it was one of the few things that still fitted me these days. I had bought it a few years ago, around the time I started up the shop and lost a lot of weight due to stress. I wore white shoes and flesh-colored stockings and dug up a lipstick and tanner from my bag that I hadn't used in months. My hair fell loose over my shoulders.

Even though I was still as dizzy as hell, I wouldn't tell Mac that. I didn't want him to play doctor tonight, so I faked my appetite and eagerness to go out to dinner. I was glad we sat in the dark of the bar, which made it harder for him to see how pale I still looked. The choice of a white dress also avoided the fact I was almost translucent. The make-up did the rest. I shivered when I removed my Burberry, but Mac didn't comment, since he was too busy checking out the menu that was already on the table when we sat down.

"Why don't you order for us?" he asked. "I'll go with whatever you choose. Your budget and all."

I ordered the same meal for us both: grilled garlic chicken with French fries and a salad on the side. When the food arrived a couple of minutes later, I managed to eat a quarter of my plate. Mac devoured his entire meal and then picked food off my plate, after I invited him to do so. We skipped dessert, but I still ordered coffee. We chatted about everything and nothing, keep it polite, easygoing and simple. Friendly and comradely, bantering back and forth.

I told him I was going to do some shopping in the morning.

He said I should still take it easy and rest.

I said I was fine.

He knew I was lying. That sort of thing.

Over coffee, Mac remarked that my eyes gave away my feelings. When I was sad, they would turn darker and intense; when I was cheerful and upbeat, they produced a lighter green with brown sparkles. I tried to see if I could find the same emotions in his eyes, but he wouldn't let me. I knew he wasn't the type of man that would give away his true feelings like that. He talked about the woman down the street that he fancied, living three houses down with a roommate. He didn't mention her name but described the blue painted house in detail.

"You should meet her one day," he said.

My headache increased while the evening continued. Truth be told, I hardly remembered half of the conversation while I fought against the urge to take my medication. I hadn't taken a single pill all day, which made me proud, but I was slowly losing the battle now. Mac noticed of course. When I reached for my purse, he stopped me, by telling me I could do this, and he would help me through it. I let go, dug out my purse and paid while I fought the pain in silence, gritting my teeth. We walked back quietly to the apartment building, where I swallowed my invitation for a nightcap, since my head felt like it was exploding.

I had fought the last hour against the chronic pain in my head, not wanting to show my new friend how bad it really was. I knew I would give up and take a pill as soon as he left me alone, which made me feel ashamed of myself. It was time to deal with my addiction as well, because I knew that I was too hooked on my medication. When I closed my eyes, Mac gently placed his hand on my forehead and asked how bad the pain was.

"It's not so bad," I croaked.

"Liar."

"You need to rest," Mac said, stroking my face lightly, while feeling my forehead. "You look like you're having a serious migraine attack, but I don't think you're running a fever. I'm not sure having dinner was such a good idea, but I know that it was important to you to take this step. Are you sure you don't want to spend the night downstairs with me? I'd like to keep a closer look on you. The spare bedroom is still yours to use."

"I will be fine in my new bed," I said. "This is my home now and I need to get used to being alone, Mac. I'll be okay after a good night rest. I'll give you a call in the morning, okay?"

"Deal."

He took me upstairs, took off my coat and white shoes and helped me into bed. I was still fully dressed in my white dress when he gently placed a blanket over me and closed the shutters. I was too tired to change into something else, and I didn't want him to undress me either.

"Goodnight, Zoey," he said.

He placed my phone next to the bed, with his number ready to use.

"Night, Mac," I murmured, closing my eyes.

I pretended to fall asleep and be done with it, but the moment that he left the apartment, I knew wouldn't be able to sleep a wink without my medication. The pain became so bad that I finally crawled out of bed to get those damned pills. I swallowed two of them with some water and chose the couch instead of the bed, still too tired to even change. An hour later, I was so agitated I felt like crawling up the walls. It felt suffocating, as if anger itself sought its way out. My mind was upset, and I wallowed in self-pity when the reality of my situation gained up on me. I was losing control rapidly.

I left the apartment in my white dress and without a coat, stumbling down the stairs, instead of using the elevator. The front door closed behind me. Outside, it was freezing cold. I started walking down the street, not knowing where I was or where I was heading. Wind blew hard in my face. Something hurt my feet. I realized only now that I was barefoot out on the streets, in my white dress, with no shoes or coat on. Neon lights shone above me, from a bar with a dark, black window that I leaned against, trying to get a grip. I scraped the palms of my hands against a brick wall. The whole thing felt like an outer body experience.

"Zoey?" I turned around. Mac approached me cautiously. "It's okay, Zoey. I'm here."

Mac reached for me, pulled me up by the wrists and allowed his hand to slide gently over the bleeding palms of my hands, before he lifted me off the ground as if I weighed nothing.

"It's okay," he soothed me, "I've got you."

I believed him without a doubt.

Monday

Twenty-Six

I WAS UP IN THE AIR. My head tilted against someone's chest, while my eyes were closed. I heaved in sickness and was lowered onto a couch, with a small bin standing next to it. I reached for it just in time and retched while my stomach emptied itself in the metal of the bin. I heaved until the horrible taste of bile was the only thing remaining. I put down the bin and rested my head on a warm pillow. The blankets on top of me felt too heavy, so I shoved them off, but he put them right back up.

"You're slightly hypothermic," he said. "Keep them on."

Mac undressed me and put me in one of his sweaters, sweatpants and socks. I hadn't even realized my teeth were clattering and I was shaking, until he wrapped me up in a warm blanket again and said I should keep warm for now. I rested my head on the pillow again.

"It's okay, Zoey," Mac said when I spoke out loud about how the world was spinning. "It'll stop after a while."

He was right. It did and it didn't even take that long. In between naps, I saw my friend move around the apartment in the semi-darkness. He was doing whatever he could to keep me comfortable. When he wasn't, he was in the kitchen. His back was turned towards me while he finished preparing breakfast. I sat up slowly, thankful that the world had stopped spinning. The sound I made, turned him around. He quickly turned off the heat. It was morning, which meant I had spent the night on his couch, instead of in my own bed. I groaned.

"Welcome back," he said, turning towards me with a pan in his hands. "How are you feeling?"

"Horrible," I confessed, tasting bile in my mouth. "I'm sorry about messing up your bin. I'll clean it."

"I already threw it out," he said. "Don't worry, I'm used to people puking their guts out. Part of the job and all. Do you remember what happened?"

"Not really."

My hands were taken care of. The cuts were cleaned and barely even visible anymore. The headache was gone, and the spinning had stopped. I remembered more details. Mac had run out of the house in his pajamas, probably awoken by the slamming of the front door. He followed me, found me and took me back inside.

I remembered lulling things to him I would never have said otherwise. My speech had been slurred and incomprehensible, as if I was drunk. He had tried to calm me down. He had refused to let me go back upstairs, even though I remembered insisting on it. He cleaned my hands and watched me puke my guts out, over and over again.

We sat together in his kitchen for the third morning in a row. He made me a cup of tea and some toast. I ate and drank carefully. My head pounded, but my stomach rumbled like crazy.

"Your stomach is empty," Mac explained. "You're probably battling a bug, since you've had problems for a few days now. Why did you leave the building in the first place?"

"I don't know," I said.

"You don't remember, do you?"

"Not really," I admitted.

"What do you remember?"

"I couldn't sleep and decided to go out for a walk. I was feeling off, so I thought I would feel better in the fresh air. Next thing I knew, you were there."

"You were barefoot in that beautiful dress of yours, without a coat. Do you realize you could have frozen to death? It was the middle of the night,

Zoey. If you had been out for a longer time, things would not have been okay right now."

"I didn't think," I said, staring at my keys lying on his kitchen counter. "I remember taking those though."

"I took care of your feet too," he said. "It took me a while to warm your body up again.

"You blacked out?"

"I guess so."

"Do you remember how you hurt your hands?"

"I scraped them against a brick wall."

"That explains the odd cuts. It looked worse than it was, so I put a disinfecting solution on the wounds after cleaning them. It shouldn't even scar. Did you take pills?"

"I did."

"Since you didn't eat all that much at the restaurant, they could have been too heavy to digest. You said before that nobody really ever thoroughly checked for the real cause of those pains, right? That your surgeon told you that they were part of the aftermath of the attack?"

"I've had a few scans, but truth be told, nobody ever suggested that the pains might not be part of the attack. They just checked the scars and internal injuries," I shrugged. "It's okay, Mac. I'm managing and nobody cares anyhow, so what's the point of trying to figure this thing out again?"

He wasn't happy with my response. I was in denial, I knew that, but I'd had enough of hospitals and illnesses. I refused to believe that something else might be wrong with me. The pain came from the attack, I thought stubbornly, because there couldn't be another possible reason behind them. Besides, if there was, I didn't want to know about it.

"Let me take over your file," Mac proposed. "I know that I said I wanted to distinguish friendship from my job as an abdominal specialist, but I can't not help you, Zoey. I told you that I have a colleague who can help you deal with your traumas psychologically, but I want to take on your case as a medical doctor. I need your permission for that."

"No."

"Please Zoey," he begged. "You don't have to go through pain and blackouts for the rest of your life. Let me just take a look at your file and consult with some of my colleagues. I won't do anything without your permission, I promise."

"Do you really think you'll be able to help me where others have never succeeded?" I asked bitterly.

"I might. It wouldn't hurt, would it?"

"I guess not."

Mac stood and put the coffee cups in the sink.

"Unfortunately, I have to work again today, but I hate to leave you alone like this. Is there anyone who can stay with you today? I don't want you wandering around on your own. I want you to take it easy. You need to sleep, Zoey. You need to heal."

"I could call Vivian."

"What about your parents?"

"I don't want to bother them with this. Besides, they still don't know that Philip and I broke up and they sure as hell won't fly over."

"Do you really think they would consider taking care of their daughter a burden?" Mac asked shocked.

"They did when I was a kid," I said.

"What do you mean?"

"I was bullied as a child," I explained. "My mom was too busy working, so she never noticed. She didn't care."

"I'm sorry to hear that, Zoey. How did you handle it then?" Mac asked.

"I created my own little universe with imaginary friends," I grimaced. "What else can you do when nobody wants to play with you?"

Mac held his breath for a second, before running his hands through his hair. He was obviously taken aback by my confession. What was I doing, throwing all of this at him? He didn't deserve any of this. I was a lousy friend if there ever was one.

"I'll call Vivian," I sighed, knowing he would want a solution before he left for work.

"Okay. It will be alright, Zoey, I promise."

"Will it?" I asked with a sense of despair.

"Yes. Take care of your hands, okay? They might still feel a bit sour, but the wounds should heal fast. I'll come by again tonight to see how you're doing, okay?"

"Alright."

Mac walked over, hugged me tight and whispered against my hair that I would be alright. He walked into his bedroom to get changed. I decided not to wait for him to come back out, so I left his apartment holding my key

Twenty-Seven

MAC OBVIOUSLY HADN'T GONE UP to my apartment after he found me. If he had, he would have seen the same mess I now encountered. My medication lay scattered over the kitchen floor; a broken glass lay next to the bottle. I had obviously taken a few more pills before I walked out, but I couldn't remember that.

The bedroom was an even bigger mess. There were socks and shoes everywhere, as if I had taken my time finding the right combination. The bed was stripped bare, as if I had attempted to change the sheets in the middle of the night, while I didn't even have a new set yet. The windows were wide open. My good hopes of yesterday were gone once I saw the mess I had made. I wanted to spend the rest of the day on the couch and sleep away my sorrows.

Instead, I grabbed the pills and took one out to get rid of the ache that bothered me so much. If this was what I would have to endure for the rest of my life, I was in for a lot of fun.

The next thing I knew Vivian was hovering over me, shaking my arm. I blinked and tried to gather my thoughts. The front door was wide open. She had stepped inside without even knocking on the door.

"Zoey," she spoke with more worry than she had ever done.

"What happened?" I croaked.

"You tell me. I receive an urgent, pleading text message from you to come over and I find you like this," she said.

"Like what?"

A shock ran through me. I was lying on the floor, with brown paper bags lying next to me, still filled with groceries. My keys still rested in my right hand. I couldn't even remember going out grocery shopping, let alone coming back here. Where did I go; how did I manage to go shopping?

"I'm losing my mind," I whispered.

I managed to sit up, helped by Vivian. I was shaking all over. I stared at the scattered groceries on the floor. There were bottles of milk, water, cola and wine, a jar of strawberry jam, different flavors of chocolate and chocolate milk. There were coffee and tea, bread for toast, honey and sugar, vinegar and vegetables. There was ice cream, melting now. A tomato had rolled all the way to the far corner of the hallway. I had bought enough food for an army.

Vivian picked up everything from the floor and stacked it all away in my cupboards, freezer and fridge. She took the keys from me. I hadn't realized I was still clutching them in my left hand, until my palm stung. I sat down on the couch, feeling nauseated again. My insides seemed to want to come out.

"Lie down."

Vivian lifted my legs and forced me to lie down on the couch. She removed my boots and dropped them on the floor. I was dressed in black slacks and a warm sweater. My coat was lying on the floor.

"You need to sleep," Vivian ordered.

I closed my eyes and sunk away in sleep as if someone had just injected me with a sedative. It was that easy.

Music played softly in the background. I thought I was back at Mac's apartment, until I figured out that the sound came from my right. Someone was playing music inside the apartment, but how could that be when I didn't even have a radio yet? I opened my eyes to find Vivian unpacking several electrical devices. To my shock, she had already installed a coffeemaker, water boiler, television, radio and a music unit that connected to Spotify.

More machines were still waiting to be unpacked. They all came on top of the utensils that my landlord had already provided. I had two coffeemakers now and two television sets.

"You've been busy shopping online," Vivian said, noticing I was awake. "The delivery came while you were sleeping. I've been having fun unpacking your stuff and trying it out. Hope you don't mind."

"Crazy," I whispered, looking around. "I don't even remember buying all this stuff. Why the hell did I do that, when the landlord has left most of his things for me to use?"

"Well, you did and by the looks of it, you have a pretty good but expensive taste. Everything here is worth its money, but I wouldn't want to pay off your credit cards by the end of this month," she smiled. "You're feeling better, aren't you?"

"A lot," I said.

It was warm in the apartment. Vivian was burning a few candles, also part of the delivery apparently, like other things that I couldn't remember buying either. There was enough soap to last me a lifetime.

"So, let's get this straight," Zoey commented. "You're buying stuff that you don't remember buying and then you pass out on the floor, which isn't your first time doing that either, is it? Did I leave something out?"

"Don't look so worried, Viv. I'm fine, really," I grunted."

"You keep telling me. What's really going on Zoey?"

"I don't know," I admitted. "I've been having these blackouts."

"Blackouts?"

"I end up in places or situations I don't remember getting into. I don't know what happens, but I do have odd dreams on occasion."

"Is that how you ended up in hospital last weekend?"

"No, I just got dizzy then. I was in an argument with Philip's new girlfriend, and it just became too much. The blackouts started quite recently and they're increasing rapidly."

"What does your doctor friend say?" Vivian asked.

"He wants me to do some tests."

"Listen to him. He's a doctor; he knows best."

"I already agreed," I said. "I'm scared, Viv."

"You're afraid of the tests. You don't like what they might find. You fear that it's serious and you don't want to know about it when it is," she remarked quietly. "You've always been like that, haven't you? You prefer denial over acceptance in any given situation."

I nodded reluctantly. Vivian's common sense put to words what I was going through. She was right: I should listen to Mac and let him make the decisions for me. Today's events had proven that quite all right.

"Come on, Zoey. Is fear more important than finding out the truth? You're frightened, before you even know what it is. It might be nothing at all. It might be fatigue or burn-out or something physical, but whatever it is, you need to figure this out," Vivian urged.

"The truth is that I'm a weakling," I muttered.

"No, you're not. You're stronger than anyone I know. You're the strongest person I have in my life, Zoey. Why can't you see that for yourself? Stop putting yourself down."

Vivian's words shocked me. She had never told me this. I always thought of her as the stronger one. I envied and admired her for her vivacity. She always came to me when I needed help.

"I'll manage," I said.

"Get real, Zoey," Vivian snapped. "You are the only one who can help yourself. Get your head out of your ass and do something to figure this out. If you don't, you'll wind up dead. Do you really want that to happen after all you've been through?"

"Mac is doing something, okay? I don't need the two of you whining on and on about this," I snapped back. "Why don't you leave me the hell alone, Vivian? I can manage; I've always managed without you and you're hardly even here anyhow, so what's the point?"

Vivian stood unmoving, as if we were discussing the weather, taking all that I threw in her direction. I felt ashamed immediately. She had dragged me out of the darkest of hells and this is how I repaid her?

"I'm sorry," I whispered. "Please don't leave me. I didn't mean what I just said."

"I would never leave you," she smiled. "I'm here to stay for as long as you want me to, Zoey. You just need to call me, you know that. I'll be here in a heartbeat."

She meant it. After all I said to her, she wouldn't let me down.

"I have to get back to work," Vivian said. "Call me, okay?"

"I will."

"Go for a walk," she suggested. "It's good outside. Cold, but good."

She was right: I hated being cooped up all day and people were walking by quite a lot, which made me feel not so alone. I decided to follow her advice and put on my shoes and coat, before grabbing my bag and keys.

The moment I walked out of the building, a stranger appeared in front of me, holding a brown envelope. He looked curiously at the building, before gazing at me.

"Zoey Mitchell?"

"That's me."

"I have documents for you."

The man handed me the envelope and let me sign for it. I knew what was inside of the brown paper. It shocked me that it had to happen this way, so fast and so impersonal. My visitor tapped an imaginary hat.

"Have a nice day, lady."

He was gone before I could utter another word. What was I to say, when the onset of divorce came to me this way? Philip didn't even have the decency to tell me in person he had already started the procedure, after telling me even yesterday that he still loved me. What kind of hold did that bitch truly have on him?

Shocked, I threw the documents in a garbage bin. Just like that, this place became ugly too. Out in the old air, I took deep breaths as I moved down the road, stopping only to gaze up at the skies. It had started snowing at long last.

"Zoey."

I looked up in surprise. In front of me stood the man who had just killed another inch of my heart: my husband.

Twenty-Eight

"I DIDN'T MEAN TO STARTLE you," Philip began, approaching me cautiously. "Can we talk somewhere?"

"How did you know where I live?" I asked shocked.

Instantly, I felt quite uncomfortable by his sudden appearance. I never gave him my address; I was certain of that. There was no reason to, especially seeing the gravity of circumstances. I wasn't ready to share that kind of information with the man I would soon never see again, if I had a choice in the matter.

"It wasn't that hard to find out," he smiled. "I called Rob, assuming you had told him where you lived now, since he's obviously still taking care of your business affairs. He wasn't that keen at first to tell him, until I reminded him that you and I are legally still married and that I was entitled to know your current location. You live down the road from here, right? Can I see your place?"

"No," I muttered, but he didn't even hear it.

Philip moved forward and tried to kiss me. I pulled back in disgust, taking my distance quickly. Why would he even attempt to touch me after what he'd done?

"What are you doing? You have a new girlfriend, and we are getting a divorce, Philip. What the hell's wrong with you?" I hissed, catching the glances of people passing us by.

"I'm sorry, Zoey," he said, obviously taken aback. "Please, can we talk somewhere private, like your place? I don't want complete strangers to overhear our conversation."

"You're not setting foot inside my apartment," I sighed, knowing all too well I would never get rid of him. "I need to go."

"Please, don't do this to me. Please, Zoey."

His pleading did the trick. I knew I wouldn't get rid of him anyhow, but I was so scared he would try to reel me back in. What a waste of emotional effort that would be.

"Do I have a choice?" I sighed, caving. His face shone brightly immediately, like a kid who just received a candy stick.

"Sure, you do," he said, challenging me." If you tell me to back off right now, I'll walk away."

"Okay then. Leave."

"You don't mean that, Zoey, I know you too well. Besides, I came with a peace offering, a few things from the apartment that are yours. I saved them for you, just in case you wanted them. There is more at home, but I couldn't bring everything. You can pick up the rest of your stuff whenever you're ready."

My soon-to-be-ex-husband handed me a small package. Inside the wrapping, I found two small statues my mother gave me when we got married. It was the only present my parents had brought, indifferent as they were about the wedding. I had put them in one of the guest bedrooms in our former house and Philip hadn't displayed them when we moved to the city, so I had practically forgotten about them. I saw this as a token of my husband's indifference towards me, so I walked over to the nearest bin and threw them in. He actually laughed, albeit nervously. What did he think: that I would throw my arms around him to thank you for bringing me a reminder of my parents' cold hearts?

We walked further down the street. I took the lead, determined to move him away from my apartment as fast as I could. We chose a small coffee bar, three blocks down, where Philip paid for my coffee and his tea. He wavered away any suggestions of food, which made me sigh in relief. My almost-former husband selected a small table all the way in the back, next to a storage room. He wanted us to sit down in privacy, without anyone able to overhear us. There were no other guests that sat so far in the back and the bar was all the way upfront. This was obviously his intent. He wanted me all to himself. It made me nervous. He sat across from me, while I uncomfortably shuffled in my seat against the wall, nursing my tea without gazing at him.

"You look better," he remarked. "It was quite a shock to see you collapse the other day. I thought you were seriously ill."

"I'm sure it was. I didn't mean to startle you."

"I know. You don't collapse on purpose," he smiled awkwardly.

"I suppose not," I murmured.

"Are you still taking that pain medication?"

"Yes, I am."

"Are you taking a higher dosage now?"

"No, I'm still on the ones the doctor prescribed. I took them from the apartment, remember? Why?"

"I was just wondering if your collapse could have had anything to do with that," he said. "They often say that people need to adjust to medication. Are you taking more; could that have caused the disruption in your system?"

"Nope," I lied. "I'm actually trying to cut down."

"I see. I don't really think you should do that right now, considering what has happened during the past few days. You've always needed it to make it through the day, so I'm guessing you're even more in need of them as you were before."

"What are you saying exactly?" I asked frowning.

"Just that I never thought less of you for taking them."

I stared at him surprised, wondering what the hell he wanted from me. So, I asked the question out loud.

"I just wanted to talk to you about a few things, Zoey," he admitted. "About – well, truth be told, I was shocked to find out you were already renting your own place. I thought – "

"You didn't expect me to wait for you to come to your senses, did you?" I stopped him. "Come on, Philip. You made it loud and clear that we were through, so why should I spend good money on a hotel?"

"It's my money you're spending," he whispered. "You did it on the first night, didn't you? I saw it on my credit card."

"So?" I snapped. "You threw me out and that card was linked to our mutual bank account. Don't start that again. It was ours, mutually shared. You sold my home, remember that?"

"I did," he said, "and that was a lousy thing to do. I'm sorry about that."

"What do you really want, Philip?" I asked strained. "There has to be a reason for you to come here now and play all nice."

"We're not enemies, are we Zoey? Or did you tell the outside world that we are ready to slit each other's throats?" he inquired.

"Nobody knows anything," I said. "Not even my parents. Why don't you tell me if we are enemies?"

"I don't think we are."

"Then why you did you start the divorce the way you did?"

"What?" he asked surprised.

"Come on. Your lawyer just dropped them off at the front door, right before you showed up. You cooked this up with him, didn't you?" I didn't tell him I threw them away.

"I don't know what you're talking about." He said, genuinely surprised.

"Oh, so your lawyer acted without your knowledge?"

"I have a lawyer, yes, but I didn't ask this. I told him I wanted to think about it before filing the paperwork. We were supposed to have another meeting in a few days. I swear that I would have told you before deciding. I wouldn't do this to you, not like this."

"Why would you even have to think about a divorce in the first place?" I asked tired. "It's all been done, Philip. You made sure of that when you threw me out. It's your decision to talk to a lawyer and take the next steps, you know. Not mine."

To my surprise, Philip stood and took the empty seat next to mine. His sudden presence made me feel uncomfortable. My mind screamed to get away from him.

"I miss you, Zoey," he began hoarsely.

With a sudden gesture, Philip put his hand on the back of mine. His fingers caressed mine. Two days ago, I would have been happy with this. Now it felt like I was being violated. His hand didn't belong on my skin anymore.

"Can't I be forgiven for this one mistake? People deserve a second chance, don't they?" he pleaded.

"It depends on the mistake," I murmured. "If you are here to ask me for forgiveness, you can rest assured: I have no intention of wasting my time hating you. Life is too short and precious for that. I need to move on, like you should do too. Despite the way you did it, I still want to get this over with as soon as possible."

He moved even closer, gazing around quickly to see if we were being watched. We were sitting all the way in the back, with hardly anyone noticing us. The bartender was busy in the front with a few tables.

"But what if I want to go back?" my husband continued. "What if I realize now that my biggest mistake in life was made of silly male stupidity and desire to discover the unknown? What if I know things now, that I didn't know four days ago?"

"That still doesn't change anything," I sighed. "The mistake has been made. It has been done. You can't take back your words and deeds and hope for the best. I can't forgive you for what you have done to me; I can't forget Elisabeth either. She broke my heart and trampled on it to make sure I stayed down."

"What if I were to tell you that I gave up the best, in exchange for the worst?" he whispered again.

"Then I would have to tell you to make the best out of the worst," I reacted coolly.

Philip reached for me. His mouth came closer to mine; I could scent beer on his breath. His lips sought their target. I couldn't escape; he had me in a tight grip. Before I knew what was happening, his tongue invaded my mouth. He was exploring me again, like he did when we were a young couple getting together. We never had that sensual relationship others seemed to have, but he still knew how to turn me on. Even though I didn't want him to continue and made that abundantly clear by pushing away his hands, he still was able to cup my breasts. His thumbs played through the cotton of my shirt with my nipples. I felt slight arousal. My body still thought that it belonged to the man who was my only lover so far, recognizing the way he used to trigger my senses, but my mind screamed out loud to stop this.

I pushed my husband away and shoved the chair backwards with a bang, so I could get up and get the hell out of there. Our lips parted so quickly that it bruised my mouth. Philip stayed behind dazed, but he didn't make a scene, as the bartender made a move to head in our direction. I ran out of the coffee bar, into the street, but he came right after me. I hurried through the streets, past curious tourists, into a small alley, before realizing I had made a huge mistake. It was a dead-end street. I was trapped.

"Why do you run away?" my husband asked. "I just want to talk to you."

His voice, movements and eyes scared the hell out of me. This wasn't the man I had married. He was upset, angry and pleading at the same time. Fright took over; I couldn't think straight.

A door opened right in front of me. Some guy walked out to take a piss. I moved towards it and forced myself inside. I ended up in the back room of a bar, one of those dingy types nobody wants to be caught dead in. I heard Philip shout after me, so I moved forward, stopping when I noticed my error. I wouldn't get any help here.

Two men eyed me curiously, staring at me with hungry gazes. Next to them, a few others were getting high. Another pair of men were watching some erotic movie on a TV-screen above the bar, chatting about it with the bartender who looked like he had shot up just recently. The two curious men blocked the front door; I could hear Philip behind me. I took a turn to the right and headed straight for the toilets behind the bar, with the intent of locking myself up until my husband came to his senses again.

I acted too late. As soon as I ran inside the ladies' room, Philip caught me and shoved me inside a filthy cubicle, following immediately. He locked the door before I even had the chance to scream. Philip pushed me against the wall and pushed his hand over my mouth. A used needle lay on the sticky floor, next to some fluids I didn't want to identify. That was what I focused on when I felt his weight behind me.

"Don't scream," he whispered in my ear, when I opened my mouth to do just that. "Promise me you won't, and I'll take my hand away. I just want to talk, okay? I don't want to hurt you."

Someone turned up the music inside the bar. Or was that the television set? The sound of grunting noises filled the ladies' room. The door was thin, but I still knew that nobody would hear me if I screamed. I nodded as a sign that I understood. He let go slowly, allowing me to breathe again. He turned me around, so that my back leaned against the sticky wall. I felt whatever grease was there in my hair, almost gluing me against the bricks.

"Why won't you give me another chance, Zoey?" he whispered in my ear.

"I can't," I croaked.

"Why not?" Philip asked softly, holding me against him. I had nowhere to go, no place to run to, so I leaned into him, grasping him tight. He saw that as a sign to go on. "You feel it too, don't you? It's still there. What made us so special, still exists."

His words distressed me. The sound of erotic groans even more. I felt suffocated and scared. The urge to get away only grew. I needed to talk some common sense into him, even if it meant nothing to the man that I was still married to.

"Zoey, please talk to me," he pleaded.

"I don't care, Philip," I snapped. "I don't care if whatever you think there is, still exists, and I'm not so sure at all if we were so good together, if you took the first opportunity you got to screw someone else. Don't use me like a toy, when you have already thrown me away once. Do you expect me to believe that you wouldn't do this to me again?"

"I want our old life back. I want you back," he insisted, ignoring my words blatantly.

"Because Elisabeth is not worth your time?" I asked bitterly. "Strange, when only on Thursday, you told me that she was the one you wanted more than anything in this world. Did you compare us during the past few days to see who was the easiest person to live with? Does it bother you to know that she's not to you what I once was? Did she show you her true colors?" He flinched at that.

"She's changed," he confessed, without looking at me. His head sunk to his chest, staring at his hands on my arms. "There are things about her that I wasn't aware of when we became - you know."

"Like what?"

"She has lied to me about her relatives. She told me her parents were gone and that she had no siblings. Now it turns out that she has a younger sister that she wants to move in with us. Plus, I found out that her parents are still alive."

"Why would she lie to you about that?" I asked surprised. "She even told me she had a sister. Why wouldn't she say that to you?"

"When? At the market?"

"Yeah."

"I don't know," he exclaimed emotionally, forgetting we were standing in a toilet cubicle. "She claims that her sister is being abused, but apparently, she doesn't do anything about it. She wants that girl to move in with us, to remove her from her abusive life, when before, she lied about her parents still being alive. I didn't choose to be saddled with these problems, Zoey. I allowed her in my life, believing she would stay the person she was before. Now I'm ending up having to deal with problems that aren't even mine."

A sense of sadness overwhelmed me. For the first time, I felt an ounce of pity for that woman. Philip was a selfish coward. The only relationships he was interested in were carefree ones, but the moment a problem arose, he backed away from the issues. Was this the man I had fallen for years ago? Had I truly been so blind all my life? I slowly shook my head in disgust.

"And now you want to come back to me because I have lesser problems than she has?" I spoke slowly. God, what a joke.

"No, I came back, because the arguments with Elisabeth have taught me that I want to be with the woman I married; the one who never put up a fight and accepted me without question for who I was. You are what I want, Zoey. You have always been the one. I see that now."

"You have a strange way of showing your love," I spoke bitterly.

"Be honest with yourself, Zoey," Philip said. "We were both to blame for what happened to us. It has never been okay again between us since the shooting and I get that. I want the old Zoey back; the one I'm looking at, even now, the feisty one. This is the woman I fell in love with. She has spunk, character and strength. She doesn't sit in a corner and mope around. This is the Zoey I need."

"Mope?" I hissed. "Really, Philip? Is that the word you can think of?

We lost our child! There will never be another baby growing inside of me. How can you say that I was moping? I was mourning, grieving!"

"No, you were self-indulgent in your sorrows, Zoey. I didn't know the woman anymore who spent her waking time sleeping or staring at the television; the woman feeling sorry for herself. I couldn't love her anymore and I thought she was gone forever. Until I realized that she was still there, buried inside that shell she had become of herself, and I was right. The push I gave you, made that woman I loved so much come back to me."

"What?" I saw red. "Push? Are you now saying you kicked me out on purpose?"

"I wanted you to rediscover yourself."

"I nearly killed myself, Philip. Do you realize what I've been through?" I shouted. "You are so full of yourself. You should take a relationship with the punches, Philip, or you will end up being miserable and lonely for the rest of your life. I think you'd better go now. You've said enough."

I trembled with anger as I stood to escort my, soon to be ex-husband to the door. He moved up as well, but he didn't leave. Instead, Philip grabbed me and held my hands backwards, forcing me against the wall of my own living room. His lips stroked my throat while I wormed to get away. His fingers moved inside my sweatpants and touched me between my legs, past the fabric of my underwear, into me. His digits found their way in, explored me and it hurt. I screamed. I bucked. I cried. I felt violated.

"Let me go," I said. "Don't do this."

He wouldn't. He still stroked my insides, until I kicked back hard, kneeing him. He backed away shocked.

"No!" I shouted.

I felt hurt between my legs from the force with which he pulled himself free. I ran away from him, until the couch was between us and he couldn't get to me quickly. Where the hell was my phone?

"You still feel it too. You want me back," he spoke happily, looking at his fingers. I was disgusted.

"You will never end up in my bed again," I hissed. "You raped me."

"Not if you wanted it too."

"I didn't. I don't!"

"I need you, Zoey," he whimpered.

"I know," I said sadly.

"I want you back."

"It's over, Philip."

"Please, Zoey," he pleaded.

"I can't."

"Why not?"

"You broke my heart."

"I made a mistake."

"It's too late to mend the shattered pieces. You know we would collide again. It's just a matter of time."

Philip stared at his moist fingers, wiping them off on the side of his pants. It disgusted me. I could still feel him penetrate me. He would have raped me even more if I hadn't fought back. I closed my eyes briefly, thinking of Mac. His face, gestures and smile popped into mind. I needed to be with someone like him: someone with a stable, normal life, someone who wouldn't throw me out during a rough patch. The anger returned; it bottled up inside of me. Nothing would ever change that. I would never forget what this man standing in front of me had done to me.

"What can I do to make it right?" Philip pleaded desperately. "I can't live with Elisabeth, Zoey. I just can't!"

"Then do something about that. Throw her out, get rid of her, but don't ever come running back to me. You can't have me back. I want to make that perfectly clear," I said.

"You are still my wife."

"Only on paper, and only for a short while to come. You know I hate you. In case you haven't checked your bank statements yet, I suggest that you do. It will confirm how much I detest you."

He paled.

"What did you do?"

"You'll find out," I said. "Get out."

Philip took my rejection hard. I guess he had really expected me to accept him back into my life just like that. In the past, we had always made up our fights with sex. Our sex life had always been okay, but not fantastic.

Did he really think I would give in so easily?

"I'm sorry," Philip whispered when he walked out. "For everything."

"I know."

I locked the door behind him, not waiting for him to step inside the elevator and leave. I didn't want to see him again. Not now. Not ever. I took a shower and still felt disgusted. I never told anyone about what happened. Not Vivian. Not Mac. It was hard enough as it was.

Twenty-Nine

MY MOBILE PHONE RANG, BUT I was too late to answer it.

"I can't make it for dinner," Mac apologized on my voicemail. "It's been hell today. I've got several patients still waiting and everything's been pushed backwards. There was a major accident with a tourist bus and I'm trying to help as much as I can. I'm going to be late tonight. Please take care of yourself, okay?"

I didn't call him back, knowing he wouldn't hear it. I would lie if I said I wasn't disappointed. I wanted to have some company tonight and I had hoped that he would be able to take my mind off Philip's fingers inside of me.

I sighed, looking around the empty apartment. Truth be told, I needed to face life on my own. I couldn't go on depending on people like Mac and Vivian to get me out of this rut. The reluctant life I had begun could become a good one, if I would just allow it to be.

To my big surprise, Vivian came back around five. She looked absolutely smashing, with a recent haircut that suited her and an outfit that would cost more than some people's monthly income. She wore a wine-colored dress that fitted her hourglass-shaped figure perfectly. A push-up bra accentuated her already full breasts. The dress stopped around the knees and had long sleeves that reached to her wrists. Flesh-colored stockings tanned her legs. I had never seen her like this before.

Here I was, in my sweater and slacks. In comparison to her, I was a mouse, just like Elisabeth.

"Do you like it?" she smiled, twirling before me.

"Why are you so dressed up?" I asked.

"I'm taking you out to celebrate."

"Celebrate what?"

"Your new freedom, your future or anything else you'd like to celebrate. Come on Zoey, I know exactly what you need. You need to get out of this place and dare to step into the night. You need to get to know new people and have some fun. I am the right person to help you out of your rut."

"I don't know, Vivian," I hesitated. "It's Monday evening and I don't feel like going. Aren't people supposed to stay at home and be boring on a weekday?"

"I do know. You're coming. Get changed."

"I don't have any decent clothes," I protested.

"Sure, you do. What did you wear last night for your dinner with Mac?"

I showed her the dress.

"Perfect," she enthused. "Get dressed. I'll do your make-up and hair for you. We will show the town that Zoey Mitchell is back out there and up for grabs. I'll fix you up in no time."

I wanted to tell her that I already had a certain doctor in mind.

As a child, I had longed for a big sister, who would take me under her wings and show me the ropes of the good life. I never had a girlfriend who helped me out, so there was still a large unexplored part of me, that not even I had access to. Vivian was the first to show me the way to the other side of me. She was certain there was a lot more to me than the troubled person I had become.

My hair was too long and hard to handle, after months of not getting it cut. She twisted it into a bun and put in a cute pin she happened to bring. She used wax and hairspray to keep the bun in place. Her experienced fingers reshaped me into someone new. With lipstick, eyeliner, eye shadow, some powder and blush she re-created me. The result was a stranger staring back in the mirror.

I looked five years younger and more attractive than I thought I could ever look. The dress flattered me for the first time because she had used a few pins to reshape it according to my now very skinny figure. It was true that I urgently needed to gain some weight to fill it out completely as I had done before, but it still looked fantastic now that she had her hands on it. From the bottom of my closet, Vivian dug out a small black purse and black shoes. It was too cold to wear them, but they looked perfect with the dress, so I decided on them.

My old Burberry had to do as coat, but I vowed to buy a new winter coat soon. I was fed up with that thing, even when it was warm and felt like home. Dressed up and giggling, Vivian and I hit the town. I never told her I was feeling sick as a dog.

The club was too small and dark for my liking. The place was as good as empty. It was after ten already, but the real party would only start around midnight, as was custom these days in private clubs. After a couple of married years, it seemed as if I no longer fit in with the club crowd. My youth had passed me by. I had been engaged and married for years and didn't recall what it was like to prowl for men. Besides, how could anyone still be attracted to me when I was too pale, too skinny? Besides, I had Mac on my mind, even if we weren't even something of an item.

Coming here felt like betrayal to him. I wanted to leave and forget about tonight, just like I wanted to block Philip's actions from my mind. I turned to Vivian and pleaded with her to go. She frowned, shook her head and told me we were not going anywhere. The night was young and there was too much to enjoy. At the bar I ordered drinks for two and sipped my too-sweet cocktail. The fluid burned in my esophagus. I coughed. I hadn't eaten dinner, so every sip was one too many.

"This was not a good idea," I muttered.

I put down the glass and looked around. Vivian was not talking to anyone but me. She ignored everyone else in the small room. I wondered how long it would take before she would find someone interesting enough to dump me for. Right now, she didn't seem interested at all. Soon, more people came into the club. Around eleven, the place was jampacked. I regretted hoping for more people now. There were different types of people surrounding us now. Twenty-somethings with girlfriends, dressed in the latest fashions but never too expensive, and students dressed in jeans and T-shirt. I felt overdressed. Vivian assured me I looked just fine.

"I'll be right back."

Vivian's slim figure slid off the chair. Before I could protest, she disappeared to the restrooms and left me, behind feeling very awkward. A few moments later, a hand passed my shoulder while another one reached for napkins on the bar. A man leaned forward so that I was nearly in eye contact with his crotch.

"What's a girl like you doing in a place like this?"

His hands reminded me of Philip. Disgusted, I gave him a push. He backed away immediately and muttered that I was a bitch under his breath. More men bumped into me. Two tried to make a pass at me. I shooed them all away with an evil grin, while trying to ignore the horrendous headache that fought its way to the surface. I popped a pill, mixing it with half of my cocktail.

Vivian returned a minute or so later and sat down. She still didn't talk to anyone but me. I looked over my shoulder and held my breath when Philip and Elisabeth walked in, just when Vivian and I had chosen a small table in the back with only two chairs. I had to blink my eyelids twice to recognize my husband's lover. My husband too, for that matter.

What the hell was Philip doing here on a Monday evening? Was this his new life now? He had nothing to look after, nobody to go home to, apart from his new girlfriend. He looked nothing like the man he used to be. She had done that to him.

Elisabeth had changed overnight. From the mouse-like appearance I had seen when she first started taking care of me, she had changed into a vamp. She wore a flimsy skirt and shirt. Her breasts and slim figure were accentuated in a tight shirt usually worn by twenty-year-olds and a black push-up bra that was clearly visible underneath her clothes. She was sensual and very sexual. If that was the woman Philip had fallen for, I couldn't even blame him. She had a power over men, and she knew it. Heads turned when she walked in. She was stunning.

"Let's go," I whispered to Vivian.

"Why?" she asked curiously.

"Philip's here."

Vivian immediately openly explored the scene. She had never seen Philip, except from a few photos I had shown her that didn't do him justice. He was much better looking in real life and fully aware of that. He stood proud next to Elisabeth, even when he told me just hours before that he had made a big mistake. The men in that room envied him and he knew it.

"Don't do anything," I hissed to Vivian when she slid from her seat.

"I'm not going to talk to him," she assured me. "I'll just go and get our coats. With people like that, this place has suddenly lost its edge."

She left me alone once again. I wanted to go after her and ignore Philip and Elisabeth, until suddenly my husband stood in front of me. I couldn't help but stare at his fingers. Elisabeth stared at me as if I had the plague. Her face described her disgust to catch me here. I straightened my back while I wondered about her real character, now that I knew my husband was afraid of her.

Philip of course acted as if nothing had happened.

"Hey Zoey," he spoke casually. "I see you are on the prowl again. Fancy seeing you here. Didn't know you did clubs. Shouldn't you be double dating to do that?"

I froze and blinked away tears. His smile faded.

"I'm sorry. Didn't mean that the way it came out."

"It doesn't matter."

I waved away his excuses and tried to find a way to get out of there without losing my sanity. I couldn't forget what he had done to me this afternoon. Vivian stood near the end of the bar, obviously taking her time getting our coats. I was angry at her when she didn't see my desperation. Elisabeth leaned carelessly into my husband and acted as if he was hers. He didn't put his hand around her shoulders though. In fact, he hardly touched her. The underlying tension was apparent to me. Elisabeth obviously became aware of the awkward silence. She apologized and left us. She headed for the lavatories next to the wardrobe section. For one long second, I thought she was going to end up talking to Vivian, but she moved past her without seeing her. They didn't know each other, but my heart still went crazy. I didn't want Vivian to get infected by their nastiness.

"Zoey, I need to talk to you," he said.

"What about?" I hissed.

"I don't know what happened to me earlier. I should never have come over. I … I didn't mean to force you into something you obviously didn't want. Everything just came out the wrong way."

"Leave it Philip," I snapped.

"I … you wanted it to, right?"

"What?" I blinked my eyelids. "You mean, if I wanted you to rape me? No, Philip, I didn't," I hissed.

People turned around to stare at us.

"It wasn't rape. You're still my wife."

"We live apart. I told you to stay off me. Does that sound like consent to you?" I asked icy-cold. "Go to hell, Philip. Don't you ever touch me again. You stay away from me, and I'll stay away from you. You fucked this up yourself."

"Is there someone else?" my husband asked nervously. "Is that it?"

I blushed. Even with the strange club lights he could see that. Mac popped into mind of course.

"There is another man, isn't there?"

"No." Was I lying?

"That's why you don't want me back. You already have someone else. It makes sense, doesn't it?" He leaned backwards as if he had just discovered hot water. "It explains why you're acting like this."

"You listen to me," I said. "I'm not going to repeat myself again. You tried to rape me. You put your hands on me when I clearly said no. If you ever look at me again, if you ever touch me again, I will file a complaint against you and your life and career will be over. Do you get that, Philip?"

Elisabeth hissed behind us. She stared from Philip to me and back again. I thought she was going to slap him in the face, but she didn't touch him, nor did she speak to me.

"We're going," she just said.

Elisabeth grabbed Philip by the arm and pulled him away. She was obviously very strong. It suddenly struck me: why would Philip allow himself to be treated like this, like a lapdog? What happened to his self-esteem? He had changed so much over the past few days.

"Thanks a lot," I muttered to Vivian.

She returned after Elisabeth had dragged my husband away.

"Where are our coats?"

"On your chair," she pointed out, seemingly amused. "You should know better than to avoid your problems. I was just showing you the way."

"By feeding me to the lions?"

"Do you have a scratch on you?"

I blushed and followed her outside where it had started to rain. We ran to a cab. I got soaking wet within seconds. Vivian laughed out loud. I caught a glance of myself in the rear-view mirror. The bun was gone, leaving strands of hair plastered to my shoulders. My dress clung to my body. The Burberry hadn't protected me long against the rain. Vivian looked as if she didn't have a drop of rain on her. I envied her for treating life so easy.

I invited Vivian in, even though I noticed the downstairs lights were on, meaning I could go and talk to Mac. Vivian accepted the invitation and followed me upstairs. She took off her coat and waited patiently while I changed into other clothes. Pulling my hair together in a ponytail, I returned to the living room.

"Better?" she asked.

"Yeah."

"You know," she began, "sooner or later that husband of yours will convince you to come back home. It's just a matter of time before he does."

"He won't," I reassured her. "Believe me, the last thing I want, is to get back together with him."

"He probably knows what he's missing out on by now," Vivian smirked. "Not only has he lost a beautiful woman, but he also lost out big time financially. You are, after all, wealthy enough to support his expensive needs."

I looked shocked.

"He didn't marry me for my dad's trust fund. He has plenty of his own. Besides, I don't want to talk about it. My marriage is between Philip and me."

Vivian leaned forward and whispered words I will never forget for as long as I live.

"If Philip's dead, he can't hurt you anymore. I would kill him for you, if you would ask me to. It would be so much easier that way. After all, he hurt you today, didn't he? I can see it in your eyes. You were frightened of him earlier. Did he assault you, Zoey?"

I stared at her in shock.

"No."

"Yes, he did. Did he rape you?"

I closed my eyes.

"Do you want me to kill him for you, Zoey?"

I was flabbergasted, not knowing if she was serious or not. She laughed, leaned back and drank her Martini.

"But, since I'm not a killer, I won't murder him," Vivian smiled. "If you want to get rid of him, you'll have to do it yourself. Anyhow, I have to get going. I have another business trip in the morning. I'll be back on Friday, if all goes well. Just call me when you need me, okay?"

I heard that before, I thought bitterly, upset that she was once again leaving me. Why was she always gone, when she was the only real friend I had left? After her departure, the headaches turned so bad that I swallowed two more pills, drank a glass of water and literally crawled into bed fully clothed, not even able anymore to change anymore. I thought about Mac. I considered going downstairs to see him, but I didn't. He needed his sleep, and I needed to at least try and pretend I could make it on my own.

I fell asleep around two a.m., only to be woken up by my phone around seven. It was the beginning of a new form of hell.

Tuesday

Thirty

TODAY WAS MY FATHER'S SIXTY-FOURTH birthday. I didn't remember, until much later, when the day progressed into the living hell it would become. I didn't even get the chance to call him and wish him well. I couldn't face him nor talk to him, after what I'd done. How could I tell the man who raised me that I had messed things up so badly? Would he even care? I was an accident, an unexpected event in his life. He had told me so himself. He had shown it many times, by deeds and harsh words. He was a tough man, someone that didn't take no for an answer. I was the exact opposite.

Something happened to me last night, but it took me a long time to puzzle the bits and pieces together, until the nightmare was truly revealed. I remember getting up from my bed and putting on shoes. I was still dressed in the same slacks and sweater. My hair was still damp. I grabbed the Burberry. It hadn't dried yet from last night's rain. It felt as if I was sleepwalking.

The next thing I remembered, I was walking the streets of New York, but I didn't know how I got from my apartment to the area I found myself in. I was far away from the Meat Packing District where I now lived, but relatively close to the apartment building where my husband and I used to share an apartment. The rain had left a sweet damp scent on the streets. I was frozen to the core, as if I had been walking for hours. I felt icy cold. The damp Burberry didn't keep me warm. My shoes were wet with water and mud. The bottom of my trousers and socks was dirty too.

I stopped in front of my former apartment building. My cold fingers and hurt hands held onto the key to the front door of the building. In all our haste to part, I hadn't given my keys back to Philip. After a brief black-out, I found myself walking through the hallway, heading for the elevator. It was warm inside. I retrieved the second key on the chain that gave me access to Philip's apartment. I unlocked the door; a breeze whispered softly in my ears and ruffled my hair. A window must be open.

I spoke Philip's name twice before entering, but he didn't respond. I didn't remember why I came. I do remember turning on the living room lights and looking around. The apartment was different than I remembered. All the mementos of our joined past were gone, stocked in boxes that were shoved against the living room wall. There was nothing left here that I recognized, except for the furniture. The apartment seemed empty and dreary. Impersonal. Cold.

I walked to the bedroom, where my husband would no doubt be sleeping. She would be there too, I knew that, but for some reason, I couldn't bring myself to care. The door was half open; I saw his familiar slender figure lying in the bed. He was alone; she was nowhere in sight. My heart melted by the sight of him. He used to look so innocent in the huge king-size bed, lying next to me when we were still happy. Philip always slept on his back, with his hands tucked beneath the blankets by his side. This was no different. At least his sleeping habits were still the same. Moonlight peered in through the half-open curtains, painting pictures on his face.

"Philip?" I whispered, but he wouldn't respond.

I stepped forward into the room, until I stood close to the bed, hovering over him. It was then that I realized he was dead. His mouth had opened; his eyes were half-closed. His gaze was broken. With an animalistic sound, I pulled back the covers, only to find out that he had been stabbed in the chest. The blankets covering him were bloodied, just like the sheets below him. In fact, the entire bed was covered in crimson red. One single, deep stab with a sharp blade, had ended my husband's life. A knife, or whatever else was used to end his life, had slashed though his chest, going straight into his heart. It killed him instantly, most likely in his sleep. He probably never even knew what happened to him. He looked too innocent for that, even in death. He hadn't put up a fight at all. The weapon itself was gone.

I bit my knuckles while I stared in shock at the lifeless body lying on the bed. Then I looked down at my hand and realized there was blood everywhere, just like there was all over my coat and slacks too. I didn't know where it came from, or whose it was. I hadn't touched Philip, nor had I laid down on the bed with him.

I held my breath. A wild, deep cry escaped from my throat. I was like an animal that had just lost its mate. I put my blood-covered hand before my mouth to stop myself from screaming out loud, but I couldn't hold it back. From the inside of my throat, I felt the raw sound building up, and then it finally bellowed out of me and there was nothing I could do about it. I stumbled backwards, terrified of what I saw, but it wasn't the sight of him that shocked me the most. It was the realization that I was responsible for his death. I had to be. His blood was on my clothes and my hands. It was on my face too. I was out of my body for a while, until I came back to my senses and my senses screamed at me that I had to get the hell out of here.

The next thing I knew, I woke up on the floor of my new apartment from the sound of my smartphone. I opened my eyes and saw the first tourists on The High Line, passing by the building. The drapes in my living room were wide open. Anyhow who would take a curious peek inside and had good eyesight, could catch me shivering like crazy. Fortunately, nobody did. Drops of sweat trickled down my face and back. I was choking on my own anxiety.

The phone stopped, only to begin again. I crawled up and drew the drapes, before sinking down on the floor again. I picked up the phone when it rang again for the third time.

"Yes?" I mumbled, struggling to wake up properly.

"Mrs. Walters?"

"Yes."

"Mrs. Walters, this is Detective Charters with the New York Police Department. We've been trying to reach you all morning."

"You have?" I replied dazed, trying to remember previous phone calls.

I couldn't remember. All I remembered was blood on my hands. Blood.

Philip. Stab. Dead.

"Mrs. Walters, are you still there?"

"Yes. Yes, I'm here."

"We need to speak with you as soon as possible."

"What about?"

"Your husband. You should better come home immediately."

It's not my home anymore, I wanted to say but I didn't. Instead, I asked the question they probably didn't expect.

"Is he dead?"

"I'm afraid he is. How did you know?"

I didn't say anything anymore, just hung up. Then I realized I had moved to the kitchen floor, kneeling as if praying, clutching the telephone to my ear. A million thoughts ran through my mind like a speeding train, overwhelming me with their innuendos that I was my husband's murderer. I had assumed that my memories together formed some sort of bad dream, but that was not the case. What I had experienced was very much real. The dream, the blood on my fingers and the knowledge that I had known he was dead, proved that I would find him murdered once I went to the old apartment.

The world itself choked me; I felt sick. I made it to the bathroom just in time to throw up the remainders of last night's dinner, until there was nothing left in me to get rid of. With my face against the cold tiles, I flushed the toilet and took deep breaths. The world became a twirling sensation, a cacophony of sounds, fears and anxiety. Philip was dead. He had tried to get back with me yesterday. He had tried to rape me, had violated me. No matter what else we had gone through, I would never forget that moment for as long as I lived. It was the worst moment in my life, and it had taken away whatever good I still thought of him.

Why had he done this to me on his last day on Earth? Why did he leave me behind with such a horrible memory? Had he finally discovered that I had taken part of his money? Had that been his form of revenge on me? He must have known by then what I had done. He never wanted me back; he wanted to punish me in the most violent way a man could punish a woman. If I hadn't fought back, he would have –

Bitter tears streamed down my cheeks, until I realized that I must have murdered him because of what he had done to me. I must have sleepwalked to his place, must have stabbed him because of the pain he had left me in. Why else would I have done this?

Like in a dream I put on the first set of clothes I found, combed my hair carelessly and reached for my Burberry, which I couldn't find. I explored the apartment in panic, throwing open closets and looking in the strangest of places for my coat. It was gone.

Flashes of memories came back to me. I had thrown it in a dumpster somewhere on my way back home. What the hell had I done with the rest of my clothes? I remembered now waking up in my underwear, with the rest of my clothing gone. Nobody else was with me, so I must have removed my clothes myself.

A memory came back to me. My head pounded when I opened the garbage bin standing near the sink. There they were: my clothes, covered in Philip's blood. I had no doubt that he bled all over me. The ramifications of my actions made me want to throw myself out of the window. What point was there to fight, after what I'd done to my husband?

Instead of doing something radical, my mind seemed to take over. I closed the garbage bin, selected another coat, shoved the fabric over my freezing body and left the apartment. It felt as if someone else had taken over from me, deciding on what to do next.

Downstairs, the door leading to Mac's apartment opened as soon as I walked by. My new friend gazed into the hallway with a weary face and ruffled hair. He seemed to be coming straight out of bed. I had no idea what time it was.

"Zoey," he spoke, running his hands through his hair. "I was waiting for you, just got out of bed myself after a long night. Want to come in for breakfast? Do you have any plans for the day? I have a day off so I was wondering if you would like to go into the city with me this morning?"

I shook my head.

"I can't," I whispered.

His tired eyes changed expression.

"What's wrong, Zoey?"

I couldn't get it out of my mouth. I just couldn't tell him what was going on, but somehow, I didn't even need to say it. Mac took me in his arms and gently held my head against his shoulder. I clung on to him and heaved dry cries. Nothing made sense anymore. I was a murderer now and I would lose him too. Everything would be lost to me.

"It's okay," he soothed me. "It's all right. Just trust me, Zoey. It will be fine. Everything's going to be okay, I promise."

"He's dead," I croaked. "My husband's gone."

"I'm going with you."

Mac pulled me inside the apartment and planted me on the sofa, while he rushed to the bedroom to change. He returned with shoes in his hands and a sweater that he still needed to pull over his T-shirt. He moved through the apartment with the self-assurance of a man who didn't cave in under stress.

Thirty-One

MAC AND I SAT QUIETLY next to each other in the backseat of a Yellow Cab. The driver took several different routes to avoid traffic jams. He drove fast and experienced through the busy city, until we reached the block where Philip and I used to live. A jumble of cars made sure nobody could enter the street. People stood outside our building, watching curiously. Mac paid the driver and left the cab first. We continued on foot. A police officer stopped us, ignoring Mac completely while he looked at me. I grasped my new friend's hand in fear, but he whispered in my ear to speak quietly and gently and explain who I was.

I held my voice firm and steady while I talked to the cop. Someone came over to speak to us, again addressing me after I identified myself and escorted us past the roadblock. Mac supported me up the stairs of my former building, but he never spoke a single word to the cop joining us.

I felt weak to the bone. At the same time, I couldn't help but wonder if I had cleaned my fingernails properly, or if I had been stupid enough to leave any traces of my husband's blood on my hands. What the hell was I doing anyhow? I was a murderer who headed back voluntarily to the scene of the crime. Was I crazy?

At the entrance of my former apartment building, the doorman was talking to a police officer. He nodded at me, asked me if I was alright and told me he was sorry for my loss. Another proof that my husband was indeed dead. At the elevator, Mac gripped my arm tighter and whispered in my ear that it would be just fine, that I would be okay, but that he would have to leave me here, since he wasn't part of my family nor was he in any way related to this situation.

"Take deep breaths," he whispered in my ear. "Deep breaths and stay calm. I'll be waiting outside for you."

He turned around and left while we stepped into the elevator. I was then escorted by the police officer inside my former apartment. It smelled of death. I turned and heaved, trying to stop the nausea from finding its way up my esophagus.

The first thing I saw when we walked inside the space where I spent months in isolation, was the woman who had ruined my marriage. She lingered in the middle of the living room with teary eyes and flushed face. Her body raged with anger. Tension just jumped off her shoulders. The fear I had felt for her before, returned. There was something so cold in her eyes, that it scared me to death. Her cold haughty face was still there, despite her sorrow and grief. As soon as she saw me, her whole demeanor changed. A police officer stood by her side and held onto her upper left arm. He was supporting her, as if she was a victim too. When our eyes locked, I saw nothing but hate.

Why couldn't she have been the one to die? I couldn't help but wonder where she had been last night, but I couldn't ask her without giving myself away. Had my hatred and fury been directed towards her? Was she supposed to be the one to die? I didn't know what to think right now, nor did I know if they were going to arrest me. I didn't even know if I was considered a suspect. I couldn't think straight. I just couldn't think. My mind was as empty as it had been, the second I woke up in that hospital bed. I had lost my husband and child in six months' time. According to the law, I was now a widow.

Maybe that's why Elisabeth hated me so much right now: She was not a widow. She was the mistress, the lover, the one who had destroyed a marriage. People would sympathize with me, not her, once the truth came out. They hardly knew of her existence. She hadn't even established her position yet. The divorce had not been finalized, and Philip had probably not even told the outside world the truth about what happened last week. Even so, even if anyone had known about her, she would not be considered important. She was the lover. The adulteress. The bad guy. I almost felt sorry for her.

When those cold eyes of hers locked onto mine, her emotions took over like an unstoppable freight train. She was a good comedian. She turned away from me and snapped that they should talk to me. Ironically enough, she had become me. Her protector was gone; she was alone again. She might not even have anywhere to go. This apartment was legally mine again, since we were still married. She was just a guest here, invited at Philip's beckon and call. I could kick her out just like that and there was nothing she could do about it. I was his heir. His wife. I could kick her out right now. I wouldn't be stupid enough to leave her here. I had no sympathy for the devil.

Elisabeth turned away from me and sat down on the sofa. There she lit a cigarette, clearing her tears amazingly quickly.

"No smoking in my apartment," I heard myself whisper.

"What?" She looked up and snarled. "This isn't your place anymore."

"The law says it is," I croaked. "Please put out that cigarette."

To my astonishment, she did as I told her. Her actions made it perfectly clear that she still believed she could outrank me. By smoking in this apartment, she showed me she had every right to be here, but my determination had put her in her rightful place. She had nothing to say in here and I had made sure that she remembered that. A man dressed in jeans, shirt and tie came over.

"Mrs. Walters?" he asked, "my name is Tom Henderson. I will be leading the investigation into your husband's death. Can we sit down and talk?"

"Where is Philip?" I asked.

"Your husband's body has been taken away for autopsy."

"Autopsy?" I repeated dully. I had immediate visions of Philip's body being stabbed through. "Why?"

"He was murdered. Didn't anyone tell you that yet?"

"No," I said numbly. "How did he die?"

"Let's talk about that in a little while. Can I get you anything? A cup of coffee or tea? Let's talk in the kitchen, shall we?"

Before I could even reply to any of those questions, Detective Henderson took me into the kitchen and planted me on a chair. I felt uncomfortable sitting across from him. My instincts were on high alert, and I missed Mac. The man took a notepad and pen and put them on the table, but he didn't start writing at first. He folded his hands and smiled reassuringly.

"Let me first begin by condoling you for your loss."

"Thank you," I replied, "but as you obviously already know, my husband and I lived separated since last Thursday."

"That doesn't mean you can't mourn his loss," the man remarked. I felt immediate sympathy for the man.

"What happened to Philip?" I asked.

"Your husband was stabbed to death, Mrs. Walters."

"When?"

"In the middle of the night. Preliminary findings state that he must have died between three and five this morning."

"I see."

I didn't look up at Henderson. Guilt was written all over my face. I stared at my fingers and remembered that sticky feeling of blood. I was to blame. All I had to do was make their lives easier by admitting to it.

"Do you have any suspects?" I finally asked, knowing Henderson was waiting for a reaction.

"Not yet. We do have a lot of traces in the bedroom. We will need to go over some details with you later. Do you have anything you might want to tell me right now, Mrs. Walters? Can I call you Zoey?"

"It's Mitchell now," I whispered. "But please call me Zoey."

"Okay, Zoey, it is. Can I get you anything? You're shaking."

He offered me a paper handkerchief. I looked at it and wondered why I had to accept it, until I realized that my hands were wet with tears.

"Thanks," I sniffed, while I wiped over my eyes.

Henderson watched me with professional sympathy.

"I know this is hard for you," he said, "but I need to go over a few things with you. Routine in a case like this."

"Yes. Of course," I whispered hoarsely.

"Where were you last night, Zoey?"

"At home, in bed. Asleep."

"Was there anyone with you?"

"No."

"Is there anyone who can verify your alibi?"

"No."

This time Henderson was jotting down my answers and his own questions. I had the chance to examine his features. He was a man in his early forties, with black hair that started to grey out here and there. His face showed traces of the years. I looked at his neatly cut fingernails and wondered if he was married with children. I had read somewhere that many police officers could not hold decent marriages, especially when they were investigating murders and child molestations. Was he a bachelor, living for his job? What did he think of separations? Did he believe that betrayed spouses were bound to kill their adulterous husbands?

"Am I a suspect?" I blurted out.

"I'm afraid you are, Zoey," he said, closing his notebook.

"Why?"

"You were his wife and sole beneficiary. Plus, he was living with his new girlfriend. Many murders happen for emotional reasons. You had a quarrel with him; you lived separated. We need to investigate your relationship with your former husband further. That's our job."

"Our marriage was over. I dealt with it appropriately," I spoke formally. "I was moving on. Living my own life and all, you know? Besides, he served me the divorce papers, and I was okay with that."

He smiled reassuringly.

"At this moment we are looking through several scenarios, Zoey. Yours is one of them. I can assure you that we haven't pinpointed any particular subject just yet."

"Might it have been a burglary?" I offered.

"Could be an option."

Henderson was not letting go of the information he already had. I straightened my back and gazed outside through the kitchen window, hoping to catch a glimpse of Mac, who would be out there, waiting for me. God, I missed him so much right now. I wanted him to take me away from here, so that we could start something new and beautiful. A part of me was relieved that my husband was gone. His death made things so much easier. It made me cope with what he had done to me.

I closed my eyes, remembering Philip's fingers forcing their way inside of me. I shivered again, something that didn't go unnoticed with Henderson. He made another note.

Thirty-Two

MY HUSBAND'S DEATH WAS TREATED like a thousand others, all murder victims. Murder happened in cities like this all the time. People were taking pictures and jotting down notes. They treated his death like anyone else's. He was an unknown man to them. He had led a life they knew nothing about. He was just another body. They didn't care about his life, or me. They merely wanted to know why he had died, what event had brought on his murder. Then they would solve the case and close it, while the murderer went to jail forever.

The bedroom door opened. I saw the flashes of the police photographer inside the room. I turned my head away, unable to think about the blood. I wanted to get out of here, but they wouldn't let me go. Of course not, why would they? This apartment, the scene of the crime, was the best emotional blackmail they had on me.

Henderson still sat in front of me, trying to find out more about me. I was obviously a person of interest to him, because I acted strange. God knows I was screwing things up all myself. I was so messed up. I had guilt written all over my face.

"I was out with a friend of mine, Vivian," I whispered hoarsely, before Henderson could ask his next question. "We went to a few clubs, had a few drinks. She dropped me off at home and left."

"Were you drunk?"

"No. I don't drink that much," I lied, remembering the evenings with Vivian where we emptied the bottle.

"Do you have blackouts when you drink?"

"No."

"Okay, Zoey. What happened next?" Henderson asked.

"Nothing. I fell asleep on the bed and woke up when you called me. That's all I can tell you."

"Why do you say on the bed?" he asked. "That's an odd thing to say."

"I fell asleep fully clothed," I blurted out.

"Were you so tired you couldn't get changed?" he asked frowning.

"I've been sick, so I took a few pills for the pain and was too tired to get changed afterwards. They're heavy stuff."

"What did you wear when you went to bed?"

"The outfit I had on when I went out." Another lie.

"Which was?"

"A dress."

"Where is that dress now?"

"At home, in my dressing room," I muttered.

"Okay, Zoey." Again, he was making notes. "Can you give me your friend Vivian's full name, address and telephone number?"

"Vivian Trent," I said. "I don't have her address. I can give you her cell phone number though. She told me last night she was leaving early this morning for a business trip. She has to travel a lot."

"Where to?"

"I don't really know. She often travels to Europe, but I don't really know why. You can always try to contact her. She should be back by Saturday anyhow, so you can talk to her then too. She'll tell you the exact same story I did."

"You say you don't have her address?"

"That's correct."

"How come?"

"We always meet in restaurants or bars," I said.

"I see. Has she ever visited your place?"

"Yes."

"But you don't know where she lives?" Henderson asked, obviously surprised again.

"Why don't you ask her why yourself?"

I gave him Vivian's number and made a mental note to contact my friend later, to inform her that the police might be calling her for enquiries. I debated if I should ask her to lie to provide me an alibi. Then I silently shook my head. No, I couldn't not do that. Vivian could never know I had turned into a murderer. She would drop me like a brick.

"What are your thoughts on Miss Davis?"

"Who?" I asked curiously.

He pointed at Elisabeth, who was smoking again, blatantly ignoring my wishes not to. Her long fingers held a cigarette, but somehow it didn't seem to suit her. Last night, all dressed up, she looked smashing. Today, she had returned to her image of the grey mouse, wearing clothes that were too baggy and sat too loosely. I wondered if she had two personalities, or if she had done this on purpose to get the police off her back. After all, she was a suspect too, unless she had a perfectly good alibi.

"Do you want to know the truth?" I asked bitterly.

"If possible."

"I hate her. She ruined, no, she fucked up, my marriage. I'm sorry to use those words, but that's how I feel about her. I want her out of this apartment as soon as humanly possible. This is still my house, and she lived here only by the grace of my husband. I detest her for what she's done to me."

"You use strong words to describe her, Zoey," Henderson remarked calmly.

"Wouldn't you when your husband cheated on you with your own nurse, while you were still recovering?"

Henderson raised an eyebrow.

"That's not what she told us."

"She wouldn't, now would she," I smiled bitterly. "She's the innocent victim in all of this, right? Ask her when she met my husband and under what circumstances. I guarantee you that it will burst her bubble of innocence."

Henderson didn't comment on that.

"I suggest that you speak with her to make arrangements after we have spoken to the both of you," he said. "This is technically your place, so you have the right to kick her out. I can tell you though that she has a perfectly good alibi for the time that your husband was killed. She was also the one that found him."

"I'm sure she has everything covered," I spoke bitterly.

"This alibi is almost unbeatable," Henderson spoke, continuing more gently. "Give her a break, Zoey. She has just lost everything."

"Why should I?" I reacted bitterly. "She has cost me everything. I had exactly five minutes to leave my own home when my husband kicked me out and another ten or so to pack up my things. I don't feel sorry for her. She's the one that ruined my relationship. If it weren't for her, Philip would still be alive. Besides, she still has family."

Henderson understood when he noticed the boxes with my things standing against the wall. Elisabeth wanted to erase every single memory of me and replace it with her own. It had taken her only a few days to get rid of my influence.

"I'm sorry for what you had to go through, Zoey," he said, placing a hand on my arm.

"Could you please tell her to leave my apartment?" I asked through tears.

"I will."

He left me alone in the kitchen and asked me to stay there, while he briefly spoke with her. I saw Elisabeth pale. She stood, threw her cigarette on the floor and walked over to the built-in closet in the hallway. She fished out a suitcase and started packing things in the bathroom. She wanted to go into the bedroom next, but she was denied access. She would have to wait until forensics was finished. She stared helplessly around the living room. She really didn't have much to pack up, except for her clothes, to which she didn't even have access. Everything else was too heavy to take and didn't belong to her at all.

"You can come back later for the rest of your stuff," I spoke from the kitchen.

Elisabeth turned to stare at me and opened her mouth. Her long hair fell slightly forward. She looked as young as a child. She didn't beg me to stay. Pride took over, forcing her to deal with the same kind of reality I had endured days before. She can go to her family, I thought. She has parents and a sister. She looked so sad. I remembered her at the hospital as a kind nurse, someone who sympathized with her patients. Now we were sworn enemies, divided by one man. Even in death, Philip still managed to ruin lives.

She looked at me. "Thank you."

Then she was gone.

After Elisabeth left, the mood in the apartment instantly changed. She took a lot of hatred and anger with her. I was relieved, until the detective sat down in front of me again.

"Are you okay, Zoey?" he asked.

"I'm tired," I whispered, rubbing my temples with my fingertips. "Can I go now?"

"Not yet. Zoey, do you get what is going on?" Henderson asked, sitting down in front of me again.

It became clear to me that Elisabeth was off the hook for now, but I wouldn't be. She had a solid alibi; I had nothing.

"Zoey, do you hear me?" Henderson repeated.

"What?" I raised my head dully.

"This is serious, Zoey. We need to know exactly what your husband's last day was like. We need to investigate why someone would want to harm him. There were no signs of burglary, so whoever did this to him, had access to the apartment. How many people have keys to this place?"

I stared at my hands.

"Zoey, are you feeling alright?" Henderson asked troubled.

"Yes," I whispered.

"Do you still have a key of this apartment?"

"Yes, I do."

"Where is it?"

"I don't know."

"Is it at your apartment?"

"I guess so."

"We need to search your premises. Will you give us permission to do so? If not, I will request for a court order."

The blooded clothes underneath the sink frightened me, but I had no choice. Let them arrest me if I had killed my husband. It was what I deserved. I was their prime suspect, not Elisabeth. How stupid of me to think otherwise on my way over, when I thought I could lie my way out of this. After all, I was the cheated wife, the one who was cast out of her home and left with nothing. Who else would have a greater motive than me? Revenge was bittersweet and heartbreaking. It was also real. I killed my husband. I alone.

"Zoey, will you give us permission to search your apartment?" Henderson repeated. "Do you hear what I'm saying?"

"Yes," I said dully.

"Are you sure, Zoey?"

"It wasn't me," I heard myself whisper. "I was at home, asleep. Please, it wasn't me. You have to believe me."

Henderson didn't respond. Neither did his male colleague, who hadn't spoken a single word all the time. I rose from the wooden chair and swayed on my legs. Reaching for the counter with both hands, I tried to compose myself. Someone grasped my arm.

"She's not okay," the man who reached for me, said. "She looks like she's in shock."

"I agree," Henderson said. "Zoey, we're going to let you go home now, but you're not to stay alone. Is there someone who can look out for you?"

"Mac," I whispered. "He's a friend; he's waiting outside."

"Good. I will have police officers coming over in an hour to search the apartment, Zoey. Do you have a spare key we could use, or can you make sure you're at home?"

I always had a second house key on me, hidden in a small compartment of my bag. I dug it out and gave it to him blindly, knowing there was no point in trying to stop them.

The police officers talked about me as if I weren't there. It annoyed me. I was carefully steered out of the kitchen, into my former living room. The bedroom door stood wide open. The blankets were pulled back, revealing the extent of it all. My husband's body had been taken away before I even entered the apartment, but his blood still seemed to be everywhere: on the pillows, the sheets, the blankets, the floor. The scent lingered in the air.

I turned away and puked all over Henderson's shoes.

Thirty-Three

FOURTEEN YEARS AGO, I SAW a friend die. We were walking to the bus stop as we did every day, chatting about everything and nothing. She was one of a few rare friends I had during my high school years. One minute she walked by my side; the next she stepped onto the street while babbling away and a bus hit her full in the back, dragging her under its wheels next. She died the moment the bus hit her; she never felt the pain. For months I had nightmares about it. One second she was alive, laughing and joking and pestering me about something stupid, and then she was dead. Her life meant nothing.

That's the feeling that I felt right now, while watching the cops do their work: that a human life means nothing. I lived in a constant sense of doom, with nothing but disaster unfolding by the minute. The buzzing sound in my ears that became a constant in my ears since this morning, made a way for a flurry of voices. When I blinked my eyelids, a friendly face hovered above me. I sat down on the couch, staring into nothingness, while a few cops cleaned up the mess I made over the living room floor.

Detective Henderson held a glass of water in his hand, while his colleagues moved around the room. His male colleague, who never even introduced himself, was on the phone. He was probably arranging the search inside my apartment, and I just let it happen. There was nothing I could do to stop it. Everything that would happen next was completely out of my hands.

"Hey," Henderson said, while he sat down next to me. "How are you doing?"

"I don't know," I answered truthfully.

"You've been through a lot," the man spoke. "Don't feel bad about puking your guts out. It could have happened to anyone. I'm used to blood, and I became nauseated too."

"I don't feel sick," I said. "I just …"

"I know. And you are still sick, Zoey. You may pretend and act as if you're not, but I can feel it radiating around you. Do you want me to take you to a hospital?"

The man's hand reached out for me, as if he wanted to help me. In a flash, I remembered Philip's fingers inside of me. I winced and backed away. Henderson probably, mentally, made another note.

"Listen to me Zoey, you need help."

"Because I threw up?"

"No," he said, "because you're obviously in shock. I want to take you to the hospital to be checked out. You need medical care."

"I'm fine," I said. "I'd just like to go home now."

"Are you sure?"

"I am," I said hesitantly, while my eyes drifted off to the boxes.

I was supposed to come back here yesterday to get the rest of my things. Looking at them sitting there in those boxes made me want to puke again. I didn't want anything that had been a witness to Philip's death.

Henderson seemed genuinely concerned, which surprised me. He was okay for a police detective, I supposed. He wasn't even that much older than me. The man gave me his card and promised to give me a call as soon as possible. I left the apartment shortly after.

Outside in the cold air, I started feeling better again. The police cars were leaving; the blockade was lifted. People were getting on with their lives. Curious bystanders, parted. Mac walked straight over to me and reached for my arm. I let him hold me against him as we walked away from the area. We didn't say a single word until we walked past a small park, where he settled me down on a bench. I closed my eyes, shivered and pulled my coat over me.

"How did it go?"

I shook my head.

"I don't want to talk about it," I said.

"Zoey, listen to me," Mac said. "I need you to take better care of yourself. People are not supposed to feel this off for long. You've obviously not recovered enough from last week's fainting spell. I want to run some tests on you in the next few days, if possible, even today. I know I've been working a lot and didn't have enough time to spend with you, but you're seriously worrying me right now," he spoke in all earnest. "To be honest, if it were up to me, I'd have you admitted right now."

"Thanks for cheering me up," I muttered.

"I'm serious, Zoey. This isn't a joke."

"So am I," I reacted coolly. "Leave it, Mac."

"Fine," he retorted. "I'll just have you go through this by yourself. Is that what you want? Do you want me to go home and forget you exist?"

I stared at him in shock, realizing he was serious.

"Would you?"

"If you want me to leave, yes."

"I don't," I whispered. "Please, don't go."

"Good. If you want my help, we are going to do this my way," Mac quickly said.

"You think I killed him," I whispered.

"No, I don't. I don't believe that for one second."

"They do," I said, nodding my head at the cops, who worked around the room without looking at me, as if they felt guilty, or afraid. "They all think I murdered my husband."

"Do you?"

I blinked my eyes.

"I don't know," I admitted. "I've been having these …"

"Blackouts?" Mac whispered, making sure nobody heard.

"Yeah, how do you know?"

"That doesn't mean you did it."

"Again: how can you be so sure of my innocence?" I asked.

"I think I know you," Mac smiled. "You're too nice to do this to another human being. This just isn't you, Zoey."

"Thanks for the vote of confidence. You're probably the only person in the room right now who believes that I didn't stab Philip."

"Any time," he smiled. "Now then, let's get you up. You need to eat something. Let's get some food into you."

He pulled me up. Despite my protests, Mac wouldn't let go of me. He made me feel like a patient, not a friend, which I hated. He was right though: I needed help. I needed to figure this out. Worst of all: I needed to find out if my suspicion of late was true. If I was schizophrenic. That thought was the first thing that popped into mind this morning, when I started having flashbacks. When I realized I had done things that weren't exactly part of normal behavior.

I couldn't even be scared about the garbage bin with the bloodied clothes. It didn't matter to me at all that I would get caught and arrested in the next couple of hours. I deserved to get caught; I deserved to be arrested and put away in prison.

After all, if I was a schizophrenic, then I was a murderer too.

We walked into a small diner, where we both had toast and jam for breakfast. I wasn't hungry, but he urged me to eat. The toast would settle my stomach, he said. He ordered tea instead of coffee, which also helped. It was after ten. They would be at the house at any minute now. I had given Henderson my key voluntarily. He said I didn't have to be there, if I didn't want to.

I excused myself and went to the ladies' room, where I stared at myself in the mirror. Was that really the former flower shop owner Zoey Mitchell staring back at me? I looked ghastly white, as if I had been in prison for years. My red hair had lost its glamour. My body seemed even smaller than usual. Bones stuck through the skin. I had lost weight again, or maybe I had been this skinny for months already. No wonder I looked like I was going to fall dead on the spot. No wonder Mac was so worried. I looked like I'd been to hell and back. I used the toilet, washed my hands, rinsed my mouth with water and returned to the table.

"Are you okay?" Mac asked.

"I'm fine."

"You need a lawyer."

I was shocked. A lawyer. Now it was for real. As soon as they entered the picture, you knew you were in trouble. Shivers ran down my spine. I looked at him in shock. He put his hand on my shoulder and tried to reassure me.

"It's just a precaution, Zoey. Next time the police talk to you, you need to have a lawyer present. I know this guy. He's good. Give him a call."

I sighed. In a few moments, the police would search my apartment. They would be looking for God knows what. They would find the clothes. Yeah, I definitely needed a lawyer.

"Okay," I said, "but I'll call Rob. He has this friend that is a lawyer specializing in criminal cases. I'll ask him for help. Rob won't tell my parents if I ask him. He'll keep his mouth shut."

"As long as you're getting help, I'm fine with whatever you choose," Mac spoke relieved.

We sat quietly next to one another in the cab. Mac didn't know what to say, just like I didn't know how to act in front of him. The cab driver looked at me through the rearview mirror, but he never spoke. We sat in utter silence.

"I don't know why you do this," I finally whispered, burying my face between my hands.

"Because I care about you," Mac said, taking my hand in his.

Thirty-Four

ROB SET ME UP WITH Greg Anderson quickly, after I told him what was going on. Rob was shocked, to say the least, and promised to come over. I asked Mac to do this alone, since he wouldn't even be allowed to stay with me while I spoke to my lawyer. Plus, I didn't want him involved in my mess. He had a life of his own and I wanted him to live it without worrying about me all the time.

Despite Mac's reluctance, I decided to meet with Rob and Greg in my apartment. Rob insisted on coming over and I couldn't refuse him, since he was my confidante and probably the closest to family I had besides my parents.

We met in a tiny coffee bar right around the corner. Mac had said his reluctant goodbye and told me he would be at home in case I needed him. I couldn't meet them in my apartment, since the cops could arrive at any minute, and I had been told not to go back there for now.

I told Greg and Rob what I knew to be facts. I didn't confide the blackouts to them and of course I didn't mention that I found bloodied clothes in my apartment either. My new lawyer didn't write anything down, but he listened intently while I tried to convince him I was innocent. I'm not sure if he believed me, but Rob obviously did. He kept on repeating that all of this was Philip's fault and that I wouldn't be in this mess if it weren't for him.

Greg asked me painful questions about the divorce and went through the details of the past five days, partially confirmed by Rob, who explained how I had bought the apartment. I confessed to both men that I had seen Philip and Elisabeth the night before at the club, expressing my shock and surprise when they showed up so unexpectedly. In the end, I also told them how Philip had come on to me the day before, trying to get us to get back together, without adding what he had done to me.

"Why didn't you give your relationship another shot?" Greg asked bluntly. "After all, you had the power to save your marriage."

"I just couldn't," I said. "He hurt me too badly."

"I need to ask you one very important question, Zoey," Greg said. "You will have to answer this truthfully. After last night's accidental meet with Philip, do you believe that he might have had a row with his girlfriend, bad enough for her to kill him?"

"She certainly wasn't a happy trooper," I replied. "Truth be told, I still don't understand how we bumped into one another at that bar. What are the odds in a city like this?"

"Did you tell him you were going there?" Greg asked.

"No."

"Are you sure?"

"Yes."

"Do you think he might have followed you there?"

I held my breath, thinking about his fingers inside of me, probing, prodding and hurting me. Was that action part of the alter ego of Philip, the one who set out to hurt and damage people?

"Zoey?"

"I …" I closed my eyes and looked away.

"Zoey, what's wrong?"

I looked at Rob and swallowed the lump in my throat.

"Zoey, it's okay," he said. "Whatever it was, you can share it with us. I promise you it won't go any further."

"When he came over, he didn't just plead to get back together," I whispered. "He …"

"Did he assault you?" Rob gasped.

I closed my eyes and nodded.

"God."

Rob leaned backwards and ran his hands through his hair.

"That bastard. I should have known, Zoey. I knew there was something off with that guy, but I never really dug deeper into it because it was so busy at the office, and you seemed to be doing okay."

"Rob, this is not your fault," I said, stopping him. "Philip didn't…, well, he didn't get the chance to go all the way. He tried to, but I stopped him on time. But he still managed to …"

"Do we need to get her examined?" Rob asked Greg, interrupting me.

"Wouldn't do any good if he didn't leave seamen," Greg said.

"He didn't," I confirmed. "He used his fingers."

"God." Rob bit his lip. "I'm so sorry, Zoey."

"It's over," I said. "He's gone and that's all there is to it."

"Is there anything in your apartment that might implicate you, Zoey?" Greg asked. "In light of what you just said, I need to ask my question again: did you go to his apartment and kill him?"

"No," I said, but we all knew I was lying.

"Are you certain?"

"Yes."

"Good," Greg said, making a note. "Is there anything else you want me to know right now?"

"No," I said hesitantly.

There were so many things, but I could not discuss them with anyone.

"I think that we might get you off the hook," Greg said. "You weren't there, so there will be no evidence leading directly to you. You moved on with your life, and you are financially independent. There was no reason to kill him."

"But?" Rob asked in my place.

"But there are circumstances that will not help your situation, I'm afraid. You took half of his money, even though it was in mutual accounts, which may implicate that you were after his money. Your husband died at a very, very bad moment, since you stand to inherit all he left. He filed for divorce quickly, insinuating that he might have wanted to get rid of you quickly. And then there is the emotional part of it. He left you while you were at your weakest. He did the dirty on you and you took it hard. Your fingerprints will be all over the apartment, because you lived there. They will be on the sheets too. They might use that against you."

"I had an alibi," I muttered. "I had Vivian. Besides, if I had taken a cab over there, someone would have seen it."

"You had an alibi for the night, but not for the time of death, Zoey. If you had left on foot from this apartment to his, it would have taken you a while, but you could have done it. You could have hidden in the shadows, making your way through the city to kill him and then head back easily," Greg stated. "I've seen people do worse than that."

I was terrified.

"I'm sorry Zoey, but I'm trying to give you the facts as they stand," Greg said. "As your lawyer, that is my job. It would be unwise for me to reassure you now that you will be fine, when there is a good chance that you might be arrested. It's not going to be an easy ride, I can promise you that."

"I can't believe this is happening," I whispered.

"You have nothing to fear, since you weren't there. We have to trust in that," Rob spoke sensibly. "Your fingerprints won't be on the murder weapon, whatever it was."

"I doubt anyone's will be," Greg said.

Both men stared at me in surprise as I moved from my seat, feeling suffocated.

"I have to go. I need fresh air. I'm going crazy right now."

"Don't leave, Zoey," Greg stopped me. "You're shutting us out. You can't afford that right now."

"I have to."

Millions of memories flashed through my brain. I was back in that hotel with Matthew. I was back in the market with Elisabeth pushing me hard against the wall. I was back in the bedroom with the knife in my hands.

"You can't run away from your problems," Rob remarked.

"Stop being so nice to me," I suddenly snapped, causing others at the coffee bar to look at us. "Sorry," I whispered, sitting down again. "I'm just so messed up right now. Everything's gone to hell in a matter of days."

"Why can't we be nice to you?" Greg asked. "Don't you think you deserve that?"

I thought about Mac and Vivian, saying the exact same thing. No, I didn't deserve it. I was a murderer. I knew that in my heart.

"You're in trouble and we want to help you," Rob said softly. "Is that so wrong, Zoey? You need help and we're here to offer that. You called me because you needed me, and we dropped everything to be with you. Why would we do that if we weren't here to help you get through this?"

"Nobody does anything without a motive," I spoke bitterly. "You're my financial consultant, Rob. If I go to jail, you lose a client."

"I'm also your friend," he said, slightly hurt.

That calmed me down.

"You are," I said. "I'm sorry."

"Are you that hurt that you won't allow people into your heart again?" Greg asked matter-of-factly.

I wanted to tell him that I let Vivian and Mac in and that I wanted to befriend him and lean on Rob, but it was so hard. I had been living beneath a self-assured façade over the past couple of days. The damage that Philip caused to destroy all that, lingered in the back of my mind all the time. He had done more than just kick me out of his house: he had destroyed my trust in people.

Thirty-Five

THE POLICE CAME AND I was slowly going crazy.

Greg was there to monitor the proceedings; Rob had left. He wasn't allowed in anyhow, since he wasn't family. Mac was downstairs. I knew he wouldn't come unless I asked him to. Even so, he still wouldn't be allowed in either.

The cops went through every bit of the apartment. Henderson was not amongst them, but another detective was in charge, a woman named Alice Slater. She asked me what I was wearing the night before and I showed her my black dress, hanging in the dressing room, just like I had told them before.

She asked about a coat, gloves and shoes. I showed her the coat I wore that morning, without telling her that the Burberry had gone missing. I showed her a pair of sweatpants and T-shirt resting in the closet and told her that I usually wear those at night. They took them, even though I hadn't been wearing them last night.

They went through my home meticulously, taking fingerprints, photos and whatever else they felt was necessary. They moved from the dressing room to the bedroom, bathroom, hallway, living room and kitchen. I froze when they opened the garbage bin and peered inside.

"Empty," a man said.

I stared at him as if he had gone nuts. I really was going crazy. The bloodied clothes were gone, as was the black bag I had shoved them in last night. I hadn't removed that; I hadn't thrown away the evidence. Then, who did? Or had I dreamt it all? Had everything that happened last night been part of some horrible nightmare that never even happened for real?

I moved into the dressing room and acted as if I was selecting other clothes, while another policeman watched me. To my shock, I found my clothes in the back of the closet, on the pile of other sweats and shirts that I had grown accustomed to during my many months at home. The clothes smelled fresh; it seemed as if they had just recently been washed. I didn't know how they had gotten there, but I was certain these were the clothes I had worn the night before. If I had washed them, I had no recollection of doing so. Then again, if all of this had been a dream, I was never even there.

I went to the bathroom and hid myself to call Vivian. The cops let me, even though they must have heard me talk. My call went to Vivian's voicemail, pleading with her to call me back at once. I ignored my parents again, knowing I couldn't face them right now. They would hover over me, suffocate me. I couldn't allow them to see me this fragile. Then there were Philip's parents too. I knew they would be notified, but I didn't want to be the one doing it. I took the coward's way out and didn't call them.

"We've got everything we need," Detective Slater said, smiling briefly at me while they packed things up.

They didn't take much, just my dress, the coat, the pair of shoes I had lied about and a set of my fingerprints. She wished me all the best and said that Henderson would be in touch. After they left, Greg told me everything went fine, and I should get some rest. He gave me a hug, promised to be in touch soon and left me alone in the apartment that was no longer my home. It felt polluted.

I sent Mac a text message. He rushed upstairs, grabbed some of my things and took me downstairs. I couldn't stay there tonight, which we both knew. Vivian was still missing in action. My new friend made some food that I didn't eat. He let me take a nap in the spare bedroom, while he rummaged around his living room doing whatever he was doing. I listened to the sounds he made and the ambient music he had chosen on Spotify, until I fell asleep. He made dinner; we didn't talk very much. We didn't have to. My head burst;

my entire body felt like it had been put through the wringer. Vivian still hadn't called me back. I knew that she wouldn't. She had abandoned me too.

My phone rang: Philip's parents. I ignored them and hid against Mac, wanting to escape this damned planet. My newfound friend held me, told me he wouldn't abandon me and said it was fine to want to escape the world for now. That's exactly what I wanted to do, if only today. Somehow, I was waiting for a bomb to explode. It would only be a matter of time before destruction followed. I was as convinced of that as I was of desperate life itself.

Like I said: I lived in a constant state of doom.

Wednesday

Thirty-Six

I WAS A LONELY CHILD, one of the children that were pestered during kindergarten and throughout high school, because they were different than others. Instead of playing with my fellow classmates, I preferred to read or play alone. By then, I had become used to loneliness. I didn't go out in search of new friends, too scared that they would mock my red hair and the freckles on my face.

With the imaginary friends I created during the years, I never was that lonely though. My best friend was named Eveline, after a character in a cartoon I loved to watch. Eveline was my age, but she had everything going for her that I didn't: blonde hair, blue eyes, bright, intelligent and loved by everyone in my fictional world. She was the life of the party. She lived in my room of course; she even shared my bed. She complained on occasion about her lack of freedom, since I wouldn't take her outside with me, and called her home a golden prison. I gave Eveline everything she wanted, but she was never satisfied. She wanted to go outside and become a real girl, with real feelings. She didn't like the fact that she was only created in my mind.

Eveline left me one day. Or I left her. I became too old for her at one point, since she wouldn't grow up as I did. She was like Claudia, the vampire child in Interview with the vampire. She stayed young forever too. When I was about thirteen, Asia suddenly showed up. She became my very best friend during a time when I had it quite rough. Asia was different than Eveline. She was nice, quiet and polite, so I took her out, to see things, until I again started to realize that Asia too wouldn't grow up. They both deserted me in the end, or perhaps, I dumped them.

At the age of fifteen, I had my first best friend, a girl who was an outcast like me. Our friendship didn't last long, since she died in that freak bus accident less than six months later. She was the first one I liked enough to confide in. She helped me out of my shell; she changed me, told me that I was beautiful, but just didn't see it yet. She never knew that I had an enormous crush on her boyfriend.

At her funeral, I stared at the boy and realized that it was my fault that she died. It felt as if she had died because of me. Her loss made me lose trust in real friendships. For a long time, I thought that every friend I ever loved would die. I didn't want to risk that, so I became a recluse again. It took Philip a lot of time to restore that trust. All the friends we had were his, because I had no one myself. My first real good friend was Samantha, and she died, also because of me. If she hadn't been working in my shop, she would still be alive today. Death surrounded me.

This morning, I woke up feeling like a freak. Philip had died because of me. Even if I hadn't pushed that knife through his chest, I sure as hell brought it on. Would things have been different, had I allowed him in my house and bed again? If Elisabeth killed him, she did it out of spite, revenge. If I did it, I had to figure out why. If someone else was responsible, then I would find them myself.

Mac slept on as I walked around in his living room. The door was half open; I could watch him lying on his side. He was so innocent like that, so beautiful. He turned, faced the incoming sun through the thin curtains and continued sleeping, despite the light. I had no idea when he had to go to work, or even if he was expected at the hospital today. I knew so little about his life. He had no routine, no steady schedule to cling to. I wanted to crawl into bed with him and feel comforted by his presence, but I didn't.

While I was making coffee and breakfast, it occurred to me that Philip was just as much a secret to me as Mac as. Who was my husband really? Did he have enemies I didn't know about? I needed to find out if he had more secrets than just Elisabeth. His mistress might be the key to answer all my questions, but could I face her? I sighed, sitting down at the kitchen table. My health was deteriorating fast. I woke up with headaches that wouldn't leave me until the day faded away again. A constant throbbing made me feel weary. Those damned pills didn't do anything for me anymore. I could take four at the same time and they still wouldn't help.

The blackouts scared me the most. At times, I simply couldn't remember what had happened just five minutes earlier, which freaked me out. Mac was right: it was unsafe to keep me out on the streets. I needed to be in a hospital bed, monitored. I was a danger to others and myself. Something had to be done soon.

Before that though, I needed to act. I put on my clothes and left a note for Mac, saying that I would be back before ten. I took his spare key. Upstairs, I sat down on the couch with my phone in hand. Without even thinking about it twice, I opened my husband's email account and tried out the three password combinations that he used all the time. The second one worked after we split up. I smiled briefly, remembering how trusting Philip had always been, even when we were having difficulties.

I scrolled through his calendar. Dating back months, I first noticed the initials. ED: Elisabeth Davis, always booked neatly in his agenda, with what appeared to be a code name for a hotel. Sometimes, there was a dinner appointment at a restaurant or bar. The bastard had taken her to hotels and restaurants we frequented a lot as well. He had been that self-assured that I would never catch them, since I was an emotional wreck. On the last day of his life, he had jotted down her initials again, this time adding a remark 'sister', scribbled in red. I remembered him talking about that sister, telling me how he hadn't wanted to be involved in her life too. Odd, that he would set up an appointment with her in his calendar, while he was already living together with her.

I bit my lip and scrolled through the list of names and telephone numbers in his contacts, until I found her. She was registered as Lisa, under an address near Central Park. I also found a fixed telephone- and mobile phone number. The thought occurred to me to check into her background, but I forced it back, not even knowing where to begin. Plus, Henderson undoubtedly had already done that. Elisabeth was just a regular nurse, with irregular wants and needs. There was nothing extraordinary about her whatsoever. What could I possibly find in her past? I was curious about the sister though. Why had Elisabeth lied about her in the first place? Now that he was dead, that vulture would probably find some other grieving husband to 'comfort' and move on. Her life didn't end with his death. I didn't believe for one minute that she had truly loved him. I contacted her on her mobile phone number.

"It's Zoey Walters," I said as soon as she answered.

I deliberately used my deceased husband's name; because it made me feel stronger. A silence followed, before her cold voice snapped.

"What do you want?"

"We need to discuss my husband. I need to talk to you."

"Why?"

"I can't talk about that over the phone."

"All right. When?"

"This afternoon."

"Where? The apartment?"

"No," I protested, not wanting her back there. "There's a bar called Jimmy's on Fifth. Meet me there around two."

"Fine." She hung up.

I went back to the apartment, just in time to find Mac waking up. He didn't even notice I was gone, so I tore up the piece of paper and threw it in the bin. I made him toast and told him I had already eaten and went upstairs for a while. He didn't remark.

"Zoey," he said, "what is going on with us?"

"I don't know," I replied. "I have no idea what I'm doing or if we are going to survive all this. All I know is that I like you, but I can't go there right now. I need time to deal with all of this."

"I like you too," Mac smiled. "I promise you that we will take it easy with whatever it is that we have together. I don't know where this is going, but I do know that you need me right now and I won't let you go through this alone. I talked to some colleagues of mine and discussed your case. If you want, you can go in today to have some tests done, by my colleague, Dr. Andy Wilson. He's specialized in chronic pains and abdominal diseases. We might have all the results we need back in two days. We can figure this out, Zoey, if you allow us the time to get to the bottom of this."

I wanted to accept Mac's offer. I really did.

"Later," I said. "I need to get upstairs and shower."

"You can stay here for as long as you like."

"That would only delay the problem," I said. "Thanks, Mac, but I need to get a move on, and you need to get to work. You said you only had today off, remember?"

"Right," he smiled, as if he didn't remember for himself. "Okay then, let me check around a bit and talk to Andy. I'll keep you posted."

"Thank you."

I gathered my things and left for my own apartment, where I started to clean up the mess the cops had left, while turning on the television, before forgetting I didn't have cable yet. I sighed and worked in silence, trying to block angry and depressing thoughts from my mind.

Until the doorbell rang. It was Detective Henderson who came to see me, and he knew exactly where to find me.

Thirty-Seven

"CAN I COME IN, ZOEY?" Detective Henderson asked, watching me casually as he leaned against the wall.

In other circumstances, the man would appear to be a friend. Right now, even dressed in jeans and jacket, he was the enemy. I froze, expecting to be arrested immediately. Henderson wouldn't have come back for nothing. He came back because he distrusted me.

"Sure," I said, trying to hide my distress. "Would you like some coffee, Detective?"

"That would be great, thanks."

Henderson walked in. I shut his front door. My visitor looked around the living room before following me into the kitchen, where we sat down at the table after I poured him a cup of coffee.

"Can I ask you something?" he started.

"Sure."

"Are you seeing anyone?"

"No."

"No other men in your life just yet?"

"Not at all," I said, while my thoughts drifted off to Mac. "Why do you ask?"

"Just wondering." Henderson said, sipping his coffee. "I came here

235

to give some more information, but if you want to call your lawyer to be present too, you are entitled to do so, and I could come back later. I promise you though, that this is not an official interrogation."

"I'm fine," I said.

"Thanks. The autopsy report came back. Philip died, as we expected, estimated between three and five in the morning. I can confirm that he was asleep when the attack occurred, so he most likely didn't know what happened. There were no signs of struggle or forced entry. It seems that the person that killed him had access to the apartment."

"And the murder weapon?" I asked.

"Probably one of the kitchen knives, since one was missing from the kitchen that could fit the profile. We haven't found it yet though. The only DNA we found was yours, Elisabeth's and Philip's. I'm afraid that makes the two of you our prime suspects. We didn't find any evidence so far of another intruder. Which brings me here today."

Henderson emptied his cup and looked me in the eye. I knew he was going to tell me something I wouldn't like.

"Elisabeth has a solid alibi, but I'm afraid you don't. We can't verify anything, since we can't find Miss Trent."

I blinked furiously.

"Excuse me? What do you mean by that?"

"It seems that you gave us the wrong information, Zoey. With the info you provided us, we couldn't get in touch with Miss Trent. Her phone number was wrong, so we tried to find her in our database and were unable to do so. In fact, it seems there is nobody by the name of Vivian Trent living in Manhattan."

"That's impossible," I whispered. "I know Vivian's number by heart. I've contacted her several times, and she has always called me back using that number."

Henderson frowned.

"You're sure that she lives in Manhattan?"

"Yes, of course. She told me so herself. Why would she lie?"

"We checked for the entire New York area, Zoey. Brooklyn, Harlem, you name it. She's nowhere to be found. There is no Vivian Trent. Are you sure she's from this area?"

"I am. She came to see me plenty of times."

"Can anyone confirm this?"

"Sure, several people have seen her with me," I muttered. "Last night as well. If you would check with the bars we went to, I'm sure somebody saw us together."

Henderson made a note.

"What about her office?"

"She works for a large software vendor. She travels all the time."

"What's the name of the company?"

"I don't know. We never spoke about her job. She always was a bit evasive about that," I said, trying to find other ways of contacting Vivian.

"It seems that Miss Trent is quite the mysterious woman," Henderson remarked, without a trace of sarcasm in his voice. He mentioned it matter-of-factly.

"Philip knew about her," I added weakly. "He didn't like her at all, because we were good friends."

"Unfortunately, we can't ask your husband anymore," Henderson remarked calmly.

I flushed in embarrassment.

"To be honest, Zoey, your alibi is not very solid," Henderson sighed. "Even if we find Miss Trent, we still have no proof that you were at home during the time of the murder. You could have gone over to the apartment easily, even on foot. It would have taken you quite some time, but it's doable. We called the taxi companies to confirm that you hadn't hitched a ride and the surveillance cameras in the nearest subway stations, confirm you weren't there either."

"You work thoroughly," I said bitterly. "I'm the one you want to pin this murder on, aren't I?"

"You have to understand that your case isn't looking too good, Zoey. You had the motive and the time to do this. The motive being the divorce papers you were served. You said so yourself that you received them yesterday."

"I did, but there is something you don't know," I whispered. "Philip showed up at my apartment right after his lawyer left. He begged me to reconsider." I laughed bitterly. "Can you believe it, Mr. Henderson? He threw me out, only to beg me to come back home."

"What did you tell him?"

"I told him to leave."

"Did he listen?"

"No," I whispered, looking away. "He wanted to sleep with me."

"Did you?"

"No."

"Did you fight?"

"No." I shook my head furiously. "There was no reason to. I told him to get out, and he did."

Henderson made more notes. It remained quiet for a while, until he rattled my world again.

"Would you be willing to take a Polygraph test?"

"Excuse me?" I asked surprised, imagining one of those television shows, where people were strapped to wires and questioned about what they did.

"I would like you to consider it. We can't force you to do this, but it might help your case. I believe that you're innocent, Zoey. I believe you. I want to believe you, but right now, you do look guilty." Henderson sounded glum. "There's obviously something bothering you and we need to find out what that is. I believe in your innocence, Zoey, but there are people I report to, who believe you're as guilty as hell. The odds are against you, you know that. We are thoroughly checking Philip's life, but he has always walked a straight line. He was not a bad guy, nor was he involved in any dirty deals. He had an affair, yes, but so do a lot of people. The one that suffered the most in this was you. This is looking bad."

"It's just a matter of time before I am arrested, isn't it?" I spoke bitterly. "You won't give me a chance, will you?"

"I am willing to give you every chance, Zoey," Henderson said. "If you killed him and somehow erased that from your memory, I will find help you. You said that you went to bed and slept in your dress until the morning, yet your dress hung squeaky clean in your dressing room. You claim you slept on top of your bed, but your sheets are wrinkled, and the bed was unmade.

You must have changed before you fell asleep beneath the covers. Therefore, you lied. Is there something you left out of your statement, Zoey?"

I remembered my freshly washed clothes.

"No."

Henderson sighed.

"You need help, Zoey. That much I can tell, just by looking at you. If not physically, then at least psychologically. There are ways of finding out the truth, but you need be willing to undergo treatment."

"What are you suggesting then?" I whispered hoarsely, feeling hot tears burn in my eyes.

"Hypnosis."

I laughed. I couldn't help myself.

"We have worked with hypnotherapy before. I can give you the number of a good doctor who can help you retrieve your memories. Wouldn't you want to know if you did this, Zoey? I certainly would."

He had a point. The detective handed me a card.

"This woman is quite good. You can go there, and she'll see you straight away. She's nice."

"Let me think about it," I spoke weakly.

Henderson gave me that reassuring smile again, touched my fingers for a brief moment and let go. I liked him. He cared, I could tell that, but he could also be doing this to trick me. When push came to shove, he wouldn't hesitate to arrest me. It was his job to do so.

Thirty-Eight

JIMMY'S BAR WAS A STYLISH venue that used to be an Irish Pub. Four years ago, the old pub burned down thanks to its previous owner, who wanted to get his hands on the insurance money. He failed of course because he was an amateur and was arrested and charged with arson, less than a week later. He went to jail for three years. His lawyer sold the place to the first potential buyer that came knocking at the door. Jimmy bought the pile of burned wood for less than nothing and tore down what was left of it. It took him five months to set up his Bar. It became an immediate success.

If only I was meeting Vivian here. I was terrified that something had happened to my best friend, but I wouldn't let anyone know that. She could be anywhere, casually sitting in some bar too with some stranger she met on the streets. She could be working hard. She could be dead. Anything could be wrong right now and I would never find out what happened to her. The thought of losing her was almost too much to bear, so I reprimanded myself quietly for thinking so negatively. Vivian was just fine, like she always was. The moment we would be in touch again, she would reprimand me for thinking only about her.

Elisabeth was already waiting for me. She had chosen a table in the middle of the bar, in between the counter and the window. She sat alone, holding a glass of water in her hand. Obviously, I wouldn't catch her having a stiff drink. She looked around wearily, probably thinking I was trying to set her up. She seemed tired. Her hair was combed backwards in a strict knot. She looked older than before. Her glasses hid her eyes. The last few times I saw her, she must have worn contacts. Her self-assurance was gone. I wondered where she had slept last night. No doubt she had found someone to stay with, probably her sister. Whichever way, I wasn't about to ask her. Once I sat down, Elisabeth shifted uncomfortably on her seat. She was nervous, even frightened. I decided to use that fear against her.

"Thank you for coming," I said.

"Did I have a choice?"

I ordered a cup of tea and removed my coat. She refused to look at me at first, until she finally seemed to realize I wasn't going to start talking before we had eye contact.

"Tell me what you want," she snarled.

I swallowed the lump in my throat and just blurted it out.

"I want to know if you killed my husband."

She paled, startled and then laughed.

"Are you crazy?" she asked surprised.

"I just want to know, Elisabeth. I'm not carrying a wire or anything, I swear, and I won't tell the police whatever you're going to tell me. I just need to know the truth."

She leaned forward, narrowing her eyes.

"No. I didn't, Zoey. Did you?"

"No," I responded a little too slowly.

She smiled, as if she knew I was lying through my teeth.

"Is that all you wanted to know?" she asked.

"No. I'd like to know what happened after you left the bar. I would also like to find out how you wound up in the exact same bar I did that night."

She smiled.

"You haven't figured that part out yet, have you? Your darling husband and I had a fight after we saw you. It was the second time we 'accidentally' bumped into you, and I figured out that he had been lying through his teeth for days."

"So, he was following me," I whispered.

"Yep. He knew exactly where you were."

"Tell me what happened next," I pleaded. "He went home and you did what exactly?"

"I went to work."

"Work?"

"Yes, work. I called the hospital and asked if they could use a helping hand. I needed a distraction, and it was a busy night, so I took a cab and left for work, where several colleagues worked alongside me. They confirmed to the police that I was working all night through. What a perfect alibi, right, Zoey?" she smiled eerily, obviously happy that she had one that was so solid nobody could break through it. Damnit.

I wanted to knock the smug look off her face. I was weakened by her sharp words. If so many people could vouch for her alibi, it would be over for me. The trap was closing.

"Why did he follow me? We were over," I said.

"We always fought over you, Zoey," Elisabeth spoke matter-of-factly.

"You were jealous because he still spoke to me?"

Her smile vanished, while her eyes became darker. Her mind seemed to be drifting off.

"Do you know what it was like for me to live up to your standards, Zoey? All he did, was talk about you. The second he threw you out, he already regretted it. He wanted you back, even if he would never put that to words. He was obsessed with you."

"I already told him to stop it," I said.

"I know. He as much admitted it." Elisabeth sighed and drank her water. "I'm so tired of this."

"You didn't love him, did you?" I accused her.

She looked straight into my eyes, tears flowing into them the moment that she spoke. I saw hurt and distress, which took my breath away. What an awful person I was. How sad she was.

"I ached for him. Do you even know what that's like?"

"He wasn't what you expected, though, was he? You wanted more than he could give you."

"He couldn't forget about you," she answered sadly. "I hated him for it, but I loved him just too much to let go. I thought we could live the dream, but all it became was a freaking nightmare. You can't know what it was like to live in your shadow. For months, I believed he was the one for me, but he didn't want to leave you. He cared too much about you. It couldn't last, no matter what. I was tired of sneaky meetings in hotels and restaurants. I was fed up with the lies and truth be told, I was selfish too. I wanted him completely, or not at all. The choice was his to make and he took it. I'm not proud of what I did, but he was unhappy, and he needed someone like me. Only, turns out he couldn't choose after all. He always went back to you."

"You destroyed my life."

"As you did mine, by killing him," she whispered. "I would have won in the end, even if it would have taken me months to do so. You ripped apart my heart. I hope you're happy now."

I didn't reply.

"Listen," she continued, softening when she saw the look on my face. "It was his idea to deal with you the way he did that night. I didn't want him to throw you out like that, but he insisted on having a clean break. I was shocked too."

"If he hadn't dumped me, would you have continued fucking him in my bed?"

She winced.

"He never took me to your apartment," she spoke feebly.

"That's right," I retorted. "He took you to fancy hotels with good room service to fuck you."

"Don't be so rude."

"Why not? You were his whore, weren't you? Besides, you should talk. You know all about fucking in hotel rooms, don't you?"

"What?"

I blinked my eyes, trying to get a grip on the conversation. Did she know about Matthew? Oh god. Elisabeth bit her lip, before finishing what she had started.

"Look, the moment Philip dumped you, he regretted what he had done, so he started calling around hotels to find you. It wasn't even that hard, since you used his credit card. He could trace you in a heartbeat. He went to your hotel room in the early morning to talk to you and find a solution for you, but when he got there, a man left the room. Philip was quite upset about that. That was the onset of his obsession with you. He couldn't grasp that you would have sex with a complete stranger on the night he threw you out, so he tried to figure out if you were also having an affair."

I was completely and utterly shocked, while I struggled with my emotions. If Elisabeth had told Henderson about this, he would assume that I was having an affair too, meaning I had even more reason to get rid of my husband. Is that why he had asked Mac if we were involved? Elisabeth smiled coolly.

"Don't worry, Zoey, the police don't know about your sordid little affair. They would look differently at the new, sad widow, wouldn't they? You are being treated as the sad widow who got kicked out of her own home after her husband started an affair while she was recovering from a vicious assault. That's the only reason why you aren't behind bars yet right now. They see you as the frail, young woman who has lost everything. I am merely the adulteress. I'm the bad guy in all of this, even with my alibi."

"You're wrong. They already think it's me," I whispered with tears in my eyes.

Elisabeth's whole demeanor weakened me. She had scored big time, and I was losing.

"That's because they're looking in the right place," she remarked.

She stood up, threw some cash on the table and left. I prayed I would never see her again. What the hell was I thinking believing I could handle her? I had only made things worse. God, I was going slowly crazy. It was over. Elisabeth had a solid alibi and there wasn't a single other suspect in play. I didn't stand a chance in hell. You had to be crazy not to see that I was already guilty as charged.

My body ached, my throat burned, my stomach churned, and my breathing stilled. The sadness and grief I had held inside for so long came fighting their way out. I practically ran to Central Park and just collapsed on the grass. My husband was dead. He was gone forever.

I looked around in despair, remembering the day he asked me to marry him. It had been a neutral affair, one without too much fuzz about the whole thing, just like the man he had been. We were never the extravert couple that would dry hump each other in public, but we were happy in our own way. I knew every feature of him, every mark on his face. I knew the way he had looked, what he loved and liked the best, the small things he had enjoyed. I remembered it all. That would never go away.

In twenty years, if I was still alive then to experience those days, I would wake up in my bed and suddenly remember my husband and the way that he was. He would stay young forever. He would never age, never wrinkle or turn grey. I needed to see him. I needed to say goodbye, but I knew that I couldn't. Henderson had told me adamantly I would not be allowed to see Philip at the coroner's office, since he was the victim of a crime, and his body would be examined thoroughly. I wanted to say goodbye to my husband, but this was not the way. I needed to remember Philip while he was alive, when he was still good to me. That way alone could I forget what he had done to me in his last hours.

The sound of my phone surprised me. I had one missed call, followed by a voicemail, left by Alice Slater, Henderson's colleague, asking me to return to the police station for more questioning. It wasn't a request, but a demand. The time had come: I was going to be arrested.

Thirty-Nine

I WASN'T ARRESTED. INSTEAD, I received a cup of coffee and an invite to have a chat with Henderson and Slater, but she hardly spoke. She just made notes and kept an eye on me. I made no illusions: I was being videotaped and watched by others too. On my way over, I had called Greg and pleaded with him to come, which he did. He arrived five minutes after I did.

His presence reassured me that I would not be alone. He was a great guy, who obviously cared about what was going on. He also happened to know Henderson, which was an added bonus. They had come across one another on a couple of other cases and obviously had mutual respect for one another. It still didn't stop the fact that I was going to be interrogated again.

The thing was this: I didn't have evidence to prove my innocence, but the cops didn't have the evidence to convict me either. They had an eyewitness, claiming to have seen a young woman entering the building around three a.m. The man hadn't seen who it was. The person wore a dark coat, and she didn't show her face. It could have been anyone.

The person could have gone inside the building to another apartment which they were checking up on right now. They had nothing but circumstantial evidence that led to me. They had my fingerprints in the bedroom, quite normal since I used to sleep in there. They had fibers of my clothes, again normal. They had a lot of evidence referring to me being in that room. They just couldn't prove that I was there that night.

They had Elisabeth's fingerprints too. They had samples of her being there as well. She was still a suspect too. In the end, there was enough to convict us both. It would have taken her ten minutes to get to the apartment, five minutes to kill her lover and ten minutes to get back. She could have done that easily, despite her presence at the hospital. If the Medical Examiner misjudged the time of death by even half an hour, it could change everything.

"If Philip died, you inherited his money," Henderson said.

"It wasn't that much," I spoke feebly. "I have more, thanks to my trust fund. He would have benefited more."

"Are you saying you didn't know about the insurance policy?"

"What policy?" I asked.

"He had a life insurance policy, worth half a million. If you're innocent, that money's yours. Didn't you know that?"

"No," I said. "Why would he do that?"

"He took one on you too. Zoey, if you had died, Philip would have inherited half a million too. We checked with his lawyer. Apparently, Philip took out the policy on your life on the day you opened the shop."

I stared into the man's eyes, seeing red. The pain in the back of my head returned, pounding hard against my skull. In a second Henderson leaned over me, asking me if I was all right. I nearly pleaded for my pills.

Greg, my lawyer, played it hard, but the police did too. They tried to get me to confess. I didn't. Henderson felt sorry for me. I think he believed in my innocence. He obviously didn't like Elisabeth. The problem was that I didn't believe in it myself. Guilt stood written on my face, and that would ultimately convict me. How could I change the way they felt, when I could not persuade them with rock-hard conviction that I was not a murderer? It was so hard.

They wanted to know what happened after Philip kicked me out. They wanted to know where I stayed, what I did to reorganize my life, what people, what man, I was involved with. They were curious about Mac, who was never mentioned before. They inquired about who this mysterious Vivian was, the only person who could partially confirm my alibi. Why couldn't they find her, or reach her? Why was her number disconnected? I shook my head, repeatedly, telling them that Vivian was a true friend who had helped a friend in need. When she contacted me, I would ask her to speak with the police, but I hadn't heard from her in for days either. I didn't know where she was.

I never talked about Matthew or his offer at the hotel. He was a little secret that rested forever with me. I didn't tell them about the violation either, but I think they knew. Somehow, they sensed I had gone crazy. I came across as a woman that sought out other pleasures because her husband had thrown her out. A woman, that would seek revenge by doing exactly what her husband had done to her. If I were such a woman, wouldn't I live for the revenge I believed I was entitled to?

Just before midnight, I took a cab home. Greg offered to come with me, but I declined. He had a family to go to, and it was pretty late already. I couldn't imagine an arrest. The image of spending the night in jail behind cold steel bars, stuck between women that would spite me on me as I would spite on them, was unbearable. They would rip me apart, because I was weak and frail. They hadn't arrested me yet, but it would happen. The despair I felt was almost as bad as not knowing.

What could I have done otherwise, I asked myself. Was there anything I could have changed? If I had allowed Philip back into my life, would he have lived today? It's a terrible thing, not knowing. When I arrived at the building, Mac waited for me. He took me inside his apartment without question. I burst into tears.

"Philip's death is not your fault," Mac said. "They know that too."

I threw my coat on a chair and ran my fingers through my hair.

"How do you know? How can anyone know? I don't remember, Mac! I don't know if I killed him. The truth is that I might have. How can I leave it with that?"

I practically shouted now as I turned towards to the man who had helped me without questioning me one moment. He was the only one that I could turn my anger to, and I wanted to hurt him. I had no one else to shout at. Mac stayed calm.

"I know you," he said. "You wouldn't hurt a fly."

"And what if I did?"

"Then we'll have to find that out."

"I've tried that," I whispered, "I spoke to someone today, but I'm not there yet. I need to push harder, deeper."

"Let me help you then, Zoey," Mac said. "I'm your friend. Stop hiding behind your skin. Plus, you need to call your parents."

"I will, later, but not right now. I don't have time for this," I sighed. "I need to arrange his funeral. I need to do this for Philip."

"You don't. His parents are in town," Mac said.

"They are?" I asked shocked.

"Yeah, I called in on some old favors. Now that they're here, they'll take care of everything. Don't put this on your shoulders too, Zoey."

"They think I did it, don't they? They haven't even contacted me yet."

"Didn't they try to call you earlier?"

"Right," I said, remembering that I deliberately hadn't answered.

"Maybe they just want to give you some time to grieve and recover. Maybe they think it was the girlfriend too."

"She has an alibi," I said.

"She's also cunning."

"How do you know? You never even met her."

"Your stories about her are enough," he said. "I trust you, not her."

"You believe that she did it?" I asked.

"Yes, I do. She had the motive, more than you."

Mac sat down on the couch with me, handing me a cup of coffee.

"What do you want to do next, Zoey?"

"I wanted to feel free," I whispered, "but my current sense of freedom is only fake. I'm living on borrowed time, aren't I?"

"You don't know that."

"I do, I know you'll be okay."

"We met only a few days ago," I protested.

"That doesn't mean I don't know you."

"You don't."

Mac stood and walked to his kitchen, where he started cleaning up the counter. I helped him by stocking the dishwasher.

"Do you want to stay here tonight?" he asked.

"I do," I said.

He smiled.

"I'll give you something to wear."

I hesitated, considering his eyes.

"Can I sleep in your bed?"

He smiled and hugged me.

"Of course. I'll always be here for you, Zoey, no matter what."

Thursday

Forty

I SLEPT BETTER THAN EXPECTED, with Mac by my side. At one point I woke up with him draped over me. It felt good. He was a friend, a companion and someone I cared about so much more than I ever expected to do. I didn't feel attracted to him in the way I had been drawn to Philip or, shame on me, Tom Henderson, who had settled in my mind since the moment we first met. Mac was a gorgeous man, but more someone I could see myself be friends with for life. It was good the way it was, and I could tell he felt the same way. He didn't come on to me whatsoever.

After a light breakfast, Mac received three calls from the hospitals about his patients. He retreated into his office, while I stayed in his living room, wondering what to do next. With time to think on my hands, I couldn't help but wonder about Vivian. Where was she? Was there nobody worried enough about her, to find her? Somebody had to know where she was, but where would I begin to search for her, when I didn't even know her address or new phone number? I played with the thought of calling Henderson and inquiring about her again but forced that to the back of my mind. He had too much work as it was, plus, he had to investigate her whereabouts as part of the case. He wouldn't believe me if I told him now that I was worried about her, that I had doubts about her too.

I tried to remember if she had ever told me details about the company that she worked for. She had said that it was an international software company that sent her abroad quite a bit. She also mentioned that she was a technical expert or something. She told me once that she worked near Rockefeller Center, like thousands of others. It would be impossible to trace her like this. There were too many possible companies she might work for. I couldn't just go out there and visit them all, could I?

I logged in on the internet, using Mac's laptop. He had told me I could use it freely. Using a guest account, I searched for companies in the Rockefeller area, coming up with hundreds of them, specializing in IT. Impossible to find her this way, since I couldn't start calling all of them and hope they would even give me that kind of information. Next, I did a search on Google, Facebook, Twitter, Instagram and LinkedIn, trying to find her name. Nothing came up again. The only Vivian Trent I found, lived and worked in Belgium and looked nothing like her. This was a dead end again, I knew that. It frustrated me that I knew so little about her. She never talked about family or friends either. I had no reference points. Troubled, I leaned back. This was pointless. I needed to think differently.

Vivian was missing, so maybe, I could file an official missing person's report. That could possibly trigger the cops, who obviously didn't believe a word I said about her. There was another possibility I dared not to think about right now: what if Vivian had given me a false name all this time? What if she never was the person I thought she was? What if she was sent by Philip to spy on me, or, what if, she had killed Philip herself? She hated his guts, always had, or she was a terribly good liar. But why? What would her motives be to lie to me all this time?

I started recalling details of my encounters with Vivian. We met on the day my daughter was supposed to be born, bumping into one another in the rain. She had an umbrella, I didn't. I was at the end of my rope, she was confident. She never asked any questions, never told me that I should shut up about my misery. She was the yang to my yin, the voice I never dared to use out loud. How strange, that this woman would replace that empty spot that was burning a hole inside of me, caused by Philip's behavior. She had become the center of my life and helped me to cling onto the things I still had., proving to me that I still had every right to exist. She was the best friend I had ever had, despite her often harsh, outspoken words. She always said the things I wouldn't dare to express. She spoke up where I shut up. She was everything I never dared to be. She gave me the confidence to stand up against my husband.

I liked her name, which suited her perfectly. Strong, helpful and beautiful. If I had known her before Eve's birth, I might have named my unborn child after her. They both had gorgeous names that I really liked. Maybe, someday, I could adopt a child. A girl named Vivian. One day, if I ever got out of this mess at least.

I looked outside, to find clouds taking over the rapidly changing skies. It reminded me of the day my daughter would have been born. Today had been rather bright and sunny, but now a strong wind was taking over, and we were heading towards a storm. I remembered walking through the cold night when Philip died. I had gloves on, and a Burberry that went missing afterwards. Why did I remember these details, but not killing my husband? I shook my head, cleared my mind and returned to Mac's laptop to turn it off. A Google-ad caught my attention.

Looking for the perfect baby name?
Meaningofnames.com will help you decide.

I frowned, staring at it, only to realize that I had typed in Vivian's name earlier and this ad picked in on that. I clicked on the link. A new screen appeared, offering me the option of finding out the meaning behind someone's name. I typed in Vivian and pushed the Enter-button. A few seconds later, I found out that Vivian meant 'Life', or 'Gracious in Life'. Eve meant 'Life' as well.

I froze. I closed Mac's laptop. My hands trembled, my head burst at the seams. I reached for my pills, swallowed down two without even checking when I had my last dosage and tried to focus on pushing away the pain.

Forty-One

MAC AND I HAD A late dinner after he returned from work. Fortunately, Henderson didn't come back today in his professional capacity, so I was off the hook for now, even though it still felt to me as if they were tightening the noose around my neck already. I did feel regret that I couldn't see that man in a friendly manner. He was still stuck in my mind in a way I hadn't experienced for quite some time. I was drawn to Henderson, but I had to force myself to remember that he was the one tying the noose.

I had prepared pasta with garlic bread with the ingredients I found in his kitchen. He ate it all, while I just picked in my food. I had taken two pills and felt how they numbed me. The headaches were slowly subsiding to a dull ache. I tried not to show Mac that I was hurting, but of course, he saw right through me.

"Headaches again?" he asked worried.

I nodded with my eyes closed, rubbing my temples when pain struck at its hardest.

"This is not okay, Zoey. You are simply not taking care of yourself. We need to get you to a doctor."

"Later," I croaked, knowing he was right.

After dinner, I excused myself quickly and moved into the elevator, for once relieved that I could leave Mac behind. I was too tired to argue with him about this. Yes, I needed to see a doctor, but that could happen later. Right now, I just wanted to sleep.

I practically crawled into the bedroom, where I sunk down on the bed and turned to my side, so that I could look outside. I had no curtains yet, so I could see the skies. Night had settled in, and a full moon stared back at me, providing me with enough light to see the clear skies. A few minutes later, Mac entered my bedroom. I had given him a spare key to my apartment, just in case something would happen.

"These headaches are driving me crazy," I whispered, before he could even speak.

"That bad, huh? I know we should have had you checked out way earlier, but it's been so busy with everything that was going on. Can I get you something? Where's your medication?"

"I already took two pills," I said, "not that they help a lot anymore these days."

"I'm sorry you're suffering so much, Zoey."

Mac settled down on the bed and rubbed my back until I fell asleep. I remembered him moving a blanket over me. I felt safe with him, safer than I had been in a long time.

When I woke up a few hours later, he was gone. My head burst; my body felt broken. I hadn't felt so bad in ages. I managed to crawl out of bed and reach the bathroom, where I searched for my pills. Before me stood Vivian, holding the bottle in her hand. I stared at her in shock.

"What are you doing here?" I gasped. "How did you get in?"

She didn't speak a word. Instead, she opened the bottle and moved the pills into her hand. There was something off about them. They looked a lot like the ones I had been taking for months now, but they were not exactly the same.

"Touch them," she said.

I moved and stroked my finger over the top of one, suddenly feeling the difference. They were rough on the edge and not soft, like my headache pills.

"You have to open your eyes and know where to look, Zoey," Vivian said.

Her voice was hard, and her eyes stood steely cold, as if she was upset with me. Before I knew what was happening, she threw the pills into the toilet and flushed them.

"What the hell are you doing?" I screamed, reaching for her hand. I was too late: everything was dumped in the loo before I could even react.

"They're not yours," she snapped.

I stared at her shocked. She walked out of the bathroom, and I followed her, but she was gone already, as if she wasn't even there. I ran to my front door startled and opened it, screaming her name. The elevator was closed and waiting on the first floor, so there was no way she could have taken that.

I ran to the staircase barefoot, opened the door and screamed her name for the second time. Dizziness overwhelmed me. I fell forward when consciousness left me. The last thing I knew, was the stairs coming right at me. Or was I the one doing the falling?

Friday

Forty-Two

I WOKE UP IN A strangely quiet room and turned my face towards the window while I tried to figure out where I was and what was going on. It was dark outside; I had no clue about the time or the day. A man stood before the window looking outside at the full man. His arms were folded over each other, as if he were guarding me. I groaned and he turned. It was Detective Henderson.

"Zoey," he spoke concerned, "how are you feeling?"

My head still felt as if it was bursting from its seams, but the pain had resided into a dull ache.

"Where am I?" I asked. "What happened?"

"You're at St. Mary's. You collapsed a few hours ago."

"Collapsed?" I asked dully.

"Your neighbors heard you scream and found you falling down the staircase of your apartment building. They called an ambulance and then they called me. You still had my card in your pocket and since they had no clue who else to contact since you were new to the building, they notified me."

"I'm sorry," I whispered. "I don't ... they shouldn't have called you."

"Well, seeing as I care about you, I'm glad they did," the man said. "You should rest for now, Zoey. All the rest will come later."

There was a look in the man's eyes that I hadn't seen before, one that told me something serious was going on.

"What is it?" I asked troubled, reaching for his hand as he turned away from me.

Henderson took a deep breath and moved a creaking chair closer to the bed.

"The doctors are going to do some tests on you, Zoey. We have reason to believe that you might have brain a tumor. Apparently, you were totally freaking out when your neighbors found you, before you had a seizure. They had a lot of trouble calming you down. I remembered that you complained about headaches, caused by stress and anxiety after what happened to you six months ago, but the doctors now think it might be more than that after what happened to you tonight."

I tried to grasp what he was saying. A tumor, I thought dully. I was going to die. If this was bad, I was not going to survive, which, considering what I'd done to my husband, would be my rightful punishment. It felt like I deserved it, and I wouldn't be surprised if those headaches were indeed related to it. I needed to think.

"I would like to be alone," I whispered and turned on my side.

Henderson didn't give up that easily. He moved to the other side of the bed, so that I could see him again. There was something in his eyes that went way beyond professionalism, or did I just imagine that? I was so messed up that any friendly gesture was enough these days to send me over the edge.

"I don't want you to be alone," he said. "Not in this situation. You're clearly very sick, something we had also noticed at the police station and it's obvious you don't have that many people in your life right now. I'd like to help."

"Trust me, you don't," I whispered in tears. "Please, go."

"Don't do this, Zoey," Henderson urged. "We need to talk about this, to find out if it's true what they think. Your doctors are already running some bloodwork, and I urged them to proceed quickly." The detective touched my face on impulse, sending a shockwave through me. I looked at him. "Don't give up now, Zoey."

"It's a fitting end though, isn't it?" I muttered.

Henderson stood there, not knowing what to say.

"Just rest," he finally muttered, "I will stay with you, if you want me to."

"I need to be alone," I whispered hoarsely. "Please give me some time to deal with this."

Henderson understood of course. He smiled weakly, gave my hand another squeeze and left the room. I lay in darkness, with only the full moon gazing back at me and knew that I had to decide about my life. If I stayed here, I would never find out the whole truth. I needed to know what I had done. Without that knowledge, my soul would never be at rest. I gazed at the clock above the door. It was four a.m. The hospital was quiet for the night; with some luck, it would take them a few hours to figure out I was gone.

I pulled out the IV-line and slipped out of bed feeling extremely weak, as if I had just run a marathon. I found my clothes in the small closet next to the miniature bathroom. It took me a minute to get dressed. Adrenaline kept me on my feet. I didn't have my bag here with my ID, cards and money, which meant I was basically without any personal belongings. My house keys weren't here either. I slipped out of the room and made my way to the staircase. As quietly as I could, I opened and closed the door and walked downstairs. I ended up in the empty reception area. Outside the hospital, a couple of taxis were waiting for passengers. I hailed one and gave him my address.

The taxi dropped me off in front of my new apartment. I asked him to wait while I went upstairs to get my money. I knew my front door would be locked, but I would kick the door in if need be. I refused to look at the woman in the elevator mirror, ignoring her distressed gaze. This wasn't me. This was some sick person who messed up her life. Once upstairs, I was in luck. My front door wasn't fully closed, which meant that my downstairs neighbors, the ones who had found me, hadn't come into my apartment. They hadn't noticed that the door wasn't shut. I stumbled in, reached for my bag and phone and hurried back downstairs, where I paid the driver and added a large tip. Then I asked him to take me to another address. He looked at me surprised and agreed.

He drove to my old apartment next, where I gave him another bonus. He took off surprised, without asking me any questions. I held my bag tight against me and entered the building, using the second set of spare keys I had stashed away in my bag after I lost the first during that dreadful night. I had taken the keys from the apartment on the morning after Philip's death, without anyone noticing. Philip had four sets made, which he all tucked away in the dressing room. It had taken me a second to find another spare, which I used now.

I removed my coat and threw it on the couch, looking around for a moment. This place was now polluted by death, and it was a complete mess. The police left traces of their interference everywhere: from the walls to the carpet, from my former bedroom to the kitchen. Nothing was sacred beneath their hands, and I felt violated for the second time in a few days. The memory of Philip's fingers traced my skin. I shivered, blinked away the tears and walked into the bedroom again, where my husband was murdered. I sat down on a chair next to the bed and closed my eyes, and I tried to relive that night my husband had been murdered.

Exhaustion overwhelmed me. Why hadn't Vivian stayed when I saw her? Why had she flushed my pills down the toilet? What had she been trying to tell me when she told me to feel them? Why wasn't she here? Why wouldn't she help me now? Why had she run off after I fell, when she must have heard it? I felt frustrated, exhausted and strained. I sat there with a pounding heart, soaked in sweat. I had to clear my mind, find her and set the record straight with Henderson about that night. Vivian somehow was the key to my innocence. She was the one I still needed to find.

I walked back into the living room, grabbed my bag and threw it upside down on the floor, dropping its contents all over the place. Another bottle of pills rolled towards me and stopped near my phone. I picked it up and slid my fingers over the plastic. They looked exactly the same as the pills Vivian had shown me earlier tonight.

I called Vivian's number. This time, I didn't get her voicemail. A friendly, electronic voice told me that the number I had dialed, was unregistered. Panic took over. Had Vivian disconnected her phone number? No, she wouldn't do that to me. I must have made a mistake. I phoned her three times again, every single time ending up with that same voice that told me the exact same thing. The number didn't exist. I opened the small notebook I carried with me all the time and found Vivian's scribbled number in the back. I typed every number in again meticulously, once more winding up on that same message.

Something wasn't right. What the hell was going on?

My last means of access to Vivian was now blocked too. Panic again settled in. I was so scared. She was lost to me. We only were in touch when I needed her, when I left her a message on her voicemail. She always came to find me. I had left dozens of messages over a short period of time, both voice and text. I knew her number by heart. This was not a mistake. She had called me back several times too, so I couldn't be wrong about this.

I became agitated when I scrolled through the received calls on my smartphone, only to come up with nothing. I had no friends left and the only people who ever called me were my parents and Philip. Mac was added to that list, as well as Rob and just recently Tom Henderson, the man who was showing me so much compassion. Everyone was there, except for her. Vivian's calls weren't registered. I couldn't find a single trace of them. I tried to remember when she had last sent me a message, only to realize that it was before Philip had thrown me out. After that, she was always there when I needed her, as if she knew I could use a friend. Frantically, I moved further down my call and text history, to find nothing again.

She must have used a private number then, but that was impossible too. I had her number. I had it! I used it. She used it to contact me. How could this be happening? Had she somehow removed my call history, and for what reason? Was that why she was in my apartment earlier tonight? Had she been messing around with my things? Or maybe she had never called me in the first place. Then who did? I really started to panic now when I tried to figure out who and what Vivian was, figuring out details I had blocked from my mind because they seemed unimportant. Why did I know so little about her? Why was she always so secretive? What did she have to hide?

People had seen her. They had spoken to her. I had taken her to busy, crowded places. We had set at tables, being waited on by managers and employees. The restaurants where we ate and the bars where we drank non-alcoholic cocktails and Martinis, must remember her. She was a stunner after all. I never went anywhere by myself. I never went to dinner alone. She was always with me, always the one who had dragged me outdoors, claiming I was cooped up too much. People had seen her. They had spoken to her. They must have. Someone out there must know who she is.

I remembered the last time I had dinner with her, now a week ago, on the night that Philip threw me out, the night she had to fly out of the blue to Paris. I remembered the restaurant, the waiter and the manager, whom I knew from happier times. I had gone there often when I was a teenager, during happier times. I had their information. To make the booking, I had called Samuel Walters, an old friend of my father's, on his mobile phone number, as I always did when I needed a table. Walter knew me since many years; he would definitely remember Vivian.

I glanced at my watch. It was nearly six a.m., and the man was most likely still asleep, but this couldn't wait. I needed to know now. I needed to make sure that I wasn't going crazy. I searched for his number. I called the man three times before he picked up, sounding sounded sleepy and extremely unhappy that I had woken him up at this untimely hour.

"Zoey," he grunted, his voice leaning towards impatience and anger. "What's wrong? Did you dial the wrong number? Do you know what time it is?"

"I'm afraid not, Walter," I said. "I need your help urgently."

"Why?" he asked, alert in a flash. "Did something happen with your parents? Are you okay?"

"They're fine, Walter. It's me that I'm worried about. I need to verify something with you, something very important. Do you remember that I was at the restaurant last Thursday? I called you earlier that day to request a table, do you remember that?"

"Yes, of course, is there a problem?" His voice sounded clear now, curious about the reasons behind my disturbance.

"I know this may sound ridiculous, Walter, but it's quite urgent. The woman that was with me that night seems to have lost one of her valuable earrings and she believes that she might have dropped it at your restaurant. They're an heirloom and she's very anxious about finding it."

A silence followed.

"Walter?"

"I'm sorry, Zoey, but I have no clue what you're talking about. You were alone at the restaurant. Who exactly are you referring to? As far as I know, you ate alone."

"I had a companion," I corrected him, growing weak to the bones. "A tall woman, blond, wearing a beautiful dress. She was stunning. It was the first time at the restaurant."

"Zoey, I think you're confusing restaurants," Walter spoke gently. "You were really by yourself that night. You booked for two, but your companion didn't show up. I remembered how sad you looked. William, my bartender, told me that you were talking to yourself all the time and felt really sorry for you. You decided to have dinner by yourself, so we set you up with the small table in the back, near the window, where you could eat privately while looking out the window. You barely touched your food though and you left a large amount of money. I was actually meaning to call you about that."

My phone nearly dropped from my hand. I shivered. I finally knew the truth. The whole truth.

"Zoey? Zoey, are you okay?" Walter asked, his voice disturbed this time. "What's going on?"

"Thank you," I managed to say and hung up.

Something screamed deep inside of me. I crawled on my husband's old couch and cuddled underneath the blue blanket he always left there. Nothing could ever get me warm again.

Forty-Three

I OPENED MY EYES AND groaned reluctantly, wanting nothing more than eternal sleep when the realization of the present struck me hard. It was around nine a.m., and I was losing it. Correction: had lost it already. Bittersweet anxiety filled my waking hours, so I just wanted to sleep forever, but I knew that I couldn't. This was all one big mistake. One big, major mistake. I needed to find Vivian and talk to her. She existed and I would prove it. Walter had mistaken my visit to his restaurant with someone else, that was the only explanation. I stretched out on the couch and looked up at the ceiling.

"Where are you, Vivian?" I spoke out loud. "If you can hear me, get in touch with me."

Then I laughed out loud, mocking my own insanity. I closed my eyes again and lingered between dreams and reality for what must have been hours, until something woke me again. A sound, a soft sound caused by someone walking in. I sat up and looked at the front door. My heart leapt when I recognized Vivian, standing right in front of me. At first, I hardly recognized her. She looked completely different, far away from the woman I had come to admire so much. Shadows hung over her, while soft light toyed with the weary expression on her face.

"You heard me," I spoke in relief. "Thank you for coming."

Vivian didn't reply. I moved up, practically ran to her and hugged her. I needed to feel the warmth of her body against mine, to reassure myself that she was very much real. Vivian did feel warm to the touch, but her body stiffened as soon as I held onto it. There came no response from her, not a single word. Her silence frightened me. I let go of her and ran my fingers through my hair, moving backwards awkwardly.

"I need some coffee," I muttered.

Without looking at her, I walked into my husband's kitchen and made strong coffee. Vivian followed me into the kitchen and watched me quietly. I felt agitated under her scrutinizing gaze. What the hell was wrong with her?

"Why won't you speak to me?" I asked, without looking at her. "Did you come to tell me that you exist only in my fantasy? If so, don't bother. I won't believe you, trust me. I know that you're real. I know it."

Vivian wore a long silk skirt and a black blouse. She had no coat with her. This time, she was beautiful in her simplicity, where before, she would always be made up to perfection. There was barely any make-up on her this time. Her hair was pulled together in a casual ponytail; her perfume was sweet. She wore a pearl bracelet and matching necklace. Pearl earrings completed the picture. Her fingers were bare.

My eye caught those pearls. I was almost fixated on them. They reminded me of the ones I would inherit from my mom, a beautiful family heirloom that would go from mother to daughter for as long as possible. I would have given them to my daughter one day, had she lived.

My daughter ..., I thought wearily.

Vivian wouldn't drink the coffee I put in front of her. Her eyes didn't dwell from my face. I remembered how she would never touch her drinks or her food, how she would sit back and watch me eat or drink something, but never did so herself. I sipped my cup until I finally couldn't take her silence anymore.

"If you have nothing to say, then leave. Get the hell out!" I snapped at her.

The cup slipped from my hands and shattered into pieces on the kitchen floor. The black liquid dripped all over the floor and against Philip's cupboards. My heart pounded inside my chest; I started to cry. Hot tears streamed over my face, before dripping on my hands. I knelt and picked up the pieces of china. I cut my fingers, and still, she wouldn't help me. She left me to my own devices, watched as I picked up the pieces.

"You're real," I cried while tying a paper towel around two bleeding fingers. "I didn't make you up, Vivian. I'm not crazy."

She wouldn't tell me otherwise. Her face was empty, expressionless. She could have been a ghost, but she wasn't. She was worse: she never even existed at all. I dropped the pieces of china in the sink and rushed to the bedroom. She followed. In the semi-darkness, I stopped and stared in the mirror, seeing what I had refused to acknowledge all this time. I saw only my own reflection, staring distraught back at me. She stood right beside me, but I couldn't see her mirror image. She wasn't there, because she simply didn't exist.

Vivian Trent was a figment of my imagination, like all the friends from my childhood had been. I had conjured her after losing Eve. She personified my daughter and the bond that I had lost when she died. Vivian was like the bird that died in my hands but never existed. She was put together by memories of my past and experiences I had blocked out. Trent: the name of a former classmate. Vivian: 'Life', just like Eve.

She had become the stronger half of me, the one that bluntly told me to move on and stop grieving, whereas I was left with the emotional wreckage I had become after my daughter's death. I had even created her after my daughter's image, after the vision I had of the child that would never really be born, exist and grow up. Not a redhead, like me, who was bullied at school, but a stunning blonde who had the world at her feet.

I needed her. God, I needed her so much. Whether she existed or not didn't even matter to me anymore. I couldn't go on without her. I turned around and she was gone. I stretched out my arms and hands into empty space. Never again would I feel the warmth I had felt when she was by my side. Never again would I feel so safe and secure and protected. I picked up a hairbrush and smashed the mirror. Shattered pieces fell all over the bedroom floor.

"Come back," I whispered hoarsely as my tears dried up, and coldness entered my heart.

Vivian didn't return.

Forty-Four

I DIDN'T KNOW HOW I made it back home, but I did. Mac wasn't at home, but even so, I would never go there again. I would never knock on his door again. He was lost to me too, like everyone else in this world. It was time to leave at long last. I had made up my mind. Vivian's loss was one too many.

I opened my medicine cabinet and retrieved bottles with painkillers, sleeping pills and acid blockers that I threw together in the sink. Those pills were the results of months of physical pain and mental anxiety. I couldn't bear to go on. Whatever excuse I sought for myself, it was one that meant nothing to me. I wanted out; I yearned for eternal rest, so I moved around the living room like a ghost and prepared for the end.

I thought about Mac, Henderson and Greg, the men I had befriended over the past days and whom I had really grown to like. Henderson and Mac especially had really gained a place in my heart, even when the detective was assigned to solve my husband's murder and thus basically trying to arrest me. Rob was on my mind too, as were my parents, who I knew would be devastated once they learned I had lied to them for over a week. I couldn't let them feel guilty about this, so I jotted down a note and placed it on the table.

My movements were automatic; my thoughts were all over the place. I no longer considered a future for myself, so I started taking the selected pills, while sitting on the couch. By the time I swallowed the last ones and drained the last of the bottle of water, my crying had stopped. I was still shaking, but certain that this was the right thing to do. I was ready for the end to come. I leaned back and waited patiently for my eyes to droop and my thoughts to drift off, but it never came to that.

The door flew open. Henderson shouted.

"God no, Zoey. What did you do?"

Within a few steps, the man was by my side and lifted me up roughly, as if I weighed nothing.

"Don't," I protested weakly, fighting him.

Henderson wouldn't listen to me. He dragged me into the bathroom. I choked as his fingers forced their way down my throat. He bent me over, making sure that all the poison left my body. I coughed and vomited in the toilet and partially over his shoes for the second time in a few days. He held me gently against him, pulled back my hair and spoke to me with the softest voice I had ever heard. He helped me get rid of the poison in my system, until I was too weak to fight him.

Henderson gave me water to drink. Plenty of it, to soothe my aching throat and stomach and to drain the last of the poison from my system. He had been there on time, since the pills hadn't gotten the chance to work their way into my bloodstream yet. He told me that he wouldn't call for an ambulance after I pleaded with him not to and repeatedly reassured me that I wasn't alone in this. He washed my face, wrists and hands and carried me back into the living room. I passed out in his arms.

When I opened my eyes again, he was still there, sitting on the carpet that covered the space between my couch and the coffee table. One hand rested on my wrist, as if to reassure himself that I would not die under his watch. I was lying on the couch, with a blanket draped over me, shivering from cold and anxiety. Henderson's eyes were a mixture of embarrassment, relief and fear. It was obvious that he wasn't supposed to be here at all and that he still debated calling an ambulance. Less than an hour ago, I had taken those pills and now here he was, and I was fine. My heart leapt, but I forced my feelings back. This was not the time nor the place to even consider beginning a relationship.

"Why did you come?" I whispered. My throat hurt.

"Be glad that I did when I did."

His voice had a neutral sound, without throwing accusations in it. He wasn't angry with me; he wasn't even disappointed. He leaned forward and stroked my face gently, touching me with so much care that it made me weep again. This man genuinely cared about me, far more than a policeman should for his prime suspects. Was I still the subject of his investigation though?

"You're going to be just fine, Zoey, but you just need to believe in it," he whispered. "Please don't ever do this again."

"I don't believe in it," I said. "Not anymore. I can't promise you that I won't do this again."

The fear in my eyes restrained the man from asking further questions. Henderson sat on the couch, took me in his arms and pulled me so close to him that I could feel the stubble on his unshaved chin. We hugged for minutes, while his hand again moved over my back. The quietness that lay between us was not uncomfortable. It was sweet and comfortable. He was a good man. A good, decent man. In other circumstances, he would have made a good husband. My heart leapt for the second time.

"Just rest for now," he whispered. "You need to recover, before we talk again. Then we'll figure this out."

"Don't leave me," I pleaded, before I could stop myself.

He grabbed my hand and sunk down on the carpet again, making sure I could see him.

"Don't worry, Zoey. I'm never leaving you alone again."

I woke up to find Detective Tom Henderson in my kitchen, cleaning up my mess. Tom, my mind said. Just Tom. He wasn't here as a detective now; he was here as a concerned friend.

When I looked around the room, I noticed that he had already fixed up the living room too. Music was playing softly from his phone, that was placed on the kitchen sink. I felt better, rested and levelheaded. With a blanket over my shoulders, I walked over to him, unable to look him in the eye. He was moving in his socks; his shoes were cleaned and drying in a corner.

I felt so ashamed of what I had done. This hadn't just been a cry for help. This had been a genuine suicide attempt. If he had not come over when he did, I wouldn't have made it. I had forced more than twenty pills down my throat, knowing perfectly that they would kill me. I hadn't considered any of the people who cared about me for one second in the process. It frightened me that I could be so selfish. That I hadn't even gone downstairs to talk to Mac first, while he had been so good to me.

I made the decision here and now to never to go dwell on that path again. I couldn't do that to them, to those who still cared about me. No matter what happened next, I would find a solution. Now that I had lived past the consequences and seen the terror in Henderson's eyes, I felt that this was not the right thing to do. I relaxed, slowly walking back from the abyss. It was like waking up for the first time in days.

"I'm sorry, Tom," I said, for the first time using his name.

I had always thought of him as Detective Henderson, but he wasn't that anymore to me.

"It's going to be fine, Zoey," he replied.

His voice sounded so gentle that I started crying, but it was a good feeling, nonetheless. It lifted the tension. The walls I had built around me crumbled down for good. So ironic that it had taken a police detective to do that. Not even Mac could get through me. I had blocked him out too, scared of what I would find inside my self-created walls.

"It's not okay," I said. "I killed Philip."

He looked at me with surprised shock in his eyes, proving that he had truly never believed that I was the one responsible. He was here as a friend and not as a cop, but he would have to report this, nonetheless. I knew I had decided to put an end to the lies too.

"How can you be so sure about that?" he asked.

"I remember bits and pieces of it," I said. "It's like some parts are blocked in my mind, but others are quite clear."

"What exactly do you know for sure?"

"I saw my husband lying dead on the bed, with blankets covering him. He seemed to be asleep as he always was, lying on his back, with his arms beneath the covers. When I approached the bed, I pulled back the blankets and saw the wound in his chest. There was a lot of blood on my hands. It wasn't a dream either; it was very real, as true as us having this conversation. I saw him that night and I know what his death looked like. How could I know all of that, if I wasn't the one who killed him?"

Tom didn't talk. Instead, he poured me a cup of coffee, handed me that and reached for my hand. I looked up at him and realized he was here as a friend. He wasn't the one who would arrest me in the end; he would leave that up to his colleagues, who would have no choice in the matter.

"There's something else bugging you. What is it?" he prodded gently.

I placed my hands around the cup and sat down on one of the bar stools before my kitchen island. I told him the truth about Vivian. He listened intently and didn't comment once. Instead, I saw in his eyes that he had already suspected this. That's why he gave me that card in the first place. He knew something was terribly wrong with me.

"You need those tests, Zoey," Henderson insisted. "All of these events lead back to your own mind. You were hallucinating and you have been for months. You spoke to a woman who was a figment of your imagination, and we need to find out why. That's why I came over, to find out why you had left the hospital like you did. I was afraid you weren't thinking straight."

"I can't have those tests," I whispered.

"What are you afraid of?"

"I don't want to know the truth. If it's bad, it's … I killed my husband, Tom. I murdered him in cold blood. Whatever I went through doesn't put that right. Philip is gone because I conjured up a vision of my own daughter. How could I ever make up for what I did? Even after what he did to me and even after he threw me out, I was still in love with him. Even when he tried to …"

I stopped, biting my lip. Henderson understood instantly.

"I know you still care," Tom whispered, touching my hand gently. "That's okay, Zoey. It's perfectly fine to still love him. You spent your adult life with him and that won't change because he's gone. Needless, you still need to figure this out. I can't …" Henderson waited for a second, looking me in the eye. "I don't know why, but the second that I saw you, I knew there was something about you. I came here on impulse, because something told me I needed to be here at this point in time. No matter what you did or did not do and no matter what you're going through right now, I won't handle your case anymore. I've asked my boss to take a step back, so I could focus on helping you. Alice took over and she is rooting for you too, Zoey. No matter the outcome, you need to get those tests done and you need to focus on a possible future. Don't you think you deserve that, after all you've been through?"

"Didn't he deserve the same?" I asked quietly.

Henderson didn't reply.

Forty-Five

TOM, I COULDN'T THINK OF him as Henderson anymore, took me to the police station, where he told Alice Slater, his colleague, that I was ready to talk. It was two p.m., but I felt like I had not slept in weeks. I was shaking, so a police officer offered me a cup of tea, while the other one handed me a slice of homemade biscuit that his wife had baked this morning. It was crispy. I sort of nibbled on it. I had sent Mac a message to tell him I was going to turn myself in, but he hadn't replied yet. I hadn't seen him for a while now. He had no idea what was going on, and I wanted to keep it that way.

I was led into a small interrogation room, where I sat on a chair, with Alice taking the seat facing me. Tom was in the room, but he didn't say a single word. I declined to have Greg by my side. It wouldn't make a difference anyhow.

"Is it an official confession, Zoey?" Slater asked friendly.

"I suppose it is."

"Would you like me to get it on camera, or would you like to talk first?"

"I'm fine with whatever you want."

"Okay then, Zoey. I need to read you your Miranda rights first." Slater turned to her colleague. "Tom, I will have to ask you to wait in the visitor's area for now. I'm afraid that, legally, you're not allowed in, since you were taken off the case at your own request."

"Can he stay with me?" I asked. "I promise I won't use his presence. I just … I need …"

"Okay then," Slater said easily, smiling at her colleague, who moved to the corner of the room. A police officer brought in three cups of strong coffee. The room was four by four, with nothing more than a table and four chairs in it. The walls were bare. Slater set up the camera to record my confession. I watched her lean fingers and felt an incredible urge to light up a cigarette, just to have something to do, while I never even smoked. Vivian always did though.

"Go ahead," Slater said, once the camera was rolling.

"I think I killed my husband, Philip Walters," I said.

"Why is that, Zoey?"

"I don't remember doing it, because I've been suffering from blackouts and hallucinations. I must have done it, because I have memories of blood traces on my hands and clothes. Plus, I remember standing by his bed. I don't know if those memories are true or false, but they must have been real."

"We know that you were sick and that your doctors want to run some tests to find out if you have a brain tumor," Alice said. "Is that correct?"

"That's correct," I said. "Mac has been urging me for some time to have me checked over, since I've been sick since the shooting, but I never had time to have them done."

"Mac?" Tom asked, veering upwards.

I looked at him.

"My downstairs neighbor," I explained. "We became friends when I moved into the building. He's been a very good friend over the past days. You've met him, haven't you?"

"Not to my recollection," Tom frowned, immediately becoming Detective Henderson again. I could practically see him making mental notes.

"Anyhow, Mac is a doctor at St. Mary's and has been insisting that something's wrong with me," I shrugged. "Turns out he was right."

"Do you believe you might have a tumor, Zoey?" Slater asked.

"I don't know. It would explain the headaches and pains that I'm experiencing constantly. To be honest, I always thought the aches came from stress after my daughter's death. My last doctor thought the same. I have been taking for the pain."

I lifted my bag off the floor and showed them the bottle with white pills. It was the only one with painkillers that I could save after Vivian's little rampage and my own suicide attempt.

"Zoey, why do you believe you're responsible for Philip's death?" Slater asked friendly.

I took a deep breath, coming to the difficult part.

"Vivian doesn't exist. She's a figment of my imagination. When I was a child, I had imaginary friends. They became my allies when I was lonely. I was bullied in school, you see. I have reason to believe I created Vivian after my baby's loss, for various reasons I can explain to you. It doesn't matter how I did it, but I know now that she wasn't real at all. I figured that, if I was capable of imagining people to deal with my loss, I must be capable of murder as well."

"Do you remember killing your husband then?" Slater asked.

I shook my head.

"Not the actual kill. I remember being outside that night, going into the apartment and finding him on the bed. I remember a pair of bloodied gloves that were thrown inside a garbage bin near the building. I had a Burberry when I walked into the apartment, but it was gone when I got home. No matter what, I was most definitely there," I admitted.

"What about the actual murder?" Slater repeated. "Do you remember how you did it?"

"No, I saw him on the bed, but he was already dead. Later, back home, I had visions of a sweater covered in blood, stuck in the trashcan in my new apartment, but they were washed and cleaned by the time you got there, and I can't remember who did that. I thought it was Vivian, but I must have done it myself. Reality and fantasy are so mingled together, that I can't recall what is real or fake anymore."

"Can you describe where you threw those gloves?" Henderson asked, disturbing the silence.

"No. It was dark. It was just a bin, a couple of yards from the building. I'm not sure if you would even be able to find those gloves after a week. It must have been emptied since then."

"Do you remember what happened to the Burberry?" Slater asked.

"No. I must have thrown that away as well, but I don't remember the details. It's probably in the same bin. You have to understand that these are bits and pieces, as if I was looking at myself, while existing outside my body. I watched myself do all those things, but I don't remember doing them."

"Would you be willing to undergo a polygraph test to find out the whole truth?" Slater asked.

"Yes."

"Are you convinced, Zoey, that you have murdered your husband?" Tom asked. His voice trembled.

I didn't speak for a while, contemplating his question, until I knew the answer for sure.

"Yes," I finally admitted. "Yes, I'm sure that I killed my husband."

I looked down and saw warm tears drip on my hands. Slater suddenly leaned forward and grabbed my fingers.

"Zoey," she spoke warmly and gently. "I believe that you did the right thing coming to us today and I believe Tom when he tells us over and over again that you didn't do this. Do you trust us enough to put your fate in our hands? We want to get to the bottom of this, but we can only do this together with you."

I nodded without hesitation. I had felt from the beginning that I could trust Henderson, and by proxy, I trusted Slater too. I remembered how gently she had been in my apartment, going through my personal things. No matter what, I trusted these people's judgement. Without hesitation, I put my life in their hands.

"Am I under arrest?" I asked when Detectives Slater and Henderson took me out of the interrogation room.

"No, Zoey," Slater said. "We are going to make sure those tests are done first, but it's my obligation to warn you that they will most likely lead to your arrest. For now, we want to focus on finding your clothes and getting you checked over. Tom will be with you at all times from now on and keep an eye out on you. We will have to go through your apartment again and process the clothes you were wearing on the night of the murder."

I nodded and signed permission to have them go through my things again. Slater, another male colleague and Henderson drove me to Philip's apartment building, where I steered them into the direction of the alley where I remembered dumping the clothes. Some police officers joined us in a separate car and started going through two massive, overloaded dumpsters that could be possible candidates.

I realized that they might actually find my clothes, since the dumpsters hadn't been emptied in weeks. More cops arrived, while I was taken back to the police station by Slater's quiet colleague. Tom didn't speak either. He was processing what was happening, I knew. Slater and her colleague left me alone, while we waited in another room, a small empty office that looked out on the streets.

"It'll be alright," Tom said. "Do you want me to call Mac?"

"I already sent him a text," I reacted. "Why?"

"He's probably worried about you."

I smiled, realizing Henderson's intent.

"He's a good friend, but I don't look at him that way, Tom."

"What way is that?" he asked, raising an eyebrow.

"Like you're doing at me right now," I said.

Henderson flushed scarlet red.

It took longer than we thought for Slater to come back. From the look on her face, things were serious. We sat down together, and I knew I was in trouble.

"We found the gloves in the dumpster," she informed us. "The Burberry and murder weapon have not been found yet. We're processing them now. We hope to have answers soon. In meantime though, we have a slight problem, Zoey. The reason why I'm late, is because I had a meeting with our police chief. He doesn't agree with my decision to let you walk for the time being and wants to have you arrested."

I nodded in acceptance, knowing this was going to happen.

"No," Tom spoke in my place, "there's no proof yet that she did it. She was there, yes, but she didn't kill him, Alice, you know that."

"I know that, objectively speaking, Zoey is the one who lead us to the gloves, Tom," she addressed her colleague. "I have to look at the facts."

"Are you convinced that she's the one?" Tom insisted.

"What I think or believe, doesn't matter. It's the evidence that counts, you know that. We talked about this when you confessed your feelings for her, Tom. That's the reason why you stepped down from this case in the first place."

"Alright then," Tom continued, not giving up yet. "What about her health? Zoey is a very sick woman who needs medical attention. I was just about to take her to the ER when you barged in on us. Tell that to the Chief. I'm taking her to see her doctor."

"And who is that?"

"Dr. Mac Ramsey," I said. "He's a surgeon at St. Mary's."

"Can I speak with you for a second?" Slater said, addressing his colleague.

I watched in strange amusement while the partners stood behind the glass door arguing about my future. Strange, now that I had made the decision to face facts, it seemed as if nothing could hurt me anymore. I would never find out what it was that Tom said, but as a result, they walked to another office. A few minutes later, they came back in.

"We've just spoken to the Chief," she said. "Tom has convinced me that the results of those tests might have an important impact on your innocence or guilt. Therefore, I have advised my boss to have you transferred to St. Mary's Hospital immediately. Besides Tom, you will have a police officer with you at all times. We can't let you go freely, because you are now officially considered the prime suspect in your husband's death."

"That is fine by me," I said.

Slater walked out and left me alone with Tom, who looked at me excitedly, as if he had just saved my life. I didn't get that. The fact that I had a small delay in going to jail didn't change anything. By tonight, I would be behind bars and charged with murder. Nothing anyone did would change that. I knew I had no tumor in my head. I would have known if I did. There were no medical explanations to clarify or defend why I had murdered my husband. There was only little old me, going off the rocks. I couldn't help but wonder how long it would take for Tom to grow tired of me.

Forty-Six

A POLICE CAR TOOK US to the hospital around four p.m. There were two officers, a man, driving the vehicle and a woman, who was going to guard me while I was being examined. Tom had made some calls before we left, so they were waiting for us. The woman slipped in the back beside me, forcing Henderson to take the front passenger seat. The three of them talked about the weather while we slowly made our way through traffic.

At the ER, I was immediately processed and taken into a private examination room, where I was left with the female police officer. Tom disappeared to find Mac at my request, who was at work somewhere in this hospital. The other cop left. I sat down reluctantly and wondered what would happen next. Before long, a nurse walked in and smiled at me. She carried a typical hospital gown with her and some medical supplies.

"Why don't you make yourself comfortable and change into this?" she spoke. "You can keep your panties on but remove your bra and any jewelry you might be wearing. I'll be back to take some blood samples. You'll be taking a ride upstairs then for an extensive CT-scan. Based on those findings, we might run some more tests."

The female officer turned around politely while I changed into the gown and crawled beneath the bedsheets and single blanket that couldn't stop my legs from shaking. It was cold in the room. I had carefully folded and my clothes on one chair, while the police officer sat on the other one, leafing through a magazine.

I dreaded the fact that I was back here, in the same hospital where I had officially lost my baby, even though Eve was long gone by the time they brought me here. It felt as if my fate was linked with this place. Even Mac was linked to it, probably operating on someone right now. Thank God Elisabeth was not working at the ER; she was the last person I wanted to see right now.

The nurse came back in. The small band-aid of last night's blood tests was still there. She pulled it off, before she used my other arm to push the needle in to tap off blood. It slid in efficiently and fast, without hurting at all. She left with six small bottles, filled to the brim with the thick red fluid extracted from my artery. A couple of minutes later, she returned with a wheelchair to take me to the basement floor for the CT-scan.

"Why don't you drink a cup of coffee at the nurse's station?" she proposed to the female officer. "I'm sure Mrs. Walters is not going anywhere soon."

I winced at the use of my marital name but didn't comment on it.

"I need to stay with her," the officer insisted.

"Where would she go? I'll make sure you get her back in one piece," the nurse smiled.

"I'll go with you then."

"Then you might as well take her downstairs yourself," the nurse said, giving the woman directions.

The policewoman wheeled me through the corridor and pushed into an elevator, before we ended up in a hallway with several doors. A couple of nurses came out the door and of course Elisabeth was one of them. She stared at the police officer behind the wheelchair and then at me, trying to figure out what the hell was going on.

"Are you arrested?" she asked blatantly.

"They found some evidence that might indicate me," I said quietly.

"What kind of evidence?"

"Bloodied gloves," I whispered.

Elisabeth paled, bit her lip and moved on without saying a single word, while the cop pushed the wheelchair past her, into a room with the number thirteen on the door. I was given another IV and a syringe with contrast fluid before I was taken to another room, where the CT-scanner was waiting for its next patient. The cop was told to wait outside, while another nurse prepared me for the scan and told me I would be given a second injection while lying on the table. They had been given instructions to scan my abdomen, chest and head.

I was strapped so tight on the machine that I could hardly move an inch. They placed some sort of plastic mask over my face, before I was slid inside the machine. Once the second injection entered my body, I felt warm and itchy for a few minutes. The machine moved over me back and forth at a steady pace, until I felt drowsy and exhausted from watching the machine do its work. The whole process lasted about fifteen minutes.

Afterwards, I was wheeled back to the ER by the police officer, back into the small room where my clothes still lay on a neat pile and the nurse waited for us.

"That wasn't so bad, was it?" she asked friendly. "The doctor will see you in an hour or so to discuss the results. We will have them shortly, so it might even be sooner."

"Thank you," I said. "Can I get dressed?"

"Sure, go ahead."

She left again, taking the police officer with her. I dressed quickly and took out my phone to call Mac, hoping he would respond. He didn't and Henderson still hadn't returned with him. It troubled me that I was left to my own devices, which gave me too much time to think. Biting my fingernails, I logged in on Netflix and picked out a random show, without really registering what was happening.

About an hour later, after I had eaten a salad, given to me by a nurse, Tom, Detective Slater, the same nurse and the attending doctor, came into the room. Mac wasn't with them, and the other female officer had left too. The look on Tom's face told me they had found something. He didn't mention Mac at all, so I gathered that he didn't go look for him at all. He was too busy trying to prove my innocence.

"What is it?" I asked nervously, expecting to find out I was going to die within the next few days.

The doctor had a file in his hands. He placed it on the table and dug up a bunch of scans and a report.

"Mrs. Walters," he said, "my name is Doctor Smythe. I'm afraid I have some good and some bad news for you."

"Give me the bad news first then," I asked.

He smiled briefly.

"To do that, I need to tell you the good news first, Zoey, which is, that you definitely don't have a brain tumor. All the tests came back negative, and the scans showed that you have nothing to fear physically. You are, in fact, in good health, despite the fact that you're underweight."

"Then why do I have these blackouts?" I asked. "Is that part of the bad news that you're about to tell me?"

"I'm afraid so and I think this might come as a shock to you. We found traces of a drug called Triazolam in your system. Not in small dosages either, but in large amounts. The blood samples we took showed that you have been taking this drug in high dosage for quite some time now.

"Triazolam?" I repeated numbly, "I'm sorry, the name doesn't ring a bell at all. It's not on my list of prescribed medication."

"Zoey, we know that your behavior lately has been at times strange. The blackouts, the depressions, the amnesia that you spoke of all relate to this drug," Tom interrupted the doctor. "Detective Slater and I did some research on it. Triazolam is a drug used for treatment of insomnia, but it's not very popular, because it has a fairly high incident level of adverse reactions and serious side effects. Amongst those effects are severe depression, periods of amnesia, hallucinations and confusion. Basically, when taken in much higher dosages than prescribed, Triazolam becomes a danger for the patient's health and will work exactly the opposite."

"I don't understand," I whispered confused. "I swear that I don't know where this drug came from. All that I've been taking was the Meperidine, which I've been taking on prescription due to my post-surgery pains. Apart from that, I didn't take anything else. You have to believe me. I've never heard of this drug."

Tom placed his hand on my wrist, to confirm that he believed me.

"In your case, Zoey," Doctor Smythe continued, "the effects became even worse because you have been taking the Meperidine for some time. There are known cases where patients who were on sedatives or pain medication for a long time, had severe reactions to the sudden additional administering of this particular drug," the doctor spoke. "Whoever gave you this cocktail, should have known this. Your medical history didn't allow this combination. If your doctor did this, he should be disbarred immediately."

"The only one that could do this, is my doctor," I said, "but even so, I would have known about it, wouldn't I?"

"You can only get Triazolam on prescription," Doctor Smythe said. "Of course, if you had access to a pharmacy, you could easily get your hands on it. Or in hospitals like this, where samples are always kept for trials."

I paled when a sudden realization struck me.

"Elisabeth works in this hospital," I spoke slowly. "She had access to my pills when she lived with Philip. I went there to get my last prescribed medication, nearly a week ago. Could she have mixed them?"

I reached inside my bag and showed them the nearly empty bottle. "I'll bet you ten to one that these are not Meperidine-pills."

Henderson took it from my shaking hands and showed them to Doctor Smythe.

"They look nearly the same," the man frowned. "You could easily get them mixed."

"Or deliberately changed," Detective Slater said. "I suggest you have these pills examined immediately, Doctor. I have this feeling we might have an attempted murder case on our hands too."

I sank down on the side of the bed, realizing that I might have killed my husband under the influence of drugs. If I had done so, Elisabeth might as well have pushed the knife into his chest herself. What had that woman done to me? Was she trying to poison me, or did she lure me on purpose in this state of mind, knowing perfectly well what the effects of added Triazolam would do to me?

Forty-Seven

WHILE WE WAITED FOR THE outcome of the results, I realized that these tests worked for and against me. Not a single person would question the fact that I had been out of my mind when I slashed my husband to death. I couldn't be held accountable for my actions, but I would also be considered my husband's killer without a doubt. Elisabeth would be arrested and charged with attempted murder, but she would never be charged with my husband's death. She would claim that his murder was not her intention at all, that I had reacted differently to the cocktail of medication than expected.

The acknowledgement of my defeat was worse than the realization that I had been mentally trapped for days. I had done things under the influence of drugs that I would never have done otherwise. I had invented Vivian, just as I used to invent kids when I was younger. Had I done that because those kids had made me feel safe? Did I subconsciously sense that I was on the verge of a breakdown?

Doctor Smythe came back in and told me the lab had confirmed that I had indeed been taking two sets of medication. He showed me the pills. There were only a few slight differences, mostly on the surface. Where the Meperidine was smooth on the outside, the Triazolam felt rougher. That's what Vivian, my own subconsciousness, had been telling me. I knew, but I had ignored it.

The doctor proceeded by telling me that I wouldn't be able to take medication for several days, so that the effects of the Triazolam would forever disappear from my system. It couldn't be flushed out, so my body needed time to restore itself. He warned me that I might experience severe withdrawal symptoms. Therefore, he wanted to admit me for a couple of days, to monitor me.

The test results and scans that they made of my abdomen and head, still didn't explain the headaches and pains, but the man had a theory about them. More tests would be done in the next few days to see if I suffered from something called Chronic Pain Syndrome, or CPS, which could be treated. I would also receive additional fluids and a special diet, since I was severely anemic and malnourished. The ordeal was far from over. All of this confirmed what Mac had told me. I made a mental note to tell him all about it when he came over to see me. He had sent me a text message, telling me he was in surgery all day and would come by as soon as possible.

Tom told me that they couldn't find Elisabeth. She had left the hospital in a hurry, literally dropping everything she was doing. Nobody could reach her; her parents had no clue about her whereabouts. She didn't want to be found, that was for sure. She must have seen what was going on; she might have dug into my medical files to find out why I was admitted and scanned. Only later did I realize that Tom didn't mention Elisabeth's sister. I wondered if she, whoever she was, was alright.

I was taken to a private room, where another IV was pushed into my veins. I was in a hospital gown again and now officially treated as a patient. I was tired and frustrated and already felt withdrawal symptoms. The headache returned in full force and my abdomen ached like crazy. Doctor Smythe gave me a minor sedative something to relax and reassured me that I would be just fine. He also reassured me that I would get help for the CPS, but that it would be a long process.

Tom and Detective Slater came in to discuss my situation. Slater told me they had put out an APB on Elisabeth for murder, since it became obvious to them that I had been used by her as a weapon. The fact that it was now generally accepted that I had driven that knife through my husband's chest, still hurt. There was no other explanation for it though. I had done this, because I remembered parts of it, which I had admitted to freely.

"For what it's worth," Tom said after Slater left the room, "Alice and my colleagues will do whatever they can to find Elisabeth as soon as possible. If she confesses, we might get lucky."

"What about me?" I asked frightened.

"We will talk to the District Attorney about your case, but Doctor Smythe already confirmed that your state of mind was definitely influenced by the medication. Since you have a clean track record and confessed voluntarily to what you remembered, we believe that they may not charge you for murder, under the condition that you will be monitored in the next weeks to come. Also, you are never allowed to take that medication again."

"Trust me, I won't," I groaned. Did you find anything yet on the gloves?"

"Not yet," Slater said. "I promise you that you will be the first to know when there is news, Zoey."

Slater left so Tom could talk to me. He sunk down on the side of the bed and held my hand between his. I looked at it and then at him and saw something I didn't think anyone would ever show me again. It was different than Philip's affection had been. My husband used to be quite cold and distant, even in his most passionate moments. Tom showed his emotions openly.

"I don't even know if you're married," I laughed through my tears.

"I'm not. Never have been. No hidden kids either. I have only myself to take care of and my neighbor's cat, who often comes by for food in the middle of the night," Tom smiled. "I do have to tell you that I work odd hours and have quite an intense job."

The word kids startled me. It made me remember what had happened to me. I pulled my hand back.

"Zoey, what is it?"

"I – I'm messed up, Tom. I'm a wreck, physically and mentally. I'm useless, worthless and a basket case. Someone like you can find someone better. I can't do this to you."

"Zoey, are you everything else than that," he spoke gently. "The moment I saw you, something happened to me. You walked into that apartment feeling so sick, so small and so scared that it broke my heart. I knew then, as I know

now, that you are a good person. Don't ever underestimate the power of your will. You survived this, remember? Your daughter was killed, your friend was shot to death, and you nearly died too. But you survived. Your husband kicked you out, but you lived. You were nearly driven into death, but you overcame. Do you know how strong you are?"

Tom leaned into me. His lips grazed past mine briefly. Before he moved back, I reached for his face, stroked my hands over his stubbled cheekbones and pulled him in for another kiss. It was absolutely perfect.

Forty-Eight

MAC ENTERED MY ROOM LATE in the evening. He was beyond exhaustion, that was for sure. He had a weary gaze in his eyes and an apology written all over his face. I saw my day reflected in his eyes.

"I'm so sorry, Zoey," he said ashamed. "I feel so guilty for abandoning you in your worst times. It was hell today. I was called in this morning for a patient with a burst appendix and it all just got worse after that."

"Don't apologize," I said, stopping him. "I'm doing fine, I promise." Mac sat down next to the bed.

"You are looking better. Zoey, what's going on?" Mac asked, noticing the dreamy gaze in my eyes. "I know that you're going through hell, but you seem … happy somehow. What happened to make you feel this way?"

"Remember that I told you about Detective Henderson?"

"Yeah – the cop you told me about, the one you repeatedly called cute, without any consideration for my feelings," he grinned. "Oh god, is he – are you and he –?"

"I don't know. I don't think so, or at least not yet," I interrupted him. "But truth be told, I have no clue what is happening between us. It's new and fresh and exciting and – God, Mac, I hope you don't mind. I don't know what you thought would happen to us, but I–"

Mac stopped me immediately.

"I like you, Zoey, but not in a romantic way, rest assured. I thought you had it figured out by now that I'm gay?"

"You are?" I asked surprised.

"Yep. Besides that, I like you because you're a good person and a great friend and I'm so glad that you're doing better. That's all I ever wanted for you, trust me. I'm not ready to build any romantic relationships with anyone for a long time to come. Where is he anyhow?"

"I sent him home," I said. "The poor man was so tired. And besides, he's not my detective anymore. The case is with someone else."

"Yeah, I've heard about that in the corridors. Trust me, this is a small hospital, so people tend to gossip. I read you medical file too in meantime. CPS huh? That makes sense. I knew there was something more going on than just pains and aches. I'm sorry I didn't catch it earlier. I should have been there for you."

"You were," I interrupted him. "You're one of my best friends, Mac. I love you for all you did for me. You're still here, aren't you? Thank you."

I reached for his hand and squeezed his fingers. Mac sat down on the side of the bed and smiled.

"You were right about everything," I said. "Thank you for that, Mac. Thanks for being my friend through all of this. If it weren't for you, I wouldn't have made it, I know that."

"Anytime," he smiled. "What about Elisabeth? Did they catch her yet?"

"I don't know," I said. "I don't think so, or Tom would have called me already to tell me."

"Tom? Is that his name?"

"Yep."

Mac smiled again and hugged me carefully. I was still shaking like a leaf and sweating like a horse from kicking off from the medication, but I had never felt better in days.

"You're doing so great, Zoey," he said. "I wish you nothing but the best. Whatever happens next, I want to stay part of your life, you hear? We're neighbors for something."

"Thanks, Mac."

"I have to get going," he said, getting up. "Will you be alright on your own tonight, or do you want me to stay with you?"

"Of course," I said. "I'm fine. Go home and get some rest, Mac, you need it badly. I'll sleep properly tonight, I promise."

He smiled and said his goodbye to me, stopping by the door suddenly when something occurred to him.

"What is it?" I asked.

"I was just curious about something. You've been so determined to find out what was happening to you, but you seem to accept the fact that Elisabeth is still out there. Aren't you afraid of her? Shouldn't the cops be protecting you against her? After all, she's the one who did this to you. Where are the cops? Why aren't they here to protect you?"

I looked at him surprised.

"Doctor Smythe convinced the Chief of Police that I wasn't a threat to society, so they said it was safe to leave me here alone for the next few days. They're understaffed as it is, so putting a guard here seemed kind of silly. What makes you say Elisabeth would come here? I'm not afraid of her anymore, Mac. She won't make a stupid error; she's long gone. She won't show up with a knife in her hands, you know."

Mac smiled.

"Of course she won't," he said. "I'll see you tomorrow, okay?"

"See you."

Mac left me alone feeling disturbed. I stared at the ceiling for a long time, thinking about his words. If he thought I was in danger, why would he even leave me alone right now? Something felt off, something I couldn't place. I shrugged and tried to forget his words, while fatigue took over. My eyes drooped as the evening turned into night, and the full moon showed itself for the last time this month.

When I woke up, I saw her hovering over me, a blade in her hand. I caught a glimpse of her eye, as I instinctively reached out to stop her, just as the door to my room opened and Tom rushed into the room, stopping her from pushing the blade through my chest, straight into my heart.

It was the same knife she had used to kill Philip. His blood was still on it. She wore different gloves this time, since she had chucked away the old ones, leaving them in the dumpster, four blocks away from Philip's apartment.

Tom didn't even threaten her. He ran to her, grasped her by the wrists and pulled her backwards. The knife fell to the ground, where it remained until Detective Slater picked it up.

The moment the lights went on, I saw her face. It wasn't Elisabeth, but someone who looked very much like her. We had found her mysterious sister. Or: she had found me.

Forty-Nine

WHAT WAS THE TRUTH, I asked myself, when I stared at the girl, sitting on the chair in my hospital room, handcuffs around her wrists? I imagined Elisabeth and her sister, huddled together, conspiring to kill me. Had she really acted so low to send a seventeen-year-old to do her dirty work for her? Or had she no clue that this girl had come to finish the job?

A doctor on call rushed into the room and checked me over. I demanded to have the IV removed, so I could go to the police station with them, despite Tom's urgency not to do so. I screamed and fought the doctor and nurses with all I had in me. In the end, they sedated me to calm me down. Tom hushed me as I went under, promising not to keep me in the dark, but I needed the rest right now.

It was a day later that I heard the whole story. When I woke up from my slumber, caused by the sedation and enhanced by the huge amounts of medication in my blood, Tom was by my side. It was over, he said. They had a full confession. I wasn't Philip's murderer, nor had I been involved in what happened that night. How could I ever fully understand the whole context of that night, when all the memories were still blurry and hidden behind a cloak of medication? It would take time, but the doctor told me it would all come back by itself, once the medication was fully out of my system. It could be days, maybe even weeks, but I would most likely remember everything again. Until that time, it was Elisabeth's sister Janie, who filled in the blanks. While I was under, she gave a full confession.

"Elisabeth showed up at the police station," Tom told me. "That tough woman she used to be, is gone forever. She didn't know Janie was planning on killing you, so it was quite a shock to her."

I imagined the mousy nurse, who had seen me in my worst days.

"She knew what Janie had done to Philip, didn't she? She knew about the gloves."

"She did," Tom confirmed. "Janie killed Philip, because she was upset with the man who had offered them paradise but provided them hell instead. You were next, because you too had stood in the way on the path to happiness. Her exact words."

All through the night, Elisabeth told Tom and Detective Slater about the dysfunctional relationship she'd had with her parents. She hinted about lonely nights, where her father had come into her room to 'talk' to her. She ran away from home at the age of eighteen, leaving her kid sister behind. She had no choice, but she swore that she would get her out of there as soon as she could.

Elisabeth moved into a small studio in Brooklyn, where she finished her education. She worked nights and weekends at a pub, working for the money to pay for her studies. She wanted to become a doctor, but she couldn't afford it, so she became a nurse instead. She was offered a job in Manhattan, where she rented a small apartment.

She learned that her sister Janie was also getting her dad's nightly calls, so she swore to find a solution. She was going to file for foster care and report her father to the cops, but child welfare already told her she wouldn't stand a chance since she was too poor to have money for two. Elisabeth had already buried the hope of getting her sister out of her dad's house, when she met Philip and me. It changed everything.

"I knew from the start that he didn't care enough about me," she admitted. "I told myself repeatedly that he loved me, but at the same time, I was using him for the money. I would have done anything to save her, and he was vulnerable, so I used that. I just needed a good income and financial status to be able to provide for her. Philip had no idea that I lived in a dump;

he never picked me up there once. He never knew how bad it was, or that I had a sister. I only told him much later, once we came to a point I managed to wiggle my way into his life."

"But Zoey was still standing in the way, right?" Slater asked her.

"Yes. I wanted her to die at first, I admit that to that, "was her reply. I begged to God for her not to survive that gunshot, but afterwards, I felt terrible for wishing that upon someone who had just lost her baby in the most gruesome way possible, so I decided to go the other way and get him to divorce her. I thought Philip would leave me when she came out of the hospital, but he didn't. He was down, so we started seeing each other more frequently. I started whispering to him after a few months that he should divorce Zoey, putting thoughts in his head. He listened to me, because I comforted him. I pushed him into leaving her and it worked."

Indeed, it had worked. He had thrown me out for her. He had allowed her to move in within an hour's time. He replaced me for her and when the truth about her sister came out and he realized she had been lying to him for quite some time, he wanted me back. Philip regretted his actions immediately and started stalking me. He had told Elisabeth it was all a big mistake and asked her to leave again. He would convince me to come home; we would wipe our past away and start anew. She couldn't handle that, not when her own life lay in shambles. She had thought she could build up a life with Philip. She had counted on his generosity and goodwill to take her teenage sister in. Only, he didn't react the way she had expected.

Philip wasn't pleased with Janie's sudden appearance. He started questioning Elisabeth about all the lies she had fed him. He changed his mind and wanted to go back to me, to beg me to return home. He signed his death warrant by doing so. That night, he admitted to Elisabeth he had someone following me, to figure out my routine. Once he found out I was at the club, he convinced Elisabeth on their night to go there too. She hadn't realized then that it was so bad, until they bumped into me. Angry, Elisabeth went to work, where she stayed all night. She hadn't lied about that. Janie came to see her, and they argued about Philip. Elisabeth told her she would move back to her old place and that she would bring Janie there, no matter the consequences. Janie stole her keys and went to the apartment to talk to

Philip, but by the time she got there, she had worked herself into a frenzy and decided to kill him, so that Elisabeth would get his money. The seventeen-year-old teenager had no clue that Elisabeth wouldn't get a dime.

She was clever enough to protect herself by using gloves and making sure to throw them into a dumpster, but she kept the knife as a token of what she had done. She had no idea I had seen her come out of the building, nor that I was there. I don't even remember why I followed her, but it was probably because she looked so much like Elisabeth that I became curious. Once I saw her with the bloodied gloves, I probably hurried back to the apartment on a hunch that Philip was harmed. When I got there, I pulled back the blankets and tried to revive him. That is why I had his blood on my own gloves and why it was all over my coat too. I still don't remember where I dumped my coat, or how I managed to wash my clothes.

I remembered bits and pieces of the events, after Tom told me the whole story after Janie's confession. Somehow, I must have sensed that I would be blamed for his death, so I ran. The moment I fled the scene, something inside of my head must have cracked. The results of the Triazolam in my blood stream, added to the emotions I couldn't handle. I went home, crawled into bed and fell asleep. And forgot what had happened.

Saturday

Fifty

IT WASN'T OVER YET. ELISABETH was devastated after Janie got arrested and would be sent to juvenile court for murder and attempted murder. The girl was nearly eighteen years old, but there were circumstances such as the assault her father on her, that would help. She was meek as a lamb, Tom told me, and she fully cooperated, so that would help too, but she would still, most likely, be trialed as an adult.

I should be happy that I was off the hook, but something was still amiss. I felt guilty about Janie and Elisabeth, but that wasn't it. Like I said, it wasn't over yet. Tom wasn't happy either.

When Slater asked Elisabeth about the pills, she was genuinely startled. Elisabeth swore on the life of her own sister that she never messed with my medication; that she never did me any harm. The shocking part was that Slater and Tom both believed her. She even volunteered to take a Polygraph. Also, when her sister was accused of poisoning me, she denied it too.

It was still far from over for me. The reality of it all was that I was going through withdrawal symptoms and would have to be monitored for quite some time, but I would find a way to cope with it. I would be fine, now that Philip's murder was resolved and I turned out to be innocent. Tom, no longer shy about his feelings in front of his colleagues, gave me a hug and held me tight against him in Slater's presence and that of his Captain. The man just smiled wished us all the best. If it wasn't for Tom, I wouldn't be here today. I owed him my life, my sanity and so much more. If he hadn't followed his gut feeling, things would have looked quite differently right now.

"Can I go home now?" I asked, despite the fact I was still shaking like a leaf.

"I'm afraid not. Your doctor was adamant about that, even when I woke him up in the middle of the night," Tom smiled, touching my face. "I'll stay with you for the rest of the night though, how's that?"

"Sounds like heaven."

Tom kicked off his shoes and crawled on top of the bed. He held me quietly against him, while he hummed a song. Philip never did that. He was always deep in thought, always looking for ways not to discuss anything. He had changed so much over the past months, after Eve had died. Before, he had been talkative at times, quiet at others. Sometimes he felt like listening to the radio, but even then, he would dwell off all the time. It was always hard to get a grip on what went through his mind.

And then, after Eve, he changed completely. He no longer was the man that I married, the man that I trusted with my life. He was a stranger, a man who hid his feelings behind a hard shell. Vivian always said I was burying my feelings, but what was he doing? It was, in many ways, even worse. God, he even did things that I never knew about, like setting up our life insurance policies. Why in the world had he done that? Had he –

Oh god. I gasped, causing Tom to nearly fall off the bed. He looked at me frantically as I placed my hand before my mouth and figured out what I had been missing for so long. Philip had given me those pills. My husband had packed my things from the bathroom and given them to me. He had told me to make sure I take them, that I shouldn't forget them. He could have easily mixed the contents of those bottles, making sure that I would take them, one way or the other.

Philip had plenty of access to the medication. He still could have easily stolen pills from the hospital supplies, seeing as he was there quite a lot. He could have snatched them off a medical cart. He could have used Elisabeth; he could have faked stolen prescriptions. It was so easy to pretend to be someone you weren't. I remembered thinking once that Philip would have been better off poisoning me, after he gave me a few pills. That was on Thursday evening, when he told me the truth about Elisabeth.

"It was Philip," I croaked. "He did this to me."

The look on Tom's face told me that he already suspected as much. They were investigating it. I saw it in his eyes; he just didn't want to shock me with this news, knowing what effect it would have on me. Philip had played a cat-and-mouse game with me over the past months. Pushing me away, wheeling me back in, pleading for forgiveness, raping me. He raped me.

Tom gasped this time. I had said it out loud. For the first time, I told someone. I used the word. I had never done that with Rob and Greg.

"I took his money," I whispered. "I took it, to punish him for what he had done to me. Was that the reason why he did this?"

"I don't know," Tom said. "We have no clue yet, but truth of the matter is that he would have been well off, if you had died first. Maybe taking that money from his bank account, proved to him that it could go the other way around too."

For the second time, Tom held me in his arms and let me cry. It was the last time I ever cried over my dead husband.

We'll never know why Philip did what he did, but it was certain now that the life insurance policy showed that suicide was included. If I would die in an accident, suicide or murder, he would get my money. He would have gotten it all. What kind of man had I married? I couldn't grasp it. Had he sent that woman to me too, asking her to shoot me? Had he given her a hint? No, I couldn't believe that, but I did believe that he might have decided to get rid of me after Eve's death. He blamed me for her death, always had. I believed that his grief made him do nasty things.

We never told his parents. It was my decision to keep this for us, even when investigation showed that Philip's fingerprints were all over the bottles with my medication in them. Even when they found old footage on tape showing how he stole medication from the cart at the hospital. He may never have known what he stole; he just took it because those pills resembled mine. Further tests showed that he probably gave them to me the day that I left the apartment. If I had digested them earlier, I would not be alive today. That, in the end, was my fortunate luck: the fact that he kept them aside until the time was right. Until he knew I had sunken deep enough to need just another little push over the edge.

After

THE MORNING LIGHT BROUGHT NEW hope for a normal life, even if it was going to be a difficult one at first. Tom and I ate breakfast together in my hospital room, where I would have to stay for at least a few more days. He had slept by my side every day, literally. He would come in after his tour of duty, bring junk food, kick off his shoes and jacket, hide his gun in the safe that he could lock, feed me whatever greasy stuff he had with him that day and fall asleep next to me, always fully dressed. We hadn't even kissed yet, or at least not properly. We hadn't spoken about our feelings, or where to go from there, but it was perfect as it was.

We selected a television channel with old movies and television shows. We re-watched series like Friends, The X-Files and even my childhood favorite, The Black Stallion. I laughed as I told Mac that night that he almost had the same name as the lead character on that show: Mac Ramsey. Mac snorted while he told me he was dead terrified of horses.

There were a lot of open wounds that needed mending, and it would take a lot of time for me to heal, we both knew that. Apart from the mental part, where I had to cope with the fact that my husband had tried t kill me, I also went into withdrawal symptoms now that the Triazolam and Meperidine were gone. Doctor Smythe had told me that I could never take pain medication again. I had to live with the aches that I felt on a daily basis, without numbing my brain.

My doctor set up an appointment at the pain clinic to give injections into my abdomen, that would hopefully ease the pain, which would then hopefully also put an end to the worst headaches. Stomach and head were connected, so it made sense that I suffered from both. He was hopeful that this would do the trick. The days at the hospital went by slowly, but Tom was there as much as he could and when he wasn't, I was still never alone.

Mac showed up quite a lot, always popping in between surgery or appointments. We talked about everything that happened, and I kept on telling him how much I appreciated him being there for me. He had called Tom after all that night, expressing his concern. He told me so.

"I just knew something was off," he said casually. "I'm so glad I followed my gut feeling. It just didn't feel right, having you there by yourself."

To my surprise, more people showed up too in my room. Old friends that I had neglected, like Simone, and new ones that I had could rely on. Rob and I talked about opening that flower shop in the Meat Packaging District and I spontaneously offered Simone a job. She accepted with a smile on her face, telling me she had already planned on moving closer to the city now that her son studied here. It was the beginning of something new.

Philip's parents never came by, which was okay. I couldn't face them in this weak state of mind anyhow. Maybe someday, we could face each other again. Tom called my parents with my approval and told them everything. My dad wished us all the best but said he was too weak to travel. An excuse of course, but one I had heard plenty of times before. Some things never changed. I didn't even talk to him, or my mom. Tom took me in his arms and told me that his mother was looking forward to meeting me. It made up for the heartache of not having proper parents myself.

After six nights, I was finally released from hospital. Tom came to pick me up after his shift. We had decided that I would go back to my new apartment, while Philip's parents dealt with the old one. They would sell it in my name, and I knew his dad would do me right. He always had. I was glad that they never needed to find out the truth about their son.

"How do you feel?" Tom asked while we sat in his car.

He had his eyes on the road, steering us carefully through busy New York traffic. It was eight p.m., but still as busy as ever. New York never slept.

"I'm doing great," I said. "Looking forward to a future with you."

"Do you want me to stay with you tonight?"

"I would love that," I smiled, "but you have a very early shift in the morning and to be honest, I would love to get a good night's sleep. Besides, if anything's wrong, I can always contact Mac. He said he was home, so I just need to send a text or head downstairs."

"When do I get to meet your new best friend?" Tom smiled. "I need to thank you for taking care of you. It's good that he was at the hospital. He sounds like a great guy."

"I know, Tom. He's been asking about you too. After all, if it weren't for the two of you, I wouldn't be here today."

"What are you talking about?" Tom asked.

"He was the one who called you that night, wasn't he? Without him, you wouldn't have known something was amiss."

Tom didn't reply. We arrived at my building, where he parked the car in the front. The lights on the ground floor were on, which meant that Mac was home. I felt happiness flood through me. My two best friends were finally going to meet each other.

"He's home. His lights are on," I said. "Let's go."

Tom looked at the house and frowned lightly, before exiting his car. We removed my bags from the trunk of the car. Tom took my keys and opened the front door. I walked straight to Mac's apartment door and rang his bell. Light shone from under the door, but he wouldn't open.

"Mac?" I asked, knocking on the door.

"Zoey, what are you doing?" Tom asked confused, putting my bags on the marble floor behind me.

"He's home," I said. "Maybe he's asleep."

The door still didn't open. Tom stood right behind me; I could feel the tension radiate off him. He moved forward and tried the doorknob, which gave way easily. I held my breath as I followed Tom in. The apartment was empty; the rooms were clear of furniture. There was no trace of anyone living here, not even a carpet on the floor. The kitchen looked as if it had never been used.

"What–" I stopped, not understanding.

Tom reached for me, but I pushed him away when I walked in, scanning the rooms, looking for a sign of him. He saved my life! Mac saved my life in more ways than one. No, this couldn't be real. He had to be here.

"Is everything alright?"

Tom and I turned around to see a young woman standing in the doorway with a shopping bag in her hand, looking at us curiously. She had a similar key to the front door like mine in her hand. She seemed vaguely familiar to me.

"Are you here to view the apartment?" she asked curiously, eyeing me, before scanning the room briefly. "Where's the real estate agent? Does she even know you're here?"

"I ..." My breath hitched.

I couldn't speak; felt that old feeling of suffocation all over again.

"Doesn't anyone already live here?" Tom asked.

The woman laughed and tilted her head slightly.

"Nope. This floor has been empty since they started renovating the building three years ago and put the apartments up for sale. Nobody seems to be quite interested in ground floor apartments these days, but we have high hopes that it will get sold soon. It will definitely increase the value of this building."

The woman reached for her shopping bag, but she stopped when she saw me clearer than before, again tilting her head.

"Don't I know you? You're the upstairs neighbor, aren't you? The one that fell down the stairs? We found you that night, but you were totally out of it. Glad to see that you're doing a lot better. Have a good night."

She left us alone in the darkness and silence. Something caught my eye. Something I recognized immediately. I walked over and lifted my missing Burberry off the floor, while my heart sunk into my shoes. I turned around to Tom, with my throat closed and my hands shaking.

He was not there.

CASTLE BRIDGE MEDIA RECOMMENDS...

If you liked this book, you might also enjoy reading the following titles from Castle Bridge Media available on Amazon or by order at your favorite book store:

The 23rd Hero
By Rebecca Anne Nguyen

ANIMAL CHARMER
By Rain Nox
Animal Charmer
Magic & Melody

Austinites
By In Churl Yo

Bloodsucker City
By Jim Towns

SOUL CATCHER
By Don Sawyer
The Burning Gem
The Tunnels of Buda

THE CASTLE OF HORROR ANTHOLOGY SERIES
Volume 1
Volume 2: Holiday Horrors
Volume 3: Scary Summer Stories
Volume 4: Women Running From Houses
Volume 5: Thinly Veiled: The 70s
Volume 6: Femme Fatales*
Volume 7: Love Gone Wrong
Volume 8: Thinly Veiled: The 80s
Volume 9: Young Adult
Volume 10: Thinly Veiled: Saturday Mournings
Volume 11: Revenge
Volume 12: Ripped From The Headlines
Edited By Jason Henderson and In Churl Yo
*Edited By P.J. Hoover

Child of Dark Water
By E.G. Rand

Castle of Horror Podcast Book of Great Horror: Our Favorites, Top Tens and Bizarre Pleasures
Edited By Jason Henderson

Cherry Dark
By R.L. Wilburn

Dream State
By Martin Ott

Dominic
By Lee Guzman

FRENCH DECEPTION
By Janice Nagourney
A Forgery in Paris
A Forgery in Lyon
A Forgery in Marseille

FuturePast Sci-Fi Anthology
Edited by In Churl Yo

GLAZIER'S GAP
Ghosts of the Forbidden
By Leanna Renee Hieber

Hellfall
By Jay Gould

Isonation
By In Churl Yo

JAYU CITY CHRONICLES
By Chris M. Arnone
The Hermes Protocol
Necropolis Alpha

Junk Film: Why Bad Movies Matter
By Katharine Coldiron

Nightwalkers: Gothic Horror Movies
By Bruce Lanier Wright

MID-LIFE CRISIS THRILLERS
18 Miles From Town
By Jason Henderson
Lost Angel
By Sam Knight

Ties That Kill
By Deven Greene

THE PATH
By David Bowles
The Blue-Spangled Blue
The Deepest Green

Strange Shape of Love
By Herta Feely

SURF MYSTIC
By Peyton Douglas
Night of the Book Man
Dark of the Curl

The Thing That Happened When We Were Little
By Caroline Kelly Franklin

Tick Town
By Christopher A. Micklos

Yesterday's Tomorrows: The Golden Age of Science Fiction Movies
By Bruce Lanier Wright

Please remember to leave us your reviews on Amazon and Goodreads!

THANK YOU FOR SUPPORTING INDEPENDENT PUBLISHERS AND AUTHORS!
castlebridgemedia.com

9 798999 178559 4